D0480199

SOUTHERN DREAMS AND TROJAN WOMEN

SOUTHERN
DREAMS
AND
TROJAN
WOMEN

A Novel by
LEO SNOW

JOHN F. BLAIR, Publisher
Winston-Salem, North Carolina

NO LONGER THE
PROPERTY OF
ELON UNIVERSITY LIBRARY

864131

Copyright © 1985 by W. Leo Snow
Printed in the United States of America
All rights reserved

Library of Congress Cataloging-in-Publication Data

Snow, Leo.
Southern dreams and Trojan women.
I. Title.

PS3569.N624S6   1985   813'.54   85-11069
ISBN 0-89587-047-9

To Ollie Martin and Dorothy Snow McGee
for the legacy of strength and dignity
that they have given to us

Acknowledgments

I AM GRATEFUL to my family, who have been supportive when I dealt with sensitive matters; to my editor at John F. Blair, Virginia Hege; and to my readers: Judy Hunt, Linda Chester, Shirley Sprinkle, Danny Lawrence, Elizabeth Hudgins, Sally McMillan, Roni Woodell, Linda Benefield, and Deborah Pickett.

One

South Carolina, 1904

"HEY YOU, nigger lady!"

Mayzelle turned to face a skinny girl almost a foot shorter than she. She had seen this white girl for the first time at dawn when the migrants arrived from their tents near the Catawba River. The white girl talked funny, a little faster than most. Lord, thought Mayzelle, when will white trash like this one stop putting on airs, 'specially in the middle of August in a cotton field. She's nothin' but a field hand, just like me. Come dusk and she'll be just as tired and just as dirty.

Mayzelle placed her thin fingers on the small of her back, gently kneading the swollen bruise as she straightened, grimacing briefly as the stinging sweat escaped from beneath her scarf. She knew that responding to the girl could only cause trouble. Still, this white girl didn't look as mean as some of the field hands.

Mayzelle cleared her throat. "If you're a-talkin' to me, my Christian name is Mayzelle . . . not Nigger."

"Mine's Lora. Lora Rebecca Mitchell. I'm glad to know you. I've been studyin' you for an hour now. You keep lookin' up the road. What you expectin', a storm?"

"You might say that. The storm has a name: Jeffries. He gonna rain all over us if'n he catches us gabbin' like we was in church."

"Was he the one here this mornin'?"

"Yeah, the ugly one."

"Which ugly one?"

Mayzelle laughed. "The one with the scar, Lora Rebecca Mitchell. The scar that runs clean from his nose up to his black hair and worms its way into a hole in his head clear to his gut."

"Is he the one looks like a chicken?"

"The same." Mayzelle glanced behind. Talking was expensive. Pay came by the bag, not by the number of words used in idle conversation.

Mayzelle frowned. "Now I know what's so different about you," she said softly. "You have black eyes. Must be part Indian or somethin'. Get to work quick, Lora Rebecca Mitchell! I see Jeffries comin'."

The familiar sounds of hooves and the squeaking buggy springs drowned the sounds of rustling cotton plants and bags half-filled with picked and pitted bulbs being dragged across the dirt.

"That him?" whispered Lora.

"Yep."

The buggy slowly pulled to where the two girls, making a great show of their speed, were stooped. Mayzelle did not look up. Lora did.

"Howdy," Lora called.

Mayzelle shook her head. This one is not too smart, she thought.

Jeffries looked across the parted rows as if his eyes were chasing the echoes of her words to the far woods.

Lora hesitated for a moment, then stepped forward and repeated, "I said howdy."

Jeffries reached for his whip and continued to survey the other workers. Lora straightened up and brushed past Mayzelle. Mayzelle caught the scent of anger lingering in the air as Lora walked by.

Lora touched the buggy frame. "Speak, Ass. Mouth won't."

Mayzelle dropped her bag.

Jeffries glared at the skinny girl who dared hold her head high despite cloth-wrapped shoes and a stained gray dress. He spit across his seat at the girl's feet and smiled faintly.

"Git in," he whispered.

Mayzelle frowned.

"You hear me?" he said, trying to sound friendly but firm.

Lora drew a circle in the dust with her foot. "What for?"

Jeffries wiped his brow and with the flick of a finger cleaned the dust out of his deep facial scar. "You not been here long, girl. I'll show you 'round. Needs be to talk to you."

Lora glanced quickly at Mayzelle. Mayzelle's face was blank.

"Might as well," Lora said cheerfully, with a deep breath. "Can we see my husband Lon near the cattle fields?" she asked as she stepped into the buggy.

Jeffries said nothing as he urged the mule forward.

After a while he whispered, "I'm foreman here."

"Yeah, I know," Lora replied. "Mayzelle said you a good foreman."

Jeffries laughed deeply. "She did? That's good news from that lean bitch."

"No need to be ugly."

"You been down to the river?" he said sharply.

"All the time. I live on the river with Lon—"

"Bet you ain't seen the meadow side to the south, have you?"

"No. But I suppose that Lon'll take me there sooner or later."

"No trouble. Mule needs water anyway. We can go there now."

He jerked the mule to the left, and the buggy bounced twice across a rain ditch going downhill towards the forest.

Lora tried to keep the fear out of her voice. "Why . . . why you doin' this, Mr. Jeffries?"

Jeffries cursed the mule and fingered his belt. "Got somethin' here a pretty little girl like you might like to have."

Lora felt her stomach fall and her voice go weak. "I think I oughta be gettin' back to work."

"What? Miss High and Mighty can give it in the field, but you can't take it out here. Is that what you saying?"

"Look, Mr. Jeffries. I need this job. I got to help my husband—"

Jeffries pulled the buggy up to a grove of persimmon trees. He slid his hand into his trousers.

Lora jumped from the buggy and started away, calling, "I'll walk back."

Quickly Jeffries followed and pinned her to the ground, his hand over her mouth. She didn't move. She couldn't.

Suddenly, from the top of the road came a loud, almost muscular shout. "Hey, you all down there!"

Jeffries stood quickly and with his back to the road turned his head. Squinting into the sun, he saw Mayzelle waving her hands wildly. "Hey! Mr. Jeffries! They's a man who want to see you in the fields! Better hurry, he look like a banker or somethin'."

Lora stood and scrambled quickly up the hill to join Mayzelle. Jeffries jumped into the buggy.

Mayzelle looked at Lora. "Look straight ahead, girl," she said. "Don't cry or do nothin' peculiar. Act natural."

"Hold onto me," Lora said, shaking.

Mayzelle put her arm around Lora's shoulder. "Why the hell you go ridin' with that man? I figured you for brighter than that."

"You figured wrong, I guess. I didn't know he was gonna try somethin'. My Lon is gonna be so ashamed."

Mayzelle stopped. "Don't tell him, fool. Why he got to know? You wanna lose this job for him and you both? Chances are I scared the piss

3

out of Jeffries anyway. Now, let's get back to work. Stick close to me and he won't bother you again. I had a run-in with him about a month ago; he tried to get into my britches, too. Came close, he did. Said he's gonna fire me if'n I didn't do it. So I let him fool aroun', you know? He touch me, but I didn't let him do nothin'. One of these days he's gonna catch me alone, knock me cold, and then take what he wants. So I stays away from him. Figure you better do the same. He's a nasty man."

"He always been like that?"

Mayzelle glanced after the buggy. "Always has been. He used to talk to us. Once he walked over to me and told me that I stank and I should go home and wash everythin' possible. Next day he came back and told me I still stank. I jes' looked at him right serious-like and told him that I washed everythin' *but* Possible."

Lora looked at the spot where the buggy had stopped, then extended her hand to Mayzelle. "Lora Mitchell, just plain Lora Mitchell."

"Mayzelle Clark."

"Glad to know you."

"Likewise, Lora Mitchell."

"Listen, friend," Lora said, her eyes growing softer, "why don't you and your man come down to our place for supper tonight? We ain't got much on these wages, but we would be pleased to share a special meal with a friend, and since we are fresh out of friends, exceptin' for you, we would be pleased to have you and your man to visit."

"Ain't got no man."

"Oh, don't matter. Jes' you would be plenty, for good comp'ny."

"I don't know. Where 'bouts you live?"

"You know those tents near the trestle?"

"Yeah? You live in one of those?"

"Well, till the end of the month. That's why the special supper. My man got a job with a mill up at Paw Creek and his bossman found us a house there for September."

"How long you lived like that?"

"In a tent? Ever since we been married, that's six months now. We got to go where the crops need workin'. Rent on a house runs clear to eighty or ninety cents a week. You live in a house?"

"In a room in a house with my people, catch the wagon ever' mornin'. That's the only part of this job that I like, ridin' that wagon over those bridges and watchin' this farm get smaller and smaller at night. You no more than I am, are you?"

"Sixteen. I'm with child, been so for three months or more. Jes' don't show it yet."

"Good thing, too. Jeffries don't want no loaded-down women workin' for him, thinks it slows 'em down. You keep up pretty good for a white girl."

"What about it, Mayzelle? Lon's bringin' home chicken."

"And how am I s'posed to be gettin' back to town? Ask Jeffries to give me a ride? Can you see it? 'Hey, Mr. Jeffries, sir, may I ride with y'all to town this evenin'?' Why, he'd turn green and shush me for fear that the Klan would spring out of the earth to slice his heart out for even entertainin' such a question."

"I guess you got a right good point."

"I guess? I *know*. Jes' ain't no way. Appreciate your askin', though."

Lora frowned, then smiled. "I know what we can do! I'll bring lunch for both of us tomorrow. I'll save some chicken for you, that's what I'll do."

Mayzelle looked away. All the other workers had moved up the rows, leaving the two women standing alone. "Girl, why you so interested in feedin' me? What you got up your mind?"

"Up my mind? I tol' you, we ain't got no friends 'round here. Everybody in the other tents keeps to themselves. And besides, I like you."

"Your eyes are turnin' weird again."

"What?"

"Your eyes, ain't never seen eyes like that. One minute they's black and the next they's purple."

"Lon's the only other person that ever noticed. Nobody else had the nerve to mention it before. I used to be embarrassed by it, hopin' no one would notice, or at least not say they noticed."

"Now, listen, Honey, I didn't mean to hurt your feeling; I think they's beautiful, like the color on butterflies' wings."

"Oh, that's all right. Lon said he loved my eyes first and then the rest of me followed. My eyes are dark until I get real excited or upset and then they tint a little. Usually can't tell it unless the light's right."

"Listen, about that chicken. You bring the chicken and I'll bring the cornbread."

"Fine enough."

"Oh, one more thing, Lora."

"Um?"

"I may be a little late in the mornin'."

"Why's that?"

"'Cause when I tell my momma that I wasted time talkin' to a white girl when I could'a been pickin' cotton, she's gonna wear me out."

The sound of the bell raced across the farm one half hour before dark. If they hurried, the migrants could get their bags weighed at the farmhouse and get home by suppertime. As usual, Mayzelle was one of the first to check out; and Lora, giving up her space in line for those who claimed to have more urgent business at home, was one of the last. But if she put off that time when she would see Lon, the feeling she had for him would grow stronger and stronger, surging through her limbs as she walked the path behind Jeffries' home to the river where the tents stood.

She watched Mayzelle pull herself up onto the wagon with the other field hands from town. One by one, the tired, quiet workers were hauled onto the wagon until at last the solemn load jerked toward the sandy road. The mules strained. and the wheels pushed a rain of sun-bright dust over the still, dark people on the rear of the wagon. Mayzelle pulled a cloth from somewhere and covered her nose and mouth. Lora stared after her as the wagon disappeared.

Lora turned and walked slowly beside the yellow-tinted green pines toward the sound of water, stumbling across a meadow of moist moss. She almost fell over a colony of crumbling mushrooms.

Lon would be at the tent before her, since the cows were brought in before the field workers were called.

Lora pulled back the heavy rain flap and entered their one-room temporary home. There was no light within. "Lon? Lon? You here?" As her eyes grew accustomed to the dark, she felt his hand pull her down to the cot. He smelled like cattle barns. "Lon," Lora murmured, "you get yourself right up and light our lantern, unless you forgot to get the kerosene again."

The burning glow of the lantern crept across his features, revealing dark, high cheekbones and a face devoid of rigor—except the eyes, wide and alert, inward-fixed, appraising every instant with a cold caution. They were the glowing, defiant eyes of a mongrel dog constantly whipped but not broken.

Lon wiped the soot from his hands onto his pants, which were large in the waist, tied with a weak gray string.

"Lon," Lora said, "I met a real nice nigger lady in the field today—is this the chicken? Scrawny thing—well, anyway, her name is Mayzelle, and she's a lot nicer than a lot of white folks livin' twenty feet away from us," she finished, lowering her voice. Lon smiled, because his Lora invariably lowered her voice *after* she had said something she shouldn't have.

She looked around. "Well, it's true! At least Mayzelle will *talk* to you. Here, get me some water to boil these feathers off if we're goin' to eat this here skinny bird tonight. Gonna take some to Mayzelle for lunch tomorrow. Now, don't you give me that look. You know I don't waste nothin'. Besides, she's my friend. Person needs a friend in the field."

Lon pulled her to him and kissed her mouth before grabbing a bucket. Then, breathing deeply, he walked into the night, clearing his nostrils of the tent musk from a hundred rains. Lon, he thought, you are the luckiest man alive. Got a fine woman—little cheeky sometimes, but a good woman—and a baby comin', and thank God, a job in the city, and a house besides. Never been this lucky till I married Lora.

She is the only woman I ever met who could make me laugh when I was tired. She's going to make a good mother as soon as I can get her away from here. But she don't complain. Never met a woman like her; makes a tent seem like a palace, cleaner than some houses I seen.

He knelt in the sand under the railroad trestle and slowly dipped the tin pail into the river. The lights from outdoor lanterns at the campground flickered from the scrub pines and caught the glint from the trestle beams above him. The sky was clear and summer violet. Fireflies covered the far shore of the Catawba, and whippoorwills called for quiet from the darkness.

Lora boiled the water. After slicing off the head and feet of the chicken, she dipped the bird into the pot. The feathers warmed and filled the tent with a putrid odor as she peeled them from the skin. "Lon, open the flaps, please. Nothin' worse than dank chicken!" She pulled it from the pan, pink and clean, washed it in cold water, and with the precision of her butcher father, gutted the bird. The cold water warmed with blood and entrails.

"There. I swear, if I didn't love you so much I'd never touch another chicken. Oh, you sit there all smug and warm on Your Highness's bed. Why do I spoil you so?" She greased the chicken, sliced it, rolled it piece by piece in flour: liver, wings, legs, gizzard, and all.

Lon got up and carried the skillet to the waiting fire outside the tent. Lora wiped her brow with a scarf and followed.

The night turned cool and the embers glowed in a death struggle. Lon twisted the metal cap from his canteen and savored the river water. He wiped his mouth and passed the water to his wife, who gently turned the container to her lips, letting her hand linger on the cold metal.

They lay together, warm and tired; his smell, masculine and sweet and hard, mingled with hers. The Southern Railway Atlanta run clattered across the trestle, and the campfire's embers rose a last time to the wind that came from the tracks. Lora pulled Lon's rough hand to her belly and slept.

Mayzelle washed the dust off her face at the sink.

Her mother paused behind her for a moment. "Mayzelle, you scrub much harder and you'll rub all the dark away."

Mayzelle brushed the dust from her hair. "Sun's gonna bleach me out anyway. Might as well be clean."

"Nobody ain't ever gonna accuse you of not bein' clean, girl. Now, get a move on. Elvin and the rest of the boys'll be here any minute expectin' supper."

"They can wait, Momma. Boys can wait a lot longer than they let on."

Her mother laughed. "You tellin' me somethin' I don't know? Why, Elvin's been complaining about late suppers since he's born, and he'll squall and carry on, but once he gets his gums on one of your biscuits, then he's heaven-bound."

"Brothers is funny that way," Mayzelle said as she took off her blouse and handed it to her mother.

"You must not be workin' very hard these days," the old woman said.

Mayzelle looked into her mother's questioning eyes, squinting in the glow of the pine fire.

"Why you say that, Momma?"

"Not much dirt in this blouse. Usually you bring in enough cotton field dust to plant a couple rows in your dress."

Mayzelle shook her head. A hint of a smile shadowed her lips. "You a wise woman. Just so happens I spent a lot of time talkin' with this real nice girl today, name of Lora. She's got purple eyes."

"You don't say."

"Yeah, and we just got to talkin' and one thing led to another and she sassed Jeffries."

"Sassed the foreman?"

"Watch your potato cakes, Momma—you gonna let 'em burn."

"Did he fire her?"

"Nope. Just drove off in a kind of a huff. That girl's got courage. Reminds me a lot of you."

"I don't know if I want you hangin' around no smart aleck. Jeffries might take a notion to fire both of you."

Mayzelle poured a cup of water into the bowl of flour. She glanced above for a moment. She could hear her sisters shouting. Must be wrestlin' again, she thought. She pushed her fingers into the dough, then stopped for a moment.

"What's wrong, Mayzelle? You in a daze or somethin'?"

"Nah, I was just thinkin' how I'd feel if Jeffries did fire me."

"I'll tell you—you'd feel foolish. Givin' up a good-payin' job like that. And I'll tell you somethin' else, you'd find a hard time gettin' another job in this town, that's for sure. And one more thing. You're gettin' marryin' age. What kinda man would have you, after you got fired from a job?"

"That's silly, Momma. I don't *feel* like I'm marryin' age. Why, you talk about me like I was some kinda chicken, toughed up in the joints like a rag-meated old hen."

"All I know is Nancy's thirteen, and she already got two proposals!"

"Fine for Nancy. I'm different."

"You can say that again, riskin' a decent-payin'—"

"Like three dollars last week workin' sunup to sundown? Decent?"

"Don't interrupt your momma. And don't pour that syrup on me. Answer my question."

"What question?"

"Why you risk a job just so you can gab with some funny-eyed woman?"

"Girl, not woman—least not yet. She's gonna have a baby, though. I guess I'm just naturally 'tracted to her. There's just somethin' about her. She acts kinda dumb, but she's tough and full of fun."

"Sounds like our mule."

Mayzelle pointed a finger across the table. "Not polite."

Her mother waltzed across the room, slowly unwinding her scarf, revealing a nearly bald head. She posed, one hand under her chin, her four teeth exposed in a devilish smile. "Excuse me, Miss Clark, I plumb forgot my manners. You see, I just a poor woman what's got no sense a'tall next to my wise and gentle lady daughter who can spend time socializin' in the fields—"

"Stop it, Momma."

A sound of crashing glass rushed between them. Sounds of violence drifted down the stairs. They hurried up the stairs toward the girls' bedroom.

"You younguns stop it! Stop it right now!" shouted the mother. "I swear," she hissed, as she separated the arms and legs of the fighting girls, "can't we get no peace in this house for a minute?"

The two youngsters, covered with perspiration, looked to Mayzelle for protection.

"Good Lord, Momma," she said obligingly, "they just playin'."

"They tearin' up this cabin, that's what they doin', and I won't stand for it. Seven people in one house! Looks like a stable in here. You girls clean up this room 'fore supper or I'll wear you out, that's a promise!"

"Come on, Momma," Mayzelle said wearily. "Your cakes are burnin'."

Her mother sniffed the air and ran down the stairs as Mayzelle put her hand over her mouth to keep from laughing. The two sisters began to giggle, but stopped when Mayzelle's bright, unblinking eyes met theirs.

9

"Y'all owe me one," she said as she closed the door.

"Momma?" she shouted impishly as she walked down the stairs. "I forgot to tell you. My friend at the farm—she's white!" Mayzelle stopped for a moment and listened for the slam of the oven door. She did not have to wait long.

Mayzelle looked around the corner of the stairwell. Her mother was staring wide-eyed, hands on her hips, lips pursed.

"Now, Momma, don't get all fired up," Mayzelle said, laughing. "Just look at you, all puffed up like some old hen."

"I ain't never! We got enough problems without you gettin' involved with some white girl. Where you been the last ten years? You askin' for trouble, don't you know that? White folks can't be friends with us and we can't be friends with them. It's just trouble, and I'm surprised that my own child, who I *used* to consider was the smartest of us all, has gone stark ravin' crazy."

Two

THEY HAD WALKED for nearly an hour along the rabbit trail on the river bank, sharing secrets and laughing easily, tripping over poison oak vines as thick as their legs, drifting toward a deeper, darker forest, thick with age and innocence.

"And Lon's a powerful lover," Lora blurted out, watching for Mayzelle's reaction. "Shocked, ain't you? But it's true. I feel like I got to tell somebody!"

Mayzelle rested against a tall scrub pine. "You full of surprises, ain't you?"

"You mean you don't want to hear it?"

"Course not, that's somethin' private. What a man and woman shares in the dark is between them, not for hollerin' in the open with strangers."

"Oh, you ain't no stranger. We got like minds. There's this touch that flows between brains that's kin. Don't you feel it sometimes? Lyin' in bed and everybody's asleep, and suddenly you think of me and you get this real funny feelin' like you want to smile cause you been touched with goodness?"

"Now I know you weird, Lora. That ain't nothin' magic, that's just friendship."

"You call it what you will. My way sounds more secret."

They approached a bend where a large rock jutted alone out of the center of the deep, moss-bottomed river. Clear water moved slowly, appearing not to move at all.

"This is it," Lora said grandly as she threw her dress to the nearest tree limb.

"What in God's name you doin'?" Mayzelle shrieked.

"I'm a-goin' swimmin'."

"But you pregnant!"

"So? My baby's goin' to grow up sayin' he was swimmin' before he was born."

"You can't do this. What if someone sees?"

"Nobody is gonna see, 'cept you." Lora stood for a moment and Mayzelle could not help staring. First time she ever saw a naked white woman.

A cool wind wrapped around Lora, carrying a clean smell, like new soap, through the glen. Her slender body hardly showed the mound carrying the child, but her breasts were huge. She swam carefully toward the rock in the river. She pulled herself up and shook her long black hair. Her eyes looked like polished agate, reflecting the brilliance of the sun on the river. She had deep dimples and a smooth complexion. Her eyebrows were dark and heavy, tilting toward her ears, giving her an impish appearance.

Mayzelle felt embarrassed, standing alone on the edge of the water. She wondered what to do now. Sit? Listen to the birds? Or join her new friend?

The quiet of the river was broken as Lora shouted across the water, laughing, "And my man Lon is the biggest and best in all South Carolina!"

Mayzelle shouted back, "I don't want to hear it!" Then, reluctantly at first, she eased into the water, in her clothes, toward the rock and her friend.

Mayzelle touched the flat rock but did not climb into view. "You know," she said, gasping for breath, "You ought not to shout all you think into the air."

Lora grinned. "Who's gonna hear me? Woodchucks? Besides, I'll tell the world that me and the boy in my belly is gonna make Lon the happiest man in the world. And our son'll grow up and marry a girl just like me and have lots of babies and live happy ever after."

Mayzelle laughed. "You got it all planned, don't you?"

Lora wiped the hair from her eyes. "Yep. Me and Lon work hard. Don't mind the hard work as long as we got time to live and be happy. I don't have room in my life for headaches and bad times."

Mayzelle rubbed her own hair, which she had kept short, down to her neck but not on it. Her skin was the color of aged, polished pine; her nose was a little broad, and her bright eyes were framed with long lashes. Her body was thin but well-toned by the work in the fields. There was a boyish quality about her appearance until she spoke, and then the words accentuated a feminine grace and dignity beyond her years.

"You a dreamer, Lora, a plain crazy dreamer. Life's gonna kick hell out of you like everybody else. What makes you think you so special?"

"Special?" Lora laughed softly. "I reckon havin' a good man who's willing to work hard to make things good for his family helps—but there's somethin' more. Let me ask you a question, Mayzelle."

"Go ahead, but don't make it too hard."

"If you could go back to a time before you was born, and make the choice whether to be born or not, would you do it?"

"What make you ask that? A person can't do that sort of thing so it's silly to answer."

"But would you? Even if you knew your own future?"

Mayzelle frowned. "Well, I seen some rough times, no daddy and all. But yeah, I reckon I'd still go through it again."

"Why?"

"That's two questions. I said you could ask me one."

"Come on, Mayzelle, don't you ever think about things like this?"

"No. I got better things to do."

"Why would you go through life if you knew all the bad things that were goin' to happen to you?"

"How bad?"

"Everything."

"Tell you the truth, Lora, I don't know and I don't think anybody else knows either. Frankly, I don't much like to think about rough times and hard livin'."

Lora leaned back on the rock.

Mayzelle took a deep breath. "Well?"

Lora smiled. "Well what?"

"Why, you know perfectly well what! What would *you* do?"

Lora leaned over and put her hand on Mayzelle's arm. "Lon makes it all worth it."

Mayzelle smiled and shook her head. "Honey, *no* man makes hard times worth the livin'. Why, you only sixteen. There ain't no tellin' what life has in store for you."

"Love makes it all worthwhile."

"You ain't in love, Lora, you in heat."

Lora sat up.

Mayzelle started to laugh and throw water from the river at Lora's face.

Lora held her hands up. "Stop it!" she shrieked. Soon the bend in the river echoed the sounds of childish laughter from the two girls at the rock.

Finally Lora took a deep breath. "I'm tired. You ready to go back?"

"No, not yet. I figure I'll stay awhile."

"Suit yourself. I'll see you in the morning."

"Right." Mayzelle watched Lora swim to shore, the light glancing off her shoulders, the clean, even strokes pulling the pink body through the gently rippling water. Lora dressed, waved, and carefully pushed her way through the pine branches covering the trail.

Downriver, behind the bushes, Jeffries watched without expression.

Mayzelle stayed for most of an hour, until she felt the chill of evening approaching. She swam to shore, took off her blouse to wring out the water, and pushed aside a limb hiding the trail.

When a hand slapped across Mayzelle's mouth, her heart jumped, and she fell, dizzy and nauseated, to the ground. She saw the foreman's face, felt the bruises beginning on her shoulders and the scratches ripping into her thighs. Soon the numbness on her face changed to a burn. In a rage, she struck him again and again across his face and head.

He was taut, muscular, and unfeeling. When she would not part her legs, he smashed his fist into her stomach. She tried to concentrate on the pain from his fist until he moved her body in quick, violent jerks.

Later, he helped her back to the road. He even said he was sorry he had hurt her arms. He said she shouldn't have tried to stop him.

She said she would kill him if he ever touched her again. She spent the night in the fields, wishing she were dead.

Friday was cooler than usual for the end of August. The field hands, smelling the moisture in the air, knew that rain would spoil the day. The clouds swept in from the west, and everyone gathered and dragged his half-filled bag to the barn across the road. Lora walked slowly, stopping a few times to watch the curtain of rain sweep over the hills, straining to hear the roar and crackle as the forest, once warm and quiet, was now loudly cleansed.

"Lora! Lora Mitchell! Get your fanny movin', girl! That cotton gets wet and you'll wish you had wings. Hurry, girl!" Mayzelle ran back, grabbed Lora's bag, and rushed ahead of the rain. Lora followed to the shed just as the icy summer storm broke upon them.

Mayzelle sat down next to her bag and shook her head. "Lordy, girl. If it wasn't for me, you'd never make it through the day. Guess it's over for you anyway. When you and Lon movin'?"

Lora opened her mouth to speak, but her words were lost in the thunder that shook the old timbers around them. "I said," she shouted, "this evening. Gonna ride into town on Jeffries' buggy and catch the wagon to Paw Creek."

"Good," Mayzelle said, her voice suddenly husky. "We'll get to talk a little 'fore you leave. Gonna miss you, girl, gonna miss you a lot."

Lora looked at the other workers standing in their little groups, and for the first time she was aware of how warm and familiar the human smell had become. She let her shawl drop to her lap and folded it into a neat square. "Mayzelle, I know that you're gonna think I'm crazy, and sometimes I guess I am; but I talked to Lon last night, and you and me, we got somethin' special and I know you ain't got no family and what with me gonna have a baby, I was thinkin' that maybe you—" She filled her lungs, then blurted, "Well, I don't know why you couldn't come with us!"

Mayzelle's eyes grew large, larger than Lora had thought that eyes could. Leaning forward, she whispered, "What?"

"I said, why don't you come with us? I'm sure Lon could get you a job somewhere in town. Lord, I don't know what I'm gonna do, sittin' around with a baby all day. Besides, we might be able to work it out so's you could live with us for free—it's a big house, bigger than we need, and you could live in the attic room."

"Honey, you askin' me to be a slave? 'Cause if'n you are, me and President Lincoln got news for you! It's 1904 and—"

Lora startled Mayzelle with a sudden lunge. "No! No! It's not like that at all! You don't understand. I'm askin' you to come and live with us and help me. I ain't offerin' no handout or nothin'. I've got nothin' to hand out nohow. But, to tell you the truth, city life scares me. I've lived in the country all my life and . . . I'll be lonely."

"Hush up, girl, I think I know what you're a-sayin'. You're right. It is crazy. I am gettin' right old sittin' around that house listening to those sisters of mine fight all the time. Course, I would miss that wagon ride. . . ." She watched Jeffries' buggy move among the field workers near the house. "I guess I'm not used to takin' chances like this."

"Wagon ride? One day, Mayzelle, me and Lon's gonna have a truck, not a wagon, and I promise you lots of rides. Lon, he's good and he's gonna make it someday where we won't have to walk everywhere."

"You bribin' me?"

Lora started to answer, but caught the gleam in Mayzelle's eyes. "You're a-mockin' me, Mayzelle Clark."

"Maybe I'll regret it," said Mayzelle, "but if I don't like it, I s'pose I can always move back here. Okay, girl, if you're sure that Lon don't care, then I'll try to make it at city life. 'Sides, time I moved on; I'm gettin' tired of the dust and God knows it'll take a strain off my momma."

"Good, it's settled. I got a little saved up that I can pay your wagon fee with—"

"You mean, *loan* me the money."

"Sure. Fine. A loan. You can go home and tell your momma, pack your clothes, and we'll get the wagon to Paw Creek at eight. Okay? Good. Oh, Mayzelle, we'll have a wonderful time. You and me and Lon. I know Lon's gonna like you. He don't say much, but he says that if I like you, then you must be pretty special."

"Girl, you're embarrassin' me with talk like that."

They stared at each other silently, with the knowledge that a commitment had been made. For a moment, it scared them both.

"What will Momma think?" Mayzelle said, awed by her decision.

"I told her I'd think about it, Momma."

The old woman did not smile or frown. Her face remained expressionless, like brittle leather, all ridges and cracks. Her mouth hardly opened. "So, you think you leaving?"

Mayzelle nodded.

The old woman drummed her fingers on the edge of the table. "Then leave," she said suddenly.

Mayzelle stood and walked to the iron stove. "Momma, I don't know why I'm leavin'."

"Then stay."

Mayzelle turned quickly. "You sure ain't much help. I need some advice. On one hand, I got to get away from all this noise and commotion. Too many people in this house. Ain't never had no privacy. And on the other hand, I don't want to leave you."

Her mother smiled for the first time. "I ain't never had no trouble out'n you. You and me and your brother Elvin raised those other kids. They all nearly grown now. You done paid your birthright dues. The only thing that worries me is your takin' up with white folks. Your daddy's prob'ly turnin' in his grave right now. You not been 'round many white people, 'ceptin' them white sharecrops. They can be awful hurtful."

"Not this one, Momma. She's different."

The old woman shook her head. "Sooner or later you'll learn that they's all the same. Not too many years ago her people used us like we use that ol' mule out back. And it's still in their blood, can't get it out. Each family of her folks is told over and over how we is just low-lifes. Don't blind yourself to that. Me and your daddy tried to hide it from you, but soon as you able to talk you see the hate that lives in their hearts. I just don't understand how you can go off and live with a white family. They'll turn you into a slave, sure enough. And if they don't, their own kind will turn against *them*, and you'll have to bear the guilt for what comes after. Nothing worse than white folks gouging their own kind, especially when it means cuttin' the bond that ties you to 'em. Everybody gets hurt—everybody loses. And you left with nothin' but a . . . a torch to carry; always burned by the guilt of knowing that you caused it all."

Mayzelle did not know whether to feel angry or sad. "I been with that girl, Lora, for nearly a month now, and I swear she ain't got no color on her, 'ceptin' for her eyes."

"And her husband?"

"I never seen him up close. Lon's real quiet, hardly ever says a word from what I been told. And from what she say, he's a gentle man who don't give no trouble to nobody and don't give a thought for what nobody thinks 'ceptin' his Lora."

"They young. When they babies come, things'll change."

"Maybe so, Momma. But I'm gonna give it a try, anyways. You always been good to me, Momma. But I need somethin' that I can't find in this house no more. I don't even know what I'll find away from here; but I got to try, don't I? I can't sit here all my life never chancin' nothin', never knowin' if somethin' better is out there."

"That's fair enough. Give it a workin' and if it don't work, you always welcome here. You know that."

Mayzelle put her hand on her mother's shoulder. "Thank you, Momma."

"For what?"

"For lettin' me go."

"No. No, I ain't *lettin'* you go. You *choosin'* this road by yourself. If'n you fall flat, I'll pick you up, but I'll not have no guilt laid on my pillow no matter what way it works out."

"I love you, Momma."

The old woman rose and walked upstairs, shouting, "Nancy? Elvin! Get in here for supper right quick, or food'll get cold and I'll wear you all out!"

Mayzelle walked to the front porch and felt the old railing. The green paint chips curled at her fingertips. I hope I know what I'm doin', she thought. Sure, Lora's white. And I'm a Negro. But we friends. She frowned. "Why can't we be friends?" she whispered.

Lon paid for the tickets and took Lora's arm. The horses groaned as the driver collected the money. Smoke from his pipe drifted toward the lone street lamp.

The wagon consisted of half a farm cart and half a Model T, somehow welded together. It boasted seven benches, four horses, and a baggage rack on the rear.

"She said she'd think about it," Lora said sadly. "I guess she did."

Lon nodded and motioned to the wagon. Another family, their baggage loaded, was already on board.

"I know it's gettin' late, but I so hoped that she would come with us, Lon. Please, let's wait just another minute." Her eyes widened with the effort to peer through the darkness toward town, up the narrow dirt road, past machine shops and boarding homes. Her smile came slowly as she saw the shadow, arms flailing, dash out of the night.

"Mayzelle! I knew you'd come!"

Mayzelle dropped her clothes box and knelt to tighten the rope around it. "Okay, girl," she said, "let's get movin'." She stood, walked up to Lon, and looked him in the face. "'Fore I go anywhere, I want to make sure it's all right with you. You the man of this family, and I ain't goin' nowhere I ain't wanted. Are you sure I can move in with y'all?"

Lon did not reply. He took the box from her hand and pointed to the back of the wagon.

Mayzelle smiled.

The night wagon to Paw Creek broke down only once; then it struggled along to its destination. Lora and Lon slept, but Mayzelle stayed awake. Lon had had to pay extra to get the driver to let her ride along, and then she had to ride on the baggage in the rear. Sleeping on a wagon was not her idea of comfort.

She pressed her forehead against the dirty back railing, trying to glimpse the small towns and the sights of the night, but the few houses that she could make out in the dark were blurred and stained through the thick dust that had covered the wagon's occupants.

She gave up watching and tried to sleep but could not. She had never been away from her home of sixteen years, and now she was traveling clear up into North Carolina. There was no one she could talk with, no one to share her fears.

So, here I am, she thought, riding in the back of a broken-down wagon with a couple of people I hardly know, being taken somewhere I've never been, and leaving everything that I've ever cared about behind me. Lord Jesus, take care of your Mayzelle, 'cause I ain't got sense enough to watch out for myself.

As she closed her eyes she thought of Jeffries. At least, she thought, I'm getting away from him. Away from his knotty hands tugging at my breasts.

She shuddered at the thought of Jeffries' wet fingers around her throat and his putrid breath seeking her mouth. She remembered clearly his bony elbows holding her shoulders down by the riverbank as he forced himself on her. She could almost feel the blood on her legs as she ran, shamed, toward the deep woods.

And then she remembered Lora. Lora took away the pain.

It was several hours before dawn when the wagon pulled into the depot at Paw Creek. Even in the darkness Mayzelle could see wide dirt streets, houses, and trees. More brick buildings than she had ever seen were stretched across the night. She grabbed her bags and waited for the wagon to clear out. Lon came back to get his things.

"Lora awake?" she asked.

He nodded and motioned for her to follow.

They walked together, the three of them, toward the part of town that seemed to glow and to light the clouds—the mill. Lora and Mayzelle sat down at the gatehouse while Lon walked into the massive brick structure. Mayzelle could not help staring at the tall brick smokestacks billowing clouds of steam and white dust into the early dawn. Lora reached over, patted her hand, and smiled.

Strange, thought Mayzelle, that this silly girl can reach me like this. But I wonder. Sometimes I wonder.

It was not long before Lon returned, fatigue burning his eyes. He bent over and kissed his Lora, then pointed to the sections of frame houses, each identical to the others. They walked to one of the houses and entered.

As the brightness in the east began to surround the mill village, they saw the outlines of the room begin to take shape. Lora looked at Lon and then wiped her eyes. Lon caught her look, and his face clouded for a moment with pain. "I'm just tired, Honey, that's all," she said. "This is beautiful, finally in our own house," she sniffed. As each part of the room became more clear, she stood and walked around, touching everything, lingering near wooden tables and chairs, running her hand over the fireplace wall, opening doors and windows. She then reentered the living room and declared with satisfaction, "Well, folks, we're *home*. We're gonna need some breakfast and some water. Mayzelle, you wash the walls and I'll wash the floors. Lon, you get some sleep on a real bed for the first time since we been married. You're gonna need it. You've got to go to work."

Lon walked to her and pulled her to him. He was a good foot taller than she, and her face just touched his chest. Mayzelle stood and went to the window. "I think I'll take a walk," she said. She opened the door to leave, turned, and said, "I better get a move on. It's almost six o'clock; the day's half gone." And with that she walked into the brisk air of a new and frightening morning.

Lon buried his face in Lora's hair. "My Lora," he whispered. "My Lora."

Three

February 1905

THE GUARD at the factory gate had been on duty for only a few hours when he saw a black-clad figure racing across the road through the rain. It was a young woman, heading straight to the gatehouse.

"What's the hurry, nigger?" he shouted, moving to meet her at the curb.

Mayzelle shouted back, "You get right on in there and tell Mr. Lon Mitchell that he'd better get home right now, 'cause his wife's havin' his baby and she's a-callin' for him. Now, hurry, Mr. Guard-man, get on in there 'fore I go in there myself!"

"Who the hell are you?"

"Who am I? Don't you recognize a . . . a . . . midwife when you see one? A mammy, a wet-nurse, a maid what's got no patience with men who ask foolish questions? Now go on, you hear? Mrs. Mitchell can't wait much longer, and if Mr. Mitchell ain't there when his boy is born, he's gonna whip you and me within an inch of our lives! Now go, man, git!"

Walking slowly, glancing over his shoulder, the guard laughed and walked away from Mayzelle to the front door. "Damn nigger," he mumbled, "givin' orders like she was somebody."

Lon was eating his lunch sitting on a window sill overlooking the muddy stream below the mill. He was reading an article in an old *McClures* by a state judge, who wrote that America was prosperous but in danger of losing that prosperity because of big corporations putting the little man out of the mainstream of capitalism. Lon hoped no one at the mill saw him reading the article.

He shook his head. It made little sense to him. Times were good and a man could feed his family. Working for a big company beat hell out of migrant farming. Either way a man always had hope.

"Lon!"

He looked at the angry gatehouse guard.

"There's some high-minded nigger out front bitching about you coming—"

Lon almost knocked him out of the way.

The guard walked over to the half-eaten lunch, took a bite out of a green onion and a piece of cold cornbread, and shook his head.

Mayzelle was not at the gate. Lon ran home alone. The door to the house was open, and knocking over a chair and a lamp on his way to the bedroom, he made his presence known. Mayzelle met him at the bedroom door and threw it open. Several women were clustered about the bed in the darkened room. Only one lamp in the corner was lit, casting an eerie glow on Lora, clad only in sweat and torn sheets.

"My God," Lon said.

"Now, don't you go gettin' everybody upset, Mr. Mitchell," said Mayzelle matter-of-factly. "No sense in gettin' upset. Everybody's doin' fine."

"Lon? Lon?" Lora's black hair was curled and wet, and rivulets of perspiration collected around her chin. One of the ladies pulled Lon over to Lora's side, where he knelt and wiped her brow. The smell of cotton fiber on his trousers reassured her.

The midwife tried to place a rag in her mouth, but she would have none of it. Between her clenched teeth she tried to shout, "No!" Lon stroked and soothed her until finally she took the rag. Then the expression on her face changed to real pain as she looked away from her husband, toward the light and then at her huge belly. She shook and shivered. One of the women pushed Lon out of the way and he drew back to strike her, but Mayzelle shot him a glance and he checked his hand.

Slowly the head, then the shoulders of the thing were revealed. Mayzelle gently pulled Lon backwards and out of the room. He covered his mouth and was led away unresisting.

Soon the closed room exploded with cheers, then a brief wail. Lon rushed back into the room, and this time Mayzelle did not try to restrain him. He fell on his knees at the side of the bed. Lora smiled at him and then led his eyes to the nearby table where the women had gathered. Mayzelle walked among them and brought the naked and wet child to its father. She grinned from ear to ear. "I sure hope you ain't disappointed, Mr. Mitchell, 'cause you are now the proud daddy of a baby girl what looks just like your Lora!"

Lon's face went pale.

"What's wrong with it?" he whispered. The room grew quiet. Lora searched his face for disappointment and began to cry.

Mayzelle leaned over his shoulder. "What you mean?"

"It's face . . . and its head . . . are all squashed up and slanted-looking. . . ."

Mayzelle could hear the other women in the room release simultaneous sighs of relief. And then laughter. Lora smiled.

The color came back to Lon's face. Mayzelle had her hand over her mouth.

"Damn it," he said. "Somethin's wrong with the girl! She's so ugly!"

Mayzelle almost put her hand on his shoulder.

"They supposed to look that way at first," she said, trying not to embarrass him any more than she could help. "All babies get squashed up a little being born. But you go on outside and wait just a little bit and your daughter's flesh will firm up into a real beauty, I promise."

Lon wiped his brow and looked at Lora. "That so?"

Lora stroked the child's back. "Of course, Lon. I'm surprised at you. I thought you knew all about such things."

Lon stood. "She looks a little like me, don't she?"

"I hope not," Mayzelle whispered.

Lon grinned.

Lora reached for his hand. "You disappointed, aren't you, Lon? You wanted a boy. I'm so sorry. Next time we'll have a boy, a son to carry your name, and we'll name him after you. I promise."

Mayzelle frowned. "Don't talk such nonsense right now." She pointed to the bedroom door. "We got a lot of cleaning up to do, Mr. Mitchell. You go on out into the living room and soon as we get the baby cleaned up we'll bring her to you."

Before he left he kissed Lora. "I love you."

She was asleep.

Mayzelle walked with him to the living room. He sat down in a chair next to the window and stared out through the rain.

Mayzelle brought him a glass of water. "She's gonna be a real beauty, Mr. Mitchell. Don't look so sad."

"What? Oh, hell, Mayzelle, I'm not sad. Long as the girl is healthy, that's all that matters. Course, we did have our mind set on a boy, but there's plenty of time for that. I just didn't figure on too large a family at first."

"My momma always said that even when you down to your last biscuit, the Lord will provide. My momma was never wrong."

Lon smiled. "Want a drink?"

"I don't drink, Mr. Mitchell, and you know it."

"Mind if I do?"

"Course not. It's a big day for all of us. You better sneak it quick, 'cause them ladies from next door will be out of that room with the baby any minute, and I don't want that baby to see no liquor on its first day."

"*You* don't want?"

"Well, I hope you don't mind, but I've got to help Lora take care of that child. You know how scatterbrained that Lora can be."

Lon laughed. "Uh-huh." He walked to the wall next to the fireplace and removed a plank, glancing over his shoulder for a moment as he reached deep into the wall and pulled out a small bottle. He poured the liquid into the water glass and replaced the board. He glanced at Mayzelle. "You gonna tell?"

She held her head up. "Don't give me one of those looks. Of course I ain't gonna tell."

The door to the bedroom opened and a short woman with red hair brought the baby to Lon. She offered the child to him. "See, Mr. Mitchell, all that swelling's gone."

Lon held the child. "Well, for a few minutes back there she did look like Lora's grandfather, but now she's—she's just beautiful." He touched her hand with his finger. "Ila," he said. "My sweet Ila."

❦

They named the child Ila, after Lon's mother, and Elizabeth after Lora's. Ila grew quickly under the stern eye of Mayzelle and the gentle touch of Lora. Lon refused to spoil or pamper the child, and he continued, without luck, to try for boys. In the years that followed the spring of 1905, Lora had two more girls, Pearl and Vera.

One per year. The cost of rearing a large family was beginning to tell. In 1908, from time to time, Lon traveled by train to nearby towns to mills that were owned by the Bradley family of Paw Creek. Mayzelle assisted Lora in the care of the girls. She stopped taking part-time jobs in the nearby fields and spent more of her time working with Lora, diapering, washing, cooking, sewing. Lon was at home less and less, and Lora seemed to save her energy for him when he was there.

Of all the Mitchell girls, Ila alone received Mayzelle's true affection. Mayzelle had once told Lora that if Mr. Mitchell wouldn't spoil the child, then somebody else had to, and that that somebody would be Mayzelle whether the family liked it or not. Lora agreed readily. Soon Ila began to display, along with the grace of her mother and the silent strength of her father, a stubborn streak from Mayzelle.

The house was large and comfortable, two stories of frame with high-ceilinged rooms. Mayzelle lived in the attic, which was off limits to all

23

members of the family on Lora's orders because she knew the value of privacy. Sometimes Mayzelle woke before dawn to find that Ila had crawled into bed with her. She protested and scolded, and carried the youngster down to the living room while she fetched wood for the fire. Ila's pranks always gave Mayzelle secret delight, especially in winter, when the extra warmth was drowsily accepted.

When Ila was eight, Lon and Lora planned a birthday party for Lon's mill foreman, Mr. Oliver. Lora and Mayzelle spent a week cleaning the house for the big event. Mr. Oliver arrived in an excited mood, possibly enhanced by the consumption of more alcohol than necessary. Lora told him the government had warned people to watch out for tainted products. Mr. Oliver laughed and said his grandfather had lived to be one hundred by taking a drink every afternoon and if it was good enough for Granddad, then it was good enough for Harold Oliver. Matter of fact, his grandfather had gone down on the *Titanic*.

Pearl and Vera handed him a gift: a pair of socks and a scarf for the winter. Soon the parlor filled with neighbors.

Ila was upstairs with Mayzelle while the cake was cut. Ila had been caught, during the morning frost, stealing apples from wire baskets at the grocery store on the corner. Such shame was not to be tolerated in the Mitchell family. Lora and Lon had not spoken to her all day.

Mayzelle listened to the laughter below. "Now, you could be down there with them a-havin' a good time if you hadn't stole them apples."

"I was hungry."

"Why, child, your momma cooks the best breakfast in this county and you know it."

"But I might die from hunger by the time she gets up in the mornin'!"

"Where you hear about dyin' from hunger? You don't know what hunger is. I remember my momma cookin' cornbread without milk. You luckier than most, I tell you that! Besides, your momma works hard! Where you think she goes after supper most nights?"

Ila shrugged. "I don't know."

"I'll tell you where. After cleanin' up after you and makin' three meals a day and worryin' whether you out stealin' apples, she goes to the mill and works 'longside your daddy. He works from dawn to deep night. You got to 'preciate that. When I was your age, I worked 'longside my momma in the devil's cotton fields. And all you got to do is get fat off'n your momma's cookin', and worry your sisters, and bother your daddy, and steal apples to shame your ol' Mayzelle!"

Ila closed one eye and looked up at Mayzelle. In a voice filled with disbelief, she said, "You worked with the devil?"

Mayzelle knew a good opening for a moral lesson when she saw one.

She lowered her voice. "Yes, little Miss Priss. The devil hisself, though he called hisself Jeffries. But I knew better. I knowed all along that he was the devil."

"How'd you know?" Ila whispered.

"'Cause I just knowed, that's all. Then I got saved."

"Who saved you?"

"Your sweet momma and daddy, that's who done saved me. Your momma walked right up to that devil and told him to leave me alone and then spit in his eye!"

"She did?"

"Shore did. And 'cause your momma's a good woman, that devil wouldn't touch her, 'cause he knew that she didn't do nobody no harm and didn't steal what rightly belongs to other folks."

"Mayzelle, I don't want no devil to get me." Ila's mouth began to twitch.

"Do what your momma tells you to do and you won't have to mess with the devil, but if you don't, he'll come up to your room one night and eat your hands and feet right off'n your body."

"No!"

"Yes! What you lookin' so sullen for?"

"I love apples, Mayzelle, I really do. I don't know if I can stop eating them."

"I didn't say you had to stop eatin' them, I just said you had to stop *stealin'* them."

At that moment Ila and Mayzelle heard a crash from below. They rushed down the stairs to loud shouts and cries of alarm.

Oliver had fainted.

Worse, thought Mayzelle, he's not breathing.

Lon picked Oliver up and carried him to Lora's bedroom, dropping the large body on the bed and slapping his face. Oliver did not respond.

"Go get the doctor," Lon shouted.

Someone slammed the front door.

Mayzelle brought some cold water and Lon splashed it on Oliver's face. Already a pale blue color was forming on the man's lips.

Lora covered her face. "He's dead. Oh, God, he's dead."

Several of the women in the crowd left, and Lon heard them weeping in another room. He ordered everyone out of the bedroom. He couldn't understand this. One minute Oliver was bright and cheerful, and the next he was dead.

"It was that liquor," Lora said. "I tried to warn him."

Mayzelle pulled Lora from the room. Lon followed and shut the door.

In the uproar no one saw Ila pull the bedroom door open and walk in. She walked carefully, on tiptoe, to the foot of the bed. She had never seen a dead person before. His shirt was loosened, and someone had removed his shoes.

Ila frowned. "Doesn't seem so bad, being dead. He's just not breathing, that's all. Course, he looks a little funny, all blue and cold white."

She stared at him without moving for a long time. She tried to imagine him alive and breathing. "Dead," she whispered. "Ain't nothin' to it."

She smiled. Later she would tell Pearl and Vera all about it and they would be so jealous. Ila alone with a dead man. In fact, there was one more thing she could do. She could touch him.

She reached over to Oliver's foot, closed her eyes, and, clenching her teeth, grabbed his toes and squeezed.

"What the hell do you think you're doing?" Oliver asked.

Ila's eyes were wide for only a second before she crumpled to the floor.

Oliver rubbed his face. "Must'a passed out or somethin," he muttered as he sat up. "Where the hell's everybody at, little girl? Little girl?"

He leaned over the side of the bed and saw Ila sprawled out on the floor. She had fainted.

He laughed. "You too?"

He pulled himself out of bed and walked to the living room, where the family and friends were trying to prepare explanations for the tragedy before Mrs. Oliver and the doctor arrived.

Oliver saw Lora with her hand over her face near the window.

"Lora," he shouted, "who died?"

She dropped a cup of coffee, and others chorused a collection of Oh My Gods and Jesus Christs.

Oliver rubbed his eyes and grinned. "Lon, my friend, this is just the nicest birthday party a man could have."

The first thing Ila said when brought out of the faint was, "Am I dead too?" Her confinement to her room was appealed and suspended.

Mayzelle and Lora spent the afternoon looking after guests who had followed Ila's example when Oliver had walked into the room.

Lora found Lon sitting on the back porch holding his sides, tears streaming down his face, catching his breath between bursts of laughter.

Oliver apologized and explained the nature of catatonic trances. Lon waved him away. He couldn't talk.

"It wasn't funny," Lora said as she returned to the guests.

Three nights later, propelled by a dark and bitter wind from the north, Lora opened the door to find the house quiet; only the fire greeted her. Looking around for any unusual signs, she took her coat off and walked toward the fire. She sat down with her thin knuckles clenched over her mouth. She placed her basket on the floor.

"Lora?"

"Mayzelle! You startled me. You ought to let me know you're around. Don't ever spook me like that again!" A trace of harshness in her voice left an ugly air in the room.

Mayzelle walked closer to the chair and caught the fire mirrored in Lora's eyes. "What's wrong, Honey?" she asked gently.

"Are the children in bed?" Lora whispered.

"Why, you know they are, been there for an hour or so. I stayed up and made some coffee for you and Mr. Mitchell." She paused and looked around. "Where's Mr. Mitchell?"

Lora's words came quickly. "I don't know, Mayzelle. I went to the train station to surprise him with some ham biscuits. You know how he likes them. But the train didn't come. They say they don't know what happened to it. My Lon's never been late, you know that. I never did want him to work out of town, even for a few days. Don't know why Bradley sends him to those other mills."

Mayzelle stroked Lora's hair. "Now, listen, Honey, Mr. Mitchell would be mighty unhappy, you showin' yourself like this. No proper lady would be blubberin' like this, and you gonna wake up those children. Your Lon's gonna be fine. Here, you come with Mayzelle to your room and lie down. When he comes in a-yellin' for you, he ain't gonna be pleased to see that squirmed-up face of yours!"

Lora reluctantly went to her room and closed the door. Mayzelle put more wood on the fire.

Ila opened the bedroom window and looked into the yard one story below. The wind was crisp, and little pools of water had frozen on the ledge that circled the upper story of the house. She pulled herself up and out onto the ledge. The wind filled out her white nightgown.

The cold made her hair light and weightless; thin wisps caressed her neck and shoulders. Her face was thin, her eyes large and brown with a rim of green circling the edges of her pupils. Her lips were like Lon's, full and sensuous. Her small, fine features gave her the appearance of a child in transition to womanhood.

"Ila Elizabeth!" shrieked Pearl, rushing to the window. "You better get in here right now, or I'm gonna tell Momma."

"Oh shush, you snitch," came the hoarse, whispered reply. "I do this lots of times. Here, come on and watch."

"What you gonna do?"

"I'm gonna skate, that's what. Watch me."

Ila's bare feet touched the frozen streams and she glided almost effortlessly across the ledge past the windows of the other rooms. Then she glided back.

"How do you do that, Ila?"

"You gotta be eight before you can do this. Only eight-year-olds have the gift. When you're eight, I'll help you skate."

"When will I be eight?"

"Now, don't you go gettin' excited. You'll be eight in another year."

"That long?"

"Yep." And with that she slid across the ice again. Her feet numb with cold, she glided like an apparition from one end of the house to the other, pretending that she was an angel. Suddenly, one foot slid off the edge and she caught her breath and grabbed the shutter of a window as she passed. She straightened up and glanced quickly at Pearl, who was covering her eyes, crying. Pearl slowly moved one hand from over her eyes, looked down to where she expected to see her sister sprawled on the ground, and then slowly looked up. Ila had her finger to her mouth. She steadied herself before continuing. A warm glow lit the window beside her and Ila peeked in. She saw Momma.

Lora was shaking. Something was wrong and Lora knew it. All the women in her family had the gift to feel danger, and that gift was suffocating her. She knelt beside the bed, and the incantation she used was magnified against the thin window panes.

In a few moments the door to her room slowly opened. One by one, three girls, each a smaller image of the other, tiptoed into the room and knelt beside their mother. They tried to copy as best they could the words from her lips, begging God to protect her Lon, wherever he might be.

"Ila Elizabeth," Lora said, "child, you're shiverin'! Come here to your momma. Why, you're freezin' to death! Come now, all of you, get in the bed before you all catch your death." The children nestled around their mother, and Ila cast a glance at Pearl as if daring her to speak of the ice-laden ledge outside. Pearl knew better.

❦

The light was low and the globe blackened by soot when Lon crept into the room. Lora and the girls were asleep. He pulled a chair near the bed, wondering whether to wake them. Sitting in the chair, he fell asleep.

It was daylight when Lon woke with a jerk. Lora was pushing the last of the children out of the bedroom.

28

How long, Lon thought, have I been asleep?

He moved to the bed and stretched his tense frame across the mattress, soaking up the warmth that had been his children. Lora came to him.

"I was afraid for you," she said. "What happened?"

"Train late. That damn mill riot in Hoskins slowed down all the trains."

"I was worried."

"I know. I'm sorry."

"But I didn't give up hope. I knew you'd be all right."

He kissed her. "How did you know that?"

"Because I will not accept hopelessness."

He laughed and kissed her again. "Sometimes you talk strange, Lora."

Lora pulled the covers to his neck. He had talked to her of unrest in the textile mills before, and she knew from the way he talked that sooner or later he would be involved. But that did not matter now.

He was warm and safe.

That was all that mattered.

"Does Daddy have to work today?"

"You know your daddy works on Saturday, but today he's goin' to be a mite late, Miss Priss."

Ila opened the door to the iron bread box behind the stove. Here, no matter what time of day, anyone could usually find a morsel of warmed bread or meat, kept warm by the coals within the heavy black stove.

"Mayzelle, this here box is empty!"

"You got it, Ila Elizabeth. Your daddy's been up near the whole night, and we gonna fix him a fine breakfast. Now, why don't you go get your sisters up?"

"Do I gotta?" Ila whimpered.

"Git."

"'Fore I go, tell me what we're havin' to eat."

"I don't say 'git' but once, young lady."

"Yes'm," she sighed.

Ila walked to the stairway as if each step brought immeasurable pain. She finally stopped halfway up and peered through the bannister. Mayzelle was placing thick slices of fatback into the iron skillet. Then she walked to the rust-flaked icebox and pulled a package from deep inside. She rolled slabs of fish, which she had cleaned at dawn, into the cornmeal until the slabs were coated from head to tail.

Imagine, thought Ila, fish for breakfast. We livin' like rich folks. She ran to her room, spreading the good news to Pearl and Vera.

29

Soon the living room resounded with the shouts of the three girls dressing before the fire. Lora and Ila moved from one to another, adjusting dresses and tying shoes. Lon slowly walked down the stairs as if savoring each moment that kept him at home, reluctant to make those necessary final moves that would lead him to the mill.

"'Bout time you got up, Your Highness," Lora said.

Lon looked at her in mock pain. He would have been down earlier had she not insisted that he sleep late.

Mayzelle and Lora placed the food on the thick elm table. As usual, the children argued about who was to sit next to Daddy, and as usual, Ila won out, bribing Vera with an orange she had hidden under her bed. Mayzelle glanced at the table and placed her food on a shelf near the sink, away from the family.

"Ila," said Lora, "you eat everything on your plate so your sisters will follow your example."

Ila looked at her fatback and then cut a glance to Pearl. The corners of Pearl's mouth were twitching and her eyes were rolling toward the ceiling.

"Momma, I can't eat with Pearl makin' fish eyes like that."

Pearl was tall, with a defensive, surprised look perpetually imprinted on her face. Her eyes were small and round and her mouth was filled with crooked teeth. When she smiled, all these features marked a happy, peaceful countenance. When she frowned, or was angry, her forehead turned red. It was red now.

"I am not makin' fish eyes!"

"You are, too."

Lon tapped his fork on the side of his plate and the argument ended. Both girls began to pour molasses onto their hot biscuits.

"Lon," said Lora, "more buttermilk? Pearl, you can have some butter for those biscuits if you want; not much left anyway. Maybe if you girls are nice, you can go to the store with Mayzelle after Daddy goes to work."

Butter? thought Pearl. Daddy ought to stay away more often if it sweetens up Momma like this. She pushed her chair to the side and moved toward the icebox, stopping for a moment to repeat to Ila that Momma had said that *she* could have some butter on *her* biscuits.

Ila sucked in her mouth and prepared to slap Pearl with a spoon of molasses, but thought better of it.

Lon, oblivious to the quarrels, slit the fish along the backbone, pulled the flesh in loose chunks from the pinlike ribs, and pried patiently at the meat within the skull.

Mayzelle looked up from her place and watched Lon licking the salt from his lips. She could always tell whether he liked a meal by the calmness that seemed to relax his stern jawline when he enjoyed the food, and the nervous, impatient tic when he did not.

Mayzelle pumped the water lever over the sink at precisely the same time that Lora gathered the plates from the girls. Before the water could gush into the waiting pan, Lon was up and at the door. Lora brought his jacket and told him that she would bring his lunch to the mill. They walked onto the porch out of sight of the children, where he kissed her. She tasted the salt from his lips and wiped his face with her napkin.

He stood patiently as she ran back inside to get a brush. When she returned, she brushed his hair quickly, harshly, to her liking—an unbroken daily ritual that allowed a brief intimacy, even in times of quarrel or crisis. In five minutes, she thought, that strawlike hair will be strewn all over his head.

She watched him walk away, shoulders bent a little more than last year and the year before. The wind destroyed her careful brushing. His hands worked over the coins in his pockets, his eyes fixed on the mill down the road.

Her future was in that man; her hopes and dreams, perhaps even some of her pain, all ran through his veins and pumped through his heart. Come a long way since South Carolina, she thought. Got three good girls and Mayzelle. All I need now is a son for Lon. Then everything will be complete.

She took a deep breath as he walked out of sight. A son. Doesn't feel right, even thinking about it.

She smiled. No matter. I'll give him what he wants most.

Ila went to Lon's plate and stared for a moment at the half-eaten biscuit that he had left. She pulled a napkin from her dress pocket and carefully placed the rough bread on it, weaving the napkin ends over the top so that no crumbs could escape.

The screen door startled her as it slammed behind Lora. Ila hurriedly hid the treasure in her pocket.

"Now, you girls go on with Mayzelle to the store while I clean up this mess. Don't forget, Mayzelle, we need butter and one talcum powder. I'm gonna wash those white coats Lon bought for the younguns for church tomorrow. Then we can brush them with the talcum."

Mayzelle opened the door, and the little Mitchell army marched in single file onto the porch and down the gray stone steps to the lawn. Ila led, carefully glancing behind to see that Pearl was not making faces. She was.

Vera followed. Vera always followed, thought Ila. Lord, Pearl could tell Vera to jump out the window and she would.

Mayzelle helped Vera down the steps. Vera had not lost any baby fat. Her cheeks seemed to be in a permanent state of expansion. The onliest child not breast fed, thought Mayzelle. I warned 'em, and they wouldn't listen—child's gonna get fat and stay that way. No sir, they wouldn't listen.

The girls, still in a line, kicked the cinders in front of each other down the path that some called a sidewalk, although it had neither boards nor cement like the rich parts of town—only cinders from the mill, piled on top of each other, competing to ruin the shoes and stockings of little girls.

They came to the corner, where a wide intersection separated the mill-owned houses from the rest of the town. Ila looked both ways, waiting for a moment when they could safely cross with no fear of beer or meat wagons running them down. As they were waiting, three black boys about Ila's age ventured from a nearby vacant lot enclosed by mulberry bushes. One of the boys grabbed a cinder and eyed Ila. Ila was aware that the cinder was about the size of an egg, and also aware that when Mayzelle looked the other way, the boy would throw it.

"Better not!" Ila shouted.

Mayzelle looked the situation over and gave a stern eye to the boy. He bowed graciously. The girls started across the street. Suddenly the peace of the intersection was broken by a loud and terrible wailing. Vera was on the ground, rubbing her leg, sobbing, looking for the bee that surely must have stung her. Mayzelle knelt and picked her up, hurrying across the street with the child in her arms. Pearl followed. Ila ran back to the corner and shouted to the boys as they disappeared into the tall grass and broken fences, "Nigger, nigger, black as tar, jumped into a jelly jar. Jar broke, nigger croaked, and they all went to heaven on a white billy goat!"

"Ila!" shouted Mayzelle. "You git your butt back across this street right now, you hear?"

Ila complied.

"Now, wouldn't your momma be 'shamed to hear that you weren't no lady?"

"Well, they sure weren't no gentlemen."

Mayzelle thought for a moment and decided that it would be best for everybody to let it ride.

"Come on, girls. Vera, you hold Ila's hand. Come on, Darlin', you ain't gonna die or nothin', barely scratched you. I'm gonna have a talk with those boys' momma. Yes sir, that's what I'm gonna do!"

The sidewalks turned from cinder to plank and the girls trotted along behind Mayzelle toward the mill store near the hotel. People swore each year that the hotel would be torn down, but its presence gave the lie to such rumors.

"You girls go on in, but don't touch anythin'."

The store smelled of linseed oil, which had been applied the day before to the oaken floorboards. Mayzelle stepped to the counter and placed her order for one box of talcum powder and one pound of butter.

"That all?" said Mr. Brinkley.

"Yes sir, that's all Mrs. Lon Mitchell wants today."

Brinkley pulled out a card from a soiled shoebox and carefully penciled in the cost of the items.

"Scrip?" he asked without looking up.

"Yes sir."

"That'll be ten cents in company scrip."

She reached into her front pocket and carefully counted out the company money that Lora had given her.

Suddenly, Mayzelle felt a jerk on her arm. "'Scuse me."

She quickly turned eye to eye with another customer, who had been standing near the pine shelves. She moved to the side without word or expression and waited for the man to place his order.

Brinkley refiled the Mitchell card and stepped back, nodding his head as he memorized the man's list of goods. "Now, that's two pounds of flour? Or was it three, Mr. Deal?"

"Two. Don't know what the old woman does with it. I sure don't eat it all."

"Here you go, Mr. Deal. That'll be thirty cents. Scrip?"

"Nope, cash." Deal leaned over the counter and motioned for Brinkley to meet him halfway. "Brinkley, I thought you didn't let no niggers in this here white man's store. Folks not gonna 'preciate that. Now, I know that a man's got to make a bit of money on the side if he's gonna prosper, but makin' it from niggers? Well, that don't seem right. 'Sides, I'll bet the mill wouldn't 'preciate that either. Gives the place a bad name. No sir, Bradley would raise hell." He spat in Mayzelle's direction.

Brinkley leaned closer to Deal and frowned, glancing at the other customers, who were trying to hide the fact that they were waiting to hear his reply.

"Now, Mr. Deal," he began loudly, "don't you go and get upset till you know why—"

"Why?" said Deal with a smile and tilt of the head.

"Because, Mr. Deal, it is company policy that nigger women what's

33

workin' for mill workers can come into the store for Mister or Missus' goods. We never allow 'em to buy for themselves. See, I mark it all down right here."

"Still," said Deal, scowling, "I ain't all pleased by it."

"Frankly, I don't like the idea myself, but ol' Mr. Bradley, he's got some mighty peculiar ideas." Brinkley lowered his voice to a hoarse whisper. "I'm just obeyin' orders. You oughta know he's mighty protective of his workers, just like family. Lon Mitchell's been a good worker, and I'm sure that if your kids had a mammy, the woman would be allowed in only as a favor to you."

Deal grunted, gathered his bags, turned, and spat as he passed Mayzelle. She walked again to the counter.

Brinkley smiled at her. "Now, where was we? Pound of butter and some talcum powder. Here you go."

The girls arrived at the door at the same time as Mayzelle and followed her to the street. Ila walked behind with her head bowed. Mayzelle walked stiffly, slowly, her face placid, her eyes distant.

They turned the corner and passed the hotel porch. Pearl and Vera rushed up the steps to the empty rocking chairs. The girls began to rock as fast and as hard as they could, their arms and legs moving in the air, their back muscles straining to gain speed.

"You girls!" shouted Mayzelle. "Get on down off that porch 'fore I tells your momma and she blisters you good." The girls jumped out of the chairs and skipped down the steps.

Suddenly, from above, came a rasping voice: "Now, wait a minute, nigger!"

Mayzelle looked to the balcony where the slurred words had been spoken. Two elderly men, both unshaven and tall, with hollow cheeks and large knobby bones, were grinning down at her. "You shore ain't got no manners like no proper nigger girl."

Mayzelle turned and walked away. The children followed.

"Hey, nigger girl!" one shouted. "You stop and listen when your betters is speakin' to ya! I'll come down there and beat you good if you don't."

She walked faster.

"I want some pussy!" shouted the other man, waving a bottle and laughing. "Good young nigger pussy. Yes sir, that's what I want and I want it now!"

"Prob'ly big enough for both of us!" screamed his friend.

The girls walked briskly, holding their heads high like Mayzelle, saying nothing, each with a vague sensation that their Mayzelle had been violated.

Mayzelle walked into the house, placed the butter in the icebox, and gathered the children around the fireplace, where she carefully, tenderly undressed them. Lora was standing over the sink scrubbing white hunks of cotton, kneading the water out and shaking them into shape over the stove. "You girls are gonna be the prettiest angels at church tomorrow, mark my word. Your daddy picked these coats special. This evenin' we'll brush 'em, and people gonna say you are real angels for sure, come to visit Paw Creek from Heaven."

The lamp was low in the living room, a sign that all was well within. Lon walked up the stairs more slowly than he had walked down that morning. He felt his way along the dark hallway to the first door and then the second. As he placed his hand on his own bedroom door, the door behind him squeaked open, and the moonlight traced his child's shape on the tile floor.

"Daddy?" Ila said.

He walked to her and knelt.

"Daddy, what's a nigger?"

Lon was thankful that she could not see his brow descend, hear his heart race, or feel his blood heat his face. She waited a moment and held out her hand. He reached for it, feeling the softness of her fingers. She placed a crumbly object into his hand and shut her door.

A biscuit. A half-eaten biscuit.

After breakfast, Ila was summoned to the porch. She sat on the steps as Lora rocked. "Ila, Honey, your daddy said you mentioned a bad word that some men said to our Mayzelle. He said that maybe I should talk to you about what them men said and answer any questions you might have. You see," she said, lowering her eyes and rubbing the rocker arm, "we got an unusual relationship here. Might say no one in town can claim to have what we got. What we got is a friend, a special friend. We know that our friend is . . . uh . . . colored, and you know that some people treat her different from what we do. And, well, Mayzelle *is* different. I'd be lyin' to you if I told you otherwise. She's a friend, though, and that wipes out all the differences. The advantages, see, of havin' her as a friend, wipe out all the disadvantages, see. But *some* of her people, they . . . uh . . . they different, and some of 'em got bad reputations, and some are lazy, and some just not up to our kind . . . you know?"

"No," Ila said softly.

Lora ran her hand through her hair. "Now, Honey, you ain't listenin' to me real good. I really care for Mayzelle. She's done a lot for me . . . and us. I don't know why, but I got a deep feelin' that she and you, bein' real close and all, gonna need each other some day. Now, why did I say that?" Lora looked confused, blank. "This ain't goin' right . . . she . . . *you* will need *her*. Now, how in blazes do I know that so well?"

"Momma, you all right?"

"Uh, yeah . . . ," Lora said quickly. "I was just thinkin'. Got real afraid there for a minute. Got a feelin' deep down, intuition or somethin'. At any rate, Mayzelle is a friend of the family and is special to us. You girls are at the age where you might notice other people treatin' her different . . . and I just want you to feel comfortable, that's all. You do feel . . . comfortable . . . don't you?"

"I love Mayzelle."

"Course you do."

"Don't you?"

Lora was perplexed. "Me? Why, yes, of course I do." She laughed. "We all love her and I hope we always will. But we can't let the way other people treat her hurt us."

"Why not?"

Lora felt her mouth screw up into a grimace. "I guess we can't help lettin' it hurt us, Ila; but somehow we got to learn to live with it."

"Why?"

"'Cause that's the way things is."

"I don't understand."

"Maybe your father can explain it to you. I done the best I can."

"What's a nigger?"

"Where you hear that?"

"Everywhere. Even you say it sometimes."

Lora felt it again, something peculiar inside. "I won't say it again. It's not a nice word at all."

"Good," Ila said. "Tell Daddy it's all settled."

"What is?"

"Everything."

Four

December 1917

FOR ONCE the town was clean. The snow had drifted in from the mountains and seemed determined to stay. Even the dirty row houses near the mill seemed washed by the melting ice dripping from the roofs.

Only two Mitchell children squatted silently in the yard, each in her own world, forming make-believe castles from the loose white powder. The sky was clear, and the thin, crisp layer of frozen top snow was alive with blinking silver lights, reflections of a warm morning sun. Pearl and Vera, in identical heavy cloth coats, black lace-up shoes, and soft cotton hats with red ribbons tied around, looked at the crowd on the sidewalk.

From her window, Ila watched a group of children, each with a cloth hat, some with brims and some without. Their coats were little more than heavy shirts with a row of buttons on the left side and sleeves long enough to cover cold hands. An older girl herded the children around a corner; her dress of red and white stripes covered a pair of sturdy men's boots. Close behind them came dozens of soldiers, kissing and hugging dozens of short-haired girls wearing long strings of beads and long black Sunday dresses. The soldiers had broad military hats, baggy pants, and stiff leggings.

Downstairs, Lora knitted red and brown socks for the American Red Cross. She and Mayzelle knitted a sweater every month to be shipped to the men overseas.

Ila sullenly watched her sisters from her bedroom window. It seemed colder in the room than it did outside. She heard the door behind her open but she did not turn around. She knew who it was. Only Mayzelle would dare defy Momma's orders.

"Child, I brought you some breakfast. Come on over here and eat."

"Don't want any."

"Now, Miss Priss, you're a-huffin' and a-puffin' and a-poutin', and you know how ugly that's gonna make you."

"I don't care!" she said.

Pearl and Vera were laughing below.

"Look at 'em, Mayzelle, stupid little girls who would be up here with me if they weren't so stupid."

Mayzelle walked over and looked, placing her hand on Ila's neck, softly stroking under her ear until the spot was warm and relaxed. "Now, Honey," she said, "it looks like you're the onliest one who was stupid. You got caught, if you 'member, not your sweet sisters."

"Well, I wasn't doin' nothin'," Ila snarled.

"You call messin' around with that Ferdinand boy nothin'? Child, if you think that, then you lucky to get off with stayin' in your room."

"We was just lookin'."

"In the church outhouse?"

"We was just *lookin'*!"

Mayzelle felt Ila's neck tighten and she stopped stroking. "Proper young ladies don't play with little boy's privates."

Ila turned, her eyes inflamed. "We was just lookin' and that's all. 'Sides, Ferdinand didn't have nothin' I cared for nohow. He looked ridiculous, like my little finger and all—"

"Child! Don't talk like that, Honey." Mayzelle pulled Ila to the bed. The old springs and mattress sagged and squeaked as the two rocked back and forth. "Your momma would die if she heard talk like that. Talk like that ain't fit for no lady."

"Then I don't want to be no lady," she sobbed. "I'm twelve—almost thirteen years old and Momma still treats me like a baby."

"Well, I was gonna say that you *are* a baby, but that ain't true. You growin' up into a right pretty young woman."

Ila put her hands to her face and leaned on Mayzelle's shoulder.

Mayzelle could not help chuckling. "Why, Ila Elizabeth Mitchell, I ain't never seen you cry and carry on like this. You been punished before for one thing or another. What's really botherin' you, anyway?"

Suddenly Ila's voice was not the voice of a child. It was soft and clear and had a tone Mayzelle had not heard before. "I'm 'shamed to tell."

"You ain't got nothin' to be 'shamed about. Your own daddy would wear you out if he heard such talk."

Ila cleaned her face with her sleeve and walked to the mirror. She showed Mayzelle the most recent *Ladies Home Journal*. A painting on the cover showed a beautiful, somewhat aloof young woman, with a broad hat, soft fur coat, and energetic disposition; one you tipped your hat to on the street, that is, if she ever walked on streets.

Ila cleared her throat. "I'm not a pretty young woman. I'm ugly! Ugly!"

The words stung Mayzelle like a whip. So that was it. She walked to the mirror and the two stared for a long time at the reflection of young and old. Mirrors don't lie, thought Mayzelle, noticing her own appearance: tough, broad cheekbones and sagging shoulders. But the child, the child was different. Suddenly she was angry because no one had spoken to the child on her own terms.

At the age of twelve, Ila no longer stood on skinny legs or breathed from a hollow chest. Her body had changed, with a suddenness that few had noticed, to that of a more mature, relaxed girl. She looked sixteen, with small but firm breasts, and her hair, so much like Lora's, was still uncut, falling in dark waves down her back. Mayzelle noticed Ila's face—a softer face, less angular than a few months ago. Her eyes, brown with a rim of crystal green, could catch the mood of anyone who dared return her gaze.

Mayzelle's voice shook as she pointed into the mirror. "Now, Honey, you ain't never known me to lie to you and I ain't gonna lie to you now. You're only twelve years old but you're a-ripenin' like an apple on a tree. You were born in February, but you were like a bud in springtime. I was there and I laid hands on you even before your daddy did. Your body ain't made up its mind which way it wants to grow, but right now I can tell you, Jesus knows that you're growin' like you're s'posed to. One day soon you gonna primp, and your cheeks is gonna turn smooth as your momma's, and your daddy gonna have to fight them young men off'n this doorstep there's gonna be so many of 'em."

Ila turned away. "I'm gonna die in this room, skinny and bony and ugly."

"I don't wanna hear no talk like that anymore. 'Sides, we got work to do." Mayzelle got up and went to the closet. The closet was not large; the clothes were hung in three sections, one for each girl. Three dresses per child: one for two days and one for Sunday, and long flannel underwear, black stockings, and bloomers. Mayzelle pulled out Ila's Sunday dress, blue taffeta with a cherry blossom print and a white border around the neck and wrists. "Here, this'll do. I'm a-goin' downstairs and heat up some water, and we gonna fix up that hair of yours. Black hair like that oughta be fixed up every day. I'll show you how to do it and you learn from me. Then I'll get some of your momma's perfume and one of my necklaces and we'll make you a queen 'fore the evenin' comes." Mayzelle was laughing. Ila could tell that she spoke the truth, and her eyes sparkled as she pulled off the dress she was wearing. As Mayzelle left the room, she turned and saw Ila smiling at the mirror, pulling her long hair from one side to the other, posing.

Pearl and Vera helped place the dishes on the table. Lora sat down.

"Don't forget to put a place for your sister, girls. She gets to eat with us tonight. I think a week's long enough up in that room. Ought to be a lesson to all of you. Lon, go up and get Ila—"

"I'll do it," said Mayzelle, brushing by the others to the stairway.

"Lon, that Mayzelle sure has been actin' peculiar all afternoon. I hope she ain't been a-pamperin' Ila."

Lon gave her a reassuring look.

Lora passed the forks. "You're right. I shouldn't 'a said that. I'm just so nervous with Mr. Bradley droppin' by and all." As she got closer to her thirtieth birthday, Lora became more anxious about receiving visitors. She spent more time in front of the mirror, pulling a stray gray hair, or brushing with quick, sharp bursts of energy. Her dimples pleased her; she could increase their size and depth with little effort. Black eyes and dimples recalled her youth.

"I've always liked Mr. Bradley," she prattled on. "Treats us like real class folk, not uppity like some. Where else you gonna find the owner of a mill come to his workman's home?"

Lon walked to the fireplace, placed another log, and returned to his seat at the table. The girls took their seats, leaving one at the far end of the table for Ila. Pearl sat next to her father.

Lora walked to the foot of the stairs. "Mayzelle!" she shouted. "You and Ila come on down before it gets cold!"

She stood for a moment, and when there was no answer, she started to walk up the stairs. Mayzelle appeared at the top and walked down, taking Lora by the arm and pulling her down with her. Lora stared behind her as Ila walked shyly from one step to another.

"Ila!" her mother said softly.

Lon turned to see what the commotion was about and then stood. Pearl and Vera, wide-eyed and incredulous, stared at Ila and then at each other.

"Why, Honey," said Lora, "you know you ought not to wear Sunday clothes on a weekday, and what on earth have you done to your hair?"

Mayzelle tapped Lora's shoulder and pointed to her own nose.

"You?" said Lora. "But why?"

Before she could answer, a knock broke the silence. Mayzelle walked to the door and opened it.

"Why, Mr. Bradley," she smiled. "Won't you come in?"

"Thank you kindly, Mayzelle," Bradley said as he took off his coat and unwrapped his scarf. Bradley's grin on his fleshy, pockmarked face seemed to fill the room with warmth. His breath heaved rapidly from swollen lungs. His eyes, set deep and dark like the stubs of mushrooms, seemed to penetrate right ahead, never moving from side to side. For a moment everyone forgot Ila on the stairway, and not knowing what else to do, she sat down on the step.

Lon walked over to Bradley and shook his hand. Bradley grinned. "Lon, it's always a pleasure to see my best foreman." He winked at Lora. "And the prettiest foreman's wife in the county."

"Why, Mr. Bradley, you ought not to lie in front of the children." Lora said in a girlish voice that made Lon blush.

"Nonsense, Lora," boomed Bradley, "it's the truth and the whole mill knows it. Oh," he said in a whisper, "I brought you something."

"You shouldn't have gone and done that," she protested.

"My pleasure. Lon, help me on the porch, will you?"

Nervously glancing from child to child to see if all was in order, Lora looked around the room. There was nothing further she could do to straighten things out, so she prepared to be overwhelmed by the turkey or ham that Bradley invariably brought by for Christmas.

The screen door opened and Bradley, followed by Lon carrying a large turkey, came back inside.

"Freshly killed!" shouted Bradley. The children laughed.

"Oh, Mr. Bradley, we thank you, don't we, Lon? You shouldn't go and do things like this. This must'a cost a fortune."

"Oh, it did," said Bradley, laughing as he pulled a cigar from his vest.

"Won't you stay for supper?" Lora asked.

"No, I couldn't do that. I got to make a couple more calls tonight, but I appreciate your asking me. I will speak to your beautiful children, if I may; one of the few joys an old man has left in life, talking to beautiful young women."

He walked to the table.

"Girls," said Lora, "get up and visit with Mr. Bradley, you hear?"

Pearl and Vera walked over to Bradley and allowed him to pinch their cheeks and tell them how much they looked like their momma.

"Why, wait a moment," said Bradley. "There's one missing, isn't there? Where's little Ila?"

"Ila?" said Lora, looking around the room. She finally spotted Ila on the stairway, folding the hem of her dress in little knots. "Ila, don't be rude, child. Mr. Bradley wants to see you."

"No," said Bradley.

"I beg your pardon?" said Lora.

"No," he said, "I wanted to see *little* Ila. What I see before me is not the little baby I saw last year. That's a young lady, probably the prettiest I'll ever see."

Ila stood and straightened her dress. Looking at her feet, she walked in the general direction of the man whose usually booming voice was now soft and serious.

Bradley reached for her hand and bent over to kiss it. Embarrassed, she pulled back instinctively. He winked at Lora and then at Lon.

Ila took her seat at the table, not looking at anyone, wishing she were dead.

"That's one lady you two ought to be proud of," Bradley continued. "Yes sir, mighty proud of." Looking at his watch, he mumbled something about the snow outside and said, patting Lon on the shoulder, "After Christmas I'll call for you. We got some serious business on our hands. Seems some boys up at the mill in Hoskins are giving my men some trouble. Might have to have a new foreman up there and in a few months, well, who knows, you might be the man I need to keep things moving. Anyway, I'll call you around New Year's and we'll talk about it. Again, thank you for a pleasant evening visit, Mrs. Mitchell, and take care of these lovely girls. Lon, enjoy the turkey. Yes, I'm sure you will. Goodbye, folks." As he walked out the door he turned and looked again at Ila, shook his head, and walked out into the falling snow.

The family gathered around the table. Lora pulled the biscuits from the warmer and the fatback from the oven. The girls whispered to each other about Ila's new appearance. Mayzelle put her dish on the cupboard.

"Ila," Lora said.

Ila glanced up.

"Ila, you look right pretty, Honey. You really do."

Ila smiled.

Lon pushed his chair back and stood. He walked over to the cupboard and took the fork out of Mayzelle's hand and the plate from the counter-top. With his head he motioned to the table. He put the plate next to Ila and brought another chair from the parlor. He pointed to it. Mayzelle shook her head. He nodded. She walked to the chair and sat. Lon began eating and passing the food to the children. He pointed his fork at Mayzelle's plate.

"Eat," he commanded.

She did.

Ψ

Ila slipped out of bed once she was sure that Vera's short, loud breathing signified sleep. In her gown, she walked to the frosted window and tried to lift it. The ice outside had frozen the wood to the sill. She held her breath and tightened her shoulders as she pushed again and again, and suddenly it was free, allowing the cold night to fill the room. She glanced to see if her sisters had been awakened. If they had, she could not sense it.

She climbed out on the ledge, which was more slippery than usual. This, she thought, is the last time. She had not skated on the ledge in a long while. It seemed more narrow than she remembered, and colder. She moved slowly, cautiously feeling her way across the front of the house until she came to her mother's window. A soft orange glow came from the glass. She looked in. Cold mist had settled on the panes. Steam and tear-like streams warped her vision.

Through the blur she saw Lon at Lora's feet, stroking her thighs, gently pulling himself across the bed toward her small breasts, his hair across his eyes, his muscles tense but gentle, his huge frame rocking in a slow, tight motion, his mouth wide and searching, kissing and probing, his eyes closed, his knees buried on either side of her on the mattress, and his strength growing at every breath.

The last time, Ila thought, as she crawled back to her own room.

"Lon!" Lora shouted from the bottom of the stairs, "You hurry up and get dressed. Everybody's waitin' on you. We don't want to be the only ones late for Christmas services!" She listened to the drawers slamming upstairs and knew that he probably couldn't find his tie. He never could find his tie. "Mayzelle, don't let the children move for nothin'. They'll get dirty in two minutes." She rushed up the stairs.

Mayzelle turned to inspect the girls one last time. "Now, Ila, you and Pearl remember your parts for the play and everything will work out fine."

Lora rushed back down the stairs with Lon in tow. He wore a heavy black coat and gray flannel slacks. His shoes were polished and his hair parted in the middle. His face was raw from washing and shaving.

Mayzelle opened the door. Lora pushed the children out in front of her and shut the door behind herself. She reopened the door and peeked in. "Sorry, Lon. Come on."

He was not angry. He winked at Mayzelle and followed Lora out. Mayzelle went upstairs.

The church shone in the night from a fresh coat of paint, its wooden planking like new, its steps polished by a light snow. The bell within the short tower on the roof sounded into the cold air as gentlemen took turns helping the ladies up the steep stairway.

The sanctuary was warm and festive. Hundreds of voices shouted to be heard above the cries of children gathered around the tree.

Ila wove her way through the maze of parents and children to the front of the church, where she stood in awe before the largest cedar tree she had ever seen. It was lit by thousands of tiny candles casting shadows from one wall to the other. Other children screamed in delight as their parents placed gifts beneath the huge tree.

The bell ceased its tolling, and everyone rushed to the wooden seats, arranged in haphazard rows with barely enough room for knees, which poked the backs of those in front. Ila, Pearl, and Vera saw their mother motion and went to her. The three girls shared two chairs beside Lora.

Minister Hatcher, tall and without doubt the most dignified man in town, walked to the front of the church and motioned to the choir. They rose as if one animal, and the church erupted in an off-key but powerful rendition of "O Come, All Ye Faithful."

Lora sang while seated. Ila mouthed the words and the other girls fought over the one hymnal between them. Silent and protective, Lon stood in the back with the other men.

Minister Hatcher thanked God for the company and for Mr. Bradley's donation of the candles for the tree. Then he asked the children in the program to gather up front.

Ila, taller than most of the girls her age, tried to slump to disguise her height. When her turn finally came, she recited her verse without flaw: "Rose on my shoulder, slippers on my feet, I'm Momma's little angel, don't you think I'm sweet?"

The audience reacted as only parents could, with sighs of pleasure and smiles as bright as the flames on the Christmas tree.

After all the children had made their valiant stands alone on the stage, Minister Hatcher began to give out gifts. For over an hour he shouted names across the hall, until at last, hoarse and sweating, he allowed Mrs. Hatcher to take over.

Mrs. Hatcher helped Minister Hatcher to his seat and then, walking stiffly to the base of the tree and wincing from the pain, she drove her arthritic hands into the pile of gifts. She waved each gift over her head with one hand while screaming the name of the recipient. Then she blew her nose. Mrs. Hatcher always had a cold.

"Ila, Pearl, and Vera Mitchell," she called.

Lora looked back at Lon, but he shook his head and frowned. Tripping over discarded wrappings and ribbons, the girls ran to the front before Lora could stop them. Mrs. Hatcher handed the small pink-wrapped box to Ila. There was no mistake; written across the front in bold letters were the names of all three girls. They ran back to Lora, who helped open the package and carefully folded the paper to be used again.

Inside, wrapped again with tissue, were three small sets of beads, each a different color. The girls eagerly reached for them, but Lora passed them out: white for Ila, red for Pearl, and blue for Vera.

The girls ran to show their father, and Lora searched until she found a card within. "Tom Bradley," it said.

❧

On the walk back home, the girls chattered among themselves about their necklaces. Lora, fatigued, said little as she walked arm in arm with Lon.

"Lon, look there."

They stopped and the children passed them, oblivious to anything but their beads.

"Look how the mists are movin' in over that mountain. Reminds me of the way it always looked in the mornin' down by the Catawba, mist comin' out of the river, like it was lookin' for somebody, day after day. Always lookin' and never findin'."

It was true, Lon thought. Blue and hazy, the mountains refused to go to sleep.

"Lon, I don't feel too good."

He lifted her chin, looked into her eyes, and felt her forehead. She felt warm. He reached around her waist and half-held her up as they walked back to the house.

Mayzelle met them at the door and helped put Lora on the sofa.

"I knowed it," said Mayzelle.

"Get the doctor," said Lon.

"No," said Mayzelle, smiling, "not yet."

She looked at Lora. "Is it?"

Lora shook her head drowsily. "'Fraid so."

Mayzelle grinned at Lon. "Pregnant," she said.

Five

January 1918

THE DAY was Sunday; the snow had fallen for two days without stopping, and the mill had shut down, a rare thing. Bradley sent word to Lon that he wanted to see him at his home, across the river. Lon had seen Bradley's home, but like most other mill workers, had never been inside, nor on the grounds.

Tom Bradley had built the home two years ago, a white brick structure with a light blue porch supported by thin columns, an oak balcony at every window on the second floor, and young chestnuts and firs lining the front garden.

Lon enjoyed the walk through the snow. Everything seemed so clean and quiet. He walked past the bridge overlooking the mill. Snow spread across the roof and window ledges like icing on a cake. He wondered why Bradley had sent for him. Probably about that Hoskins mess he had mentioned a few weeks earlier. I'm just a mechanic, thought Lon. What use could he possibly have for me at Hoskins? There's plenty of good mechanics there.

Several children were playing on the front balcony when Lon approached the driveway. Three young men were pushing a touring car into a garage. Lon walked to the front door and had barely knocked when it opened.

A young woman in a gray dress with a white collar smiled and said, "Yes?"

"I'm Lon Mitchell. Mr. Bradley sent for me."

"One moment, please." She closed the door and Lon heard a faint clicking noise from somewhere inside. Then he heard a voice like a cannon's roar shouting, "Let him in!"

The door quickly opened and the girl stepped aside. Lon walked into the hallway.

"Your coat?"

Lon removed his coat and looked for a mat to wipe his wet shoes. There was none. The wetness of his clothes began to seep onto the marble floor. The girl did not seem to mind.

Tom Bradley came to the hall and motioned Lon to follow him. They went into a study immediately to the right of the hallway. The floors were wooden, with scattered rugs. An enormous billiard table, several couches, and more lamps than Lon had in his entire house filled the room.

"Sit down, Lon, my friend. We've got some business to discuss."

Lon noticed that Bradley was not as jovial as usual. He had a frown that he seemed to try to smile away, but it wouldn't go.

"Lon, we've got trouble at Hoskins. I know I mentioned it to you the other day, but it's got way out of hand."

Lon understood. He nodded.

"Yes," Bradley sneered, "the union. Textile bunch from up north trying to stir up trouble. The same ones that violated our mill over in Hearshaw two years ago. I thought that experience would teach them a lesson, maybe even be the death of that atheistic, dishonorable bunch of rogues. But I was wrong, Lon. They have more power than we thought. Seems always to be that way when you're dealing with the devil's workers. Traitors, all of 'em; anticipating the end of the war, trying to take advantage of good men like you and me."

"Yes sir."

Bradley leaned over to Lon and whispered, "You know that the Committee on Public Information wants us to send in the names of those who harm the war effort. I'm sure you've read about it in the newspapers. I'm makin' a list as long as my arm of those unpatriotic men who would undermine this country's defense. It is your patriotic duty to join me in this sacred cause. Now, Lon, you know how I feel about my mills and my people. I treat them good, don't I?"

"Yes sir." Lon relaxed. He had heard this before, dozens of times, at mill picnics and baseball games.

"Yes, pretty good is how I treat them that's mine. I work all day, every day to see that the goods we make get sold and then I pay you what's rightfully yours, don't I?"

"Yes sir."

"Damn right I do! And I won't have no bunch of outsiders creating dissatisfaction within my mills. No sir, I won't have it. I can't have it. They want better wages. Hell, nobody in the South pays better wages than me. Business is getting better every day. What with the war in Europe and all, we're getting a good share of orders that will increase business, and I can guarantee we'll increase wages. That's a promise. But some people. . . ." He leaned forward, his eyes wide. "Some people can't wait for what they justly deserve. No sir! Some people got to get greedy and ask for more than what's right and more than we can afford. We can't just throw a new raise at you people every time you get an itch, no sir. It would be like giving a baby candy when what he needs is milk. Don't you agree?"

"Yes sir."

Bradley stood. "That's my thinking, boy. I thought you would agree. I've been watching you for a long time. You've got class. You don't talk much and that's a quality that I admire. Yes sir, I admire that in a man, speaking only when he has something important to say. Well, I've got something important to say: They're not going to do it! They're not going to organize Hoskins mill or anywheres else as long as I'm breathing. Already several of my workers have joined. They don't think I know, but that's the weakness of those rascals, not knowing that I know. They've already had a meeting. While most Christian folks have been worshiping Christ over Christmas, these scalawags held a meeting! A political meeting! Can you imagine? Anyway, they're getting ready to organize over at Hoskins, and when they do I want several of my trusted . . . loyal . . . silent . . . men there so that I can know what they're up to. You understand me?"

"In a way."

Bradley sat down next to Lon on the couch. Lon could smell the witch hazel in his hair. His breath was sharp with a cheese smell. "Lon, if and when th·y do decide to organize, I need to know quickly, so that I can make my move to crush them! That's what you're for . . . to let me know."

Lon frowned.

"Now, boy, don't get to feeling like you're betraying your friends, your class or anything. Because you're not. No sir, you'll be doing them a favor. If they cut into my business, I'll have to let lots of them go. Cut into business and you cut your own throat. Why, everybody knows that, now don't they?"

"Yes sir."

"Right. It's your Christian duty to help me with this thing. We've got to stop them socialists while we can or pretty soon the whole damn South will go under. We're doing real good up against the northern competition, and I've got a feeling that the union is nothing more than a Yankee conspiracy to destroy what we've got. Now, you're not real educated, Lon, and you wouldn't understand such things. So you've got to trust me. You do trust me, don't you?"

"Yes sir."

Bradley smiled. "Come with me. Now that this is straight, I want you to meet my new manager for Hoskins. Whenever you hear of trouble there, whenever you hear of anything, I want you to get a message to this man. I've handpicked him. Might say I made him what he is today." Bradley chuckled. He noticed the puzzled look on Lon's face. "Oh, it's just a private joke, Lon. You'll understand."

They walked down the hall into a large reception room, lighted by a glass roof. "Italian wood and glass," said Bradley. "I had that roof imported. Can't see it from the outside, so you get surprised on the inside. When it rains, I just stretch out with a bourbon and watch the rain pour all around me."

Lon nodded.

"Vance!" shouted Bradley to the walls. "Vance!"

A side door opened and a short young man walked in.

"Vance, this is Lon Mitchell, one of my foremen at the plant."

Vance walked over to the men and reached for Lon's hand. "Glad to meet you, Lon." He turned to Bradley. "Dad, have you decided that this is our man?"

Lon looked around, uncomfortable.

"Yes, Vance, Lon's our man. Lon, not only is Vance the new manager of the Hoskins mill, but he's also my son. Vance here is a University of Virginia graduate. During the hard times ahead I'll need both of you."

Vance smiled. He smoothed his hair with one hand and reached for a cigar with the other. His face was pear-shaped, his hair parted in the middle. Lon couldn't help looking at the son's hands. They were beautiful hands, pink and slender—protected.

"One more thing . . . no, two," said Bradley. "You boys will be leaving for Hoskins next Monday. And secondly, as a way of showing my gratitude, I've found a position at the mill downtown, Lon, for your daughter Ila. She's old enough now to get into the family business." He chuckled. "A strike after the war would certainly jeopardize her new job."

Lon said thank you and walked away. He glanced back one more time as he put on his coat and opened the door. Vance Bradley was still smiling.

Lon didn't like the idea of putting Ila to work in the textile mill. But Bradley insisted that she work there. Lon relented. The extra money wouldn't hurt. Besides, Bradley was right, the girl was nearly thirteen and needed to learn what real responsibility was.

Ila worked in the spinning room with several other girls. She worked from six in the morning to six at night with a lunch break at noon. She watched frames run through guides. Then she flicked a quill at the bottom of the frame, which pushed the thread into another weaving pattern.

After a month, Ila went into the spool room and then in another month into the finished-denim room. Throughout the mill the smell of oil, the oppressive clanking sounds of metal, and the choking heat followed her. Even with the giant windows open in the spring, the steam was inescapable.

Tired and irritable, Ila arrived home after dark, changed her clothes, washed her face, and helped Lora cook supper.

The one real pleasure that Ila looked forward to was the pay. She had her choice of company scrip or cash. She always took the cash: fourteen dollars for fourteen days' work.

Once in a while Mr. Bradley himself came down to watch her work. He made sure her supervisors did not work her too hard. Once Bradley said something about making her a file clerk in his office. Imagine, she thought, in his own office. A day didn't pass that he did not find time to speak to her and comment on her hair or dress. A nice man, she thought, a real nice man.

For six months Lon took an early train to Hoskins textile mill and a late train back. Bradley paid the fare.

It was true that the union had signed up a large number of men, almost a fourth of the four hundred employees by July. They approached Lon, but he demurred. He didn't join anything, he said. So they left him alone. There was some talk of striking, of walking out, but it was mostly talk, and was reported as such to Vance Bradley, who in turn picked up his phone and told his father. Still Lon remained until the second Wednesday in July, 1918.

Lon was eating a piece of bread on the steps near the loading dock. Cann Byrum, a lean dock loader, sat beside him. "Which way you goin', Lon?" he asked seriously.

"Whatd'ya mean?"

Cann put a jar to his mouth and drank the warm water.

"You heard me," he said as he wiped his mouth. "What you plannin' on doin' tomorrow?"

"Tomorrow? What's tomorrow?"

"Where you been, sleepin'? The big meeting. Big boys done called one for tomorrow to talk about our demands after the war."

"You don't say."

"Yep. I'm just remindin' the members . . . and a few of the non-members."

"Why you askin' me?"

"We need your help."

Lon shook his head. "It's not right. And you know it. I got a right to work. We're doing okay, profits are way up. Unions would just hurt us. I got babies to support."

"You the only one with babies? And a wife? Look, I like you. You do a good job and you've got a lot of friends here that follow your example. I don't want to see you get . . . you know, messed up."

"You're talkin' out your ass."

"No, not me, Lon. But I thought I'd give you some advice. When that open meeting starts, make sure that you either stay home or join us. This shithole has been makin' fifty, sixty percent profits for the last year. Did you know that? And still we've got men makin' nine and ten cents an hour for seventy-hour weeks."

"Ain't my problem."

"Well, I thought I'd tell you. I'll be seein' you."

"Yeah, right."

"Lon?"

"Yeah?"

"Be careful."

Lon had every intention of being careful. He had hoped that he would not hear it, hoped that it would never come. But he knew that the mill was dangerous, older than the one at Paw Creek. The equipment was abused and the steam overpowering. Bradley must be doing all right because he had just bought another mill. Things couldn't be too bad for him. Besides, Cann and the others didn't want much. A clean place to work, and money equal to that work. But Bradley, he was the boss. Been good to me and mine, thought Lon. He's the boss.

Lon worked the afternoon with no break. Several times Vance walked onto the floor checking things out. The workers liked Vance. He smiled all the time, and last week when Vester Setzer lost three fingers, Vance paid the hospital bill. Word of that sort of generosity spread quickly.

Cann Byrum stopped to speak to Vance about the blades in his machine, something about getting them replaced before he had to go back to the stockroom. Vance said he would check on it tomorrow. Vance walked down to Lon's station and stared at him for a moment, watching him repair the loom. Vance knelt.

"How's things?" Vance asked, smiling.

Lon looked up at him and pulled away from the loom. They both stood. Strange, thought Lon, how short the boy is. Not much younger than me. Nervous type. Lon pointed to the ventilation shafts in the room. "Rain leaks in," he said.

"Does it? I never noticed before."

"Yep, got to get it fixed by tomorrow."

"Why?" asked Vance.

"'Cause of the storm."

"What storm?"

"The one that's a-comin' tomorrow."

Cann Byrum walked over to Lon. Vance looked at Cann, and Cann looked at Lon.

"What storm?" asked Cann menacingly.

Lon laughed. "You mean you haven't heard? Curtis Tallent told me that a hurricane's off the coast and that it oughta rain here for the next week or so. Why, everybody knows that."

Cann laughed weakly. "Oh yeah, I forgot. Just checkin'. Gotta protect my garden, you know."

Lon went back to work.

Vance continued to look at the vents. They were new. Nothing wrong with them. Vance knew that Lon knew that.

Lon had done his job. Warned Vance as best he could. He couldn't risk going to the office. Too many workers were watching him. If Vance got the message, fine. If Vance didn't understand, then that was fine, too. It didn't matter. Lon couldn't stand this job any longer. Even Lora had noticed that something was wrong, but she had sense enough not to nag him about it. Tomorrow, he thought, maybe I will stay home. My job is done here.

Vance stepped into his office and shut the door. He opened the window and looked at the sky. Rain clouds. Sure enough. He looked at the newspaper on his desk, wet with coffee stains. Storm off the coast. A big storm. But still.

"Hello, Dad?"

"Yes, Vance. Where the hell you been?"

"Trying to get you on this damn phone. Now, I haven't got long, so listen. I don't know if this means anything or not, but something strange is going on here. Our friend down in the weaving department's been acting unusual."

"You going to pontificate about it or tell me straight out? What is the matter, boy?"

"Well, it's about a storm and some vents."

Tom Bradley felt pleased with himself. Two telegrams and three phone calls had done the trick. Vance said he could handle it. A fine boy, that Vance, thought Tom. A good boy. Going to make a fine replacement for me someday. Maybe this experience is a godsend. A test of the boy's mettle. Tom Bradley smiled. Nothing more he could do. The problem would be handled tomorrow and then things could continue as they always had—slowly and manageably. Now, what was it I was going to do this afternoon? he asked himself. Then he remembered.

"Mrs. Crotts!"

Mrs. Gracie Crotts had been his personal secretary for seventeen years. She was the only person in the mill who could type.

She walked into his office. "Yes sir?"

"You know that Mitchell girl on the floor? Ila Mitchell?"

Mrs. Crotts thought a moment. "No sir, I don't believe I do."

"Well, what with the orders coming in from Europe and the backlog of filing, I thought that you could use some help around here putting things in order. . . ."

"Why, no sir!" said Mrs. Crotts, offended. "I can do it all."

"Now . . . now, Gracie, bring the young lady up here and I'll interview her personally. Then we can decide."

"But Mr. Bradley . . ."

"Yes, Gracie?"

"Nothing, sir. I'll get the girl. What's her name again?"

"Ila. Ila Mitchell. Down on the floor."

As soon as Mrs. Crotts left, Bradley shut the door and tested the lock.

Within a few minutes Mrs. Crotts knocked on the door. Bradley opened it.

"Mr. Bradley, here is the Mitchell girl."

Bradley looked coolly at Ila. "Yes, I see. Well, come in, girl, I've got to talk to you about something we need done here; someone to help Mrs. Crotts. She's one of the best we have here and I don't want her overworked." He looked at Mrs. Crotts. She beamed. "So, have a seat over there on the lounge. Mrs. Crotts, here's an order for some yarn. Go with Bishop down to the warehouse and make sure he gets the right kind. He's been messing up orders lately. If you see that he doesn't get the right kind, then fire him."

Mrs. Crotts smiled, took the order, and walked out. She felt bewildered but at the same time pleased that Mr. Bradley would trust her with the power to fire someone.

Bradley listened to the sounds of her footsteps as she clumped down the stairs. Then he rose and locked the door.

"Privacy," he said with a smile as he walked over to Ila.

Ila smiled back. "Is this about a secretary's job?" she asked.

"Not exactly, but we might work something out. What I have in mind is starting you as a file clerk and then moving you into Mrs. Crotts' job when she retires."

"Oh? Is she retiring?" asked Ila, surprised. After all, Mrs. Crotts was older than the mill, a permanent fixture.

"Someday down the line when the time is right, Darling."

Ila looked around the room at the tall bookshelves, the family portraits, and the telephone.

"I've never used a telephone before," she said.

"Oh, well, we can remedy that, child. As a file clerk you might have to call all sorts of places for information that I might be needing."

Ila shook her head. "I'm not sure that I can do the job you want me to do . . . I'm so used to working downstairs. I don't know nothin' else."

Bradley sat down next to her and placed his arm around her back. "Come now, don't be modest. You're from a smart, class family and I'm sure that you can do anything that you set your mind to."

"I'll try, sir."

"Try, nothing," he laughed. "You *will* do what you have to do. I'm sure it runs in the family."

"I don't know what you mean."

"Why, the perseverance of your family, of course. Your stock, your patience, your working ability. I have a high regard for your momma and your daddy." He patted her knee. She recoiled. He rubbed her leg. She froze.

His voice was softer now, smooth and glossy. "I am going to rescue you, child. I'm going to give you such pleasure as you have never known."

Ila choked. "Mr. Bradley, I don't—"

"Hush," he whispered, swallowing. "I don't want . . . to hear it. . . ." He pushed his fingers down over her dress and through her fingers until he was squeezing her flesh. She watched him close his eyes and try to pull her closer. Her muscles were tight and she resisted. A moan left her lips, and she hoped no one outside could hear. She gathered her strength and pulled herself away. He stood and grabbed her arm. "Come back. I'm not going to do anything to hurt you. I couldn't hurt you. You're too beautiful to hurt."

Ila was near tears. "I don't think . . . I don't think we oughta be doin' this, Mr. Bradley."

"You shouldn't think, Ila. Let me. Let the man do the thinking. I know what's right and what's wrong. I wouldn't do anything wrong to you. I merely want to give you affection. You need affection, Ila, I can tell that."

Ila backed up to the window and twisted her head to look below at the river. Bradley walked to her. He put his hand on the back of her neck. She felt a chill. "No, I can't, Mr. Bradley. It's not right."

He pressed closer. She felt his warmth and his harshness. "No!" she shouted.

He backed away quickly, his face shocked. He looked behind to the locked door and listened. Nothing. No one had heard.

"Listen, Ila. I haven't time to waste. You've got to see the world as it really is. I have needs and you have needs. I can satisfy yours and it won't hurt a thing. You'll feel good. That's all you need in life, to feel good."

"I got to get back, Mr. Bradley."

His face was red.

The phone rang.

He let it ring and watched Ila walk to the door with her back to him.

"Ila," he shouted. "You say anything about this to anybody and your daddy will be looking for work somewhere else! You understand me?"

She unlatched the door and walked out.

Bradley picked up the phone. "Kirby? Yes, Bradley here. Going to be trouble at Hoskins tomorrow. Take what men you got, pay them double, drive them down to Hoskins tomorrow morning, and break it up. You got that? Yeah, other teams from other mills will be there. Give them what they want to break it up. Make sure they bring their guns. We'll pay for the ammunition. Make sure they know that the group at Hoskins is Yankee-inspired, socialists, atheists . . . yeah, it works here. It ought to work there. Sure. No, I won't be there, but my son will handle my end. Watch out for him, do what he says. Yeah, see you. Do it up right."

Lon got on the morning train as usual. He arrived at Hoskins and walked to the mill. Several hundred men were gathered at the gates, asking arriving workers to join them in an organization meeting. Several employees, trying to get past the line to work, had been pushed around. Others stood silently across the street, watching, waiting. Vance himself was there, talking to Cann Byrum, trying to talk him into calling the whole thing off. Because of the noise, Cann had trouble talking to Vance. Vance smiled as if the whole thing were a picnic, a short-lived exercise in play. Vance was waiting for the trucks.

They soon arrived. Fifty men, selected from various Bradley mills out of town. All of them armed. The problem, Vance noted, was that several of the strikers were armed also. The men on the trucks had been told that the meeting organizers were communists.

"I'm not impressed," said Cann.

"You soon will be," said Vance as he walked to the trucks.

Vance spoke to the drivers for a short while, then turned, pointed to the gate, and yelled, "Okay, let's clear them out of the way! The more time we sit around here, the more money the mill loses. Simply walk over and push them out of the way. If they don't want to work, that's okay with me. But these other men do want to work. Don't think of them as men, think of them as locusts. Locusts who will do anything to destroy the South. Go get them! Let's get this thing over with!"

The men jumped out of the trucks and walked toward the strikers. Lon watched from the drugstore. He couldn't believe this was happening. He heard the shouting and the cheering from the onlookers on the sidewalk. He watched Vance directing his little army, pushing one group, then another, always smiling. Lon would never forget that smile, cold and cruel.

Lon didn't hear a brief groan as a bullet went through Vance's eye and ripped out the back of his skull.

More shots were fired, screams echoed across the town, and by night two other men were dead.

Lon stepped onto the train and sank into his seat. He had trouble hearing and his stomach kept turning. He looked out the window and hoped he would never see this place again. He tried not to think about it.

He thought of Lora, sweet Lora. She would make the terrible things go away. She would surround him with peace. He would feel her huge belly and the quick kicks from his wombson and forget today. And Ila would be safe in bed and he would make her quit the mill. She was really too young to work there. Besides, Mayzelle needed help around the house; she wasn't getting any younger.

A man across the aisle, looking out the window into the dark, was smiling. What was there to smile about in the dark?

Mayzelle closed the door to Lora's room. She walked quickly down the hall and opened Ila's door. Ila was getting ready for bed.

"Child, you get dressed right quick. Go down to the mill. Tell old man Bradley to send the mill doctor, Doctor Eggers. Your momma won't be much longer. She's goin' to need a doctor on this one. Hurry, girl! It don't look good!"

Ila moved quickly. It was only nine o'clock, and sometimes Bradley stayed at the mill until late. The mill doctor wouldn't come to anyone's home without Bradley's permission.

"Oh, God. Oh, God," Ila repeated over and over, ignoring the mud and bush limbs, cutting through backyards and jumping fences and sewage streams. "Oh, God, please let Momma be all right, please let Mr. Bradley be there, please, God! It's my fault, God. I'll promise anything. I'll do anything!"

Bradley's hands shook as he put the receiver down. He stared for a moment at the paper he had taken notes on and the words underlined again and again: Vance dead. *Vance is dead.*

He was locking his office as Ila ran up to him.

"We need the doctor," she said, out of breath. "We got to have him now! Momma's goin' to have a baby and Mayzelle says that she's got to have a doctor!"

Bradley stared at the girl and listened to her ragged breathing. Then he started to walk down the steps.

Ila followed. "Mr. Bradley, did you hear me? Momma needs help!"

Bradley did not seem to be listening.

She grabbed his coat. He swung around and slapped her. "Leave me alone." His voice seemed to come from deep inside. It was a hurt voice, an angry one. She had never seen him like this. She did not understand his mood. He walked to the front gate, with Ila begging behind him.

"Sure," he finally said. "I'll send the doctor as soon as I can." He stared toward the train depot for a moment, then added, "But on one condition. You want the doctor? You play my game. You understand me?" His voice was flat, without emotion.

Ila stepped back. He moved his hand to hers. He did not look cruel this time, or evil. He looked scared. She thought of Momma and Mayzelle and of Doctor Eggers. She took his hand. They walked into the darkness, toward his home across the river.

He led her behind the wall of trees in his front garden. It was deserted and dark. He laid her gently on the ground. She clenched her teeth and tried to hold back the tears. He lay on top of her; she had to breathe quickly as he tore at her dress.

With her eyes closed tight, Ila remembered Momma and Daddy naked in the lamplight through the windowpane. She had seen their secret and it was awesome, but this could not be the same. This was ugly. *I'll do anything, God, anything*. She thought he moved and she gasped. He was not moving, not trying to move; his great belly was heaving spasmodically.

She was not crying, yet she felt warm tears. She opened her eyes. Bradley was sobbing. He rolled over by her side. She got on her knees and touched his shoulder. He sat up, stood, and walked on alone.

"Don't forget Doctor Eggers," she shouted. "You promised!" she screamed.

Lon's train had not arrived from Hoskins when his son was born. Mayzelle met him at the station. He rushed to greet her, mumbling something about being late, searching her face for news.

"Why you here?" he said.

"It's Lora," she said, her eyes bright and afraid. Lon had never seen her afraid. Lora always said that Mayzelle wasn't scared of nothin'.

"What you mean?" he whispered, his voice as faint as a child's. He looked up the road as Mayzelle placed her hand firmly on his shoulder. She had never touched him before. Her fingers were bony and pressed deeply into his flesh.

"My Lora?" he asked as she turned her face away.

"No, your son. Your son came and he was so beautiful and so like an angel . . ."

"Say clear!"

"He was squallin' and we washed him. Doctor Eggers, he never come. So me and Ila cleaned him up real good and placed him on his momma's stomach so he calm down . . ." Mayzelle took a deep, wet breath and spat the words out. "Your son's dead. He cried, and slept, and died."

Six

September 1918

"Ila, that you?" Lora called.

"Yes, Momma."

"Hurry up and change clothes so we can get supper on and done with. Your daddy's got to go back in tonight."

"Yes, Momma."

"You tired, Honey?"

Ila sat down and looked into space for a moment, then said, "Momma, you ask me that every night and every night the answer is the same."

"Well, Honey, you know I'm just interested, and so's your daddy."

Lon was sitting at the table writing a letter. He had written the same letter four times. He did not write very well and he had to make sure there were no mistakes. He made plenty of mistakes. A grown man, he thought, and I can't write any better'n my children. He cursed the paper and threw it on the floor. Maybe another pen, he thought. This one don't fit my hand. He opened the tin sewing box, dumped the buttons and thread onto the table, and pulled a fountain pen from the pile. No ink, damn it.

He found a pencil and sharpened it with his knife and began, for the fifth time, to write a letter to important people—powerful people who would throw a poorly-written request away, not wanting to dirty their hands on the dried sweat of an honest man, a prideful man.

Ila walked over to him. "Daddy, who are you writing?"

He showed her the envelope: Alexander Textile Mills, Greensboro.

"Greensboro? Don't tell me you gotta go traveling clear up to Greensboro. Why, that's all of a hundred miles. When would we see you?"

Lora came over and pulled Ila away from her father as he continued to write. Lora spoke softly: "Ila, sit down a minute. Now, I ain't told the other girls yet 'cause we ain't sure." She looked toward the man at the table and then held her daughter's hand. "Your daddy wants us to move, all of us. He feels that he would have more opportunity and maybe more money at a place like Alexander Mills. Bradley's been good to us, but he don't pay as well as the other mills."

Ila froze at the mention of Bradley's name. Good to *who*? she wondered. She was conscious of the deep fire covering her face. Moving? Away from home?

"Daddy makes good money, Momma. Course, I don't know how much he makes, but I'm sure it's lots more'n me."

"Shhhh, Ila, you know he takes awhile to put things down on paper. He needs his concentration. Let's not talk about it anymore."

Ila reached into her purse and pulled out a stick of chewing gum.

"How do you eat that stuff?" said Lora, offended.

"I don't eat it, Momma, I chew it. Here, have some."

"No thank you, it's unnatural and ladies don't eat things unnatural."

"I *chew* it, Momma!"

"Shhh. No matter. Now come on and help me get supper ready. Too late to change your clothes."

Lora walked to the stove. Ila pulled the gum out of her mouth and put it under the sofa's arm.

Vera, sitting in the corner with her doll, waited until Ila had left, then pulled the sticky wet substance from its hiding place and popped it into her mouth.

"Vera! Momma! Did you see that?" Ila rushed over to the child and began to pry her mouth open amid the screaming and raving. With arms knifing the air, both girls were pulling hair and shouting, but Vera managed to swallow the gum.

Lon pushed his chair back, crumpled the letter, and went to the back room. When he returned, he had his thick leather razor strap. He walked quickly to the couch and began flailing. The two girls separated in shock. Vera rolled under the couch and Ila was beaten to the fireplace, grimacing at each biting blow that cut deep into her dress and her flesh. Ila covered her face and head. Lon continued to release his fury until Lora intervened.

"Lon," she said meekly, "You're a-tearin' up my mantel." The papier-mache had been covered with cloth that the girls had knitted during the winter. It now hung helplessly, in shreds.

Lon glared at her. "I'll buy you another one." He stalked out.

Lora went to Ila.

"Don't touch me!" she hissed. "Just don't touch me now, Momma."

Ila walked up the stairs and into her room and then, for the first time since the beating had begun, she cried.

Lon collapsed on a thick stuffed chair and covered his eyes.

Lora knelt beside him. "You shouldn't have done that, Lon. You should beat me before you beat your children. I love you, Lon, and I feel worse than you'll ever know, hurting because our baby died. Nobody knows or can know what we *can* suffer." She put her fingers through his long, dark hair. "We can't let this put us in that graveyard with him. We got other kids who love and need us. Your family needs you, Lon. What happened was God's will."

Lon choked. "There ain't no God, Lora. There ain't. I'm not goin' to believe in a God who takes our baby like that. . . ."

"Lon, Honey, listen to me. I don't know how God works. But I don't think of our baby as being dead, like a stone or lump of clay; he drifted off to someplace between a physical and spiritual life. Life can't die, Lon. It wouldn't make any sense. God is the life energy in you and me. And when we see the love we have for each other in our eyes, we see part of God in us. You know, Lon, I think there is one thing God can't do: I don't think He can love Himself. That's why we are here—to love that part of Him in each of us."

Lon wiped his eyes. "Well, damned if I'm gonna love Him."

Lora massaged his neck and held back her tears. "Well, I think He needs us about as much as we need Him."

"I don't need Him."

"Whether or not you believe in God ain't for me to worry about. But I'll tell you this, Lon: The more important question is whether God believes in us."

"Don't go preachin' to me, Lora."

She closed her eyes.

"Damn it, Lora, why'd He take my son?"

"*Our* son. Our son ain't in that grave, Lon. Our son is *not* there. You and me take care of each other 'cause we tend to our own kind. The part of our boy that is part of God has returned to God. I saw God in his eyes. God put energy, life, and the love of good in each of us."

"How can you be so sure, Lora?" he said.

"Because the same God who took our boy gave me you, and if I don't believe in God, I can only believe in Hell."

Lon pulled her to his lap and stroked her hair. He smiled. "My Lora, you are really something. I never been this low in my life and then you come in and lift me up. My boy is dead, and Vance is dead, and I had a part in each, as if I had pulled the trigger—"

"No!"

"Hush, it's true. I know it. I thought I could live with that Hoskins job as part of my duty. But this, this was just too much." He wiped his nose. "You know somethin', Lora? I think I'll just take you into Charlotte this weekend and we'll go dancin' and have us a good fish dinner somewhere."

She said nothing.

He tweaked her nose. "What you say?"

She kissed him. "We got plenty of time. I need you more than God does."

W

The machine seemed duller than usual, the frames slower. The heat smelled of burned oil and the walls sweated with a mixture of steam and dirt. Ila's eyes were glazed, and occasionally, when she forgot to push the thread into the proper guide, the thread bunched up and the machine stopped until she repaired it. After this had happened several times, she turned the machine off and went to sit by the window. The other girls had heard of the beating and could not help noticing the hastily-sewn patches on her dress, but they said nothing.

Ila watched the muddy stream weave in and around the huge rocks below the dam. Several boys, no more than seven or eight years old, were swimming a few hundred yards downstream, where the water seemed calmer. Ila felt an icy hand on her shoulder and, startled, knocked a cup off the window ledge. She turned.

The hand held out a box of chewing gum. Lon's face was drawn and heavy from a sleepless night. Lon held out his arms and Ila rushed to him. "I love you, Daddy," she said.

"My Ila," he whispered, smiling.

W

The reeds on the riverbank below the cemetery seemed to be waving to the other side. The rain from the night before made the tree leaves look as crisp and moist as waxed fruit. Clover churned about the headstones. The wire fence around the hill was hidden by honeysuckle vines and blackberry briers. A breeze washed the skins of cherry seedlings.

Lon visited the grave one more time. He knelt and tried to see the baby in his memory; tried to see what his son could have been, would have been had he not left so soon. Whispering against the wind, Lon begged to be forgiven for not being there. If he had been there, the child would have lived. Lon would have willed the child to live; his love would have had breath. His face touched the wet grass and his lips pressed into the earth. He opened his eyes, wiped his face, and stood. He saw another man across the hill in another section, leaning on a stone marked VANCE BRADLEY. The two men saw only a blur of each other through the blotted tears, and both were quickly blinded by a dark shadow that walked between them, stopped, and looked from one to the other.

Ila stood, with shoulders bent, between her father and Tom Bradley, a victim of each.

Lon and Ila walked away, knowing that the weeds and vines from the river would cover the small plot in a year. There was no grand tombstone, no fancy marker. There was no money for a granite lamb or a marble angel. Two small boards, nailed into a cross, leaned toward the father as he moved swiftly away.

❦

Lon slammed the door behind him. "Lora!" he shouted. "Mayzelle! Ila! Pearl! Vera! Get here now!"

The normal noises of the old mill house gave way to creaking sofas and chairs, scampering footsteps, and questions of alarm. Lora came from the kitchen with a pan of muffins in her hand, unconcerned that muffins were falling all over the hall.

"Lon, what's wrong?" she asked.

He smiled. "Everybody sit down." Pearl held her hands over her ears, afraid of this sudden change in Lon's mood. Lon spoke slowly: "We're goin' to Greensboro—the gate city of the South!"

He told his stunned family that Greensboro offered a new and better life for them all. He showed them a newspaper sent by his future employer. True enough, the city was not some hamlet between farm tracks. It was a real city; with brick roads and railroad lines and mill power to spare. Downtown Greensboro was a remarkable display of office buildings, hotels, and cultural centers. There were theaters, trolleys, parks, and even a college for women.

"Look," Ila said, pointing to the open pages of the *Greensboro Daily News* on the kitchen table. "Fannie Mart in *Woman of Destiny*. Listen, Daddy: 'Fannie Mart makes her photodrama debut in a picturalization of the comedy. Miss Mart in the part that has won her international fame, from Paramount Pictures.' Oh, Daddy, I've just got to see that!"

Pearl rolled her eyes. "Really, Ila, you acting like some kind of hick or something, like you never seen shows."

"You don't appreciate culture, Pearl Mitchell, and you never will," Ila said. "Here's an article more in your line: 'For indigestion, constipation,

63

biliousness, lazy, tired feeling, take Cobles Liver Pills. You gonna have to get a big box of them for your biliousness."

Pearl frowned. "Mayzelle, is Ila talking dirty?"

Lon hit the table with his fists. "I got to leave tonight to get things ready for you. Mayzelle, I'm depending on you to take care of my darlin's."

Mayzelle turned to the girls. "Y'all get your packing started. We got to be on that train in one week."

A week later, with Lora and the girls finally on the wagon, Mayzelle prepared to lock the door of the house that had been home for so long. She started to leave when she saw the Greensboro newspaper still on the table and walked to it. She thumbed through the pages, getting an impression of the new city. She read aloud: "'One of the "Peek-a-Boo" hats of black tulle and bronze satin, by Lady Gordon. Here is something also entirely new which the tailor-made maid cannot wear at all, and which is designed especially for her "fluffy sort" of sister.'"

"Fluffy sort." Mayzelle chuckled. "That'd look good on my Ila." She shook her head and turned off the lamps for the last time.

The train was black and gray and formidable in the pre-dawn darkness. The air was cold, and any movement seemed to stir up the chill. The children, bundled up in several dresses and coats, boarded the passenger car. They were followed by Lora and Mayzelle.

"Wait a minute!" said a voice in the dark.

Mayzelle turned. She tried to make out the stranger, but the one depot light glared directly into her eyes.

"Hold on just a minute, nigger! You ridin' this train? Then ride in baggage!"

"I know that," said Mayzelle, trying to control her irritation. "I was just makin' sure the children were comfortable."

"Well, now you have! You goin'?"

"I'm a-goin'," Mayzelle shouted inside to Lora, who was trying to quiet the children. Lora understood.

Mayzelle picked up her cloth satchel, slung it over her back, and started without a word to the baggage car near the end of the train in the dark. The railway conductor followed.

Lora leaned over to make sure that the children were warm and glanced out the window. Mayzelle passed by and waved. Lora smiled and waved back. The light was so dim she caught only a glimpse. She watched as Mayzelle disappeared around the corner of the train.

Suddenly Lora's eyes bulged and she moved closer to the window. For a moment, for just a moment, she thought she recognized the face of the railway worker who had told Mayzelle to go back. No, she thought, it was the light. It could'a been anybody.

At the last baggage car Mayzelle threw her luggage in and climbed into the half-empty storage area.

The conductor, right behind her, asked sharply, "Can I help you in?"

"No," Mayzelle said, "I can get in."

He followed her inside. Just before he closed the huge door, Mayzelle made out his face.

Jeffries.

"What you doin' here?" Mayzelle demanded angrily.

"I work here," he said. She imagined him grinning in the dark.

The train jolted forward. Mayzelle hissed, "You just stay on your side, you hear?"

The sound of the train wheels slapping at the track did not cover the sounds of him removing his belt. He laughed.

Lon met them in Greensboro and hired a car to take them to the Alexander plant near the northern outskirts of town. Unlike Paw Creek, Greensboro was too vast for them to walk from one side to another. The girls huddled near their mother, gazing at the huge buildings and paved streets that were unknown in their former home.

Alexander Mills covered twenty acres and was located between two large streams that passed through Guilford County. The buildings were three-story combinations of brick, steel, and glass, and Ila counted seven smokestacks. The mill homes were nearly all of a rectangular similarity. Lon's house, across the creek, was larger.

The car stopped and everyone piled out and ran to the house.

"Lon, it's beautiful! It really is!"

The brick house had wooden columns over a planked porch and a swing hanging from one side. Two oaks seemed to blot out the second story. Mayzelle called the children back and slowly, laboriously, they unpacked the crates. Lon paid the driver, and they entered their home for their first breakfast.

That evening, Lon went to the mill for his shift, taking Lora with him. Not long afterward, Lora came running back. The house was well lighted, and the trees stood out like giant pasteboard cutouts against the light. Lora ran into the house, and without taking off her coat, she jumped two steps at a time up the back stairway to the attic room and banged on the door.

Mayzelle opened the door. Lora's hair clung like knotted strings about her face and her eyes were inflamed. She gasped for breath.

Mayzelle pulled her into the room and cleared off a chair near the window. Still gasping for air, Lora choked out two words: "He's dead."

"Who's dead?" Mayzelle said calmly.

"Jeffries! Jeffries! He followed you to the baggage car. They found . . . they found him on the side of the tracks. He's dead. Dead." She was shaking uncontrollably, and Mayzelle grabbed Lora's shoulders and forced her to look at her face.

"What you talkin' about, Lora? I don't know what you talkin' about!"

"You mean—you mean you didn't know it was *him*?"

"Why, Lora Mitchell, if you don't talk sense, then I don't know what I'm gonna do."

"But he followed you . . . into the dark. Then, you didn't know, did you? Of course not! You didn't see his face. You didn't know who he was. It was dark." Lora sighed. "Thank God for that. Mayzelle, that fellow, that Jeffries—they found him dead 'longside the tracks miles out of Greensboro. They're sayin' that he fell off the train!"

"Jeffries?" asked Mayzelle, concerned.

"Yes, that's him. The overseer what worked us half to death way back in South Carolina fourteen years ago. Seems he had only been workin' for the railway 'bout a year. But . . . but, oh, my God, what have I done? What have I done?"

"Lora? What you tryin' to tell me? That you thought I might'a *pushed* him?"

"Lord, forgive me, Mayzelle, but when I saw him or thought I saw him followin' you, I saw some meanness in his face. Oh, my Mayzelle, will you ever forgive me?"

Mayzelle stood up. "Nothin' to forgive. Now, you go on down near that fire and stop talkin' nonsense."

Lora wiped her eyes and shook her head. "I'm gettin' old, Mayzelle. Havin' all these children's done rattled my brains."

Mayzelle smiled and pushed her out of the room. The door shut. Mayzelle walked to the window.

Folding and unfolding her fingers and looking at her hands, she leaned against the cool pane and felt the old paint crumble from the wood frames. "Nothin' to forgive," she said. "No sir, nothin' to forgive."

She could almost feel Jeffries' raw hands around her neck and his stiff fingers clawing. She could have given in, she thought; could have spared all this on Lora.

Mayzelle was on the street before dawn, walking along Summit Avenue, across Buffalo Creek, holding her breath to keep from gagging on the chemical fumes that the creek carried from the mill. She walked fast, pulling the shawl around her neck to keep the morning chill away. Already cars and trucks began to wake the city.

After two hours she turned onto the broad street leading to the train station and stopped. She thought about turning around but decided against it and continued. The sun was beginning to heat the roof of the huge railway structure. It looked more like a Chinese mausoleum than a station. An elderly black man was bent shining the shoes of a conductor. She walked past them as if she knew where she was going and what she was looking for.

The main lobby was crowded with smells from the night before: dozing passengers, soldiers, dirty floors. She saw a policeman at the far end of the hall taking notes and she watched him chat, laughing, with a young boy cleaning windows. Soon the policeman walked toward her. She held her breath and turned away. He walked out.

She turned and walked to where he had been standing near a door with a small window. She looked around, then looked in. There on a baggage wagon was a body with a large piece of denim covering it.

She had to know. Had to be sure. No one was in the room. She turned the door knob. It opened.

She walked in, turned the coverlet back, then closed her eyes. It was he. Jeffries. His face was black and puffy, but it was he. There was the scar, and his mouth was opened as if summoning words that she never wished to hear again, words from the dark of the baggage car demanding the services of an animal, for animal pleasure.

"Hey, nigger! What you doin' in here? Git out, you hear? Git out!"

She turned, dropping her shawl. The young window washer, his face screwed up in righteous anger, pointed to the door. "What you doin' with that man? Huh? You here to mess with that body? You better leave, you better!"

She walked past him and felt his window brush strike her legs. She turned and looked into his eyes. He was thin and blond. His shallow blue eyes took on a tinge of question. For a moment he looked down at the body and then at Mayzelle. He started to speak, but her frown stopped him. She left the building.

She had survived at a terrible cost. She had a secret that could never be told. It would hurt too many people. But she felt she had done the right thing, the only thing possible when confronted with the awful stench of Jeffries' frenzy. She had survived. Survival could be brutal, and only time would tell whether it was worth it.

Seven

Ila SIGNED UP full time at Alexander's textile mill. She worked in the spinning room, threading raw cotton called roping through spinning frame rings until the yarn twisted tight. Her father worked upstairs and her sisters worked in another part of the plant.

Ila was about 5′2″, but not conscious of her height. Her hair was still dark and thick, sometimes covered with a scarf to keep the mill dust out. She never cut it. She had large breasts for her age, but Mayzelle showed her how to dress with modesty.

One day in November, just before the end of the first shift, the lights across the huge ceiling flickered on and off, and the whistles from the boiler rooms began to scream across the town. Within minutes, church bells pealed.

The word spread from department to department. Machines stopped and men and women let go with long-suppressed rebel yells.

The war is over!

Some of the older ladies dropped to their knees in prayer. Ila tried to step around them without disturbing their peace.

"Ila! Ila! Isn't it wonderful?"

"Yes, Margot. It's wonderful. Let me by, will you? I got to go!"

"I'll bet you do, Ila. Goin' to see that beau of yours upstairs? Maybe get a little kiss?"

"I'll see you later, Margot. Got to run."

She was delayed several times by other girls who, caught up in the excitement, could think of nothing better to do than to run from one to another in the spinning room, kissing and crying. Ila stepped around them, pushed them into warm machines, and fought her way to the stairway.

Upstairs the men at the machines had gathered near the supervisor's office. Passing a bottle from lip to lip, they spilled some of the clear liquid on the floor as one man after another jerked it from the mouth of the celebrant before him.

Lon was sitting on the floor laughing with the others, until he saw his daughter walking briskly down the aisle. He frowned and tried to catch her eye. She didn't see him. He looked across the ruddy faces of those in the crowd and saw *why* she didn't see him.

The bottle, half empty now, was in the hands of a dark, thin dopper named David Tolbert. Tolbert turned the bottle up and gulped the burning liquor. Finally, choking, he passed the bottle on. He wiped his mouth with his sleeve and shoved his way to the aisle where Ila stood waiting.

He swaggered through the crowd, his eyes bold and dark, his face retaining unblemished baby fat along the chin. His hair was dark, falling across his forehead, giving him the look of a thin child with a crooked frame. He had large elbows, hips, and knees. A bold slash of color from his deep-set eyes to his ears and a blush of honor betrayed a man drunk with pride but vain enough to try to hide it.

"I guess you heard," he said.

"Yes," replied Ila. "I guess everybody has."

"We, uh, that is, me and other boys been celebratin'."

"I can see that, David. I had hoped," she said, lowering her head, "that you would want to celebrate with me."

"I do," he stammered. "I mean, just as soon as we finished, I thought maybe we could go out to Battleground Park. Everybody in town is goin' out there."

"Well," she said thoughtfully and a little wistfully, "I hope that you have a good time."

"No! Wait a minute. I was a-hopin' that you would go with me, that is, if your daddy would let you."

"I'm not sure, David Tolbert. Daddy might agree, but my momma might not."

David pleaded, "You will ask your daddy, won't you?"

"I'll see what I can do, *Mr.* Tolbert." Ila spun around and walked quickly to the stairway. David's green eyes, brightened by the booze, followed her. Lon's eyes followed David's.

"Oh, Momma, you got to let me go! Daddy won't mind. I'm sure of that. Everybody at the mill likes David. Besides, we're goin' to Battleground Park and everybody's goin' to be there. Even Daddy's goin' to hire a car, so we'll all end up together. It's not like a date or anything! Please?"

"Well, all right," sighed Lora, "as long as we are all there. Wait a minute. Pearl! Pearl!"

"Yes, Momma," came the reply from upstairs.

"Pearl, you get on down here. Ila and that Tolbert boy are goin' to the battleground and I want you to go with them."

Ila gasped. "Momma! No! Not her! She'll embarrass me to death, a-clingin' to me while I'm with my beau . . ."

"Your beau? I thought he was just a fellow worker."

"Oh, Momma, you know what I mean. We won't have no privacy at all with Pearl stringin' along."

"That," said Lora, "I had considered."

Pearl came clopping down the stairs. "Ila? When we leavin'?" She ran her tongue around her lips and winked at Ila with a perverse sense of delight; anything to upset Miss Ila Priss.

Sucking in her cheeks, Ila sat down on the sofa.

"Ila, answer your sister!" Lora commanded.

"Soon, Pearl. You just go on back upstairs and I'll call you when David arrives."

"Not on your life, sister dear!" said Pearl, laughing. "I'm gonna stay down here with you till he comes. I know you. As soon as he comes you'll slip off and leave me."

Lora went to the window and called, "Girls, come here. Your father *did* rent a car! And what's that he's got with him? Now, I declare. Look at that. Crepe paper and bunting. Come on out and let's decorate the car. Come on!"

Pearl ran out the door and began to wrap the car with red, white, and blue streamers. Ila sat on the porch, staring down the road. She didn't stare for long. She saw David weaving down the sidewalk. He always weaved when he walked, as though his long legs would buckle under him at any moment.

"David!" Ila shouted impatiently. "Hurry up! We're gonna miss the train!"

Lon put the bunting down and gave Lora a stern look.

"Oh, Lon. Why not? Don't look so harsh. The boy means well, and besides, the war is over and Pearl's goin' with them."

Lon nodded and walked into the house.

"Momma, we're goin' now." Ila kissed Lora and ran to meet David.

"Ila, you forgettin' somethin'?"

"No, Momma," shouted Ila.

"Yes you are!" screamed Pearl. She threw the paper streamers into her mother's arms and ran down the street to join the couple.

The train was crowded with excited townspeople, all in a festive mood.

"Why, this is better'n Christmas!" sighed Pearl.

Ila looked at David and then at the child behind them. "Stupid," she whispered.

David put his arm around Ila as the train started up.

Pearl turned red, yanked on Ila's arm, and whispered in her ear, "I'll tell Momma."

"And she will, too," Ila said loudly to David.

He grinned, winked, and removed his arm.

The house was quiet. Mayzelle and Lora served the food and sat down. The children were tired from the day's celebration. Lon was tired also. He ate slowly, delicately.

Pearl broke the silence. "Momma? You know what?"

"What, Dear?"

"David Tolbert put his hands all over Ila today."

Lon dropped his glass.

"What?" shouted Ila. "Why, you liar! Momma, that ain't so. He put his arm around me on the train 'cause I was cold."

Lora looked at Lon and then at Pearl. Pearl was sipping soup with a slurping noise.

"Ila," Lora said gently, "Now, your daddy and I are tryin' to raise you girls to be ladies, and ladies don't, I repeat, don't allow gentlemen to put their arms around their shoulders no matter how cold it gets!"

Lon grunted.

"Besides," Lora continued, "I don't think you ought to get so involved with a man his age. He's a good ten years older than you and I'm not sure but that a man like that would use a sweet girl like you."

"Momma," said Ila in a heavy, frustrated voice, "I like him and he likes me and that's all there is to it. We ain't even had a real date yet. He asked me to go to the moving pictures with him Saturday, but I ain't answered him yet."

"Well, that's real nice of him, ain't it, Lon?" asked Lora.

Lon ripped a biscuit in half.

"You do trust me, don't you, Momma?" asked Ila.

"Course we do, Honey. It's just that he's so much older'n you, and you've got so little experience with men."

Pearl put her spoon down. "How 'bout that army soldier that Ila met last summer? Remember? You and Daddy had to bail him out of jail 'cause he got in a fight with another man over Ila . . ."

"That will be enough, young lady," Lora said sternly. Pearl picked up her spoon.

"But, Momma, as long as you trust me there's no real harm in my seein' him, is there?" Ila asked.

Lora thought a moment. "No, I reckon there's not, as long as you're properly chaperoned."

"Good, then do you and Daddy mind if I go to the movie with him?"

The movie was *The Perils of Pauline*, and Ila had seen it several times. Ila paid her dime, and David paid his. Pearl looked in her pocket for her dime but couldn't find it.

"Ila," she shouted. "You got another dime? I lost mine!"

Ila grinned and shook her head as she followed David into the theater.

"Want some popcorn?" Ila asked.

"Ain't got no money," said David.

"Oh, that's okay," chirped Ila. "I just happen to have found a dime just before I left home." Ila bought the popcorn and laughed at the thought of Pearl fuming outside.

The movie ended. Ila stood up, but David pulled her back down.

"Will you marry me?"

"What? You got to be crazy. We ain't been dating but twice now. And you're too cheap, David Tolbert, to buy my way into the show."

"But I want to marry you."

"Why?"

"'Cause I love you."

"Well, I'm not so sure I love you."

"Do you like me?"

"Yes."

"Do you like it when I touch you and kiss you and hold—"

"Hush, people goin' to hear you."

"Well, do you?"

"Yes, I suppose so."

"Then let's get married."

"Daddy will kill you."

"Not if he don't know we're gettin' married."

"You mean *elope*?"

"Yep."

"That *is* romantic. You would marry me? You ain't just kiddin' me? 'Cause if'n you are, my daddy will—"

He pulled her close, ran his hands down her back, and kissed her with a violence that made her forget what she was going to say.

"You will?" he asked.

"Yes," she answered.

He kissed her again. All over her face.

"David?" she whispered, catching her breath.

"Yes?"

"The show's over."

He closed his eyes and moved his mouth to hers.

She pushed him back. "David, don't you think we're rushing into this? I mean, there should be a courtship, and a proposal, with my parents present, an engagement ring and maybe a few engagement parties . . . like in the newspaper?"

He kissed her again.

She breathed deeply and put her arm around his neck. "This ain't proper, you know . . ."

"Stop laughing," he said. "Your lips move funny when you laugh."

"I'm a proper girl," she said softly. "I'm not going to do anything that ain't proper, for you or no other man . . ."

"If you don't stop giggling, Ila Mitchell . . ."

"David, you're gonna make my lips raw and Momma'll kill you . . ."

He sat up. He looked hurt. "You gonna stop laughin' or what?"

The theater lights came on.

"You don't want to marry me, David. You just want to fool around. I ain't crazy. My Mayzelle told me about fellows like you. I don't give up no lady potential for somebody with your reputation."

"I'll have it all arranged by Friday."

"You're sweet, David."

"I'll get a license . . ."

"Uh-huh," she smiled.

"And a car . . ."

"Uh-huh," she said loudly.

"You don't believe me?"

She reached for his hand and pulled him to the aisle. "No," she said, and she ran to the lobby. He ran after her, his eyes dark and wide.

73

On Friday morning, David went to Cliffman Jewelers and bought an engagement ring. Ruby and gold, ten dollars. He dropped by the Mitchells' and tried to press it into Ila's hand, but she wouldn't take it, fearing her mother would find it.

David smiled, waved goodbye to the family, and jumped into a car that he had hired.

"Why on earth would that boy hire a car?" asked Lora.

"I don't know," said Ila. "I really don't know."

David drove to Rockingham County, where he was not known, and applied for a marriage license.

"Where's the young lady?" asked the clerk.

"Sick."

"How old is she?"

"Eighteen," he lied.

"Son, I got to have proof she's eighteen or I can't give you this here license. Now, you go get a relative or somebody to swear she's eighteen, and it's yours."

David was gone fifteen minutes. He came back with a short man.

"This a relative?" asked the clerk.

"Yes sir," said David. "It's her father."

"You her father?"

"Yes, shore am, been her father ever since the day she was born."

"How old's your daughter?"

"Eighteen, I swear it."

David folded the certificate and walked the old man to the courthouse steps.

"Where's my money?"

"Here," David said. "Five dollars."

"Thank you, son. You must be crazy wantin' to marry a woman bad enough to pay five dollars for her. Next time you down this way to get married again, I'll be sittin' on the same bench."

David drove back to Greensboro and picked up Ila.

"Well?" she asked.

"Well," he replied.

"Now, David Tolbert, you tell me what you're a-doin' with this car. You actin' mighty peculiar."

"Got a good reason to, Ila. I bought our license." He pulled it from his coat and handed it to her.

"Oh my God! It *is* a license!"

"Course it is. Tomorrow Preacher Campbell's goin' to come over to my house to marry us. Ten o'clock. Hope you're there. My folks'll be gone."

"I don't know, David. This is happenin' a little too fast for me. I'm still worried about Daddy. He don't care for you too much, you know."

"I know. But you do and that's all that matters."

"Yes, I s'pose you're right about that."

"Ten o'clock?"

"Ten o'clock. One thing, though, David. How am I goin' to explain bein' gone all day tomorrow, much less all night tomorrow night?"

"My sister Beatrice. She'll ask you to spend the night. It's all settled."

"No, it's not completely settled. There's one person I gotta tell."

"Not your daddy!"

"Lord, no. I may be crazy a-marryin' you, but I ain't no fool!"

"Mayzelle, can you come up and help me, please?"

"After I finishes the dishes."

"They can wait."

"No they can't."

"I'll help you do 'em later."

Mayzelle looked at the dishes, then at Ila.

"Girl, this is a first. I ain't never known you to ask to wash dishes before. You must be awful sick."

"Now, don't tease me, Mayzelle. I really do need your help."

"Yes, I can see that. Just a minute and I'll be right up."

Mayzelle walked into the room a few minutes later.

"Where the other girls?"

"I sent 'em away."

"You sent Pearl away?"

"I gave her a dime. She took the others to the porch."

"Honey, you surely gone mad."

"Maybe so."

"What you doin'?"

"I want to dye this white hat. I want it black, and I want to sew this plastic rose on it."

"You got any shoe polish?"

"Yes, here it is. Will you sew the rose?"

"Might as well. Don't slop that shoe polish on the quilt or your momma will kill you. Now, what is it that you need from me besides sewin' a rose, which you can do yourself?"

Ila put the hat down and walked to the closet. She reached deep into the back and pulled out a small brown box.

"I want your honest opinion. What do you think of this?" She opened the box and pulled out a thin white nightgown with lace sleeves.

"Mighty skimpy. Won't keep you warm a'tall. Where'd you get it?"

"I made it. My weddin' nightgown."

"Your what?"

"My honeymoon nightgown. Don't you like it?"

"Well, it's mighty nice, bit thin though, but what with a husband and all you don't need it too heavy, I s'pose."

"Oh, I'm glad you like it, then."

"I ain't never heard you speak of marriage before. I guess it's natural, though, a girl your age. Got anybody special in mind?"

"Yes."

"Who?"

"David Tolbert."

"David Tolbert? That good-for-nothin'? Why, he's a tom-bird if I ever seen one. Yes sir, a real tom-bird. He's got women all over this town from what I hear. Why don't you favor on somebody more your own age, like Grant McCombs, and in four years or so you can marry."

"Grant McCombs is stuck on himself."

"And David Tolbert ain't? Why, he's as vain as they come."

"Well, it don't matter. It's done anyway."

"What's done? What you talkin' about?"

"I'm a-marryin' David tomorrow."

"What?" Mayzelle said. "You crazy or somethin'?"

"Shhh! Please whisper! You'll have Momma in here and then everything will be ruined."

"You got to be foolin' your old Mayzelle. I mean, that's all there is to it, you got to be foolin'."

"No, he loves me and, well, I think that he would make a fine husband. He's got the marriage certificate and everything else and we're gonna do it tomorrow."

Mayzelle stood and walked around the room, touching the curtains and the wooden walls, shaking her head and moaning in a low hum.

"Mayzelle, I thought you would be happy for me."

"Oh, Honey, happy ain't the word. I'm in a shock. I ain't never been in such a shock. You gettin' married! Your momma and daddy? When you gonna tell them?"

"I ain't."

Mayzelle sat down near the window. "You ain't, huh? Well, listen to me: That's not a nice thing to do to them after all they done for you. Yes sir, I know that for a fact. You gonna break your momma's heart is what you gonna do, and I . . . I love you and I ain't gonna allow it. No sir. No sir,

I ain't. I'm gonna go down and tell them right now. And after your daddy beats you, then *I'm* gonna beat you." Mayzelle rushed for the door.

Ila caught her sleeve and pulled her back to the bed. "Please, Mayzelle, I need him. Can't you understand that? I'm not a little girl no more and Daddy and Momma gonna hold me back all my life if I don't get out of here. Don't you understand?"

Mayzelle put her hands to her head. "I don't want to hear no more, Honey. You old enough to make your own decisions, but I don't like to see your momma hurt. She been hurt enough and so has your daddy. This is gonna hurt him worse than when he lost his boy. His oldest girl runnin' away to marry some ganglin' goose-eyed tom-bird."

"He ain't a tom-bird," snarled Ila. "You got no right to talk about him like that, Mayzelle, no right a'tall."

Ila lowered her head and tried to hold back the tears.

Mayzelle patted her head and smiled. "I'll help you, youngun, but I don't know what your momma and daddy's gonna do. Lord help you, things always work out like they's supposed to; guess there's not much we can do to change 'em. If you love that man, then I'm with you. You *do* love him, don't you?"

Ila looked away and nodded her head.

"Then it's all set, ain't it?"

Saturday morning, in the quiet of dawn, Ila moved about the room dressing slowly, making no sound. All I need, she thought, would be for Pearl to wake up and start asking questions.

She closed the door gently, agonizing over each squeak of the hinges, then tiptoed down the stairs into the cold living room. She grabbed her coat from the rack and turned the door handle.

"Ila?"

She jumped and slammed the door.

"Ila? What on earth? Where you a-goin' this time of mornin'?"

"Oh, Momma, you scared me. I thought I would go over to Beatrice's early so we could go shoppin' uptown."

"Oh. Well. Have a nice time. It's right nice of Beatrice to invite you over. You'll have to return the compliment. Tell Mrs. Tolbert I said hello."

"I will, Momma," she lied. Mr. and Mrs. Tolbert had gone to the country to visit cousins in Stokesdale. "'Bye, Momma." She shut the door.

The morning air was cold and yet she felt strangely warm, almost sweating with fear and excitement. She walked to the Tolbert's door and rapped sharply.

Beatrice opened the door, rubbing sleep from her eyes. Her torn blue robe was wrapped loosely around her large body. She tried to hide the egg stains on her sleeve. "Ila? What you doin' here this time of morning?"

"Oh, shut up, Beatrice, and let me by." She rushed into the Tolbert kitchen and found David shaving over the sink. He washed his face and turned to her with a smile.

"Well, my wife to be. Good to see you so early. Mustn't get in too much of a hurry, you know."

"David, where's the preacher?"

"He's not due till ten. Come on and let's make some breakfast. You look like you could use some."

"Make breakfast? How can you eat at a time like this?"

Beatrice came in and sat down at the table. "Will somebody please tell me what's goin' on?"

"Gladly," said David. "Beatrice, tonight you have invited Mrs. Tolbert here to stay over."

"Mrs. who?"

"Mrs. Tolbert, Beatrice, your future sister-in-law."

"Lord God, David."

"Cut it out, David," said Ila. "You're a-scarin' that child half to death."

"I'm sorry," said David. "Beatrice, hold on to yourself real good, Honey. Today at ten o'clock, I am marryin' this here young lady."

"Lord God!" said Beatrice.

"Will you stop sayin' that?" shrieked Ila.

"Lord God," whispered Beatrice.

"David? Do we have to sit here for the next three hours? I don't think I can make it."

David walked over and kissed her forehead. "You'll make it. You just stick with me and you'll make it all right."

Beatrice came out of her shock and managed to say, "Congratulations," to Ila.

"Lord God," replied Ila.

"Ila," said David, "why don't I send Beatrice up to the store for some of those chocolate apples you like so much?"

"Good idea," Ila said.

"I ain't dressed," said Beatrice.

"Get dressed," said David, his teeth clenched.

Beatrice pulled her great weight from the table and walked solemnly out of the room, shaking her head as she went.

David sat down next to Ila.

"Now, Honey. Don't you go and get upset. We've only a little time to wait and then it will be all over."

"All over? That's a nasty way to put it."

"You know what I mean. You just got weddin' jitters, that's all."

"I guess you're right, David. It's just a big step to take. I suppose I can wait a few hours."

Beatrice, clothed, walked through the room and out the door, still shaking her head. David and Ila smiled foolishly at each other. Then came a loud knock at the door. David went to the window.

"Oh my God," he said. "It's that nosy sister of yours, Pearl."

"Let her in."

"Come on in," said David. "If it isn't my beautiful friend from up the road."

"Thank you kindly," said Pearl, amused. "I just wanted to see if everythin's all right down here. Where's Beatrice?"

"Gone to the store," said David.

"Why don't you go find her?" said Ila in a low voice.

"No thanks. I'll just wait on her."

"But Pearl," said David, smiling, "it's gonna be a while. She went clean on down to the railroad store."

"I'll wait," repeated Pearl.

"Suit yourself," said David, as his smile crumbled.

The three sat at the table drinking coffee until nine o'clock, when Beatrice finally came back.

"Where you been?" snapped David.

"At the store, where you sent me."

"It don't take that long to go to the store."

"Well, I stopped and ate a couple apples on the way back. Knew you wouldn't mind."

"What apples?" said Pearl.

"These here chocolate ones that David sent me for."

"You want one, Pearl?" asked David, leering.

"Well, I guess one wouldn't hurt me."

"A dozen wouldn't hurt you," said Ila. "You're skinnier than a buzzard now."

Pearl drew back in horror. "No thank you, David. I guess plump Ila here would need the chocolate more than me."

David looked at his watch and realized that once the preacher arrived, Pearl would go screaming back up the road.

"Beatrice?" he said. "Why don't you and Pearl go to the picture show? My treat."

79

"Oh, good!" said Beatrice.

"'I don't want to go," said Pearl.

"Okay," said David. "You don't have to go if you don't want to go. I'm not going to make you go. I was going to throw in an extra ten cents for candy and such, but if you don't want to go . . ."

"Let's go," said Pearl. "Where's the money?"

David reached into his pocket and pulled out a dollar bill. "Here, take it."

"Whole dollar?" said Pearl, genuinely surprised.

"Yep. Now beat it 'fore I bash your face in."

Waving the dollar bill under Beatrice's nose, Pearl stepped out the door with exaggerated dignity.

"David," said Ila, "I don't know if I'm gonna make it or not."

"Sure you will. Just hold tight. Close your eyes."

"What?"

"Now, go on and do what I tell you to do. Close your eyes."

"You not goin' to do nothin', are you?"

"No, Ila, not till later, anyways. Now close your eyes or I'll throw your treat away."

Ila obeyed.

"Now open them," he said.

She did. "Roses! Oh, David! They're beautiful!"

"A weddin's not much without flowers for the bride. Matches your hat, too."

"Oh, David, nobody's ever given me roses before."

"Nobody's ever loved you as much before."

"Anybody home?" a deep voice yelled from the porch.

"Who's that?" whispered Ila.

"Just the preacher," said David. "Preacher Campbell. Come on in, Preacher!"

Preacher Campbell was a short man with thin hair combed forward, making him look a little like Nero. He was dressed in dungarees, a tweed jacket, and a red tie.

"Let's get on with it, boy. Where's your witness?"

"Oh, Lord," David gasped. "Beatrice was supposed to be our witness. I forgot about it when I sent her to the picture show."

"You sent her to the movies?" said Preacher Campbell. Preacher Campbell felt that the moving pictures were the devil's work.

"No, not exactly," said David, clenching his hands. "I sent her to make sure Pearl Mitchell got there all right."

"Oh," said the preacher. "Can't have a weddin' without a witness."

David rushed to the door and looked up and down the street.

"Hey, you, little boy," he shouted. "Yeah, you. Come here a minute and I'll pay you a dollar."

The little boy playing in the mud across the street stared at David for a moment, confused. Then he got up and ran into his house. His father came to the door.

"What's that you want with my boy?" shouted the boy's father.

"I need a witness for a wedding!" screamed David hoarsely.

The boy and his father chatted for a while on their porch, then the boy walked over to the Tolbert house.

"Preacher Campbell, this is Timmy. Timmy, say hello to Preacher Campbell."

"My name's Tommy."

"Okay, Timmy, Tommy, what's the difference? You just watch what happens and I'll give you a dollar. All right?"

"All right," said the boy. Tommy never looked into anyone's eyes, possibly because he had a cross-eye condition that caused people to wrinkle their noses when speaking to him. He found they were more interested in his wandering eye than in the content of his speech. Consequently, he was the neighborhood cynic.

"Is the bride ready?" boomed an impatient Preacher Campbell.

"Yes," stammered Ila.

"Where is the marriage certificate?"

"Right here, Preacher, filled out except for your signature and the boy's there."

"Wait a second, son," said Campbell, suddenly quite serious. "This here is a Rockingham County license. That means you got to be married in Rockingham County."

Ila brought the roses up to her face.

"No!" shouted David.

"Yes," said the preacher.

"Jesus," whispered Ila.

"You can say that again," said Preacher Campbell.

Just at that moment Beatrice came slamming into the front door. It was locked. "Open up in there, you hear, open up!" she shouted.

David unlocked the door.

Just as he opened the door, he saw a red flash go down the street, headed toward the Mitchell house: Pearl.

"You told?" asked David, his voice shaking.

"Had to," said Beatrice, trying to catch her breath. "She said she'd break my arm if I didn't tell her."

David paced, desperate. "Preacher, for an extra five dollars, will you ride with us to Rockingham County to get us properly married?"

"Now?" asked Campbell.

"Now," said David. "Right this second."

"Well, boy, if it means that much to you, I guess I can—"

"Fine," shouted David, pushing the preacher out the door and dragging Ila behind him.

"Everybody in the car!" shouted David. "No, Timmy, not you. You can go home. Beatrice can take your place."

"What about my dollar?" cried the boy.

"Here's your damn dollar. Everybody in? Let's go."

The back wheels of the Ford coupe that David had rented spun in the mud as the car chugged forward at a slow but sure pace. Ila sank down in the back seat with Beatrice as the car passed her home. There on the front porch, pointing and shouting frantically, were Lon, Lora, Pearl, and Vera.

"Lon! Stop them!" screamed Lora. "That man's goin' to marry my baby. You've got to stop them!"

Lon shook his head and whispered in Lora's ear, "How the hell am I goin' to stop them when I don't even know where they're goin'?"

Mayzelle walked to the porch and helped Lora inside.

❦

Resting his Bible on the back of the seat, the minister knelt on the front seat of the car. David and Ila knelt on the back seat, facing him. Beatrice stood under a sign that read, "Rockingham County." They had parked under a persimmon tree off the road.

"David," Preacher Campbell intoned, "I'm just a country preacher what lives in the city. Some folks look at me and my manners and get some laughs outa my uneducated ways and this big stomach. Some make fun of us country preachers 'cause we get a little bit carried away by the spirit sometimes and holler a bit more than maybe we oughta holler. But those people who see us in that way forget sometimes that we have to deal with simple folk who work most of their lives in the heat of the mill, spending their strength for another nickel for bread or another shirt for their boys, and when I work with these people, I am humbled by the good I find in each of 'em despite their hardships; and in that humility I remember where and how I fit in the work of this world. So, David, consider this here car a sanctuary, 'cause God's love has come to the people in it; and consider the sky around us the ceiling of the greatest cathedral you'd ever hope to see; and consider my words to be a holy force. Forget the way I

82

look, or the rough leather of the seats, or the sound of my voice. All I want you to hear is the language of God speakin' from my heart.

"And Ila, take these words also to your soul: It is an important step you're a-takin' here. You ain't allowed to change your mind once you accept the truth you see and hear today. You understand that, Honey? Good. Then, we are here gathered in the sight of God and man . . . ."

It was dark when the Ford stopped in front of the Tolbert house. Ila noticed that every light in the house seemed to be on. She waited as David paid the preacher.

"Five dollars all right?" asked David wearily.

"Is that girl worth five dollars?"

"I think so."

"Then five dollars is what it is. Goodnight, children. And good luck."

Beatrice went into the house first and held the door open as Ila and David entered.

David's parents were sitting at the kitchen table. At first glance the pair looked like twins. Both were tall with olive skin clinging to thin bones. Their hands were webbed and liver-spotted. Both had a serene, almost mystical look about them. Each seemed absorbed in some irreversible impending tragedy. Mr. Tolbert was bald and Mrs. Tolbert was balding. She always wore a red and blue scarf about her head. Both Mr. and Mrs. Tolbert wore red flannel shirts.

Pearl was sobbing over a mug of milk.

David pulled out a chair and eased Ila into it.

"Son," said Mr. Tolbert sleepily, "Pearl done told us what you all went and done this afternoon. You got a hell of a lot of explainin' to do to me and Mr. Mitchell. He's mighty upset. Mighty upset!"

"Pa," began David, "I'm old enough to marry when I please. It's done and that's that. Ila can live with me upstairs until we find a place of our own."

Mrs. Tolbert smirked. "And when will that be? We got trouble enough feeding ourselves and the boarders. Who's gonna foot *her* bill?"

Ila began to speak but David stopped her. "I am her husband and I'm gonna make do in my family. We'll pay rent just like everybody else. Agreed?"

Mr. Tolbert looked at his wife. She nodded. "All right, son," she said. "We're expectin' you to live up to that bargain. As for you, young lady, we expect you to pull your own weight around here. No special favors to any other boarders and none to you. We got five people livin' here 'sides you and they comes and goes and would make a fuss if we gave anybody any special attention. You understand?"

Ila nodded.

"Good. Now, somebody try to hush this here child up. Pearl's been a-cryin' all afternoon 'bout her sister gettin' married. Ila, you say somethin' to your sister. She's been near hysterical. I can't stand hysterical children."

Ila rose and pulled Pearl to the porch.

"Now what you blubberin' about? Don't you see that I got enough trouble without you a-blubberin' all over creation?"

Pearl wiped her eyes and her nose. She searched for the right words. "Ila, I'm . . . we . . . gonna miss you. I don't know how we gonna make it without you."

Ila took a deep breath and said, "Now, look. I've made my decision and we all got to do the best by it. I know that one day you will get some young man and then I'll stand by you. Now wipe those eyes. How's Momma and Daddy?"

"They mighty upset with you. Momma's in bed and Daddy, he just rocks in front of the fire sayin' cuss words over and over."

"I figured Daddy would take it pretty bad. He never did like boys around me. I didn't think Momma would let it bother her for long, though."

Pearl sniffed. "Mayzelle been tryin' to talk to her. Every time she does, Momma just gets up and moves to another part of the room. Daddy's talkin' about takin' a walk down to Mo Rafferty's and you know what he does when he goes there—drinks all night. Mayzelle told him it would only hurt Momma, so he said he wouldn't go."

"Well, Pearl, let's at least be glad of that. I figure in a couple of days, when they simmer down, I'll come home and try to talk things over. You go on back home and tell 'em I love 'em. One more thing I want you to do before you go. Deep in the back of our closet is a little brown shoebox with some green string around it. Bring it back to me as soon as you can. Tonight. Will you do that for me?"

Pearl nodded.

"Good. Now get on home before they get mad at you, too."

Pearl walked into the dark. Ila turned and went into the kitchen.

Mrs. Tolbert looked down into her coffee cup. "David's up in his room. I expect you'll want to go there."

Ila went upstairs. She helped David clean out his bureau to make room for her clothes.

Within an hour Mrs. Tolbert knocked at the door. "Ila! You got a visitor."

"Who is it?" Ila asked.

No answer.

Ila walked down the hall and slipped down the steps to the parlor. Lon stood at the door with a small brown box in his hand. He held it out for

Ila. She ran up to him, hugged him, kissed him, and went back to David without a word.

Lora slumped back into the rocking chair. Lon stood by the fire.

"It's your fault, you know," she said casually.

Lon looked up, startled.

"Yes," Lora mumbled, "I always knew it would end like this. Ever since you beat her that day over the gum."

"Now, Lora, don't start—"

"Don't look at me like that. You know it wasn't right. Man should never beat his daughter, no sir. I should have stopped you. I seen it coming as she clung to that wall, bleeding like a trapped rabbit. I seen it in her eyes, Lon Mitchell."

"Lora, that was a long time—"

"She's lookin' for a kinder man, that's what she's lookin' for. And I guess that's what she thinks she's found. She don't know one thing about bein' married, not one—"

"Lora, shut up!"

She stopped rocking.

Lon walked over to her and pulled her up.

"No, leave me alone."

"Come on."

"Lon, I don't want to lose my Ila."

He saw the hurt in her eyes. He recognized it.

"I know. You won't lose your Ila. Ila's a smart girl and she's gonna be fine. Lots of girls get married that young."

"That was when you and I was young, not now. Young people got it too easy these days, they don't know what hardship and hard work is like."

"They'll find out soon enough, Lora. That's part of living, too, you know. Let 'em live and grow and learn like we did. We didn't turn out so bad, did we?"

"Well," she said, beginning to smile, "at least *I* didn't."

Lon slapped her lightly on the bottom.

"Do that again, Lon Mitchell, and I'll have Mayzelle beat you up good."

"And I guess she could do it."

"Lon," Lora said as she stared out the window, "you think tomorrow I ought to take some food and clothes over to Ila and . . . that boy?"

"That might be a real good idea."

"I'm just scared for her, Lon."

"I know."

"No, Lon, this is a different feeling that you can't know."

Eight

"MORE WOOD," grumbled Mrs. Tolbert as Ila poured a bucket of water into the huge iron pot. Ila's eyes burned from the hickory smoke drifting across her face and to the sky. As Ila ran to the woodshed, Mrs. Tolbert threw the clothes into the pot, gently scraping the lye soap over each article with a wooden spoon.

"Hurry up, girl, 'fore the damned shirts melt away!"

Ila scooped up an armload of wood and raced back, dumping the over-sized twigs to the ground. Kneeling, she placed them one by one into the fire until she could feel the steady heat grow stronger. Her tears mingled with the sweat from her brow as she squinted through the woodsmoke haze that turned everything in the neighborhood blue. She hated washing clothes.

"Don't daydream," commanded Mrs. Tolbert.

Ila pushed her stick into the boiling cauldron and drew out heavy, steaming clumps of cloth, shirts and pants, underwear and dishrags. She quickly dumped the collection into a basin of cold water, then reached into the basin and kneaded the contents like dough, forcing the dirt and soap out with her reddened fingers. Then she reached behind for the scrub board, thrust it into the water, and moved the clothes roughly up and down, rinsing and squeezing until no water was left. Finally, she threw the clothes into a basket for them to be hung on the line.

"Ila!" shouted Mrs. Tolbert. "When you finish the next load, you can get on inside and wash those kitchen floors. Damn mess, bunch of pigs for boarders, never have seen the like! They eatin' me outa house and home . . . and for three dollars a week! Cheap bastards! Now, don't let that fire go out, you hear? Ain't you got some sense of your own? I don't know which is lazier, you or my David. Course, I know the answer to that one. David won't never 'mount to nothin', no sir. He's a dreamer. You'll find that out soon enough. He runs away from problems. Hope he never finds you to be a problem!" She giggled, a guttural, rasping laugh. "Course he might'a been somethin' if he hadn't married so young. But, oh, he's tied down now . . . he'll see what life's about . . . and you will, too! Yes sir. Life gonna whittle the both of you down, little by little, year by year. Not that I wish it on you." She spat. "Nope, wouldn't do that. You won't believe this, but I always hoped he'd have it better than me and his old man. Ha! Fat chance for that . . . it's a laugh, it is. Maybe he got his dreamin' honest, huh? He'll just have to live with it, expectin' the worst in this life . . . that's all you can do. Bear up as long as you can . . . with no hope. No, none . . . no hope at all in life." She stopped stirring the clothes and gazed off over the mill smokestacks and beyond.

"When I was young," the old woman said gently, "I always wondered why my kinfolk, especially the older ones, was always so joyful when they talked about dyin'. 'Seein' Jesus,' they used to say. I had an aunt once, Aunt Meegan I believe it was. She always used to say, 'I'm ready to go.' Took me a couple of years to figure out where she was goin', exactly. She always smiled when she said it. Said it all the time. Ain't it a shame that all we got to look forward to is dyin'? If Aunt Meegan was right, then we go to heaven and have such a good time. Lord, I hope she was right. Look at me." She wiped her eyes. "A-sweatin' and a-carryin' on . . . What? Damn, Ila, you let the fire go out! Go get some more wood, do you hear? Don't just stand there a-gawkin', Ila, git! Ila? Ila, what you starin' at?"

Ila spoke slowly. "I ain't gonna end up like that, Mrs. Tolbert. People can make the best of themselves no matter how old they are. David and I love each other. He's gonna make something of himself because I'm gonna stand behind him all the way and help him all I can, like my momma did for my daddy. We gonna build a family we can be proud of, one that can stand the shocks of the rough bends in our life. Hard times come to everybody, Mrs. Tolbert. You ain't something special. The only difference between you and me is that you mope and complain and act like you already dead. But I'm not gonna give in like you have. I wouldn't trade places with you and your boarding house and your money for all the . . . ." She stopped.

Mrs. Tolbert was looking at her with an almost awed expression. "We'll see, Mrs. David Tolbert . . . we'll see," the woman said softly.

"I ain't never seen a girl get so pregnant so fast," David's mother said.

Mr. Tolbert grabbed a pail. "Got to go milk the cow," he said.

Even while she was pregnant, Ila worked hard around the house. David loved everything she did. He loved the way she kept the room cleaned. Loved the way she helped his mother. Loved the way she fussed after him. But little by little, as she gained more and more weight, she lost more and more of her patience, and by her ninth month, she was grouchy.

One of the boarders had a child named Susan. Susan was only a year younger than Ila, and she visited every afternoon and played house while Ila worked. Susan sometimes brought dolls and dressed them up and down, made and unmade Ila's bed, and pretended to be married.

"Here, hand me that dumb doll," Ila said one day.

"Why?" asked Susan.

"'Cause you got its hair all wrong. I'll fix it for you. Here, comb it like you see in those newspaper ads for those women's clothes up in New York."

"I ain't never been to New York."

Ila brushed the snags and tangles out of the doll's hair. "Hand me that bow over there on the dresser. Yes, the blue one." She caught a glimpse of herself, sitting on the bed with the toy in her hand. "My God, what am I doin'?"

"What's wrong, Ila? You sick?"

Ila handed the doll to Susan. "Take a walk, girl. I ain't got time to play with dolls."

"What's the matter?" asked Susan. "You ill or somethin'?"

Ila tried to smile but couldn't.

"Ila? Ila? You look bad sick. You want me to get Mrs. Tolbert or somebody?"

Ila shook her head. "No," she panted.

"Just the same, Ila, I think I better go get Mrs. Tolbert. She's downstairs in the back workin' in the garden."

That was all that Ila could remember. She was not sure who shouted to her, but the room soon filled with voices.

Lora.

"Honey? Can you hear me, Baby? You gonna be all right. Me and Mayzelle are here and Doctor Nesbitt is on his way. You been sweatin' and rollin' a lot."

"Momma? Momma? Oh, Momma, I've just wet all over."

"You what?"

"Wet . . . wet," whispered Ila weakly.

Mayzelle walked over and looked. "Water's broke. Won't be long now."

"Momma, Momma?"

"Right here, Honey."

"Where's David?"

"He's on his way, Honey. We sent Beatrice to get him."

"Momma, I think I'm gonna die."

"No, no, Honey, you gonna be all right. You gonna give birth here in a little bit."

"I hurt, Momma. Real bad. In my back. Momma, when am I supposed to have . . . bearin' . . . down . . . pains?"

"Good Lord, child. You havin' 'em now?"

Ila pushed three times and Rossie was born. Doctor Nesbitt never did show up. Mayzelle washed the baby after Lora had cut the cord with scissors.

Ila spoiled Rossie. When the child was old enough, Ila talked David into buying a carriage for him. The wire frame was covered with wicker in the shape of a car, with hoods, sides, a top that let down, and even a little sticker with *Body By Fisher* printed on it.

The child seemed to cry a lot, and Ila always fixed him a sugar tit. She took a clean cloth, placed a lump of butter and sugar in it, closed it, soaked it in milk, and popped it in his mouth. Rossie begged for the treat.

One day Ila went downstairs to the kitchen to get a broom. Mrs. Tolbert was in the kitchen talking with a neighbor. She turned with a start at seeing Ila in the doorway. Mrs. Tolbert walked right up to Ila and said, "Eavesdroppers don't ever hear no good about themselves." And then she turned around abruptly.

Ila ran upstairs and grabbed her child from the crib, laid him on her bed, and began packing. David came home from work to find that all his clothes had been folded into neat little bundles with strings around them. Ila was sitting in a chair near the window, rocking the child, trying not to cry.

"What's the matter?" asked David.

"Nothin'," she said.

"Nothin'? Then why you cryin'? People don't cry for nothin'. Tell me, I'm your husband, you got to tell me."

"I can't stand it anymore," Ila said, the words suddenly coming faster than the tears. "I work from sunup to sundown and all your mother ever does is complain or criticize and I keep this room and this boy clean and the boarders complain about his cryin'. I can't help it if he cries! I do the best I can, David. I really do! Oh, David, hold me."

He knelt next to the chair and put his arm around her.

"What do you want us to do?" he asked.

"Oh, I don't know. Get out, I suppose. We got to get out of here. To a place of our own. To the country. Your cousin's got a farm in Ellisboro. That's not too far from here. You're always talkin' about how you would like to go back to farmin'. Let's do it, David. Let's get out of here and show 'em all. I'm tired of bein' beholden to your folks and my folks. Please, David, let's *go*."

David looked at Rossie, carefully touching the child's long hair.

"I wouldn't mind farmin' again, that's for sure. Mill life never did please me."

"Then you will? You mean it? We can go to a farm? David, that would be so wonderful, a place where your children could grow up away from the stinking mill and the stinking river and the stinking wagon that hauls the sewage!" She was up with the child, almost dancing around the room. "David, just think of it! Alone, you and me and the child. We can make it there and not be beholden to nobody!"

David smiled. "Now, I don't know if Luke has still got the farm to rent. The ground's not the best around but it will do. I'll tell you what. I'll drive there Saturday and see what I can do. No promises, but I'll see what I can do. Okay?"

Ila put the boy back in his crib and lay on the bed. She motioned for David to join her.

Finally, she thought, we can be on our own, independent at last, free, secure, and happy. We can live our own life. Build a family that's strong. Life in the country can only help.

"It's hard work," David said.

"Can't be much harder than what I'm used to around here."

"Might be harder. I like farming, but I don't know if you're cut out for it or not."

"Then I'll just have to show you, won't I?"

Ila would never forget the spring of 1920, when she moved her family from Greensboro to the country. David had gone ahead and she and Rossie followed a week later.

The train ride seemed to relieve all the frustrations of the months of living with Mrs. Tolbert. The train went slowly enough that she could gaze out on the miles of corn and tobacco rows. She breathed the heavy pine odor coming from the forests and the fragrance of apple and peach orchards by the tracks. She waved at the naked little boys swimming beneath the bridge over Elk Creek. She held her son up to watch a herd of cattle race to a barn at the sound of the hay bell. She smiled at the sight of horse-drawn carts being passed on dirt roads by shiny new cars.

She was fulfilled at last. A husband who loved her. A son with brown eyes as bright as Easter, and a new life where the pace would be one she set for herself.

Soon she saw the sign for O'Neil's Grocery and pulled the conductor's cord. Signs covered the place in dark greens, reds, and blues. *Ice-Cold Coca-Cola Sold Here. Supreme Ice Cream.* Newspapers from Winston-Salem, Greensboro, and Charlotte were stacked in front. A crowd of people came in and out, some in salesmen's suits, most in farmer gray. Children wore white smocks or baggy pants.

Attached to the grocery store was a Ford garage shaped like a tent. Thin shuttered planks shaded a gas pump based in concrete. The pump resembled a tall man whose skin had been ripped off, leaving screws, pipes, and cranks surrounding the skeleton.

The train slowed to a halt, and Ila jumped off with Rossie in her arms. She walked across a newly plowed field, her feet sinking in the bright red clay, which was moist from a morning rain. Rossie began to shout and Ila saw what he was shouting about—a rabbit crouched in a nearby turnip patch, trembling at their approach. Ila tried to walk silently, but the rabbit bolted into the blackberry briers.

This is a good place, Ila thought. She walked to the edge of the field and down a dirt road, carefully following the instructions that David had left her. Soon she came to a hill and knew that this was the place. On the hill, surrounded by locust trees, stood a weathered frame house with a roof needing repairs and a well half-covered by pine boughs.

Ila walked up to the house, stepped up to the porch, and walked in. The screen on the door was rusty, but no matter, David would fix it. The inside of the house was as plain as the outside. A stove, a fireplace in one room, and an iron bed in the bedroom. Ila walked to the back porch and leaned against the column. No smokestacks, no open sewers, no house other than this one for miles. You could scream if you wanted, she thought, and no one would care. She looked across the woods at a column of smoke a few miles away.

"Neighbors," she said. "Good distance for neighbors."

She drew in a deep breath and shouted at the top of her lungs, first in one direction and then in another. Echoes slashed across the fields and into the woods and hills. She laughed, jiggling Rossie on her hip. David should be home soon. Seeing a pile of wood chips in the back, she began to collect them for the fire.

David worked hard. He planted tobacco and corn the first year but only tobacco the next. Ila grew a house garden to supply the vegetables. With help from some neighbor women, she produced almost everything that was eaten in the house. David bought some pigs and a cow with his first tobacco money. Later, eggs came from a few chickens won in a poker game.

One of the neighbors taught Ila the art of canning. Soon she had great stores of blackberries, tomatoes, apples, and peaches, watermelon preserves and pickles, damson fruit and cherries, string beans and squash.

Yet life on the farm was far more harsh than Ila had imagined. Every day she woke with one thought: This is not the way things are supposed to be.

Where's Mayzelle? she thought. Mayzelle could help me figure out what's going wrong.

Ash was born in 1921.

Nine

Greensboro, 1925

A DEEP CRY came from within the wooden church, a sound like a final lament from a wounded beast. No other sound disturbed the dark cemetery or the box-shaped houses drawing evening shadows across the dirt alleys.

The Reverend Max Chapman had the congregation in his hands. Even the babies ceased crying, and Mayzelle broke out of her drift toward sleep. The black congregation was on the edge of their seats. He had them and he would not let them go. He ignored the wet collar chafing his dark throat and the sweat washing across his large brown eyes. Even Reuben, his son, seemed to be listening, anticipating the inevitable fireworks display of words that would bring the small, cramped congregation to its feet, shouting and praying.

Reverend Max did not disappoint Reuben.

"And deep . . . in the recesses . . . of that cancer of evil, a-smotherin' and a-chokin' the goodness seed that God planted in you from birth, is a piece of Jesus, a-cryin' in His Father's name to be freed from the chains that you—yes, *you*—placed on the power of God!" He let his hands move across his close-cropped white hair, bristling with almost uncontrollable energy. He felt the shout begin in his gut and travel through his veins until he could hold it no longer: "On your knees! God Almighty, you get on your knees and bless His name! Bless His name for forgiveness, for a-stayin' with you all these years, a-holdin' out His love while you defiled his temple, and defiled your flesh, the flesh of His babies! Bless His name for not strikin' you dead upon this very holy ground, for lovin' you so much that He allowed the filth of your transgressions to abuse and taunt the Holy Spirit!"

And they did kneel, and the chorus of amens filled the church until Reverend Max could barely hear his own words. Reuben smiled at his father and offered him a clean handkerchief when the service was over. Fatigued and cleansed, the congregation filed out the door, shaking the preacher's hand, complimenting him on the unusually moving sermon.

"Why, Mayzelle." Reverend Max beamed. "It's so good to see you in the house of God again. When was it last? Easter? I don't remember things real well, but it don't matter, s'long as you make it regular habit."

"I'll be back, Reverend Chapman. I sure enjoyed the sermon."

"Thank you, thank you much. Oh, you know my son, Reuben, don't you? He brought that new stained glass window all the way from France after the war. Reuben, this here is Mayzelle Clark, she lives over near the mill."

Reuben stepped forward and took Mayzelle's hand. "Pleased to meet you, Miss Clark." He walked her down the steps toward the sidewalk.

She thought about pulling her hand from his for a moment, but felt he would interpret the movement as rudeness, or worse, dislike. After all, he *was* handsome. And young. Probably about twenty-one, or two. She couldn't tell.

"I thought you were up north somewhere, Mr. Chapman," she said, imitating Lora's most formal company's-come-to-dinner manner.

"Well, I was," he said. "I finally got a job in a machine parts factory in Richmond. Took me a month to find the job and I don't have to start until three weeks from now. Thought I'd spend the extra time visiting my daddy. I don't get to see him much, you know."

"Yes, I know. He's a fine preacher. Best I ever heard. Wonderful the way he can start off slow like that and build to a fine finish what's got everybody thinkin' about God and all."

"Clears my sinuses."

"What?"

"My sinuses. Get clogged up every now and then—gas in Europe during the war. I served with the Twenty-Fourth Infantry. Daddy's sermons are so full of steam they have a way of draining . . . all colored, you know."

Mayzelle looked quickly around and nodded politely to those standing by. "You mustn't talk like that," she hissed, turning back to Reuben. "Somebody might hear you. Break your daddy's heart!"

"No. I kid around with him all the time. Listen, can I walk you home in this drizzle?"

"That's not necessary. It's a two-mile walk . . . in the rain."

"But I'd love to."

"No, really. I don't want to put you out."

"No bother. No bother at all, Maybelle."

"That's May*zelle*."

"Oh, I'm sorry. I don't hear so well."

"The war?"

"No, all that shoutin' and hollerin' inside."

"Don't start that again. I don't like that kind of talk. It's blasphemy."

"God's got a sense of humor."

"How you know?"

"My daddy told me."

"Well, I guess it's all right then." She laughed. Maybe he's twenty-three, she thought as they walked the road.

"How come you live over there?" he asked, pointing.

"What you mean?" she said, pulling her coat closer to her neck as the wind from passing cars rushed on them.

"You know, in the white folks' section. I don't know no other blacks livin' over there."

"Negroes. I'm not black. You can plainly see that. I got a job keeping Mrs. Lora Mitchell's two girls, Vera and Pearl. There was three, but Ila got married and moved to the country someplace."

"Oh, so you're a nanny."

"A what? What you calling me? I don't like bad names, so you better watch it, young man."

"A nanny? That's what they call women who keep children in England. You know, educates them, teaches them the social graces. Is that what you do?"

Mayzelle laughed. "Sort of. Mainly I cook and wash. But I do educate them. I raised those girls. I'm like their second momma."

"You seem proud of your work."

"I am." She smiled. "There's a lot of love in that family and I'm lucky to be a part of it."

"I'm glad for you." He pulled her closer to him.

She pulled away. "What you doin'?" she asked sternly.

"The sidewalk's ended. Figured you'd want an arm to lean on so you wouldn't fall."

"I'm not going to fall," she said loudly. She fell. Reuben pulled her up, laughing.

"It's not funny, a-laughin' at people's misfortunes."

"I'm not laughing. Not really. I just find you interesting."

She brushed off her coat. "Take me forever to get this coat clean. Now, you just move your hands back to your pockets, young man. I've heard about preachers' sons, and you ain't going to take advantage of me."

"I wouldn't dream of it," he said softly. A car chugged by and the lights caught his eyes.

"I didn't mean to suggest anything," she said, embarrassed. "Just that it's been such a long day. And I don't know you and all."

"I'd like to get to know you better."

"That's crazy. You must be a good fifteen years younger than me."

"War added that much to me in the first month."

"It's not the same thing."

"Yes it is."

"We got a mile yet to go, Reuben. Maybe you just better not say no more."

"Can I sing?"

She shook her head. "You drivin' me crazy."

"Well, if I can't talk, I might as well sing."

"Go ahead," she said, laughing, "talk your fool head off for all I care. I'm not going to listen." She began to walk faster.

"You ever been to Europe?" he said seriously.

"Now, that's a stupid question. I'm a farm girl. I was born in Nedar, South Carolina, lived in Paw Creek awhile, and now I'm in Greensboro. That's the total of my world travels."

"You'd like Paris," he said cheerfully. "You'd fit in real good there. For a farm girl, you got city class. Sort of an international flavor."

"Chicken's got flavor, not women."

He walked ahead of her, backwards.

"You fool, you gonna kill yourself," she said.

"Some women taste like ginger, some taste like cinnamon, but you . . . I figure you taste like barbecue. Tangy."

"You askin' for a punch in the face, Reuben. I don't like this here dirty talk."

"I ain't talkin' dirty," he shouted. "I don't mean to give no offense. Flavor comes in all things. Nature grants all living things smell and taste, don't you think?"

"I think you talkin' like your daddy."

"More like my momma. *She* had an education."

"That so?"

"Yep. Learned some Latin and French in New Orleans, she did. *Parlez-vous français, Mademoiselle? Aimez-vous moi?*"

Mayzelle stopped. "Look, you've impressed me, okay? Now, will you walk right? You makin' me crazy."

"Only if I can take your arm."

She thought a moment. He could be twenty-four. Maybe even twenty-five. One thing for sure, he's nothin' but muscle and grins. Not a brain in his head.

"All right," she said quietly. "Come on."

"Aren't you glad I came along?"

She said nothing.

"Well, *I* am," he said and kissed her ear.

"That does it! You go on back." She shook off his arm. "I can find my own way home."

"Okay, okay. I won't do it again. I promise. I just couldn't help it."

"You keep your hands to yourself! Go on home, you hear? Right now, I mean it."

"No. I've got to follow my assignment to the letter: Protect and defend the lady from all harm."

Lady. The magic word. Mayzelle stared at Reuben. Can't figure him out, she thought, calling me a lady.

"You ought not to fun with me like that," she said.

"What you mean?" he replied, confused.

"You know what I mean, calling me a . . . a . . . you know."

"Lady?" His eyes brightened. "But you are. Don't you know that? Hasn't anyone ever . . . told you?"

"No reason to."

"Can I see you again?"

"You're too young."

"I'm twenty-one."

"That's what I said, you're too young. I'm thirty-one." Thirty-seven, but he don't know, she thought.

"Then I'm thirty-one. Age is a creation of man, not God."

She smiled. "Your daddy tell you that?"

"No, I learned that at the battle of the Marne. I learned that death doesn't distinguish between men and boys, and neither does friendship."

"I could use a friend, right about now," Mayzelle said wearily.

"You have those children."

"Not that kind of friend. Look, over there." She pointed. "Half a mile and I'll be home. Looks like it might rain harder."

Lora brought the coffee to the men in the living room. Lon was sitting on the floor throwing kindling into the fireplace. The two visitors sat uncomfortably on the sofa. She handed each a cup. The bitter odor of the liquid competed with the burning wood fumes.

"I hope you gentlemen don't mind your coffee black. I forgot to get some cream this morning, what with Vera havin' a cold and all. Person have to be half-fish to walk out in this weather."

The older visitor nodded grimly. "Coffee's fine, Mrs. Mitchell. Real good, it is."

Lora watched him place the cup on the table without tasting. She frowned. He's going to let it sit there and get cold, she thought. I hate it when men waste food. I'll heat it up for Mayzelle when she gets in from church. At least she'll appreciate it.

Lora looked around the room. The two visitors were looking at her, expressionless. Lon was frowning.

She was amused. "Well, I've got lots of things to do in the kitchen, so you men go ahead and talk."

She walked out of the room, noticing out of the corner of her eye that the visitors seemed to relax as she left. Lon's frown remained.

"Lon," said the older man gravely, "we didn't want to come here tonight . . . but policy is, uh, policy requires us to discuss the problem before any action is contemplated."

"Yeah," said the younger man. His red hair was parted neatly down the middle. The veins on his nose almost seemed to glow. He pulled a handkerchief from his pocket and held it to his nostrils.

The older man patted the younger on the knee. "Relax, Walter. The committee assigned the talkin' to me."

The younger man wiped his brow. He seemed feverish.

"Now, Lon. Let me be frank. Me and my boy, Walter Junior, has been friends of yours for a couple of years now. Maybe that's why the committee sent me instead of some stranger." Lon noticed that the older man whispered when he said "committee."

Lon stood and walked to the rocking chair by the window. He sat down, never breaking eye contact with the older man.

"Lon?" Walter Senior whispered. "Do you mind if we speak man to man?"

Lon shrugged.

"It's the nigger."

Lon blinked his eyes.

"She's the only nigger in this part of town, and frankly, we—uh, the committee is concerned that you and your woman would allow a nigger to live right here in the house with you. Now, a-workin' for you is a different matter. Anybody can understand havin' a nigger washin' clothes and cookin'. Why, I remember we used to have a nigger cook for us years ago and it was the bestest food I believe I ever ate." He held his knees and looked at the fire. "But livin' under the same roof is—" his voice became shrill, "—just plain disgraceful." He looked up to find Lon's eyes locked not on him, but on his son. He looked to the boy.

Walter Junior was smiling. "What Papa is tryin' to say, Lon, is that we want that nigger outa this house. The Klan . . . the committee . . . has done decided that either she goes . . . or you and your family goes."

The old man shook his head. "My boy Walter has a fresh mouth, but he has laid it on the line. We met the other day in Jamestown. We don't like the idea of a nigger standing there in our backyard right in front of our children playin'. Gives 'em ideas, don't you know?"

Lora opened the kitchen door. "You gentlemen want some fresh coffee? Oh my, look at that . . . why, Walter Senior, you've not even taken one sip. Is somethin' wrong with it?"

Lon smiled. Lora's words were dripping with a caustic sweetness, filling the already tense air with restrained anger.

"Why, no," said the older man, trying to be courteous. "I just forgot about the coffee, what with me and Lon deep in discussion."

"Discussion musta been mighty deep to forget *my* coffee. Lon says my coffee is the best he ever tasted. Ain't that right, Lon?"

Lon's smile grew broader. He relaxed slightly. She's gonna kill them, he thought. She'll charm 'em to death.

Lora walked over to the sofa. "May I sit down?"

"Certainly, Mrs. Mitchell. Move over, Walter Junior. Let Mrs. Mitchell have some room."

"You sure you don't mind?"

"Course not," said Walter Junior with a nervous laugh. "It's your house."

Lora slowly eased herself down on the sofa, carefully arranging her blue dress. "Well now, tell me, Mr. Propst . . . and Mr. Propst Junior . . . what do you and the Klan have against my Mayzelle?"

The old man's eyes bulged. "You shouldn't have been listening, Mrs. Mitchell. That was private men-talk."

"Couldn't help but hear you, what with that raspy voice of yours yellin' at my Lon."

"I wasn't yellin'!"

"See? There you go again, disturbin' the peace of my house. What business you got with my Mayzelle?"

"It is no concern of a lady."

"It is a *lady* what you talkin' about."

"That's a matter of opinion."

"That's a fact, is what it is. Mayzelle raised my children, and in return she gets board and room. She's gettin' the short end of the stick. Those kids care about her and I care about her. She ain't leavin' and we ain't leavin'. *You* the ones leavin', right now." She smiled like a piranha.

"Settle down, Mrs. Mitchell. We didn't mean to offend you. Me and my boy here are just carryin' a message. Lon knows what ignoring that message can mean, don't you, Lon?"

Lon wasn't smiling anymore. As much as he enjoyed his wife's indignation, he realized that the old man spoke the truth. The Klan had ways of forcing its opinions on others.

Walter Junior sneered, "You understand what Papa is saying, don't you, Lon?"

"Shut your mouth, boy," said his father. "Look, Lon. I'm sorry if I disturbed your wife, here, but this ain't no time to get emotional or sentimental. I'll tell you what I'll try to do. If you build a shed out back for the ni—uh, for Mayzelle—to live in, then maybe the committee will accept that as a gesture of good will. Think about it. At least it's a compromise you can live with."

Lon stood. "We'll think about it, Walter." He showed the father and son to the door.

After they left, Lora tugged on Lon's shirttail. "What we gonna do?"

"We'll build the shed. Can't fight the Klan. No way."

"How am I gonna tell Mayzelle?"

"Tell her the truth," said Lon softly. "She'll understand better than we do."

Mayzelle used her key to get into the back door. She walked quickly through the darkness toward the stairs that would take her to her attic bedroom. She walked down the hallway but stopped abruptly when she thought she heard a noise in the living room.

Mice again, she thought. Glad Lora's asleep. One thing in the world that scares Lora, that's mice. Don't matter what size or color, she gets the look of death on her face when she sees or hears one of those things. Begged her more than once to let me set traps, but she won't hear of it. Hates 'em but can't kill 'em. Might as well see to it.

She pushed the living room door open and let her eyes run along the floor. The dying embers from the fire flared up a few times, and the clock on the mantel clicked harshly.

Mayzelle frowned. Don't like that clock, she thought. In the middle of the night, two stories up, I can hear that clock clicking up through the plaster walls. But Lora likes it so. Lon got it cheap at some auction in town. Lora can't sleep when it ain't tick-tockin', and I can't sleep when it is.

Her eyes were beginning to get used to the dark. Where was that mouse?

Suddenly her heart jumped and she reached for her mouth. Something on the sofa. She slipped to the fireplace and eased out a poker.

"Who's there?" she said loudly.

The huddled mass on the couch sat up.

"Lora? That you?" Mayzelle shrieked.

Lora yawned. She could see only the silhouette of Mayzelle. "Yeah," she said softly. "It's me. What time is it? Must'a been a real barnstormin' church sermon to keep you out this late." Lora forced her eyes open wider. "What's that in your hand?"

Mayzelle looked down. "Oh, this. Just a poker. I was gonna brain you with it. Thought you might be a burglar."

"Sleeping on the couch?"

"Does sound silly," Mayzelle said, laughing. "But it's been a silly night."

"What you talkin' about?"

Mayzelle eased over to the couch and sat cross-legged next to Lora. "I met a man."

"Oh, Lord. I knew it was bound to happen."

"He's nice. Maybe a couple years younger than me. Preacher's boy, name of Reuben."

"That's a nice name."

"Yeah. I keep sayin' that name, and the more I say it, the prettier it gets."

Lora yawned again.

"Come on, Lora, let's get to bed. It's cold in here."

Lora placed her hand on Mayzelle's arm. "No. Stay here a minute. There's somethin' I got to tell you. I don't really know how to tell you, but I figured it couldn't wait till morning."

Mayzelle frowned. "One of the babies sick?"

"No, nothin' like that. Besides, Vera and Pearl ain't babies no more. They'll probably run off and get married like Ila did."

"Ila married a good man. I hope I can do the same."

"Now, you know you can't do that. What would I do without you?"

"That's a good question. But the girls almost grown and I figure their second momma can raise a family of her own now."

Lora smiled faintly in the dark. "Yes. Yes, I suppose so."

"If they ain't sick, what's the matter that we got to sit here in the cold?"

"We had company tonight, Mayzelle. Walter Propst and his son. They work over at the mill with Lon. I don't like neither of them, but they play on the factory softball team and everybody thinks they just good old boys. But they ain't. They're Klansmen, Mayzelle."

Mayzelle's voice took on a muted tone, not fearful or strained, but cautious. "What they want?"

"They want you . . . to move out . . . but me and Lon think they'll accept it if we build a little room, like a cottage, out back . . ."

"I'll leave."

Lora stood up. "No. Listen to me . . ."

"I'll leave as soon as I can."

"But all we got to do is get you a room out back, and there's plenty of lumber around. Lon don't mind building it."

"No. I'll leave. They'll hurt you—and my babies—if I don't."

Lora's tone changed to one of anger. "Now, listen to me, Mayzelle Clark, we been through too much together for you to just give up now and walk away from a fight."

"Fight? Woman, what you talkin'? We talkin' about the Klan. They burned three churches in Georgia last month. I can read the papers, y'know. They lynch people like me and they whip the whites what favor us. I can't take no chances of them doin' that to you. No ma'am. You can talk till Christmas and I ain't listenin'. It's just one of those things that I have to do."

Lora spoke softly again, pleading. "But they'll let you stay if we just build a little place out back."

"Like a cabin? And then they'll want me to pick cotton and maybe offer you my firstborn, or maybe you could sell me at auction."

Lora took a deep breath. "Don't talk like that. I hurt when you talk like that. I've never had cause to regret inviting you to live with us since those South Carolina days in the field. You helped us set up a new life—nursed sick children, taught them right from wrong and how to fight for the good things of life. You saved me from Jeffries and comforted me when Lon was away on business. No one has had a better effect on my Ila than you. I honestly believe that you gave her the backbone to get through that marriage at such an early age."

"Now, Lora, I've always felt like you and I were like—"

"Sisters?"

"Yeah, like sisters, sort of. Inside this house I've been treated like a member of the family. I earn my way, but I never feel like a maid or slave or chamberpot cleaner. And because of what we feel for each other, I will have to move across town. I don't want no harm to come to you and Mr. Mitchell."

"That's exactly why you have to stay. You've taught all of us that we can't run away from our problems, we got to have courage and face 'em with the help of our family. That's what makes us so strong, the family.

And you're part of it. I've lost a boy, my Ila lives far out in the country, and I don't want to lose you. You give me strength."

"I love you, Lora Mitchell. You a little crazy sometimes, but you still a fine person. I'm sorry to upset everythin' so. I been livin' near this all my life. Never get used to it, but it does sorta toughen a person up. It's gonna take me a couple days to find another place. I'll ask Reuben tomorrow afternoon. He can help me. We're supposed to meet at his daddy's church to talk about some other things."

"I'm scared for you, Mayzelle."

"I'm scared for all of us. Maybe God's punishin' me."

"For what? You never done a bad thing in your life."

Mayzelle saw a glint of firelight catch Lora's eyes—a flash of cold black and then warm blue. Only bright sunlight brought out the dark purple of her youth. Lora hadn't changed much. At thirty-seven she still had the charming innocence of those early days on the Catawba. She's a little less romantic, though, Mayzelle thought. A little tougher, maybe.

Lora seemed to know what Mayzelle was thinking and said, "I'm never going to be strong without you."

The next day Mayzelle and Reuben walked near the mill. She tried to bring up the Klan problem, but each time she got serious, he made her laugh. She liked this young man. Hour after hour of being with him, she liked him more. Why is it, she thought, that some people take years to fall in love and I'm cursed with deep feelings in a matter of hours. Same feeling I had with Lora, in a way.

Evening came and still they talked—of quiet river fishing, of strong music, and finally, of Reuben's plans to leave for Virginia. Mayzelle and Reuben spoke softly in the dark, empty church sanctuary. Only the faint gleam of the sunset through the stained glass window above the church door vied for their attention.

"Kinda pretty," Mayzelle whispered.

"Yeah, you are," Reuben said with a grin.

She rolled her eyes. "No, silly. I'm talkin' about the window you brought from France for your daddy."

He feigned surprise. "Oh, that. It's okay. I kinda like it."

"It's small, but the cut casts a powerful beam. Yesterday afternoon, I was sittin' back in the church, a-watchin' your daddy speakin' on the Sermon on the Mount, and for a few moments that sun pushed the colors right into his face. He didn't even flinch."

"Daddy can't half see anymore."

"Don't you take anything serious?"

"You. I take you serious."

"I thought we had that settled. Just friends, remember?"

"No, *you* got it settled. I'm still unsettled."

"I'm gonna miss you, Reuben. I don't exactly know why, but I will."

"Oh, I'll be back from time to time, and when I do come back, I'll head straight for the mill village and pop up in that kitchen. Besides, Richmond isn't that far away. Maybe you could come visit me up there sometime. Virginia is a pretty state."

She felt the sadness sweep across her chest. Her voice was strained. "I'll write you and let you know where I'll be, if that's all right."

"What you mean—where you'll be? You'll be carin' for that white family, won't you?"

The spotlight of colors on the wall seemed to blur and move toward his face.

Just like his daddy, Mayzelle thought. "No, I got to be movin' on. Maybe back to Nedar, with my momma."

"But I thought you were going to stay with the Mitchells forever, the way you talked last night."

"That was before the Klan started puttin' pressure on Mr. Mitchell."

"The Klan?" He eased toward her. "What you talkin'? What happened?"

And she told him. She would have to move. The Mitchells were threatened and she would have to move. Simple as that.

"It's a shame," he said angrily. "I thought things would be different after the war, but I was wrong. No matter where you go they make you conform or make you move on. Shameful way of livin'." His voice grew louder and echoed across the walls and ceiling of the sanctuary. "Damn shame . . ."

"Shh, don't blaspheme. Not here."

He stood and walked to the pulpit. His fingers caressed the polished wood of the lectern. He seemed to be wiping dust from the carved crosses on the side panels. "I went over to fight for something I believed in. Not many of us over there, you know. Figured that when I came back things would be different. But things will never be different. Only person over there who treated me different from here was an old priest. German and American artillery had smashed his church into rubble. Only thing left was that glass window up there. I helped the old man go through the rubble. We pulled out what we could—a cross, a communion cup. Only thing in that church undamaged was that window. I told him about daddy's church, and he gave it to me. Just like that. Can you imagine? Just said, 'Take it to your father.' Only thing in that church that was complete and he gave it to me. Ain't that strange?"

"They's a lot of good people out there. Even whites."

"Well," he said bitterly, "ain't many in this town, is there? Even the folks you stayin' with don't have the guts to stand up to the Klan—"

"They can't! I understand that, and deep down I think you understand it, too."

"No!" he shouted. "I don't understand it. I can't understand it 'cause to do that is to accept it! And I'm not ever going to accept it." His eyes lit up as the beam of light crossed his face. "I got it!" He slapped his head. "Why didn't I think of it before? You can come to Richmond! There's plenty of jobs there, won't take long to find one, and we can be near each other. Maybe this is what Daddy calls the Lord's will—takes you out of a bad situation and plops you down into my arms."

Mayzelle looked away. "Don't talk like that, Reuben. I'm not sure. Lord, I've only known you one day."

"You're sure. You know how I feel about you. You can't deny that you feel the same way. I ain't talkin' about marryin'. I'm talkin' *feelin*', lovin', holdin' onto somethin' sure—even if it is only for a little while." He walked to her, pulled her off the bench, and kissed her on the forehead.

"I ain't sure," she protested weakly.

"I'll make you sure," he said as he pulled her closer.

The front door of the church slammed open.

Reuben looked up quickly as Mayzelle turned her face away.

Lora.

And the Reverend.

"Oh, shit," Reuben hissed.

At first they just stood there, Lora and Max, looking perplexed, but quickly the looks became frightened. The Reverend spoke first. "Reuben, come here! Here—you too, Mayzelle."

"Now, Daddy, I'm a grown man, I can—"

Lora rushed to him. "Listen to your daddy. We got bad news. We got to get out of this church right now. Walter Propst Senior just came to my house. He and my Lon been friends for some time now, even if he is blind to what the Klan has done to him. His son and some of his son's friends are a-comin' to this church tonight, and they gonna burn it down. Walter was afraid somebody might get hurt and so, out of friendship, he came for Lon. But Lon's at work and I sent Vera to get him. Come on, let's get out of here."

Mayzelle grabbed her coat and rushed for the door.

Lora held the door open. "Come on, Reuben!" she shouted. "We ain't got all day. They'll be here any minute. We got to move."

"I ain't leavin'," Reuben whispered somberly.

Mayzelle stopped. Max turned to his son. "Don't be a-talkin' foolishness, boy. Not now, not here! They a-comin'. They gonna burn this church down and anything in it, and I'll not let 'em have my son. You my only boy. Now let's get movin' like Mrs. Mitchell here says."

"Run away?" shouted Reuben. "Again? Always running away. Didn't anybody think to stay here and fight for this? It's our church and we got a right to protect it, didn't anybody ever think of that?"

Max looked to the floor. "The time ain't right, son. Maybe your children can fight; we can't. It'd be foolish. Now come on, we'll talk about it tonight. You're upset. You don't know what you're sayin' or doin'. Tell him, Mrs. Mitchell, tell him to come with us!"

Lora swallowed hard. The Reverend's pleading was nearly hysterical. "Reuben, one man can't stop 'em. Walter Junior is bringing a whole bunch of 'em. I called the sheriff. He said he'd do what he could to get here. Let the law handle it, Reuben. For your daddy, go with us. For Mayzelle."

Mayzelle ran up to Reuben. "Come with me, Reuben. We can leave for Richmond tomorrow morning, make a fresh start. I'm ready now. I know what I got to do. But I can't do it without you."

For a moment she saw his face turn gentle, and his eyes seemed soft— but only for a moment, as he briefly considered her plea.

'No." He shook her hand free. He reached into his coat pocket and pulled a small army-regulation pistol into the fading light. "I know how to fight. And I'll shoot any of the sons-of-bitches who try to touch my daddy's church."

"It's God's church!" shouted Max. "Not mine. Let God take care of His church. If it is His will that it be burned down, then so be it! We got no right to question His will! For His sake, come!"

Lora grabbed Mayzelle's arm. "Come on, Mayzelle. Come on with me."

Mayzelle tried to resist but was pulled from the church in time to see the truck drive up into the cemetery.

"That's them," Max said. "I know it's them. I got to stay with my boy. I got to stay with him!"

"No!" Lora shouted. "Reuben's got a gun. Maybe if he fires it a couple of times they'll just turn and run away. They just cowards. You two go over into the trees over there. I'll be along in a minute."

Four men piled out of the truck, knocking flowers over on the graves as they pushed each other toward the church.

Drunk, Lora thought. Stinkin' drunk, all of 'em. She noticed that one carried a rifle and young Walter, leading the pack, carried a can of something—gasoline?

"You boys stop right there!" Lora shouted sternly.

Walter grinned. "Look at that, won't you? Uppity Mrs. Mitchell. Skinny ol' Mrs. Mitchell. You come down here to protect your nigger's church, Mrs. Mitchell?"

The men with him laughed and patted each other on the back.

"God ain't never gonna forgive y'all if you're plannin' what I think."

Walter looked around. "God? Woman, you're stupider than I thought. *God* is why we're here." He walked closer to her. She held out her hand when he was close enough for her to smell the liquor on his breath.

"God don't like niggers no more'n we do," he said. "Why, everybody knows that niggers is the sons of Cain. They marked with Cain. And we gonna burn down this place where aborigines worship Baal."

"You crazy drunk, Walter Propst. You better take your buddies back on home and sober up 'fore you get in any real trouble. Sheriff's on his way right now, and he'll put you all in prison. Your mommas'll be real proud then, won't they?"

Walter drew back his fist.

"Don't!"

Reuben, standing in the doorway, spoke in a heated voice. "Mrs. Mitchell, you walk away. This ain't any of your concern."

Lora moved slowly toward the woods.

"Who in the hell are you?" Walter shouted.

"I'm the man what's gonna kill you if you don't move away from this church."

Walter laughed. "I see you got a gun. You better put that thing down before you hurt yourself."

A shriek went up from the woods. "Reuben!" shouted Mayzelle. "The church! They set fire to the church!"

The roaring noise of flames swelled through the back of the sanctuary. Walter's friends were running around the church, dousing the shingles and windows with gasoline.

Reuben pointed the pistol toward Walter's head.

Walter grinned. "Go on, nigger, pull the trigger and your daddy's a dead man."

Reuben put his arm down and backed into the church, closing the door. He walked up the steps to the balcony toward the stained glass window. He knocked out one pane with the butt of the gun and began firing at Walter's feet.

Walter jumped back as the bullets came close to his shoes, and then he ran back to the truck.

Mayzelle ran from the woods, Max behind her. "Reuben. Come out, Reuben! Please come out, Reuben!"

The sheriff's car pulled up as Walter and his friends fell over one another trying to get into their truck.

Reuben wiped his eyes. He fingered his window. His broken window. He saw his father in the yard below on his knees. He saw Mayzelle screaming as Lora kept her from rushing into the church. He saw Lon running toward the church with a stick in his hand.

Reuben sighed. He started to walk down the steps, but the flames had begun to engulf the stairway. He retraced his steps. As fire scorched his clothes, he crashed out of the window, his window, and the sheriff heard Reuben's neck snap when he landed.

Mayzelle would not leave Reuben's body for a long time. Finally Lora touched her shoulder and begged her to come home. Mayzelle shook her head, but as her tears fell on Reuben's face, Lon reached around her waist and carried her home. Soon she was beyond tears, and Lon could feel the strength go from her body. He was moved by how soft she had become, and suddenly he feared for her spirit and was embarrassed by the depth of that fear.

He knew then what Lora had always known: Part of their strength came from Mayzelle.

The Mitchell household had never been this silent. Pearl and Vera crept from room to room, occasionally standing sentry at Mayzelle's bed. They had never known Mayzelle to be sick. She slept off and on for several days. She asked for Reuben when she was awake. Lon said that she had a sickness of the mind, not of the body, and that she could help it if she wanted.

"Hush," Lora whispered. "You'll wake her up."

"Maybe that's what she needs," Lon said.

Lora looked at him briefly, tilted her head back, and raised one eyebrow. Light from the sunset came in through the small window and fell on her face. "Ain't you due for work 'bout now?" she said.

Lon kissed her on the forehead. "She'll be all right. We need her more than God does, remember?"

Lon left the door open as he walked down the stairs. Lora heard his footsteps echo through the house. She smiled, knowing he was trying to walk quietly. The weight and forcefulness of his walk prevented that.

Lora took the washcloth from Mayzelle's forehead and dipped it in a basin of ice water on the windowsill. She noticed an empty glass next to the basin. Lon had left it there. How many times had she asked him to take his things back to the kitchen when he had finished? Shaking her head, Lora stood, picked up the glass, and turned to the door.

"Lora?" Mayzelle said.

Lora dropped the glass.

Mayzelle was sitting up. Lora ran to the bed and reached for her hand.

"Hold me," Mayzelle whispered. Lora did. And together Lora and Mayzelle wept into the night, talking of little things, of how beautiful the girls were, and what a proud man Reuben had been.

"Why do men have to be so prideful?" Mayzelle said. "They stand up and talk about principles and tell you they got to say what they believe and fight for what they love, and we can't seem to find a way to tell them that there's no need for that kind of pride."

Lora nodded. The skin around her eyes was burned from brushing away so many tears. "They think it makes life worth living if they have some cause. They don't know that family is the only cause. Or maybe they do know. Maybe they think that by taking up causes, and going into politics, and speaking up at camp meetings, they protect us. Maybe that's what they think. I don't know."

"Where's Mr. Mitchell?" Mayzelle asked.

"At the mill. He's been worried about you. He carried you home. Do you remember that?"

"I remember some. I remember waking up and asking for Reuben, and I saw your face like death telling me he was gone. And I . . . I hated you for telling me that. I'm ashamed of that now."

"Don't think about none of that . . ."

"And when you told me, I wished I was dead, a-layin' in the ground next to him. And part of me wanted to die for being angry with you. And then I slept."

"He shamed them, you know," said Lora. "Reuben shamed them all. Walter Junior's gone. Nobody knows where he went. His own daddy beat him up that very night, and he had to leave home. Sheriff says Walter Senior drove the boy out of the county and told him not to come back. Then Walter Senior came over to see Lon, and he said that as far as he was concerned, you could live with us forever, and nobody would ever bother you or me or anybody. Reuben shamed them. He was a good man."

A good man, thought Mayzelle. Why didn't good come back to him? Momma always said you reap what you sow. If you do bad, then bad comes back to you. What about the people who do good? Why do they suffer for the bad that others do?

Mayzelle saw Jeffries' face, felt his hands, and she put her hands over her eyes. When would the punishment end?

Then from downstairs Mayzelle heard the voices of Pearl and Vera. She opened her eyes.

"How long have I been a-layin' here?" she asked.

Lora frowned. "It don't matter. You stay here as long as you need. You're not well."

"Don't bother about me," Mayzelle said. "You go down and take care of them younguns."

"You taught them to take care of themselves, remember?"

Mayzelle closed her eyes again. The new lines in her face relaxed very slightly. "I wish Ila was here," she sighed.

Lora took a blanket from the tall wooden wardrobe, unfolded it, and lay down on it beside Mayzelle's bed. She, too, thought of Ila.

Ten

Ellisboro, 1926

MAYZELLE CARRIED her bags off the bus and sat down on a plank beside the muddy dirt road. She gently unfolded the crumpled letter in her dress pocket and read, for the seventh or eighth time, the directions to Ila's home in the country.

It had been a year since Reuben's death. Mayzelle felt that accepting Ila's invitation might help to ease the lingering loneliness.

After a half-hour walk, jumping mud puddles and avoiding rusting trucks gliding across the changing ruts, Mayzelle came to the beaten-down shack that Ila had described as her "country home." She stopped short of walking up the steep drive. There was a strange woman on the front porch, dancing. No music—just a woman with fluffy curls and a shameful short dress, dancing by herself from one end of the porch to the other.

And then the woman opened her eyes.

"Mayzelle!" she screamed. "Oh my God. You're here! I can't believe it." She rushed down the steps and began to touch and feel and hug.

Mayzelle dropped her bags and held Ila back. Both were crying.

Ila began to laugh. "Come in the house. I want you to see my baby, Ash."

"Baby? Why, that boy's a man by now, ain't he?"

"Five. He's still my baby."

"They always be babies, just like you're still mine."

"I only feel like a child when I'm around you, Mayzelle. Come on, let's have some tea and talk and talk for days and nights. David can cook his own food this week. We don't have no time to mess with men this week. This week is ours. There's my baby now. Say hello to Mayzelle, Ash."

Ash ran to the back bedroom.

Ila laughed. "Just like a man, don't you know."

Mayzelle pulled a chair from the table. "Where's David?"

"He's workin' in the fields. Won't be in till nightfall."

"How's he gettin' along?"

"I don't rightly know. Man works himself half to death. Too tired to do much of anything. I get lonesome sometimes—Rossie, Ash, and me, all alone up here on this hill. But I hope we'll have permanent company soon."

"What you mean, permanent company?"

"Another baby. I want to have another child."

Mayzelle smiled. "Really? I thought you only wanted two."

"Did at first. But like I said, gets lonely sometimes. Cannin' peaches ain't my idea of havin' a big time, and at least havin' a baby gives me plenty to do."

"I'm glad for you."

Ila poured the mint tea into mugs. "Here's one for you and one for me. Now, how's Daddy and Momma and Pearl and Vera? I miss 'em all."

"They all doin' fine. I think Pearl's 'bout to get married. She falls in love with a different fella every other week."

"That sounds like Pearl."

"And I'm gettin' along best I can. Your momma keeps me plenty busy. She'd have a cow if she saw you in that short dress. And what did you do to your hair?"

Ila smiled faintly. "It's my Clara Bow style. I got tired of those high-button shoes and ankle-length dresses. When Rudolph Valentino died after that appendix operation, I got so down on myself that I decided to fix myself up a little. Figured I might as well take care of myself. Livin' in this wilderness does funny things to your mind."

"This looks like paradise to me. Fresh air, dusty road, corn and tobacco fields. Pure beautiful compared to the smell of the textile mill back home."

"Yeah, but people so spread out, nothin' to do but go to church or eat. That's so borin'. I had hoped that David would take me to parties and such . . . but there's not many shindigs up here. Every now and then a dance, but they few and far between. Biggest thing to happen up here was when two federal agents disappeared over the river lookin' for moonshiners. Oh! I saw a moving picture show! Pola Negri in *The Cheat*. I cried when they put a hot iron to her shoulder. I keep a scrapbook on Pola and Clara. You want to see it?"

"Maybe later, Honey. I feel like a nap now. Then I'll get up and fix you and David some supper."

"Oh, *would* you?" Ila beamed. "It'll be just like old times. Nobody in the world cooks just like you. And while you cook, I'll sing."

Mayzelle laughed. "Child, you can't sing!"

Ila stood and walked to the sink and began to rock back and forth, as if in a trance. She slowly raised her hands to the ceiling and sang quietly, "Yes . . . we have no bananas, we have no bananas today. We have string-beans and onions, cabbages and scallions . . . and all kinds of fruits, and say . . ."

Feels good, Mayzelle thought, listenin' to my Ila bein' happy.

Mayzelle clapped her hands as Ila danced across the kitchen floor. She forgot that she was tired and did not take her nap. She was afraid she might miss something, something good and pleasing. She closed her eyes and thought of how things might have been, of her and Reuben maybe dancing like this through the night in Richmond.

She forced herself to think only good thoughts.

She was with her Ila now.

She was needed.

After supper, when the children had been put to bed, Ila and Mayzelle sat on the front porch steps. David leaned on the smooth porch rail. For several minutes no one said anything, each watching a night served with stars. The crickets seemed to get louder as the evening passed.

David had tamed a turkey, which he called Earl. The turkey ran to and from the barn making gobbling noises as David threw corn on the path.

"Look at them stars, will you, Mayzelle? Momma used to always say that the stars were angels holding candles for those who had gone to heaven."

Mayzelle put her hands around her knees and turned her head to the side. "Lora always had a interesting way of puttin' things. I'd rather think that the stars are angels holdin' candles for all of us down here."

"How you holdin' up, Mayzelle? I know it's only been a year. . . ."

Mayzelle's eyes moistened. "I'm holdin' up fine as long as I can lean on my Lora and my Ila."

David looked the other way. "Barn's about to fall in. Gonna have to do somethin' soon or we're gonna lose the tobacco in it."

Ila pointed at him. "Don't go talkin' farmin' while we got Mayzelle with us. She don't want to hear about that old barn."

David shrugged. "Just thought she might like to know."

"Don't mind him, Mayzelle. David only thinks about work."

"Not so," David said coldly. "I think about *good* work. Doin' a good job on something means you got to take time to think about it; there's a difference between thinking and feeling. You and Mayzelle are sittin' out here feeling your way down the memory road. But I'm thinking. There's a difference between thinking and feeling."

Ila laughed. "Then pray tell us, sir, what is the difference?"

"Well." He spat. "By thinking I can tell you what thinking is. By thinking I can tell you what my feelings are. The difference is I can think about feeling, but I seldom feel about thinking."

Ila stood up and brushed the dust off her dress hem. "I feel you been thinking too much, David."

"I'm gonna have to fix that barn roof soon."

Mayzelle yawned.

"Let's go inside," Ila said. "I want to show you somethin'." Ila walked over and kissed David behind the ear. "I'll help you with the barn in the morning."

He smiled.

"Come on, Mayzelle, I want to show you my treasure," Ila said. They approached a door at the rear of the old house. "You're not gonna believe this, but David was at an auction the other day and some old schoolteacher was selling most everything he had, and David picked up a few trinkets for me." Ila opened the door and motioned for Mayzelle to go in first.

Mayzelle walked to the middle of the room with her mouth open and a look of reverence on her face. Books. Hundreds of books from floor to ceiling all along the walls. Maybe thousands of books.

Ila smiled broadly. "I'm real proud of 'em. I can learn a lot about the world from these books. There's a stack over there about the Great War, and a couple on religion, and quite a few on business ethics."

"Business what?"

"Ethics; you know, cheating customers and such."

"Oh. You plan on reading them all?" Mayzelle said.

"Yes," Ila answered seriously. "One by one. Lot of mystery books, and some school books that might help the boys someday."

"Between washing, and canning food, and repairing barn roofs, when do you ever get the time to read?"

"I make time. Reading will set you free. It says so in one of those books in that corner."

Mayzelle put her hand on Ila's shoulder. "You seem so happy. What's your secret?"

"Now, if I knew, then it wouldn't be a secret, would it? I don't really know if I can explain it. I suppose that I'm happy when I can get along with the rest of the living things in this world. I don't let storms and lightning bother me. I don't let shrews in my potato beds bother me—well, not much anyway. I suppose I'm happy because my husband is good. David has some mean streaks in him sometimes, but as long as the good times hold up, we're gonna make it. We work too hard not to make it."

"You sound just like your momma when she was your age."

"Really? That's a sweet thing to say."

"Where do I sleep?"

Ila started to chuckle. "You got a choice. You can sleep with me and David—just kidding—or in the barn."

Mayzelle saw the light in Ila's eyes. "The barn with the bad roof?"

Ila grinned. "The same."

"What if it rains?"

"Oh, you know I'm just kiddin'. You can sleep in the kitchen next to the woodstove. Warmest place in the house."

"Goodnight, Ila."

"Goodnight, Mayzelle." Ila looked to the floor. "Oh, Mayzelle?"

"Yes?"

"It gets lonely sometimes. Thanks for comin' up here."

"Me and Lora gets lonely for you, too, but Lora said not to tell you."

"I'm glad you did."

David woke early. "We gonna have a big breakfast for your friend?"

Ila rubbed her eyes and hit David in the chest. "I suppose so. Any meat in the root cellar?"

"You know there is. Go get it."

"Me? Why don't you go get it? I got to cook it."

"She's *your* friend."

"She's a friend to all of us. You can tell anything to Mayzelle . . . or most anything."

"You get it."

"Let's both get it."

He pulled on his pants and she folded her arms and walked in her night-gown with him to the root cellar. It was cold among the potatoes and strings of onions and dried beans.

He leaned over to cut the rope holding the ham above the ground.

"You still got a nice-lookin' rear end," Ila said.

He stood. "Don't go talkin' like that. You know I don't like you to talk like that."

She walked over to him and pinched his rear.

"Stop that."

She did it again. He grabbed her arm and pulled her to him.

"What you gonna do if I don't stop, Mr. Tolbert?" she said.

He smiled. "In here? It's awful cold in here."

"Are you man enough to keep me warm?"

He brushed her curled hair away from her face. He held the back of her neck and kissed her. He started to laugh.

"What's so funny?"

"You'll have to lay on the potatoes."

"I certainly will not."

"Too late," he whispered as he pulled her down.

A week later, Ila and Mayzelle stood by the grocery store. Ila pointed to the bus. "Seems like I should be gettin' on there with you."

The sunlight wove through Ila's hair, highlighting the red burnish. Mayzelle sighed and forced a smile. "I loved the visit. You grown into a fine woman. Now, take care of that family of yours, and if'n you get in any need then call for me, you hear?"

"Yes, I hear, Mayzelle."

"I never have felt right about bein' away from you. I worry about you all the time. You look so tired."

"Tired? Why, I've never felt better."

"That's not what your eyes tell me. You workin' too hard out here in this . . . wild country."

Ila touched Mayzelle's arm. "I'll be seein' you soon, I hope."

"Yeah, real soon." Mayzelle stepped toward the bus. "At least there's plenty of room in the back on this trip. I can get some sleep, maybe."

Ila watched the bus pull away from the grocery store. Suddenly she felt alone and cold. A different kind of loneliness gripped her, causing her head to ache. She rubbed her eyes.

Ila was alone when Judith was born in 1927. David was in Winston-Salem trying to sell his tobacco. Ila had spent the day making lye soap from the fat of a hog David and Rossie had butchered. She took the fat, poured some Red Devil lye with it into a large pot, and boiled it. She took the bones out—or what was left of them—cut the remaining mixture into bars, and put the bars on a plank while she prepared another batch.

They needed the soap. The last bar of the last batch had been eaten by

Earl, David's pet turkey, who had promptly collapsed and died. David had almost cried when he found out about it. Ila had laughed for several hours.

Granny Avery, a neighbor, had helped Ila with the soapmaking but had gone home at dusk. Ila felt the pains that evening. She could not move, and Ash and Rossie were crying in bed. "What time am I goin' to have this baby?" she asked herself, looking at the clock. "Lord, Ila," she said, "don't go havin' no baby by the clock." She fastened a rope to the footboard and pulled on it when the time came.

When David returned in the morning, he found a daughter, still bound by the dried umbilical cord to her sleeping mother. They called her Judith, after one of David's aunts.

In 1928 Ila gave birth to Deidre. For some reason, while carrying Deidre, Ila could never get enough of the short-stemmed cherries that grew in the backyard. She carried a bag of them everywhere she went. Granny Avery taught her how to turn the fruit of the orchards into wine. So during the last month of her pregnancy she made and bottled wine, lots of it: cherry, blackberry, persimmon. It was not long after Deidre was born that David discovered a box in the cellar filled with empty bottles.

One afternoon, David came in and washed the red dust off his hands over the sink. He did not seem to be pleased. Ila was eating her favorite snack for the day. She had taken an egg yolk, mixed it in a bowl with brown sugar, and poured it into a bowl of wine.

"What you so huffy about?" she asked David between slurps of her sticky dessert.

"Got a letter this mornin', Ila."

"Well? Who's it from?"

"Your momma."

"You read a letter from my momma?"

"It was addressed to me."

"You? What on earth for?"

"Ila, put that damn stuff away for a minute and I'll tell you."

She pushed the bowl away.

"It's your sister . . . your little sister . . . Vera."

"Oh my God," choked Ila as her hand went to her heart.

"No, no, not that bad. She's not dead or nothin'. It's just that—"

Ila blurted, "Let me see the letter. The letter!"

David handed it to her. "Ila, your sister's got what they call the grand mal, epilepsy. Your daddy was sitting at the table . . ."

"I can read!" she snapped.

". . . and her neck and head flew back and her hands turned back."

"Oh my God, David. My poor Vera. Epilepsy. They hold her down and have to tie her up. Oh, dear, sweet Vera."

"Honey, I'm sorry. We can go back to Greensboro if you—"

"No!" she shouted. Then, in a quieter voice: "If Momma needs us, she'll send for us. There's nothin' we can do there." She rose and folded the letter, putting it in a box above the stove.

"Ila, there's somethin' else I been meanin' to talk to you about. Those bottles in the basement . . ."

"What bottles?"

"In the root cellar, near your wine. You been drinkin' all that stuff?"

"Lord, David, that bunch of wine's been down there a long time now. I drink a little bit with old Granny Avery when she comes up. 'Sides, there's not much else to do with you in the fields all the time or up in Winston."

"Well, I was just wonderin'."

"Wonderin' what?"

"Well, I just don't want you drinkin' so much, that's all."

"David Tolbert! If that's all you got to worry about, then maybe you better think again. You worry about that tobacco and the price we get, that's what you better worry about. We got four children to raise, and I don't think that we gonna be able to do it on just that garden patch out there. Those younguns need clothes, and you sittin' there talkin' about a little wine!"

"Oh, all right. Sorry I brought it up."

"You oughta be." She sat down and pulled the bowl back to her place.

"I'm gonna feed the pigs," he said as he left.

She sipped on the syrupy spoon. "Grand mal," she whispered. "Poor Momma."

❦

Granny Avery pulled the pony cart into the front yard of the Tolbert house. She was at least eighty, but she still made it a habit to visit as many homes in the area as possible. There was no newspaper, and so she appointed herself newskeeper for the area, spreading gossip from one house to another, bestowing old secrets in return for new ones. Two other women piled out of the cart and headed for the door. Ila greeted them.

"Granny Avery? And Bertha, and Celina? Y'all are a bit early for a quiltin' bee, wouldn't you say so?"

Granny Avery, who had never been a grandmother, patted Ila on the head. "Honey, while your man's away, the mice will play."

Everybody laughed.

"When will David get back from Winston-Salem?" asked Celina, a widow with a perpetual twinkle in her one good eye.

"Not till 'round noon tomorrow," replied Ila.

"Good," crowed Granny Avery. "We can piece this here quilt tonight in one sittin', if everybody's agreeable. If not, everybody can walk home."

"I'm with you, Granny Avery," said Bertha. Bertha was the youngest of the women.

"Anybody else droppin' in?" asked Ila.

"Not as I know of," said Bertha, "'less the Cooper sisters come by. They said they would, but you never can believe them."

Granny Avery went outside and brought in a bag, slowly emptying the contents on the kitchen table. "Here they are, every extra cloth patch in the county. You're the only girl around here what ain't had a quiltin' bee, and I figure it's high time."

"Thank you, Granny Avery. You've been mighty kind to us."

"P'shaw," said Granny Avery. "We got to help each other 'round here. God knows the men won't help us."

Again the room vibrated with laughter.

Rossie, Ash, Judith, and Deidre watched from the iron bed. Celina walked over and closed the door.

"Now," said Celina. "Let's get started. Ila, you cut the scraps into even squares. Bertha, you can help Ila with the cutting. Now, who was supposed to bring the thread?"

"I did," answered Granny Avery. She looked at Ila. "Honey, I've been in the dust all day. You got any of that famous cherry wine left?"

Ila laughed. "I saved a couple bottles just for this occasion. Y'all make yourselves comfortable and I'll get it."

After Ila walked out the back door, Celina leaned over to Bertha. "I surely ain't gonna drink that devil's brew. No sir, not me."

"I am," chuckled Bertha, "if for no other reason than to be a-doin' somethin' that my Charlie don't know I'm a-doin'. Men! Think they can have all the fun behind our backs. I'll show 'em."

"I'm with you, girl," said Granny Avery. "But remember to drink that stuff slowly and sparingly. Got a bite to it, it does."

Ila slammed the door. "Oh, this is the best I've got. And the last until I make a new batch next year. I hope y'all like it."

"Got a pretty color," said Bertha. "Hold it up to the light. Real clear."

"Tastes pretty good, too," Granny Avery said as she turned her mug up. Ila refilled it.

"Celina," asked Bertha between sips, "do you think we should put the red print next to the yellow, or the green?"

Celina filled her mug and tried to put the cork back in the bottle. "Whatever you want to do, Bertha. I don't care. Why not ask Ila?"

Celina passed the bottle to Ila.

"I really think you ladies know best," said Ila. "But I do like the green. It matches David's eyes."

"Yes, I see," said Bertha. "It does, doesn't it? Red would match my Charlie's eyes."

"Ought not to talk about Charlie like that," Granny Avery said as she rethreaded her needle. "Everybody in the county knows what a good man your Charlie is."

"Yes," chuckled Celina. "Good to everybody but Bertha!"

"Celina!" shrieked Bertha. "You watch your mouth, Honey. They's children in the other room."

Celina put her hands to her mouth in mock embarrassment. "'Scuse me," she said in a girlish voice. "I don't know what come over me. Must'a been the wine a-talkin'."

Granny Avery smiled. "Forgive Celina, Ila. She ain't used to anything other than corn squeezin's from ol' Ned Walden's still."

"That ain't so," protested Celina. "I'm used to squeezin's from other men 'sides Ned."

Ila laughed. "At least that's one thing I don't have to worry about. David's too tired to squeeze much of anything."

"I know what you mean," said Bertha. "Charlie and every other farmer around says that this is gonna be a real bad year for crops. I don't like the looks them men got in their eyes this year. Hard looks, like they're thinkin' of bad times. You can always tell when bad times is comin' by the look of a man's eye, whether it's hard."

"Oh, I don't know," said Celina impishly. "I can tell by what else is hard."

"Oh, shut up," Granny Avery said, laughing. "Here, Celina, have some more wine. Maybe in a while you won't be makin' no sense, and then we won't have to listen to you."

Celina accepted the wine and began to giggle. Fairly soon, Bertha began to giggle with her. "What's so funny?" asked Ila.

Celina bent over. Bertha stammered, "Granny Avery, she . . . she . . . oh Lord! She sewed the patch to her sleeve!"

Granny Avery, bemused, pulled up her sleeve and the quilt traveled with it. "Lord'a mercy!" shrieked the old lady.

Around midnight, Judith came into the kitchen.

"Why, lookee there, what we have?" cooed Granny Avery.

"Judith, what you doin' out of bed, Honey?" asked Ila.

"Milk," said Judith. "Milk. I wanna milk."

"Why, Honey, it's cold outside and we can't go out there and milk that old cow. You go back to bed and in the mornin' I'll get you all the milk you want."

"Aw hell," Celina said with surprising sternness for a woman who had drunk half a bottle of wine. "The kid wants milk. I'll go milk the damn cow myself!" And with that she rushed for the door, grabbing a pan as she went. Bertha followed her out, and Granny Avery shouted for them to come back.

Ila rushed to the front porch. "Oh my God, Granny! That cow's in heat! She'll kill those girls."

"Serve 'em right. Look at them, chasin' that cow like they was young-uns. They'll have the devil to pay in the mornin'. Look there! What's that down by the road? A lantern. You 'spectin' company, girl?"

"No," Ila said, concerned. "I have no idea who it could be."

"Got a gun?" asked Granny Avery.

"Yes."

"Git it."

"Yes'm." She rushed into the house.

Granny Avery called her back. "False alarm, Ila, put that old blunder-buss back in the house. No need to go a-shootin' your own husband." Granny Avery smiled.

"My hus . . . husband? David? What's he doin' back?"

"I got a better question, Honey. How you gonna explain you and me smellin' like tarts at a fair and those drunk ol' birds upsettin' your cow?"

It took David two days to say why he had come home early that night. Tobacco prices in Winston-Salem were unusually low and he had had to sell quickly before they got any lower. He was lucky. Other farmers barely made enough to cover their costs. He told Ila that they would have to move.

"Move? Why? Where?" she asked, unable to believe what she had heard.

"Down to Madison. There's a little farm there that we can buy, not rent. I've saved up a little money. Ain't but nine acres, but that's more than we need."

"But why? We're doin' all right here. You couldn't ask for a better place to farm, near our friends. It's taken us years to make this place pay and now, all of a sudden, you want to move! Well, I ain't havin' no part of it. You move. Me and the children stay."

David laughed in a bitter way.

"You're not tellin' me somethin', David. I never heard you talk like you're talkin'. You're a smart man, and you're not tellin' me somethin'. Out with it. I got a right to know."

David lay down on the couch. "I got in a fight with Luke." Luke was a

121

cousin by a step-grandmother of David's, and he neither looked, talked, nor thought like a Tolbert. He had the features of a well-bred gentleman, the language of a breeder of dogs, and the manners of a banker at the height of a foreclosure.

"Luke? Your cousin Luke? Why, you and he fight all the time. We're makin' money for him out of this dirt. That's all he cares about!"

"A real fight this time," murmured David. "Luke says he can't let us use the barns, that we gotta rent them from him, too."

"You got to be kiddin'. *He's* got to be kiddin'. We ain't rentin' no barn from nobody! He's got some nerve. I've got a mind to go down to his house and give him a piece of my mind!"

"Won't do no good."

"Why not, pray tell?"

"Luke's laid up."

"What? Laid up? Sick? What's the matter with him 'sides his green greed?"

"Seems some fella beat him up and cut his face with a knife."

"Serves him right, David, the way he's tryin' to walk over us. Who else is he tryin' to walk on? Some poor so-and-so what's got less than us, probably."

"Not exactly. A fellow named David Tolbert, his cousin, cut his face up after arguing over the barns."

Ila was speechless.

"He took a swing at me."

She sat down, holding her stomach.

"A man can take so much and then talkin' don't do nobody no good."

"When do we move?" she sighed.

"Soon as we can. Luke's laid up like Caesar himself, complainin' and threatenin' to have me arrested. We better move before the week is out."

Eleven

Madison

IT IS STRANGE, thought Ila, how puny nine acres seem after working on fifty acres. But at least it is ours, all nine acres for nine hundred dollars. Every penny we had, and now we got to start over. Maybe, she thought, just maybe 1929 will be a good year if we work hard at it.

The house outside of Madison was even more run down than the one in Ellisboro. It had two bedrooms, but David closed one of them up during the winter to save heat. Events beyond his comprehension later forced other farmers to give up their homes to the banks. David was spared that humiliation because he had borrowed four hundred dollars from Lon, and with that added to the five hundred he and Ila had saved, he was able to pay for the house and property without need of a mortgage.

But money was scarce. They had four children and no savings. Crops were sold for almost nothing. David spent half his days roaming the county looking for odd jobs. He cut firewood, rebuilt roofs, anything that would earn a dime or quarter to pay for flour.

Sometimes David spent hours stuffing newspapers in the cracks along the house wall outside. The children laughed at his puny efforts to defeat the wind. They didn't care, because when the cold got too bad, the four children slept together, a mass of entwined arms, legs, and warm breathing.

Ila was lucky. She managed to get a job at a pajama factory in town. She worked twelve-hour days on production. She worked on a quota basis. A certain number of cuffs had to be sewn before she was paid. She hated the job, but found a friend.

Florence Kellam was the same age as Ila, twenty-four. She had three children, was a widow, and lived only a few miles from the Tolberts. Florence and Ila rode into work with Major Canipe, the shift supervisor. Flo Kellam had bony elbows, constant indigestion, arthritis in her wrists, and red hair that curled in large waves on each side of her head. Her blue eyes were dark like storm clouds, her mouth thin and small. She always looked hungry and ate constantly, except when she was copying poems from books to share with Ila.

The women became close friends. One morning Florence gave Ila a rose and told her to put a fruit jar over it in the ground and it would root. It did, along with their friendship.

Neither of them had a car, and on weekends they alternated visits, each walking the three miles. Sometimes if one wasn't able to make it, a note was placed in the bottom of a child's shoe, and the child was sent as secret messenger. When Jamie arrived with a message from Florence, Ila knew to take off his shoe and read the note, thus preventing a nosy husband or neighbor from learning the secrets of the two friends.

Not that the secrets were earth-moving. Often the notes contained little more than a recipe or a used piece of gossip, occasionally an attempt at poetry.

Among Ila's prized possessions was an old and torn book that Florence had given to her for her birthday. It was a play by some ancient Greek, Euripides, entitled *The Trojan Women*. Ila read it over and over. She never tired of it. In the play the Greeks captured important women of Troy and put them into slavery. Ila felt close to those women of long ago, who had lost children and husbands in war. One of the women, Cassandra, was raped in a temple. The Greek god Poseidon promised revenge. Another woman, Hecuba, attempted to endure the slavery even though she was assigned to a hard-hearted master. Hecuba seemed to hold out hope despite her troubles. Hecuba kept her dignity.

Ila liked that. Hecuba endured even the murder of her grandchild; she held her head high with pride, despite the blows of fate.

It *is* a good story, Ila thought. The land of the Trojans is burned and ravaged by events beyond the control of the mothers and wives. Yet the victims conquer their conquerors by showing a stronger spirit.

Ila could identify with that.

Trojan women.

Broken promises.

The hard times.

It's all the same.

But Hecuba tried to kill herself. That confused Ila. She couldn't understand going through all that and then giving up.

With four children to rear, a job to keep, a friend, and a thinning husband, Ila found little time to read, but she made time while eating, while riding to work, at lunch, after the children were asleep and David's snoring began. It helped take her mind off things, things that seemed to be closing in on her. Friends gave her old books and magazines, and her library grew as the pressures mounted.

Nineteen twenty-nine was not the good year that she had hoped for. Neighbors began to move. Even nearby churches boarded up for lack of members.

Each year that followed seemed to be worse than the one before. Winter only made things seem worse. The house was not well built. There were cracks in the walls that froze over. Pillowcases wore out, and without material for new ones, she had to make them out of flour sacks. Her heart felt heavy as she treated the children's constant sicknesses and watched David eat less so they could have more.

Christmas was the hardest time of all. She went through every dime-store in town, fingering toys and shaking her head when she saw the prices. There was nothing she could afford. She remembered the Christmas days of her youth, when there seemed to be an abundance of everything—maybe there wasn't, but there seemed to be.

She found some patterns in a dress shop and sewed dolls out of rags: a rabbit, a dog, an elephant, a girl. She dressed them herself, using buttons from torn jeans, dishrags, burlap, anything she could find. She went too far on the girl. She stuffed it with hay until the breasts bulged. But she left it unchanged. Add four boxes of animal crackers to the four dolls and that was Christmas.

She sold her engagement ring and bought David a shaving set—mug, soap, and razor. It was the only time she had ever seen him cry.

In spite of all the trouble, this would be remembered as the best of all possible Christmases. The prayers of thanks for the blessings on the family were genuinely given. Each member knew the survivor's creed: Things could always get worse. As long as they had hope together, as a family, survival was possible. The laughter of the children filled the house as David teased Ila for the shaving mug and chased her to the bedroom in an attempt to tickle her feet. Soon the bed sagged with Tolberts saying "Merry Christmas" to each other.

Winter was by far the worst time. There was nothing to look forward to but spring and summer. Spring and summer offered hope. That was when everything Ila touched seemed to grow and yield enough fruit and vegetables for canning. Still, they had no cow; the animals had to be left at Luke's to pay back rent. With no meat, or milk, or protective clothing, the children grew thin. David and Ila had only two solutions: work and hope.

One day in the summer of 1934, Ila was asked to work overtime at the pajama mill. Overtime meant some extra money, so she agreed, only to learn that her friends had driven home without her. She was the only woman working in the department, and she had no way home. And it was raining. And David would be trying to calm the hungry children. And there was no flour for the morning gravy. And she would never be able to afford to get the church dress that she had put on layaway three months before. And so she cried and walked the three miles through the rain to her home.

With her tears joining the rain, her clothes soaked to her back, her eyes aching from sewing in a dark room for five years, she walked through the mud, angry at herself for marrying a farmer, angry at the farmer for not providing better, angry at her friends for leaving her, angry at her mother for not stopping her wedding, and angry at the rain and the mud and the sounds of night along dark country roads.

David met her at the door and rushed her near the fireplace. She pushed him away.

"Don't touch me!" she snapped.

He moved back.

"Don't ever touch me again."

"You've got a right to be mad, Ila. But we've been worried to death. Just now the kids have finally fallen asleep and I've been to two neighbors trying to borrow a car to look for you."

"You couldn't call me from the store, could you?"

"The lines were down."

"Doesn't matter," she said. "I'm just a dog anyway."

"No, you're not! You're my wife."

"No, I'm a dog, and to prove it, if you touch me again, I'll bite you," she snarled.

He touched her and jumped back as she bared her teeth and her eyes widened in a frenzied stare.

"I said get back. I'm a dog, not a person, and I'll bite anybody touches me. I'm a mad dog. You hear? A mad dog, and I'll give you rabies, and I'll give the children rabies."

"Oh my God," whispered David.

Ila got down on the floor in front of the fire and moaned and whimpered.

David knelt beside her. She growled at him as he tried to cradle her.

"No, Baby," he said. "It's gonna be all right. Really, you'll see, things will get better."

"Get away from me!" she screamed, and then she was on him, clawing and biting, doing her best to draw his blood, digging her fingers into his throat. He slapped her with the back of his hand and she scurried into a corner, barking and whining.

"She's mad!" David said, feeling cold. "My Jesus, she's mad!"

He turned from her. All the children were standing at the bedroom door, wide-eyed, shocked. The children never looked related by blood. Rossie, at fifteen, had grown too plump for his nightshirt, probably from his continued addiction to sugar. Ash was thirteen, the same height as Rossie but dark and handsome, resembling Ila in some ways. Judith, at seven, was skinny and rosy-cheeked, with brown eyes as big as nickles. And Deidre, at six, was small for her age; her face was oval and her blond hair thick, smooth, and soft, like red fox fur.

David called for Rossie. "Boy, I know it's wet outside, but your momma needs help. I got to stay with her. You take Ash and you go down to Doc Fletcher's house. Tell him to come quick. Get your clothes on and get goin'. Don't tarry or I'll wear both of you out. Now git!"

He pulled a chair in front of Ila. She had her face pressed to the wall, humming and singing nonsense sounds. He looked around. "You girls go on back to bed, and stay there till I call for you!"

Judith grabbed Deidre and pulled her back into the darkened room. They crawled under the covers of the bed and held each other tight.

Doctor Michael Fletcher did not like to be awakened. Sleep was one of his few pleasures in life, and he did not like to forsake it for anyone, ill or well.

He tried to ignore the pounding on his door but finally answered it. Two wet boys shouted at him.

"Now, hold on, you boys. One of you speak, not both. You, you're bigger, speak."

Rossie stammered, "My momma. She's bad sick. Daddy said to come get you right now."

"Right now? Can't it wait till morning? How bad sick is your ma?"

"Mighty sick. We never seen her like this before. Please, let's go! They's waitin' on us. She might die!"

Ash broke down sobbing, and Doctor Fletcher pulled the boys into the house.

"You boys wait a minute till I get my clothes on. You're the Tolbert boys, ain't you? Well, I know your mother from church and I never known her to be sick in all these years. Sickness catches up with all of us sooner or later. Finally catches up, it does."

Doctor Fletcher's truck pulled up in front of the Tolbert house. The rain had stopped. The doctor jumped out and headed for the door. It opened as he got to it.

"What's the matter, Tolbert?" he asked bluntly.

"I finally got her to bed, Doc. She's not actin' right. I think she's gone crazy!"

"Crazy, huh? Lots of that runnin' around. Let me look at her."

Fletcher walked into the room. David brought in a lamp. Fletcher looked first at the bed with the shivering girls in it and then at the other.

Ila was sitting up, wide-eyed and silent. He walked to her. Suddenly she began a low, gutteral growl.

Fletcher stopped and raised his eyebrows. "You get these kids out of here. I want to examine this woman alone."

David obeyed.

With the door shut, Fletcher sat down at the foot of the bed and chuckled.

"Well, Ila, I hear you finally went off the deep end. The land of the fuzzy-wuzzies. No matter, I s'pose we can send you to a mental hospital. No real problem getting you admitted."

She made an attempt to bark at him.

"Now, don't bite me, Ila. I'm just a poor doctor. I can't afford the shots. Now, why don't you tell me what's really bothering you? You're no more crazy than I am, so stop acting and let's get down to business." He pulled some tobacco from a coat pocket and reached into his bag for a pipe. "You got some mighty dark areas under those eyes, Ila. Not been getting any sleep, have you? Eyes like yours used to be clear and bright; now they're dull and red. Spoils a pretty picture, it does."

He lit the pipe and watched out of the corner of his eye as her hands moved to her eyes. "Another thing, you got wrinkles that you didn't have last time I seen you. And when's the last time you washed your hair?"

He watched the tears fill her eyes. She wiped them away, leaving huge, swollen red marks that would be blistered tomorrow.

"Now, talk to me while they're out of the room. You got 'em scared to death. Is that what you meant to do? Scare 'em out of their wits, your own loved ones?"

Ila looked away and in a scarcely audible voice said, "I want to go home. I want to go home to Momma and Daddy and my Mayzelle."

"Well, Ila," he said cheerfully. "Don't you think that there's a better way to get there than by making a fool of yourself? Why don't you leave? There's nothing stopping you."

She looked at him sharply for a second.

"I suppose you do have a problem, now that I think of it," he said. "You got some children and a husband out there to think of. I tell you what, why don't you take 'em with you when you go? I suppose you and David have talked this over, right?"

"No," she said. "He wouldn't understand."

"Have you tried talking to him?"

"No, it wouldn't do no good."

"Well, in that case, you got little choice. You stay here and make the best of things or you leave your family. The choice is yours. I'm going to give you something that will make you sleep. Tomorrow morning I want you to drop into my office for a chat. We can talk better when you're a little more clear-headed. Now, go to sleep and I'll take care of your folks for you."

She reached for his arm. "You won't tell them, will you? I couldn't stand that."

"No," he said. "That will be up to you."

David knocked at the door.

"Come on in, David," Fletcher said. Ila closed her eyes.

"David, your wife has had a mighty rough time lately, but after a good night's sleep I think she'll be as good as new. I want her in my office in the morning to check her over some more. Meanwhile, she needs lots of rest and sleep. Think you and the children can handle yourselves for about a week?"

David was shaking. "Thank you, Doctor. Me and the children will be just fine as long as Ila gets better. We couldn't do without her."

"I'm sure you couldn't," said Fletcher. "Now leave her in peace tonight, and I guarantee you that she'll be much better in the morning. I gave her some pills. See that she takes 'em."

"What's the matter with her, Doctor?"

"Oh, I guess exhaustion's as good a word as any for it. But don't worry, her mind's as sharp as yours or mine, probably sharper. I'd bet on that."

The rains seeped deep within the soil, rearranging the delicate crystals of decay until the earth could hold no more, until the water spilled out, carving new streams and plowing old ditches across fields and down hills into the swollen, heaving valleys.

Summer lightning cracked across the forested middle girth of North Carolina.

In all the clamor, no one noticed the sudden white, crackling death of a persimmon tree on the Rockingham County line.

❦

Ila woke feeling stupid. David was asleep on the couch, and the children were sleeping on the floor, curled up in blankets near the fire. She washed and dressed without waking them. At dawn she began the long walk to Doctor Fletcher's.

He was sipping coffee in his study when he became aware of another presence in the room.

"Oh, so there you are!" he said. "Bright and early. Looking much better than last night, I can tell you that. Here, sit down."

She sat down in a wicker chair near his desk. Her fingers kept feeling around her eyes. Fletcher noticed.

"Don't worry about those crying scars. They'll go away in a couple of days."

"Oh, I'm not worried."

"Well, that's a sudden change. Have you had a chance to think about your idea of running away from home?"

"I thought," she began slowly, "that by me acting crazy, David would get the idea that this place isn't good for me, and maybe, on his own, he would decide to take me back to Greensboro. I'm the one who forced him out here, and I guess I'm too prideful to admit I was wrong."

"And what would he do there, in Greensboro?"

"I don't know. Something. Anything. Maybe a mill job."

"You couldn't buy a mill job these days and you know it."

"I suppose so."

"Listen, to start off, you've got to take much better care of yourself. You must be at least thirty—"

"Twenty-nine."

"Well, doesn't matter. You've had four children and you can't run around doing everything that a fifteen-year-old does. You work at the pajama factory, don't you?"

"Yes."

"Maybe you can arrange to work fewer hours."

"They'd hire someone else."

"Maybe you could quit?"

"David hasn't got a job."

"Well, something will work out. Until it does, try not to worry so much. Worrying never helped any situation. No sir, that's a fact."

"I'll try."

130

"Besides," Fletcher mumbled, "a pretty young woman like you doesn't want to end up looking like an old corn shuck before her time."

"I ain't been pretty for a long time."

"My eyes tell me different," he said softly.

"Nice of you to say so, but you're just tryin' to make me feel good."

Fletcher hesitated a moment, playing with his pen. "Maybe that's part of it, but to tell you the truth, without being forward, I appreciate your beauty and your honesty. Those are two qualities that you don't often find in a woman."

She started to speak but couldn't find any words.

"Now, don't blush, I'm not trying to be forward."

"Oh," she said, smiling, "I don't mind. Feels good to be complimented for a change."

"Well, that's a relief! I don't usually give too many compliments."

He leaned forward, his hands shaking and his knee rocking back and forth. "Frankly, Ila, I've always admired you; a secret admirer, you might say. You're a good-looking woman."

She blushed. "Oh, now you are lying!"

"No, you can look in my eyes and tell that's not true."

She looked up and realized that she had never really seen his face at all. It was a strong, young face. He must be thirty or thirty-five, she thought. A gentle face. His nose is a little crooked, and his teeth are too straight, but it's a lively, friendly face.

"Ila," he whispered, "I don't know how to say this, or even why I'm saying this, but . . . but this evening after house calls, I will probably stop by Melton's Pond to rest and enjoy the dusk. Would you meet me there?"

Ila's eyes tightened. She got up to leave.

"No, Ila." He hurried after her. "Don't take it wrong. I just like your company . . ."

She slammed the door.

That summer David found a part-time job at a sawmill that had bought up patches of cheap woodland in the county. Ila began to hoard money for the first time in her life. She buried coins in jars in the flower beds in the back of the house. The buried jars gave her a feeling of security, a feeling that she had not had in a long time.

Florence Kellam visited more often. She brought her children to play with Ila's. While the older boys wrestled in the dust or climbed the rafters in the outbuildings, Ila would read to the younger children. Ila held Deidre on her lap, on the edge of the bed, arms wrapped around the little girl's waist, both holding a small book. Ila read slowly, emphasizing the sounds so Deidre and the others could hear them clearly. Deidre stared intently at the letters on the pages, occasionally reaching out and touching the words as if she could feel the horses or princesses that the letters signified.

One hot and humid July afternoon, Florence suggested that they all go swimming in the quarry down the road.

"My children can't swim," Ila said.

"No matter, they can watch and play on the bank. *We'll* go swimming."

"I don't know," Ila said. "I'm not such a good swimmer myself."

"Look, Honey, it's so hot we're gonna fry unless we do somethin' about it. I say let's do somethin' about it!"

"All right, I guess there's nothin' left to do around here. You get your younguns and I'll get mine." Ila went into the house.

Florence turned to her eldest son. "Jamie, go fetch the other younguns and let's go for a walk."

"I'm tired of walkin'," grumbled Jamie.

"Let's go," replied Florence. "Me and Mrs. Tolbert are goin' swimmin'."

"Swimmin'? You mean it? Let's go!"

"Not y'all, Jamie. You got to watch the children on the bank. You know you can't swim."

"We can wade!"

"Well, maybe. We'll see."

In a moment the door slammed on the porch and Ila hurried out with Judith. Rossie, Ash, and Deidre were already waiting with the Kellam children. Florence walked down the road and everyone followed.

The sky was clear and blue, except for a thunderhead that looked like running ink in the northwest. The children stopped to tease cows in neighboring pastures. Florence gathered flowers and talked about poetry. Ila made jokes about Florence's bright hair, begging to cut it to the scalp.

It took the crowd an hour to walk the two miles to the abandoned quarry. Countless rains had filled the granite bottom. The water was clear and still.

A group of twelve or so Negroes moved down the road, carrying pails and bags loaded with fresh bass and catfish toward their sharecrop homes across the valley.

Florence waded in, shivering from the chill, laughing at Ila who, on the bank, shook her head. Florence rushed out of the water, grabbed Ila's arm, and amid the shrieks from the children, pushed her in. The children sat on the granite bank and splashed each other. Rossie and Jamie quickly tired of the smaller children and walked to an apple tree at the quarry entrance, where they conspired to smoke cigarettes at the edge of the peach orchard near school on the following evening. Rossie found Jamie's knowledge of the world outside the farm to be more intimate and exciting than his own.

Ash climbed onto the bank and watched the younger children splashing and giggling. He pretended not to care that Rossie and Jamie had not invited him to the tree to talk of manly things. He looked across the water, watching his mother frolicking like one of his younger sisters.

"We'll swim out to that log!" shouted Florence.

Ila spat a mouthful of water and raced Florence toward the center of the lake.

"Ila?" said Florence in a strained voice.

"Yes?" she replied, laughing.

"Let's stop here."

"No, girl, you did the challengin' and I'm a-gonna beat you!"

"No, Ila, wait, Ila!" Florence cried urgently.

Ila stopped and swam toward her friend.

"Oh God!" screamed Florence. "I'm sinking!"

Ila put her arm around Florence's neck, but Florence wrapped her legs around Ila's waist and they both went under. Ila pushed Florence away and came up for air. The children were crying and screaming on the bank. Rossie and Jamie ran down the hill toward the water, tripping on jagged rocks. Ila pushed her hair out of her eyes and looked around. Florence was gone.

"Rossie!" she screamed. "Go get help!"

All the children followed Rossie toward the road. Soon the only sound was Ila's heavy breathing as she pulled herself from the water. The frogs had stopped croaking. A gentle rain began to fall.

The funeral was in Summerfield at a church near the school. Florence had been dressed in a plain brown dress, one of her favorites. Ila leaned on David. After the coffin had been removed from the church, Ila walked over to Jamie Kellam. Jamie took one look at Ila and walked away. David helped her outside. She fainted.

She woke in her own bed. One lamp, turned low, lit the room. David reached for her hand. She jumped, startled.

"Honey, you all right?"

"Yes," she whispered, thinking of Jamie.

"You want anything? Need anything?"

"Yes." She rose. "I need some air, I'm gonna take a walk."

"Now? It's past midnight!"

"Now," she said firmly.

She put her coat over her nightgown and walked past him. She went to the boys' bed and woke Rossie. They walked outside. In the moonlight she scribbled a note on a piece of paper from her coat pocket and told him to put it in his shoe.

"Where you want me to take it, Momma?" he asked sleepily.

"To the doctor. And hurry."

Rossie ran off in the direction of the doctor's home, and Ila walked toward Melton's Pond.

She walked around the pond several times, waiting impatiently for Michael Fletcher. The moon was not bright enough to reflect the willows on the far side of the deep pool, the cold fingers of moss dripping off the muddy bank. Ila waited several hours, numb from the cold and the anger within. The pond whispered with gentle waves made by active water spiders and the sound of fish breaking the surface. Crickets, thousands of crickets, screamed at her to go home; he's not coming. He's never coming. It's a joke. Flo's joke. Dead Flo's lungs filling with water, and Ila splashing hysterically nearby, a hand on her leg, a kick, then nothing. One step, then two. It was easy, slipping in the mud to her knees, reaching for the water pulling her down to Flo. Her breasts met the stinging, creeping chill as she slid into the water, and the crickets listened, and she listened, and she heard a baby cry. Judith? Ash? Rossie? Deidre?

She pulled herself out of the mud, choking on the green mold, pushing away from the hole, away from everything. She stumbled home ashamed, more ashamed than she had ever been. She walked quickly. Then she ran, afraid that she might turn back.

David had never known his wife to work so hard. She washed the floors of the shack every day. She spent more time in the garden and helped the children with their schoolwork. She smiled little. He did not understand her, but then he had never understood her. She wanted to get out of Greensboro to the country and now, he thought, she wants out of the country, yet she works as if possessed. He watched her for signs of fatigue and began to treat her as if she were a child, making her lie down, placing cold cloths on her head when she complained of pains. He spent a lot of time thinking of her, of them.

He was still proud of his body. There was still, he thought, some thunder left in his muscles. He worked hard in the field and stopped every now and then to watch the sweat curve down his neck to his chest, across the muscled breast and down to the hairline to his navel, and disappear. Not an ounce of fat, he thought, all lean. And all worthless.

No one saw or admired him alone in the fields. No one touched him except the children, kindly touches of pity from wise children who knew that he would die without a pat on the head. Like a dog.

No one told him the things he wanted to hear. He ended up talking to the mule, an old mule at that. The only good thing about this mule, he thought, is that he listens and seldom comments. Better than a woman. Though in some ways, sometimes, Ila worked twice as hard.

Ila, he thought. She hasn't changed that much, not really. Except her spark, her wit, seems to be asleep. A little fleshy around the chin, maybe. A little broad in the ass, sure. But sometimes, early in the morning, she curls close to him until she wakes, and then she moves away and up. He hates it when she wakes. The bed gets cold and the distance between them colder.

Well, what did she expect? She knew what she was getting into when she married him. He never claimed to be anything special, some damn knight in shining armor to wake Sleeping Beauty from her numbness. But he provided. By God, there wasn't anybody who could say he hadn't provided; working the fields, the sawmill, and most any other dirty bastard work that he could take just for the pennies for her flour or for medicine for the children. Sick bunch of children. All the time sick.

That was what really bothered him. Sickness. Diphtheria, smallpox, Victoria Flu. You name it and everybody gets it. Every week in the Madison newspaper there's a list of unnamed babies who die. *The Lord Has Taken Her Home. His Angel, He Missed Him. Baby's With Him Now.* Mourners singing "How Great Thou Art" and "Shall We Gather at the River."

And if they live? They'll just go through the same things we go through. They'll work in the mill, get lots of good North Carolina dust and cotton in their lungs, grease in their intestines, and maybe, if they're lucky, go two or three years without having someone they love die. It's so damn unreal. Nobody understands it and everybody pretends it don't exist. Tragedy breeds tragedy; guilt breeds guilt.

Gets so you expect it, wait for it.

I'm getting down now, he thought. Better rest a bit, Ila will be here in a little while with the water and maybe some apples and bread. Gotta think good thoughts. Think of the good times. After all, the kids are mine, flesh and blood mine. They don't seem too unhappy. They grin a lot. Me and Alvin got drunk last Saturday. That was good. Soon I'll be able to buy Ila a new hat for church. She'll yell and scream and tell me to take it back and buy some flour or sugar, and I'll get mad and tell her to go to hell, and she'll tell me she's already there.

And then I'll leave. Sometimes I think that's what she wants. For me to leave so that I won't have to see her like that. And I do as she says.

"Whoa, you damn bastard, whoa there!" He had been so busy thinking that he had failed to realize he was plowing straight across the dirt road.

David heard her laugh a hundred yards away. There she was, in that same old dirty dress. But her face is clean, he thought, always is. And her hair is freshly washed.

He lifted the plow and moved the mule to the locust trees. He found a cool spot, checked first for hornet nests, then sat, waiting. He watched her come to him, slowly, making no sound. She carried the jar of water in one hand and a basket in the other. Apples and bread, he thought. Every day, apples and bread. He leaned back against the tree and felt the bark scrape his skin. He raised himself up and brushed off the itchy pieces of wood. He pulled a handkerchief from his pocket, placed it under his head, and leaned back on the grass. He stared at the heated sky above him.

Ila kicked his feet. "Hey, lazy man. Don't you go to sleep on me, you hear? I brought somethin' to eat."

He opened his eyes and nodded. "Bread and apples?"

"Yeah, how'd you know?"

"Funny."

"There's bugs on the cabbage again."

"What am I supposed to do about them?"

Ila shrugged. "Just thought you'd like to know, that's all. No need to jump."

He sighed. "I'm not jumpin'. I'll mix up some poison after supper."

She laughed. "They'll be ate up by then, but it don't matter. Don't much like cabbage anyways."

"Neither do I."

She frowned. "You don't? I thought you did."

"Nope, I ate it 'cause I thought you liked it."

She smiled. "Here we been married a couple hundred years and still don't know each other."

"Goin' to church Sunday?"

"I might."

"You need a new hat."

"You been sayin' that for years."

"Really, hair like that ought to be held by somethin' pretty."

She looked away but could not help smoothing her hair. She had not yet put it up. It fell long and dark across one shoulder. She wiped the moisture from her brow. "Too hot to work today."

"Weeds grow fast when it's hot. You know that."

"I know, just thought you might want to go down to the creek with me for a while. You know, just to do somethin' different."

"What's down at the creek?"

She took a deep breath. "*I* will be, for one thing."

He sat up.

She looked at his face, dark and painted with dirt.

He shook his head. "I can stop for a little bit, I guess . . . but the money. After I finish our field, I promised to plow Zack's. With a broke back, he's paying good money. I can't lose that."

"Yeah," she said, suddenly formal. "That would be a shame."

"Maybe tomorrow?"

"Yeah," she said as she got up and brushed her dress. "Maybe tomorrow."

He watched her walk back down the road. She stared at the dust. He knew that look, and he didn't like it. Her head, he thought, is bent. That prideful neck is beaten. He felt scared and at the same time he felt a burst of heat from his loins as he drew up his knees.

David sat on the porch with the children, watching the fireflies light up the sky. Gonna be rain, he thought. They're searching for rain.

Ila made the children go to bed. The girls slept in one room now. Rossie and Ash slept on the floor near the fireplace.

Ila opened the screen door. "You comin'?"

"In a minute," David said.

Across the woods he could see the glow from other homes. Yet his house was dark, cold, quiet. He stood and let the screen door slam behind him.

"Goodnight." The voice was warm. Judith.

"Goodnight." The voice was alone and haunting. Deidre.

"'Night," said David as he entered his bedroom, carefully closing the door. Ila had already turned the lamp down. David whipped off his belt, dropped his pants, and crawled into bed. The sheets were fresh and cool. He sought the scent of Ila's hands, her flesh. She turned on her side, effortlessly reaching for the lamp, turning the wick out. Through a crack in the wall David could see one star, blinking through the clouds. He reached for Ila's shoulder, presing lightly. He felt her tense and move away. She hugged the edge of the bed. He always wondered why she didn't roll off onto the floor. He frowned in the dark and moved his hands to his stomach.

He moved one hand and tried not to think about it. Night after night, this was the way it was. He tried not to think about it.

Her breathing was regular now, soft but noisy enough to let him know that she was trying to sleep. She needed her sleep. She would have to get up before dawn, make breakfast for the children, and send them down the road to school.

Suddenly his hand reached to her shoulder. He heard her whisper, "No."

He repeated, scornfully, "No."

He wrenched her back to the bed and crawled on top. She tried to push him off. "The children," she huffed.

"The children," he repeated softly.

He tore at her gown. He could not see her, but he knew what she looked like. Her face contorted, angry, afraid. Her legs tight. Her elbows dug into his chest. Yet he was determined. And so was she.

She could not think. She could only see, against the red glow inside her mind, Bradley's heaving flesh smothering her youth, and holy Lora pushing hips upward, swallowing Lon's shadow.

The bed springs began to creak and sag, reflecting the angered weight. He thrust quickly, horribly, and heard her choke in his ear. "No," he whispered, "No . . . no . . . no." He thrust again until he was sure he had her, and then he moved and rocked violently, and still she groaned and spat. Her breath was heated and her sweat mingled with his. She wrapped her arms around his back and her nails clawed their way to his neck. He tightened his legs between hers and moved his knees so that she was forced to move up and back.

And then the cry came, like that of a wounded child, and he stopped and listened as his lungs emptied and he fell limp.

She was crying. At this moment, David thought, *she is crying*. He stayed in her for a moment and then withdrew slowly. She gasped as he left her, then again turned on her side.

"David, what's happening to us?" she said, weeping.

He did not answer.

"David? We can't live like this. Something's happening to us—the way we feel about each other. You hurt me, David."

He found it hard to breathe and to swallow.

"David? Help me, David. We can't be like this with each other. This isn't right."

David turned to her and put her arm over her chest.

"Hold me, David. Don't let me go."

Now David put his face to her hair. "I'm sorry. I don't know . . . ."

"We can't do this to each other, David. What's happening to us? You don't love me anymore."

"That's not true," he said. "It's just that . . . so much has happened . . . so many changes I can't keep up with them. Times are gettin' worse." He could hear her crying. "Ila, don't cry. Please. I won't ever do that again. I just went crazy. I didn't want to hurt you. I hurt when I hurt you."

"We're gonna be all right, David. Tell me we'll be all right. We got to beat this thing that's tearing us apart. We can't let it destroy us and these younguns. We can beat it, can't we, David? For us and the children?"

He nodded in the dark. "Yes. For us and the children. No matter what happens to you and me, we still gonna love each other. Let the world throw the best punch it's got. We'll show our children how to really live. Life means more than just existing. Our boys and girls got to know that."

"David?"

"Yes."

"Sometimes I get the feeling something bad is gonna tear us apart. I'm scared for us, David."

"Don't be," he said. "If we go around looking for trouble, we won't have time to enjoy the time we have with our kids."

"We're getting' old, David."

"Nah, we're gettin' just right." He pulled her to him. She put her face to his neck.

"Hold me," she said. "Hold me and I'll be all right."

"We got a lot of good times ahead of us, Darlin'. I ain't beat yet. I'm a fighter, just like that Mayzelle of yours."

Twelve

March 1937

WHEN DAVID READ in the newspaper that Southern industry was expected to grow, he smiled. He had been hearing that story since 1930. He read that the yearly income of a farmer in North Carolina was about $400. He laughed at that also. He didn't make half that much. At least he wasn't a tenant farmer. That's where the real poverty was. The article said that government plans to spread factories out would help solve union troubles. There was also an article saying that syphilis was the cause of death for a large number of new babies and insane people.

Strange world, David thought.

Along with the newspaper was a letter from Lon in Greensboro. David opened it. As he read, a smile spread across his face.

"Ila," he shouted. "Ila, come here! Hurry!"

Ila ran in from the clothesline. "What's wrong?" she asked, alarmed.

"Old Lon did it again. I don't know how, but he talked his supervisor into holding a job open for me at the mill in Greensboro. If I want it. Hell, yes, I want it. He said we have to move as soon as possible."

Ila looked from side to side, from pantry to bedrooms. "I can be ready in a day."

Judith and Deidre helped Ila pack the few things they owned. Judith folded the flour-sack pillowcases. Ila told her to put them in the fireplace.

Judith said she would. Instead, she placed them in her own small bag.

Ash helped pack David's tools from the barn. His hands moved through and around his pockets, unconsciously folding and unfolding, his flannel shirt pulled out of his overalls on one side. His face was hard, defiant, his mouth tight and teeth clenched—an obvious victim of lashes from forces he couldn't see: greed, economics, drought, and storm. He was, Ila thought, the most beautiful young man she had ever seen—because he had the look of a survivor.

Rubbing her eyes, Mayzelle washed the last of the dishes and sat down on the couch. The letter from Ila was too good to be true. Of all the children, she missed Ila most. Pearl had married a fireman and moved to South Carolina. Vera had married a schoolteacher in High Point.

Mayzelle heard the screen door slam. Probably Lon home for lunch, she thought. She sighed and pulled herself up. Suddenly, her tired face rose into smiles. She placed her hand on her mouth and ran to the door.

Ila.

The two women hugged each other, touching faces and feeling hands and hair.

"Oh, Ila," cried Mayzelle. "Oh, my baby's come home to her old Mayzelle."

Ila's children swarmed through the door, overturned a table, and headed for the stairs, examining everything in sight.

Mayzelle laughed. "Lord, Honey, you done went and had a mess of 'em! Well, don't worry, Mayzelle gonna try to take as good care of them as she did of you."

Ila hugged her once more. "I want to cry," she said, "but I'm all cried out. I didn't really know how much I loved you till I left you. Been regrettin' it ever since."

"Don't talk like that, Honey. Don't."

Ila brushed her face with a towel that was on Mayzelle's shoulder. "Mayzelle, if you can take care of them younguns you're a better woman than I am. Didn't you notice? They's mostly grown now. The boys are like young bulls, and the girls are just now *noticin'* young bulls."

"I can handle anything!" boasted Mayzelle with raw confidence.

"We'll be stayin' here till David gets some land. He's bound and determined to build us a house."

Mayzelle nodded.

"What you doin' now, Mayzelle?"

"Anything you wants me to do, Honey."

"Let's go downtown. There's somethin' I've wanted for years, and I'm gonna buy it today. Most of our money's got to go for land, so I best spend for what I want right now."

"I'm ready, Miss Priss, anytime you are."

As they headed for the door, Lora hurried into the room behind Ash, berating him for neglecting to give her a kiss. She was breathing in short, spasmodic contractions.

Mayzelle frowned at her. "Sit down, Lora, before you have a heart attack."

Lora reached for Ila and they embraced. "I missed you, Honey," Lora said. "That's the hardest thing about raisin' children, seein' them leave."

"They always come back when they hungry, to their Mayzelle," Mayzelle said.

Lora walked around Ila. "Country life been good for you, toughed you up a bit. Still big up top, Ila. You can't hide that."

Ila was surprised at the blush on her own face.

Lora laughed, kissed Ila, and for a moment their eyes met, black on brown. Without speaking, each saw the history of the past few years written on those dark mirrors.

"Welcome back, daughter," Lora said.

Ila walked out on the porch. Mayzelle followed. They caught a bus downtown. Ila found a good seat in the front and Mayzelle went to the back. Thirty minutes later, Ila walked into Cliffman's Jewelers to buy a replacement for her engagement ring.

David bought two acres of land on Battleground Avenue, on the outskirts of town. On part of the land was an old stable. He boarded it up and moved in until he could start building the house. Ila planted a garden behind the stable. Soon the house began to take shape. David came home from work at five and worked on the house until nine or ten. Rossie and Ash helped him. Soon the foundation was laid of cinderblocks; the floor and walls of pine; then a tin roof and a porch with huge wooden columns, cement steps, wide windows, and high-ceilinged rooms. It took two years to build the house. The family moved in before it was completed. Each family member who was not at work or at school was expected to do something on the house each day—painting, sheetrocking, or laying bricks. It was a house built by each member of the family, and each had a sense that the house was his or hers by earned right, not by birth or kinship.

David seemed to have a talent for building cabinets and doorways, attic spaces, and anything else involving precise work. He was proud of his work. On the night that he, Ila, and the four children moved in, David wandered from room to room, commenting on how difficult each part had been to build. "It is a good place for us to spend the rest of our lives," he said. "It is comfortable. There are no uneven walls, no holes in the roof, no out-of-square places on the porch."

Ila thought she was in a dream. She suggested he build a smaller house on a back lot to rent. He began construction in 1940.

Deidre and Judith began dating. Rossie married a girl, Pansy, from Summerfield, and moved away. Ash married Maureen, a girl from Mc-Leansville, and moved in with her family. He got a job at a bank.

The building and loan corporation charged twelve dollars a month for David's construction materials. Ila didn't have to work with the rent money coming in. She spent most of her time looking after the property, growing and canning food, and helping Lora when she could. She planted walnut trees, fig bushes, peach trees, and apple trees. She made locust beer and took occasional trips to the country to pick up moonshine from a man named Sossomon McDowell.

And then the war came.

In 1941, Rossie and Ash enlisted in the army. Food ration coupons became a way of life, one that was still better than the one Ila had experienced in the country. The war brought fear and death, but it also brought jobs and prosperity of a sort.

In the summer of 1942, Ila asked daughter Judith to travel with her to Summerfield to purchase the month's supply of liquor from the Mc-Dowells. Judith did not want to go. There were better things to do on summer afternoons than wander around in the woods at the McDowells. Besides, Momma shouldn't be drinking that foul stuff. Even Daddy was drinking it now, secretly at first, then more and more in the open. It was almost as if those two were in a race to see who could drink more. Sometimes both David and Ila drank too much and ended up laughing and swearing at each other on the front porch until it was time for bed.

Ila banged on the door with such force that Judith felt it would break open. "I'm hurryin', Momma, keep your shirt on," she shouted as she applied fresh lipstick. She took pride in her appearance, using lipstick and makeup to soften her angular features, washing her hair daily in the sink to keep the sheen. People always commented on her eyes, almost as dark as Lora's. Her gaze was intelligent and lonely.

Ila's voice was almost gentle. "I want to get there before dark. Judith. You hurry. I'll be a-waitin' in the car."

"Oh, Momma, do I have to go?" said Judith plaintively.

"No, you don't." Ila's voice worked up and down. "You can let your poor old momma go all the way out to the country by herself, maybe have a flat tire or engine blowup, or maybe run off'n a bridge, or get robbed at a gas station, or maybe get hurt by those barbaric McDowell people. No, you don't have to go for my sake. You just sit here and rest up from your hard mornin's work. . . ."

"All right, Momma. All right, I'm coming." Jesus, Judith thought, it's a wonder Daddy could put up with her all these years. Seems Momma always gets her way, no matter what happens. And what do I get? A dark room at the back of the house with a dresser straight out of the Dark Ages and a bed that sags and creaks whenever a body breathes. All I'll have when I get old is a bad back and lots of memories of sweaty rides to Summerfield.

Ila wrapped a scarf around her head and put on her extra-large sunglasses, placed the car in gear, and squealed out of the driveway.

"Slow down, Momma!"

Ila smiled. "Now, don't you get too smart with me, young lady. I've been driving for two years now and I don't need no lessons from you."

"Yes, Momma. By the way, when you run off the road, don't let me know."

"I raised a house of smart alecks, that's what I did." She drove out of the city in a very few minutes and relaxed when she found the highway to Summerfield. The convertible top on the car was down, and wind rushed over the windshield. Judith wished she had brought a scarf. Her hair was being whipped across her face and against the back of her neck. She eased down in the seat, trying to escape the wind. It was useless to ask Momma to stop and put the top up. Momma loved the wind.

The road to Summerfield was shaded part of the way by tall pines and old oaks. They crossed a creek before arriving at the small community with its ramshackle houses and little frame country stores. The smell of fertilizer and oil hung in the air as clouds of dust drifted over the car.

A few miles on the other side of the community, Ila turned off the main road and allowed the car to ease down a smooth, hard-packed dirt road leading into the woods near a large stream. A log house hunched deep on the riverbank as if it had been washed up on shore. A barn, near collapse, was silhouetted, tall and alone, in the pasture.

Sossomon McDowell came out of the barn and almost ran to the car. He welcomed his customers as if they would be his last, all smiles and waving arms.

"Ila Tolbert!" he shouted with a hoarse voice. "You bringin' the sunshine into this hollow sure enough." He stopped briefly to wrench some yellow-bells off the bushes. "Here's some late springtime for you."

Ila laughed like a schoolgirl. "Why, Sossomon McDowell, you old coot, don't you try to sweet-talk me, or I might figure you've done raised the prices around here. And I warn you, if you have, you've lost your best customers. Times is hard, you know."

Sossomon turned sheepish for a moment, brushed back his gray hair, and leaned on the car door, avoiding her eyes. "Why, you know," he said, "I couldn't raise prices on the likes of you. The only reason I can't *give* it to you is 'cause the bank owns more of this house than I do."

Ila smiled. "I'm just a-kiddin' you. Let me out. Me and Judith plan on gettin' back 'fore dark, so you just load up the regular three gallons."

"How about four?"

"Three. No more."

"Then how about testin' the stuff with me on the back porch? It's a wonder how the stuff makes the waters look after a few drinks."

"I got to drive back."

"Can't your daughter drive?"

"Well, I guess . . ."

Judith shook her head with amusement. "It's all right, Momma. I'll drive careful."

"Well, maybe a drink or two. 'Sides, I want to hear about your boys. By the way, is your sweet daughter Esther here?" Ila asked, smiling.

"Sure is. She went behind the barn to get your load."

"She's lookin' more and more like Anna every day—God rest her soul."

"Yes. Let's talk about you . . . oh, clean forgot, you enjoy door-opening! Here, I'll open your car door and then I'll scoot right over and help sweet Judith. Judith and my Esther can have a long talk with us or maybe take a walk."

Ila walked toward the house with Sossomon, and Judith followed.

Ila stopped a moment, squinting her eyes toward the front door. There was someone in the hallway; she could see the shadow. "What one is that?" she asked, pointing.

"That's Arthur."

"Arthur? I thought he enlisted."

"He did. But the boy gets lonely now and again and goes AWOL for a few days. Don't amount to much. Those sergeants come and get him. He don't cause no trouble, and 'sides, it gets him a couple days of being home and that don't hurt nobody. I figure it does him lots of good, sends him back in good spirits. Me and the sergeants got to be good friends. Course, if he keeps it up, they'll boot him out, and the boy won't like that."

"Arthur must be awful immature."

"No, I don't rightly think so. Arthur is a man—yes sir, no doubt about that." He turned and pushed Judith to the front, shouting toward the house. "Hey, Arthur! Come on out! We got company. Mighty pretty company!"

Judith looked up to the heavens and waited for the blush. It came.

And then Arthur opened the screen door and walked into the sunlight. The breeze blew his carefully combed hair out of place, and his eyes almost twinkled within the pine shadows waving across his body. He was tall and thin, but muscular in a taut way. His teeth seemed a little crooked, his lips wide and thin, his nose thick and tanned, and his eyes large and soft blue, framed by dark eyelashes. He walked quickly, in great strides, up to Judith. "Come," he said softly. He pulled gently on her arm.

Ila harrumphed. "No. Now, I don't know about this. Esther would like to see Judith, I'm sure."

Sossomon pushed some dirt out of his way with the point of his boot. "Now, Ila, my boy's the gentlest. You know that. Let him take your little one down to the stream to see the ducks. You don't mind, do you, Judith?"

Judith was glad someone had asked her. She wanted to say that she minded very much, but his eyes were so clean and deep, and his hair was like silk straw. When he smiled, deep indentations ran like rivers from his eyes to his jaw.

"Yes," she said softly. "I'd like to see the stream and the ducks."

There was something about the way his army khakis fit him, loose and free. His hands were large and bony and seemed to give him some discomfort; he walked with them behind his back or in his pockets, fumbling with keys and loose coins. He was seventeen, but looked older.

He asked her name. Why had she never visited before? When was she coming back? What was her favorite food? Did she drink? How old was she?

No, she didn't think drinking was ladylike. "Fifteen," she mumbled.

And then, once out of sight of the house, he asked her if she had ever been kissed.

She was surprised, not at the question, but in the way he had put it, as if it were the most natural thing in the world to ask.

"I'm not sure that's any of your business."

He smiled again. "You're right. It's not any of my business. I'm sorry I asked. Papa always told me to speak out and sometimes I forget that I'm not with kin. Sometimes I feel like everybody is kin, and they ain't. I learned that in the army."

"Why did you go AWOL? Aren't you scared they'll put you in jail?"

"Oh, I been in jail before *and* in the stockade. I never stay long. If there's a way in, there's always a way out."

"You're a strange one, Arthur."

He looked hurt.

"No, I don't mean it bad; it's just that I never met a boy . . . I mean, a man . . . like you before. You seem so open and honest."

"I ain't."

"What?"

"I ain't open and I ain't always honest. I just say whatever pops into my head."

"Oh. Well, I suppose we better be gettin' back. Momma gets worried when I'm out of her sight too long."

"It doesn't matter."

"Well, of course it matters!" she said sharply. Or did it? "Well, I don't want to get her all flustered, or I'll never hear the end of it."

"You ain't seen the ducks yet."

"I've seen ducks before."

"But you've never seen *these* ducks."

"What's so special about these ducks? Ducks is ducks."

"They're mallards."

"Mallards? You mean wild ducks, with all those pretty colors—blue and gold and green?"

"Yes, they're kin."

She laughed. "Okay, I might as well see the ducks. Can't stay Momma's little girl forever."

"You have just spoken a great truth," he said.

He put his arm around her shoulder. And it seemed natural there.

❧

For the next three days she went back to see him, to be with him. Ila made Deidre go along. Deidre didn't mind. She and Esther talked and cleaned and cooked and went fishing with Will, Arthur's younger brother.

Judith was in love, or thought she was in love. This rugged, skinny soldier took her driving and swimming and, more often than not, deep into the cool shadowy woods, beyond the holly and birch and into the thickets surrounding a black pool, an ancient mirror of the sky. Lying on a blanket, they talked. They shared as much as possible because they both knew that soon his sergeants would come and take him away. This would be his last trip home before being shipped overseas.

He was the first man to return her affection, and the force of that affection both frightened and pleased her. She knew that there were a great many things that she didn't understand, and being loved by a man was one of them.

Judith had never been a very popular girl in school, not in the same way that Deidre was popular. Judith dated three or four boys, but only when accompanied by friends or family. A date consisted of a Wednesday night prayer meeting at Orangewood Baptist Church, or Saturday night choir practice, or Sunday night service. Sometimes she went along with a few friends for an outing at the Battleground Park.

She felt plain and simple, but never humble. Her hair was brown, long,

147

full, and uncontrolled. Her face was angular with full lips. Her cheeks were freckled, complementing the red-gold strands of hair that appeared on her head in summer. Her friends said she was nervous and unsure of herself. But they didn't know about Arthur.

After a picnic of ham and potato salad in the pine woods, Judith told Arthur of the significant events of her life, which included moving to the city from the country, being bossed around by Mayzelle, and meeting Arthur.

"And that's my whole life story," Judith said.

"Pitiful," said Arthur as he leaned over to kiss her mouth. She pushed him away forcefully. "No, now you've got to tell me about you. I've known you all of three days and you've hardly told me anything. I want to know everything about you."

"Everything?" he said wickedly.

"Every dirty little detail."

"I'm not sure I should."

"You want a kiss?"

"And more."

"No. Not a kiss, not even a smile until you tell me your whole life."

"It's pretty boring."

"I figured that."

"All right, but I might lie some. Never know."

"Oh, I'll know all right. I've got the edge on truth in these woods. I can look into your eyes and tell whether you're lyin' or not. It's a trick I picked up from Grandma Lora. She can always spot a liar."

"If I do lie, it will probably be by accident. So don't tell me; it may be a lie I believe in, and you don't have the right to go around destroyin' people's lies. Some people live by lies. It's their right."

"Get on with it, Arthur McDowell, or I'll mess up that pretty straw-blond hair of yours."

"Promise?"

"Arthur, I'm gettin' irritated."

Arthur rolled on his back and pulled her head to his chest.

"There was a time," he said, feeling sleepy, "when I guess I was as young as you are."

He pulled a Camel cigarette from his pocket and lighted it. A frown etched his face. "West Virginia," he said. "God, I hated that place. No," he said, correcting himself, "I guess I loved it then. Looking back, I guess I hate it now. But not then. Then was something else."

In Beckley, West Virginia, Arthur had helped his mother, Anna, run the farm while Sossomon worked in the coal mine. Arthur wanted to work there also, but Anna refused to let him. Sossomon seldom lost an argument with his wife, but he lost that one.

"Never again," she had said, "will one of my children work in that hole!" She had a good point. Richard, the oldest, had died in a cave-in two winters ago. Now all she had was Arthur, Esther, and Will. Anna was a good woman, small, quiet, and gentle, with sad eyes. She held her anger inside, and was known to have caring hands that seemed to cure the most troubled soul. She believed in hard work and strict discipline. The children listened to her. She lived only for her family. She loved marigolds and zinnias; as near as anyone could tell, flowers and church were her only recreation. She went to a little hard-shell Baptist church with close to fifty members. She lived her religion, never bragged on it or pushed it. She was part Dutch and was considered to be the real strength of the family.

Sossomon adored her. He was tall, with large bones and ears. His smile covered his face. When he squinted against the sun his eyebrows made him appear sensitive and gentle.

He could be strong. Once, he killed a man in Beckley in an argument.

"In these times," he told his sons, "a man carries a gun. That's quick justice in this town. Mines and hard farming make people mean. You stand up for yourself or no one else will. You make me and your momma proud by being strong."

He left Beckley and moved his family to Surry County, North Carolina. He put together a little farm and Arthur and Will worked alongside him hoeing the tobacco; every plant, every row. The work was formidable. To supplement the income, Sossomon made liquor for the government until prohibition came along. After that he continued the tradition privately, saying to whoever would listen, "How the hell can they tell us to make the stuff for years, and then tell us it's wrong tomorrow? Man's been drinking since olden times and he's not going to stop now."

On weekends, Arthur and Will hunted raccoon, rabbit, and squirrel. Will loved dogs. He promised himself that his future would be secure with a good wife—like Momma—and good dogs like Daddy's. Arthur had no plans for the future. This was the way life was and always had been: hard but fruitful. He thought he could provide everything a family needed if he were willing to sacrifice. Arthur and Will grew strong. To cherish this philosphy of living, they had to be strong. Weak men didn't survive in the farm business in Surry County.

In 1940, Sossomon McDowell was arrested for moonshining. He had a cousin put up bail and court money, but at a price. Sossomon turned over the mortgage to his farm as collateral for the cousin's help.

Sossomon couldn't pay him back. The cousin foreclosed, confiscating two barns full of tobacco.

Sossomon moved his family again, this time to the outskirts of Greensboro, to a small farm with an expanded log cabin.

Arthur liked Greensboro. There was plenty of entertainment here that was lacking in Surry. First, there were girls—lots of pretty girls who liked long rides in the country, sassy girls who had no reputations left to ruin, and forbidden girls who did.

He was young and as innocent as any farm boy could be, considering the nature of the work. He was also a little vain about his looks. He had a smooth face and faded blue eyes. He kept things to himself and loved his mother.

When Anna died, Esther said it was like something died in Arthur. This was true. It was also true that something dark was born in him at the same time. With his mother's death, Arthur's life began to lose its reality.

Someone took a picture of Anna in the coffin before the funeral service. In that place, hers was a beautiful face without line or worry. Yet she had had plenty to worry about. There were those who said she had worked herself to death. Legends grew about her formidable compassion. As Anna lay dying, she told Esther not to worry so much over nursing her; there were more important things to do for the boys.

Then Sossomon started to drink more than usual. Arthur drank also. They missed her. They could not help remembering her kindness. Neither man would ever be free of a love that reached beyond death.

Several times, on Monday mornings, Sossomon went downtown to collect his boys, Arthur and Will, from an overnight stay in jail. The story was always the same: Work through the week, carouse through the weekend, fight anyone who wanted, make love to anyone willing, and try to forget.

Arthur didn't mind a good fight. It was a perfect way to get the frustration, hurt, and anger out of his system. Will tagged along and was often required to defend Arthur's honor. And Arthur was honorable. People couldn't help liking him.

Anna had always depended on Esther to help rear the boys. She worked as hard as Anna ever had. The boys respected her because of her ability to keep their secrets. Her blue eyes always reflected the mood of those around her. She was loving and gentle but if provoked, she could swing an iron skillet with ease.

The war came with little warning. The Greensboro newspaper said that Pearl Harbor was not as great a victory for the Japanese as the enemy claimed, but still, Greensboro worked on a plan to protect its water supplies from German saboteurs. Arthur thought it was ironic that the same man who delivered the declaration of war to be signed by President Wilson in 1917 also delivered the document to Roosevelt. Arthur decided to help avenge the crimes of the Japanese. He loved his country, the land, and his freedom. Nothing suited him more than a walk through the woods with his dogs. He considered it a freedom bestowed by democracy.

That was all there was to tell, up to now, to this place and time.

Arthur shook the chill from his face. Judith was asleep. Had he told her all, or had he dreamed that he had told her? It didn't matter.

He had told her about everything except Milly, his first love, an older girl who had married a deputy sheriff. A dangerous frown passed across his face.

"Arthur?"

He jumped. Judith woke. It was Will. "They're here, Arthur," he said. "You got to come now. Pa says to hurry, they're gettin' ornery."

"I'm comin'," Arthur said. "You go back and tell 'em that I'm on my way."

Will turned and ran back through the bushes.

"Arthur, I don't want you to go," Judith whispered.

"I know."

"And you don't want to leave me."

He straightened. "I'll be back."

"Promise?"

"Yeah, I promise. Nothin' will keep me from comin' back. And when I do, I'll come straight back to you. And we'll come back here and finish what we started."

Arthur walked toward the path.

"Aren't you going to wait on me?"

Arthur did not turn around. "No, I'm not. I'm gonna climb in that Jeep and not look back. I'll write you, and I'll come back and marry you when the war's over."

Judith ran toward him.

"No," he said gruffly.

She watched his back straighten and saw his neck muscles tighten as he walked away from her.

And then he turned and smiled at her, and she remembered that smile, at that moment, in the nights that followed.

He wrote to her, always addressing his letters to "Brown Eyes." She soon learned, by talking with other girls in town, that this was his method of keeping his girlfriends separate since he was not good at remembering names. Some of the girls to whom he wrote compared letters, only to find that they were exact copies, except for the greeting: "Dear Blue Eyes," or "Dear Green Eyes."

This did not bother Judith. She had been amused by his attentions, but she was, after all, *plain*. He was handsome and energetic. And that's the way things would be, now and always. Or so she thought at the time.

Arthur joined the army weighing 170 pounds. He trained in Georgia, Arizona, and California. He fought in North Africa and on the terrible beaches of Normandy in 1944.

Across an ocean, surrounded by groves of apple and pine, Sossomon stayed up late at night, after Will and Esther had gone to bed, sorting out the postcards, photographs, and letters Arthur sent from the army posts. On the back of the photos, Arthur had scribbled notes such as, "Daddy, does this look like me?" The reverse would show a Minuteman pose, Arthur proudly holding his rifle. A soldier, no longer a boy, the strain of boot camp barely showing on his face despite the thirty pounds he had gained. Arthur was the epitome of strength, and Sossomon took pride in the reflection.

While the photos showed the man, the letters were written in the language of a homesick farm boy. The conflict between the adventure and the approaching uncertainty was reflected in his handwriting, the nervous tension apparent.

In France, his leadership earned him a promotion to sergeant, but he was demoted to corporal for fighting.

At first he didn't really care. He was a soldier and proud of it. He became an expert marksman and a boxer, and he survived, but not without wounds.

After D-Day, he wanted to go home. Home to Sossomon and Will and Esther. The French girls were exciting, but he did not love them.

He fought with the First Army to the Siegfried line, a strong German fortified line. It could be breached only by a combination of aerial bombardment, tank attacks, and infantry. Arthur went into the Battle for the Siegfried at 200 pounds. He came out weighing 160.

He seldom spoke of the fighting for every yard of ground, of the buddies dead, and of the enemies killed in hand-to-hand combat. He had cut a few throats and killed more men than he cared to remember. He *would not* remember; he would block it out, if possible. But while clearing a German town of snipers, he lost that ability.

His job was to search through houses and spray bullets into the rooms with his machine gun. His friend Gene Kirksey waited at the rear of the house in case the enemy ran out a back door.

Gene Kirksey was skinny and short. Sometimes Arthur suspected that Gene lied about his age. A lot of boys did that to get off the farm. Gene could be fourteen or sixteen; no real way to tell. He spoke with a deep Southern drawl and chose his words carefully. The only physical characteristic he had in common with Arthur was the unexpressive nature of his blue eyes. Their eyes never gave away their thoughts, and this could be an advantage in situations that required bluffing. Gene had a small mouth and his ears were set back too far on each side of his head. Arthur thought Gene was ugly and told him so. Gene said his looks didn't matter if Arthur had to choose for a buddy between a movie star or someone who could shoot straight and true. They were friends.

At one house, Arthur kicked open the door and sprayed the hallway. Then he went through the other rooms doing the same. The house seemed empty when suddenly he heard a clicking noise behind him. He turned and fired.

"Arthur—you've killed me," were Gene's last words.

Arthur's life was marked from that day.

He was no longer a boy from Surry. The war was no longer an exciting test of courage and manhood.

In Paris, awaiting orders to be shipped home, he had a photograph taken in a side-street shop. It was a good picture. He stood straight, his Scotch-Dutch toughness enhanced by a smartly pressed uniform. His blue eyes seemed dim and distant, but his cap cocked to the side gave the impression of defiance.

He wanted to go where there was love. The war had deepened his awareness of life and kin, while also impressing upon him the brute reality of an existence he couldn't control.

He needed healing—in the woods around Greensboro, at his father's table, or in the back seat of a convertible—for he was deeply wounded. He needed his mother's healing touch, but she was dead.

He thought of Judith.

Thirteen

DAVID TOLBERT was saving a little money from the rent of the small house. For weeks he complained that the money wasn't enough. So Ila returned to work part-time at the mill. Coming home from work the first day, she planned on soaking her feet in a tub of hot water. The wind was colder than usual as she pushed open the front door.

All thought of a heated footbath vanished.

There was no tub.

"Hell," she whispered, "there ain't no furniture!"

David came to the door and walked toward Ila. "Now, Honey, don't get upset. I'm just makin' some more money for us."

"More money, hell!" she screamed. "You just get my furniture back into my house right this minute."

"Now listen to me," he said sternly. "The widow what's movin' into our big house is going to pay us five dollars more than the last tenants of the small house. You figure it up. That's sixty dollars more a year. Not bad money, that isn't. And we gonna need it. Our girls got to have a proper dowry. We can live in the smaller house."

"What dowry?" she said, shaking.

"Why, you know as well as me that they both gettin' to be at the marryin' age. Deidre sneaks down at night to meet fellows when the train roars by outside—"

"Why, that ain't so!" shouted Ila indignantly.

"Well, Honey, it's true, and I wouldn't of mentioned it, but those girls are gonna get married someday whether we like it or not, and they got to have a proper dowry."

"I never had no dowry!"

"But our girls are different! We're movin' up in the world. They got to marry into good families what can support 'em better than we can."

"Maybe so, but I don't like it. Don't like it one little bit. I'll try it for a while, but if I don't get used to it, that widow or whoever you're a-movin' in will have to leave." She thought a moment. "Sneakin' out when the train comes by? Why, I never! Come right out here, Deidre. You and me, we got to have a little talk—yes, right now! Proper young ladies don't do that sort of thing. No sir, *proper* young ladies . . . ." Somehow, for some reason, the word "proper" stuck in her throat.

The widow, Mrs. Pearson, had been in mourning for three months. Her husband had been killed in the Pacific. Widowhood gave her a sense of dignity that she had never known. She found that black highlighted the unblemished, unlined beauty of a young face that, until now, had seldom known misfortune. If she could have her way, she would mourn forever.

David helped her move into the larger house, while Ila tried to make the smaller one livable. The smaller house had only two bedrooms, and furniture had to be stacked in the corners.

Judith was the first to notice the change—a change that had escaped Ila's attention. "Isn't it strange," Judith said, "that Daddy seems so much more alive these last few months?"

"Well," Ila said. "I'd not noticed. But now that you mention it, he does seem a bit perkier."

"I think," Judith said, "that he's going through his second childhood."

"He's what?"

"You know, second childhood, when men think they're little boys again. Daddy's acting that way. I saw him up in the tree picking pears for Mrs. Pearson."

"When did he do that?" Ila asked.

"Last week. It was the funniest sight, Momma. I wish you could'a seen it—Daddy sprawled out on those top branches like a flying squirrel, picking this one and that one, making sure that they were the pears she wanted."

"Is that so?" Ila said, in an uninterested but strained voice.

"Yes, it is so. He's going with her to pick out a washing machine tomorrow. She's so helpless. I feel so sorry for a woman like that, lost her husband in the war and all. It must be a terrible thing."

"Yes, terrible," said Ila. "Right terrible. What's this about a washing machine?"

"Deidre heard Mrs. Pearson ask Daddy if he would help her pick it out and bring it home. Daddy's so nice, he couldn't say no."

"No, your daddy couldn't say no, that's for sure. Did you hear where they're goin' to get the machine?"

"Ronald Jackson's, probably. He's got a sale on downtown."

"Ronald Jackson, huh? Washin' machines are right expensive. She's hardly got any money, to hear her tell it. Wonder how she's goin' to buy one of those things."

"Must have saved her money a long time, Momma. Same way you save yours."

"I work for mine, Honey. She don't do a lick of work anywhere, near as I can tell."

"Strange, isn't it?"

"Yes, daughter, mighty strange."

Ila went to her room and shut the door. She washed her face and took her shoes off. Her feet and legs were still those of a young girl, soft and pale. But her face and hands were as tough as new leather, and her hair was spotted with gray. David has not fared much better, she thought. But he's still handsome in a rugged sort of way. He wears his hard times well, for a man. Of course, it would be natural for some woman to be attracted to him. He still has those boyish eyes and that brutish swagger. But he will never look at them. He's way past them days of cattin' around. And he sleeps well now; lost his appetite for fights long ago. In fact, he's a bit prudish now, wearin' pajamas and all.

She laughed out loud. "Lord, listen to me. Suspectin' David of messin' around with another woman. That's a laugh. Him with two girls at home and two sons in the war. Such a laugh. I must be gettin' tired."

She went back into the kitchen and began washing dishes. She looked thoughtfully at the dish in her hand. The picture of a bluebird in the center had worn off long ago. The imprint on the back of the plate had read "Made in Japan," but when the war came, proper ladies destroyed their Japanese dishes. Not Ila; she scraped the words off the back. Anything to save a nickel. Nickels made dollars.

"And if David is fooling around with that woman," she said, "I'll kill him."

"David, don't gobble your food like that."

He looked at her, wide-eyed, and began to chew slowly.

"What you in such an all-fired hurry for, old man?"

David swallowed the sausage. "I ain't as old as you think, Ila. No sir, I'm gettin' my second wind, that's all."

"Is that why they put you on as an elevator operator at the mill, cause you're so young?"

"That's not funny, Ila. You know my gall bladder's actin' up again."

"Yes, I know, and your stomach's gonna act up if you don't take your time eatin'. Besides, you ain't answered my question. Where you goin'?"

"What makes you think I'm goin' anywhere?"

"No reason to put your hat and coat across the breakfast table, is there?"

"Well, now that you mention it, I got to go uptown."

"Why?"

"Business."

"What kind of business?"

"Got to pay some bills," he mumbled.

"I paid 'em all last week," she said.

"Got some you don't know about."

"Really?" she said. "I guess that is possible." She looked at her ring. He was staring at her but she did not hear him speak.

"Oh, what's that, David? I was daydreaming."

"Oh, nothin'. Just that I won't be back till lunch time, probably."

"Well, you go ahead. I've got some work to do in the garden."

He left.

She gathered the plates from the table and looked outside the window. No activity around the Pearson house. David was walking fast—much too fast—down the street toward the bus stop. She looked at her ring. The morning sun seemed to make it come alive.

"Judith!" she shouted. "Get my coat, we're a-goin' downtown."

She left Judith on the street and went into the Jackson Appliance Shop.

"Well, hello, Mrs. Tolbert. Ain't this a coincidence. Your husband was in here a few minutes ago. I bet you're mighty proud of that man."

"What you gabbin' about, Mr. Jackson?"

"Oh, don't go puttin' on airs, Mrs. Tolbert. Any woman would be proud of that new washer that's going to your house."

"Washer? What washer?"

"Why, the washing machine that Mr. Tolbert done bought. Paid cash for it, he did. You *did* know, didn't you? Mrs. Tolbert?"

The door slammed.

Judith was leaning on a car. "Momma, Daddy just went into that cafe. Let's get him to buy us something."

"What cafe?" she said, her voice deep and husky.

"Why, Hamlin's, right across the street. I see him."

"You stay here, child. I'll be back."

She walked across the street and opened the door to the cafe. David and Mrs. Pearson were in a booth, laughing. Mrs. Pearson, in black, had her hand on the table. He touched it, smiled, and looked up.

The smile vanished.

Ila kept her head up and her eyes began to moisten. I'm not going to cry, she thought. I'm gonna brain him.

She walked over to the table.

David stood, flustered, his face red.

Ila forced a smile. "May I join you?"

"Sure, Ila. Uh, take this seat. Let me get you a coffee."

"No, thanks. That's a mighty pretty dress you have on, Mrs. Pearson. Black looks so good on you."

Mrs. Pearson's normally white complexion looked a little clouded. "Why, thank you, Mrs. Tolbert. I was just tellin' David here how much I admire the way you dress, wasn't I, David?"

David nodded.

Ila reached for Mrs. Pearson's hand and held it tight. "I am so glad you noticed what a hard-workin' woman can do with such a tiny little budget. I've always been proud to re-do my clothes to the latest fashion. As a matter of fact, I'm makin' a little gift for you, Mrs. Pearson, for all the kindnesses you've shown to our family."

David looked up, as if he had been awakened from a deep sleep. Mrs. Pearson looked to him for help. He looked the other way.

"A gift? Why, uh, that's real kind of you, Mrs. Tolbert. I really have another appointment I must make."

"Honey, don't you even want to know what the gift is?"

"Surprise her, Ila," David said gruffly.

"Why, David, you know how much I love surprises. You of all people know that."

"All right, Mrs. Tolbert. What's the gift? I really have to be running."

"I'm sewing you a pillowcase of silk, with gold-threaded doves of peace, so you can rest your pretty head."

"What do you mean, rest my head?"

Ila leaned over and whispered, "When I finish beatin' the hell out of you, you'll need the pillow for your coffin, you bitch."

"Ila!" David said.

"Shut up, David. This is between me and your paramour."

"I've got to leave," Mrs. Pearson said, standing and walking away.

Ila stood. "Leave right, Honey," she shouted. "You pack up your ass and get off my property today, you hear?"

David put his hand over his eyes.

"I want a separation," she said.

"Nothin' happened, Ila."

"Wrong, David, plenty happened."

She left, meeting Judith at the door.

"Throw it all out. Every last piece of this junk!"

"But, Momma, what will Daddy say?" Deidre cried.

"Listen, girl, do as I say, I know what I'm a-doin'."

Deidre and Judith shrugged at each other as they pulled a sofa to the front porch.

David ran into the house. Ila ignored him.

"Ila, what are you doin'?"

"I want that woman out," she shrieked. "Out of my house now!"

He grabbed her shoulder, but she jerked away. "David Tolbert . . . I thought I would never . . . ." The angry words would not come.

He walked out.

Ila ran after him. "Oh, no, you don't, David Tolbert. I won't let you get out this easy. I been to a lawyer."

He stopped and slowly turned around.

"Hah, I knew that would stop you."

"About the separation?"

"Yes," Ila said, "the separation." She licked her lips.

"You really want one," he said flatly.

"Yes, I do. And you know what? I get half of everything and all of the back lot with the rental house on it."

He looked surprised.

"You didn't know that, did you, David Tolbert?"

He smiled. "No, I didn't."

"Why you smilin'?"

"Oh, I thought about us bein' separated, you livin' in the rental house and me in the front one. Wondered whether you'd let me borrow a cup of sugar every now and then."

"Hell, no, I wouldn't loan you a sack of manure, David Tolbert."

He laughed. "No, I guess you wouldn't at that, Ila. Well, you can have the separation if that's what you really want."

She frowned. "If that's what *you* really want."

"I don't know how to go about it or even where to start. Mrs. Pearson was just a friend, Ila . . ."

"Don't start that, David."

"Well, hell, she was. I didn't mean to hurt you. I didn't know what it looked like till you walked into the cafe."

"Just a little friendly flirtation, like in the newspaper stories, right?"

"I'm a man, Ila. You can't stop a man from smellin' the bread when he walks past the bakery."

"But he don't have to sample none, either," she said, blinking back the tears.

"Oh, Ila, let me make it up to you. I'll do better. I'm sorry I done it and I didn't want to hurt you or the kids. That's all I can say. Don't make it worse than it is. I love you, Ila."

"Don't you dare tell me you love me, David. *I* love *you*. I been through hell with you so we could get somewhere, and you go and try to blow up the whole thing over that skinny little woman. I thought surely I looked better to you than that."

"Only when you're shoutin' at me, Ila."

"You makin' fun don't make things any better, David."

"Come here," he said.

"No. No kiss and make up on this, David."

"We been through worse," he said.

"I ain't kissin' you."

"Just one."

"And then you'll leave me alone?"

"Promise, old girl."

"I ain't no old girl."

"One."

She smiled. "Well, maybe just one."

He put his arms around her.

"It's moments like this," she whispered, "when I realize how really gullible I am. If I so much as see you lookin' at another woman, you can say goodbye to everythin'!"

"You don't have to worry about that."

She wondered if he meant it.

On the porch of the rental house, Deidre sat down on the floral couch. Judith sat beside her and sighed. "Ain't love a romantic thing? It's sweet to see them make up."

Deidre grinned. "They better tell us what to do with all this furniture in the yard. It looks like rain."

Judith laughed. "I knew she wouldn't go through with it."

"Huh?" Deidre said. "I wasn't so sure."

Judith felt a raindrop on her nose. "Mayzelle used to say that there are two things that are impossible to kill: love and life."

Deidre rolled her eyes. "Mayzelle's like Momma. She reads too many books."

Fourteen

April 1945

LON HAD Lora wear his coat when the wind became cool. Mayzelle had brought a folding chair and never took her eyes from the track. The whistles and clacking of steel on steel could be heard before the light pierced the darkness. They were not alone. Hundreds of others stood by the roadsides or near the flashing caution lights. The city was strangely quiet. Special trains had come through here before on the way to Lee's forces in Virginia, or to Wilmington docks for Pershing's, or to Georgia training camps, but this train was different. As it passed, Mayzelle caught a brief glimpse of Roosevelt's coffin.

Lon reached out and touched her shoulder.

Late that summer, rumors began to circulate, saying that the war would soon be over. Judith had not understood the atomic bomb, but she understood the wild shouts and rebel yells that spread through Ila's house as Maureen came in with the news: Japan had surrendered. A few minutes later, Deidre, Maureen, and Judith were on Elm Street with thousands of others. Judith noticed that a lot of people were crying, and everyone was excited. She could barely hear Deidre because of the car horns sounding from one end of town to another.

"What?" she shouted. Deidre pointed to the cars surrounding them.

Judith saw Will McDowell with a group of boys in an open car stalled in the heavy traffic. Will spotted her at the same moment. Judith remembered Arthur. She hadn't received a letter from him in several months.

He's probably engaged to some English girl, she thought. But Will is a kind boy. Maybe he can give me some news.

Will tried to hide his bottle when Judith forced her way through the crowd to the car.

"You remember me, Will?" she shouted.

"Honey, who could forget you? You're Arthur's girl."

She forced a laugh. "Arthur has a lot of girls, Will."

He grinned. "He should be home in a couple of months! Want a drink, Judith?"

"No, thanks, Will. I'll see you later."

The other boys in the car tried to get her to ride with them, but she ignored them and pushed her way through the crowd.

She had never seen so many laughing, crying, joyous people in one place. At the corner of Elm and Market, she saw some Negroes come out of a side street and get into a car. She thought she recognized one—Mayzelle? Yes. Judith shouted and waved.

But Mayzelle didn't see or hear Judith. The young driver of the car got out and opened the passenger door. Mayzelle kissed him on the cheek.

Judith couldn't stop staring at what, for her, was an incredible scene: Mayzelle having a good time with other—she bit her tongue—other *colored* people. Judith wondered for a moment why she should feel so shocked at the idea of Mayzelle enjoying someone else's company. The question bothered her. Someday she was going to ask Mayzelle about these feelings.

Ila opened the door. The soldier smiled.

"Yes?" Ila said, irritated. She was canning pears.

"Mrs. Tolbert, I guess you don't remember me."

"Yes, I do, you're that McDowell boy. What you want?"

Arthur nodded towards the living room. "Can I come in? I'd like to see Judith."

"Oh, I guess so. Come on in." she walked to the foot of the stairs and shouted, "Judith, that boy—that McDowell boy—uh, Arthur, yes, Arthur McDowell's here to see you."

Judith almost fell down the stairs. She rushed to the door and saw him standing in the living room, near the fireplace.

"Arthur," she whispered, her eyes moist. She ran to him.

Ila walked briskly into the room.

"Now, see here," Ila said. "We'll have none of this. This is a Christian home! It's not proper, young man, and you know it."

Arthur stepped back from Judith, reluctantly. "I apologize, Ma'am. I was wonderin' if you would let Judith go to the show tonight."

"No," said Ila, with an air of insulted dignity.

"Momma!" Judith said. "I can't believe the way you're acting. I haven't seen Arthur in three years! For heaven's sake, I'm not a little girl anymore!"

"Oh, yes you are; too young for an unchaperoned date."

Arthur stepped toward Ila. "Mrs. Tolbert, I had every intention of inviting you to go along as our chaperone."

Judith felt like crawling into the fireplace.

Ila was taken off balance. "Well, young man—I've got a lot of things to do around here—what picture show were you planning to see?"

"*Lady in the Dark.*"

"With Ginger Rogers?"

"The same."

"Well, I'll have to check with my husband. David! David, come off'n the kitchen table for a minute."

David walked slowly into the room. He took off his reading glasses for a moment and reached for Arthur's hand. "Good to have you back, son."

Ila put her hand on David's shoulder. "Arthur wants me to chaperone him and Judith tonight to the picture show. What do you think?"

"Does it matter what I think?" David said softly.

Ila sucked in a breath. She chose her words carefully. "No, not really."

After the movie, Arthur drove to Hamburger Square and bought everyone a Coke. Then he drove them home as Ila explained how best to repair old shoes. At the door he kissed Judith quickly, gently, on the mouth.

Ila pulled her into the house by the hair.

"See you later!" shouted Arthur, laughing. "I've got to keep a promise!"

Whistling, David shook the man's hand and walked into the house.

"What you so chipper about?" asked Ila.

"There's only one thing we got to be chipper about," he mocked.

"Riddles? This time of day? Be straight with me, Mr. Tolbert. What you got up your sleeve? And who was that old man out front?"

"Money," he said, pushing her aside as he headed for the kitchen.

Ila smiled. "Money? What for?"

"He's our new . . ." David rinsed his mouth with buttermilk from the icebox.

Ila stomped her foot.

He coughed. ". . . new tenant, for the rented house. He's payin' twice what we asked from others."

"Others? What do you mean *others*?"

"Oh, nothing." David's grin was gone. "By the way, what's for supper?"

"Don't try to go changin' the subject on me. I've lived with you long enough to know when you're a-holdin' back. Out with it 'fore I bang you up 'side the head with this skillet."

David sighed, eyeing the heavy iron pan in her hand. He sat down. "Well, he's a little different, that's all."

"Different! How? He a drunkard?" she demanded.

"No . . . no, don't go imagining things. He's a German, that's all."

Ila gasped.

"No, Ila, an *American*-German. He's fifty-three years old, and he's been here since long before the war. For God's sake, it's 1946, not 1941."

Ila whispered, "You didn't . . . you couldn't. My Rossie, your *son*, lost three fingers in that war, and you have the gall to give aid to the man whose kinfolk did it? You've finally stooped so low . . . I would have never imagined it . . ."

"Ila, will you stop carryin' on so?" shouted David.

"Well, Mr. Tolbert," Ila said icily, composing herself, straightening her back. "What's done is done. I'll have nothing to do with that heathen."

"That's fine with me, *Mrs.* Tolbert. I'd rather you keep your fat nose away from Mr. and Mrs. Spainhour. Keeley Spainhour's his name—"

"Is she German, too?" asked Ila.

"Well, I didn't rightly ask."

"You didn't ask?"

"No, didn't think it was any of my business."

"You didn't, did you? Well if she turns out to be a heifer or a nigger you'll be a-wishin' you'd of asked."

"Shhh . . . ," David said, his hand over her mouth. "You want Mayzelle should hear?"

Ila slapped his hand away. "Mayzelle's over at Momma's, thank you. 'Sides, she's not a nigger . . . she's part of the family."

"Uh-huh, sure she is."

Ila left the room.

Spainhour and his wife moved into the rental house. Ila peeked through her curtains from time to time trying to catch any activity around the house. There was none.

Judith collected the rent. She did not understand why her mother didn't do it. Ila had handled the family books ever since that Pearson woman left. But Judith had other, more pressing things on her mind. She had no time to worry about strange old Mr. Spainhour or her mother.

Arthur worked his way into Ila's confidence. He bought her a parakeet, and for this bribe he was allowed to escort Judith unchaperoned.

Ila looked up from her newspaper and stared at David. "He *is* handsome. But he's poor."

David smiled wryly. "At least you find something agreeable in the boy."

"Don't get me wrong," she said. "He seems like a real good boy. But we should find someone more suitable for our Judith, someone she can marry."

"I suppose we could go find a millionaire uptown."

"Why is it that every time I try to start a serious conversation with you, you turn it into something vile? I swear, I shouldn't ever talk to you." Her eyes were tight and she fought to keep her jaw from twisting in anger.

He eyed her briefly, then said, "I'm sorry. I shouldn't upset you. You've got enough on you."

"Yes." She paused. "I should say so. Judith and Deidre are gettin' wild on us. It's your fault, you know, always caving in to their every whim and wish. I'm just glad my father had the good sense to be firm and discipline us."

"I remember," said David, "when I knew a wild youngun myself. And she wasn't too godawful disciplined. Matter of fact, she ran off and got married without her father's consent. Yep, I remember that well."

Ila moved away from the table. "That was a long time ago, and times were different."

"What makes you think," David said slowly, "that your daughters are any different from you when you were their age?"

She took a deep breath. "I've got to get the clothes in, it might rain," she said.

Arthur had come back to Judith, just as he had promised. All those years of waiting, of going to that horrible, boring, dirty school, pretending that she was in prison and that he was going to rescue her; all the fantasy, all the nights of grief, all the letters torn up and the letters mailed; all had been worth the wait. He was back, and he didn't look like he had ever been away. He had filled out some. He looked a little wiser. His eyes were a little dimmed. But he was still handsome, and still able to work all day and carouse all night.

She had never seen a man so lithely built. He hunted and drank and laughed a great deal. Everything he does, she thought, he does to the limit. Yet he loved her with a gentleness that surprised her. She found excuses to visit the McDowells more often.

He took her to dances in the country and once in a while to some rough honky-tonks in Summerfield. She was afraid of these places at first, until she realized that he was treated with deference everywhere he went. He was accepted in every one of the bars, and the respect people had for him was liberally mixed with a fear of his fists.

His friends crowded around a booth and drank and gossiped and relived fights and feuds. Sometimes Will, after more than his share of drinks, talked about Arthur's prewar women friends; then Arthur would look at Will coldly, until the brothers' eyes met. As soon as Will quieted, Arthur reached over and gently pushed the hair out of his eyes.

Judith did not understand the way Arthur's friends greeted her. They seldom talked to her if Arthur was out of sight or hearing. They asked his permission, with their eyes, before speaking to her.

She was young and naive. She had not yet seen jealousy and the exercise of its power. Seeing it, she did not recognize it. She felt complimented by his attention and by his possessiveness.

He had one habit that she did not approve of but never mentioned. Sometimes, when visiting the Tolbert house, if he happened to see Spainhour in the backyard, or on the sidewalk, Arthur taunted him with shouts of "Hey, Kraut! You lost the war, right? Maybe you should go back to Germany! They need you there more than here."

Spainhour ignored him.

It was an ugly part of Arthur that Judith ignored. Arthur didn't like for people to disagree with him.

Judith was with Arthur, talking with Esther about her father's crop and the weather that would have to come within the next few weeks before any money could be made on the tobacco. Arthur had just poured himself another cup of coffee when Sossomon came into the room from the porch. He had been in town all day, getting parts for the tractor. At least that was what he was supposed to have been doing. It quickly became apparent that he had been doing more when he fell across a chair.

Judith stood quickly and reached for him, but Arthur stopped her. He glanced to Esther, who nodded and went to pull back the sheets on Sossomon's bed. The sheets smelled of mildew and were grey with sweat. Arthur lifted his father and carried him to the bedroom. Judith turned her head, thinking that Sossomon would not want her to see him with his mouth open and saliva dripping down his cheeks.

Arthur returned, smiling falsely, the dimples refusing to appear. "He . . . he gets like that once in a while ever since Momma died. We just put up with it. He doesn't do anybody any harm. Let him sleep it off and he'll be fine. I'm . . . uh, real sorry that . . ."

"No," said Judith. "Don't worry about it. It's all right. Really it is. Ash and Rossie get like that once in a while."

Esther came into the room. "Arthur?" she said.

He looked at her. There was something in her eyes, a question that she didn't know how to form.

"What's wrong?" he said.

"I don't know. But he's quieter than usual. You know . . . ." She looked at Judith. Judith knew then that something was not being said, probably because of her presence.

Arthur laid his hand on the back of his sister's neck.

"I know," he said. "But don't worry. All he needs is to sleep it off."

Esther sat down at the table. "Judith, I guess you should know. Papa throws things around when he gets like this. Sometimes he hurts himself real bad. I guess . . . I've known him to just pass out like that, and his face . . . Arthur, it was so cold."

Arthur tossed his head back. "Woman, listen, people pass out all the time. No need to get in a bother about it. But if it will make you feel any better, I'll stay up with him tonight."

Esther sighed. "Judith," she said. "You can spend the night in my room." She looked at Arthur gratefully. There was no need to thank him. She had known from the beginning that he would stay with his father.

Sossomon McDowell died at three in the morning while Arthur slept in a wicker chair next to his bed. The doctor said that it was a brain hemorrhage. Sossomon had not had anything to drink. He was buried in a wooden box next to Anna in Oak Hill Cemetery in Greensboro. Only those who dug the grave noticed that thin, fibrous roots from a blackened maple had encased the coffin of Anna and would eventually cradle that of Sossomon. No headstones were set.

Once, in the fall, Arthur did not show up on Saturday, as he usually did, to take Judith riding in his car. Deidre and some friends from church, young men with clean faces and strong voices, had decided to go to the battleground. Since Arthur was apparently not coming, Judith was invited along.

She saw Arthur as they drove under the shade trees and beneath the burnished maples of Oak Hill Cemetery. His head was bare and he was standing over Anna's grave. He saw her as the car passed. She wanted to tell the driver to stop but thought better of it.

Arthur came to the door that night and asked her to go with him for a cup of coffee. She walked with him, talking excitedly about the warm beauty of the day and wondering why he had not stopped by to see her as he usually did.

He was strangely quiet. The boyish mirth was gone, replaced by a sallow complexion and a haughty air. They entered the restaurant and he ordered two coffees.

"Arthur, why didn't you come see me today?"

"Who were they?" he asked. His voice, she felt, demanded rather than asked.

"Who were who?"

"You know, in the car." He looked across the room, as if he expected to see someone he knew, as if he didn't care whether she answered or not.

"They were my friends," she said impatiently. "Nothing more."

"Those boys," he said softly, "didn't look like just friends."

She was confused, not hurt, by his tone. "Arthur, what are you trying to say, that they were boyfriends or something?"

"You said it. I didn't."

"Don't you know how much I care for you?" she said.

His eyes darted from sugar bowl to napkin holder to salt shaker, but never to her face. He stirred his coffee, slowly, tightly, with controlled strength.

"Don't you?" she repeated.

"Singing," he said.

"What?"

Finally he looked at her. "Singing, and laughing and carrying on. I know their type. What did you do later on? Go for walks in the woods? Did they kiss you? Did they . . . feel you?"

"You're serious, aren't you? she said softly. "You really are serious. You *know* me . . . or at least I thought you did. I've not had many dates in my life, Arthur McDowell, and I've not done anything on any of them that I would be ashamed of. What you saw was a bunch of good church friends having a good time and if you don't believe it, then there's nothing else I can tell you."

"You've told me all you have to," he said. "I'll take you home."

She did not see him again for a month. She saw Will uptown once in a while, but he would not speak to her.

One Sunday morning as the Tolbert family moved to the front porch on their way to church, she saw Arthur rocking on the porch swing. The ever-present smile was fixed on his face, as if he had just seen her for the first time. He winked at her. She came to him. He ignored her family and told her to stay with him instead of going to church. He insisted. She stayed.

David Tolbert smiled at Arthur and waved as he pushed Ila down the path, telling her to mind her own business.

It was then that Arthur apologized for the way he had acted, and asked Judith to marry him. It all happened so fast she felt she was in a dream.

They decided to elope to Danville, Virginia, and keep the secret from Ila.

Arthur walked her to the door. "Aren't you getting tired of this?"

"Of what?" Judith said fearfully.

"Of living apart."

"But Momma would die if she knew."

"She's tough as nails. Besides, *she* eloped, didn't she?"

"And broke *her* mother's heart."

"Her mother don't look too broke to me."

Judith laughed. "Grandma Lora is tougher than all of us. She and Mayzelle have been the strength behind this family for years."

"We've got to tell them."

"Soon. Real soon. I promise." Judith tried to smile.

"No. Now. Tonight. What we're doin' ain't natural. We shouldn't have to sneak around. I want to spend my *nights* with you, not just the days. Besides, I've got to take a full-time job soon so I can get us a house."

"I'm afraid to tell Momma, Arthur."

"I'm not. She likes me."

"Not that much."

"Then when and how?"

"Wait a minute. There is somebody that can break it to her. Old Mayzelle. She still comes over to help out around the house. We can ask Mayzelle to break the news to Momma. Momma does everything Mayzelle says. Mayzelle's the only one who can order my momma around and get away with it."

"What if she won't do it?"

"Oh, she will. I know my Mayzelle. She helped raise me, you know."

"You can forget that, Miss Priss."

"But Mayzelle!"

"Don't holler at me. You'll wake up your sweet grandma. She needs her rest. I can't imagine you not havin' the courage to tell your momma! If you're grown enough to run off and get hitched like that, then you're grown enough to face up to your momma."

"But you know Momma . . ."

"Yes, and I know *her* momma. All mommas is the same. Your momma ran off with David Tolbert way back when, and I don't think my Lora ever got over it. She blamed Lon."

"Why did she blame Grandpa?"

"Oh, he was bein' pressed too far, and he beat Ila real bad—but that's none of your business. Your problem ain't then, it's *now*. You get your little self over to your momma and tell her right now!"

Lora walked into the room. Her eyes still flashed a tint of purple, and she was shaking her head. Mayzelle rushed to her. "Here now, you needn't be gettin' around like this without your cane."

Lora looked up at Mayzelle. "To hell with the cane. I ain't a cripple yet. 'Sides, what right you got tellin' me what I can and can't do? You're same age as me, ain't you?" Lora pinched Mayzelle's cheek. "But I love you anyway."

Mayzelle laughed. "Still a fiery woman. When you ever gonna calm down?"

Lora looked at Judith. "Now, ain't that a stupid question?"

Mayzelle helped Lora to the chair. "Now, what's this problem you got, Judith?" Lora demanded.

Mayzelle took quick note of the appearance of each woman: Lora, sitting without a hint of slouch, taut face showing her age, impish eyes; Judith, a cross between Ila's black-haired beauty and David's quiet intensity. Mayzelle caught a trace of connection between herself and old Lora and young Judith—a tenuous web of support and love among women who have survived.

Mayzelle spoke before Judith could say anything. "It's nothing."

Lora looked at Mayzelle and wrinkled her nose. "I may be old and a little weak, but I ain't addled. This child got married, just like my Ila did. I heard. And she's scared to tell her momma 'cause she thinks her momma's some kind of monster."

Judith protested. "No, Grandma, I don't—"

"Now, I know what I'm a-talkin' about. And I'm the one what's gonna tell you what to do. You get on over there and tell your momma what you done. If you don't, she'll feel like you don't love her enough to tell her. Believe me, I know what I'm a-talkin' about. It happened to me and opened a lot of questions. She might yell a little. But deep inside, later, after she's done cried out, she'll remember what love was all about. I think she forgets now and then; but no matter how hard you try, you can't bury that kind of love for long. It keeps creepin' up at the strangest times. You understand what I'm sayin' to you?"

"I think so."

"It don't matter, you just do what I tell you. You will not regret it. Your momma's been through hell, but she's been through heaven too, and she knows what both worlds is like."

Judith nodded out of courtesy, not understanding Lora at all.

Ila leaned on the window-frame. She was tired of washing windows. Winter would be here soon, and the steam from the kitchen would stain them again soon enough. She looked across the front yard, out beyond the walnut trees, watching the cars race west toward the winter pastures, layered across the hillside, divided into uneven plots by rows of cedars covered by dormant honeysuckle.

One thing she didn't miss about the country was the honeysuckle. The weed devoured everything—roses, cedars, azaleas. Its deadly tentacles slept in winter; its mission halted, brown, furry spiderlegs rooted deep in the soft underlayer of strong-scented wood. She missed country skies and bright sun against the blue promise of spring storms—rain, promises, and dreams, she thought, delayed or never kept. Winter on its way, but first a brief goodbye to fall. Time to look to the promise of spring dreams.

Judith and Arthur walked into the room cautiously, afraid to disturb the daydreams of the proud woman at the window.

Ila sensed them. She turned, blushing at having been seen unarmed, alone in her thoughts. She put her hands on her hips and lifted her head. "Y'all need somethin'?"

Judith sat down on the blue flowered sofa. "Momma, I think you better sit down."

Ila searched their faces for tragedy, impending bad news of some sort. She had come to expect the worst whenever a surprise seemed imminent. "Tell it straight," she said, satisfied that Arthur's serious face held no harm. Besides, even as a child, whenever Judith approached calamity she folded and unfolded her fingers, lashing them almost in a continuous unbroken rhythm. This time her hands lay still.

Judith blurted, "Momma, me and Arthur got married the other week. We know we should'a told you but we were afraid of how you might take it." There, it was done. She searched her mother's face for the sign of anger or sorrow that crossed like clouds over a still lake.

Ila looked to the ceiling. "Your Daddy ain't gonna be happy." Figured it, she thought. Could'a been worse news.

Arthur nodded. "I'll tell him, Mrs. Tolbert."

"I should think you would," Ila said, as she walked to the porch.

"Momma?" said Judith. Ila turned. "I'm sorry. I should'a told you. I didn't want to hurt you."

Ila smiled. "Well, at least *you* had the nerve to tell me face to face."

Ila walked to the kitchen and took the newspaper from David's hand. She grabbed his shoulder. "You might have to cough up that precious dowry sooner than you thought."

Fifteen

December 1947

"ARTHUR AND JUDITH need a house," Ila repeated slowly, as though making a point to a child. "We have one for rent and you refuse to evict Spainhour?"

"Wouldn't be businesslike," David said.

"Then I'll do it," Ila said. "I have to do everything around here anyway."

"I forbid it," said David, "and that's final."

Ila knocked on the door.

Mr. Spainhour opened it. When he recognized her, he invited her in.

"No, thanks," Ila said. "I just thought I'd be a-tellin' you that you and your missus has to go find some other place to live."

"Oh? I don't understand."

"Well, our daughter's married now and needs a place of her own. I figured you'd understand."

"But I don't," he said sternly. "We have paid a lot of money."

Ila lifted her head and gazed into the clear blue eyes. He really doesn't understand, she thought.

"You gotta go," Ila said. "I'm sorry, but my daughter comes first. I give you till after Christmas. You and Mrs. Spainhour will have plenty of time to find another home."

"She's gone," he said dryly.

"What?" Now Ila didn't understand. "Gone where?"

Spainhour shrugged. "Gone. Just gone. I don't know where. You see, we have been persecuted by people like you for a long time now. 'Mr. Tolbert,' I say to her, 'Mr. Tolbert, he is not like others.' But she say it is not him that she is talking about. It is all the others who stare and make jokes because of the war, who spit on people like me for something we had no part of. She is *American*. I can't blame her. Who could live with such shame? I ask you that. Who?"

"I'm sorry," Ila said softly, then raised her voice. "But I can't help any of that . . . I've got my own problems . . . you have to go."

Ila and Arthur went to court and got an eviction order. Spainhour would have to move within thirty days after Christmas.

Soon after the eviction order was served, the letters began to arrive. Ila was stunned by the obscenity of the letters: vicious suggestions of immorality and perversity; words like *incest* and *bitch*, and worse. She was not sure what to do with these letters. She could not show them to David for fear of his weak heart: *Your daughters are lower than whores*. And Mayzelle would only worry herself sick: *The nigger sucks the blood from your household*. No, showing the letters would do no good. Unsigned sickness could be infectious. Better to hide the letters behind the piano. Better to forget them.

Spainhour. Had to be him, Ila thought. No matter, I won't give him the satisfaction of knowing that I know. Besides, he'll be gone after Christmas. Don't want no police around here to spoil Christmas.

The scratching on the kitchen door finally pierced her thoughts. She put the letters away and walked quickly to the door. "Lady! Come on in, girl. Where you been?" The dog whined deeply, pawing the carpet and nuzzling Ila's leg. She knelt and rubbed the dog's ears, letting her fingers ride easily, massaging Lady's neck. The dog rolled on its back, closed its eyes, and feigned sleep.

Ila smiled. Arthur had given her the collie. At first she complained about another mouth to feed, but in time the animal had won the right to her affection. Lady was Ila's dog and everyone knew it. Lady would answer to no one else. No one was sure whether Ila owned the dog or the dog owned Ila.

Ila carried Mayzelle's bags to the car, carefully avoiding the melting slush from the sidewalk. Mayzelle followed, her heavy black shoes stomping bits of ice as she walked briskly.

"Mayzelle?" Ila shouted over her shoulder. "You be careful. I don't want Momma Lora to be a-hollerin' that I let you fall and break your neck."

"You don't worry about me, child. I'm goin' home to my *own* momma, broke neck or no. I ain't seen her in two years. Lord, that's a long time!"

Ila opened the car door and told David to crank up the engine. "It's freezin' out here. What you tryin' to do, save two cents worth of gas?"

David frowned and pressed the gas pedal. A cloud of dark gray smoke rolled from under the car. Ila helped Mayzelle into the back seat and handed her a basket. "Some chicken for the train ride. You got a long way to go."

Mayzelle took the basket and eased back. "I come a long way, you know. Ain't much trouble reversing the process."

David lighted a cigarette. "We're gonna miss you at the Christmas party. Everybody's gonna be there: Lon and Lora, all the kids."

"Yeah," said Ila with a sigh. "All the dirty dishes, dirty clothes, and dirty floors a-beggin' to be cleaned. And David, don't you tarry at the railroad station. We got to get that wood in tonight and scrub those floors in the mornin'. You hear me?"

He did not answer.

Mayzelle laughed. "Yeah, I'm real sorry I'm gonna miss all that work."

Ila turned toward the house, shouting over her shoulder, "Got a lot to do. You be careful, Mayzelle!"

Mayzelle nodded as the car roared down the driveway, spraying gravel and clumps of old snow into the air.

Ila turned on the porch and waved goodbye. Something inside made her feel like running after the car and telling Mayzelle to stay.

Ila felt afraid. Silly old fool, she thought. Just the chill in the air, that's all.

She remembered a line from the book Florence Kellam had given her years ago: *I am led captive from my house—come, sad daughters, brides of disaster. Come let us mourn the smoke of Ilion.*

She wanted to see the words, but couldn't remember exactly where she had placed the book.

Deidre had been married to Dan for only a few weeks. Arthur suggested that they accompany him and Judith to spend Christmas with some cousins in the foothills of Surry County. Judith did not look forward to the long ride in the snow and slush on the backroads. She didn't like the idea of spending Christmas away from Ila's. Arthur insisted. He said he would keep her warm in the back seat of the Jeep all the way to the Blue Ridge if necessary.

Arthur pushed the gearshift into first and pulled the Jeep into Ila's driveway. He got out and took a deep chestful of morning air, sensing the chill off the snow-covered lawn. He wouldn't have noticed the color in the ditch if he hadn't stopped on the porch to light a cigarette. He walked across the snow toward the ditch and then dropped his cigarette.

Old dog must have been hit by a car sometime during the night. Neck broke. Must have been knocked into the ditch. Can't tell Ila. Not on Christmas Eve.

He picked Lady up by the neck and took her behind the old stables near the railroad tracks. He would bury her later.

Judith pulled on her coat and kissed Ila on the cheek. "You sure you don't mind? Surry's a ways."

Ila said she did not mind. After catching up on some work at the office, Ash was planning to dress up like Santa Claus for his two children, Robert and Cathy. Maureen would help Ila with the cooking.

"I've worked like a dog for two days," Ila said to Maureen as she wiped her forehead that night. "If you hadn't agreed to share Christmas Eve over here, I don't know what I would have done."

"It's a pleasure, Mrs. Tolbert. Ash is really looking forward to surprising the children tonight."

"How late is he gonna be?"

"Don't know. He's got some last minute shopping to do. You know Ash: always in a hurry, never getting anything done."

Ila laughed. "Yes, he gets that natural from his father."

David looked up from the paper. "Puttin' us men down again?"

"No, Mr. Tolbert," Maureen said, as she handed him a piece of cake. "Just pointing out areas that need changing."

"You're sweet," David said, and he meant it. Maureen had short brunette hair that curled around the nape of her neck. Her eyes were expressive in a subtle way and gave the impression of self-assurance and a bright intellect. No one ever saw her argue in public.

David combed his hair before he settled back in the rocker. He was proud of his hair, never changing the part in the middle. His hair was as dark and thick as when he worked the fields during the Depression. Ila still combed it, just as Lora had always combed Lon's, when David left the house in the mornings.

Rossie reached across the table. "Let me have some of that coconut pie over there, Maureen."

Ila slapped his hand. "Don't point, Rossie. I've been telling you for years to leave that sugar alone. Look at you, bigger than a water tank now. I half expect you to want a sugar tit."

Even David laughed at that.

"Not funny," Rossie said, licking his fingers.

177

David stood. "Ila, that was the finest dinner I believe I've ever had."

Ila stopped working for a moment. "Glad you liked it, David. Too bad Momma and Daddy couldn't make it through all that snow."

David nodded. "Well, they gettin' up there in age, can't take no chance on slipping on the ice."

Rossie stood and put on his coat. "How is Mayzelle doin'? I ain't seen her in a long time." He put on his cap. Rossie had reenlisted in the army and was on leave.

"If she was in town you could go over and visit her. She would love to see you. She helped raise you boys and girls, you know."

Rossie walked to the back door. "Near as I can tell, she raised just about everyone in this family."

"Some truth to that," David yawned.

Ila put the cake on the table. "Aren't you staying to see Ash surprise the children with his you-know-what suit?"

"No, I got to get over to my own family. Summerfield's a good ways in this mush."

"Tell 'em we said hello and Merry Christmas."

David could hear Rossie's car warming up. "Needs an oil change," he said casually.

Ila stacked the dishes. "Maureen, I'm going in the back room to iron the Santa suit while the children are sleeping. When I get done we'll make some eggnog."

David rested his head on the back of the rocking chair. "Shouldn't Ash be here by now?"

At that moment, Ash was cutting across the rental house property, trying not to slip on the snow. He was still handsome, with a neighborhood reputation as a charming young man. He was the most articulate of the Tolberts, even winning arguments with Ila using a convoluted logic that left her spellbound.

As he approached the back door of the Tolbert house, he heard a shout: "Ash. Ash Tolbert!"

It was Spainhour calling from the rented house.

What's he want this time of night? Ash wondered.

"Come here, Tolbert. I got a message for you."

Ash walked to Spainhour's front porch. He felt the snow melting over the edge of his boots.

"I got to hurry, Mr. Spainhour. What you want?"

Spainhour pointed a pistol at Ash's face.

"You."

"Ila? Ila!"

She went into the kitchen. "Yes, David. Don't shout, you'll wake up the babies."

"I'm going to take a nap now in the chair. Be sure and wake me when Ash gets home."

"I will. And I'm sure the children will, too. Maureen, you think we ought to wake them now?"

"No," Maureen said, "not yet. Let them sleep a little longer."

"All right. You're gonna love the Santa suit. I got to iron one more part and it'll be done." Ila walked to the bedroom and shut the door.

Maureen sat at the table with her coffee and her spice cake, watching David nap. She liked David. He had dreams. Judith had said that he was saving his money to buy a chicken farm someday. Maureen couldn't imagine Ila working on a chicken farm.

"I won't harm you, Ash, if you just tie yourself to the chair," Spainhour said. "That's all you have to do and you'll be safe. Now, very quietly, come into the house. That's right, very slowly."

At that moment, Ash decided that giving in to Spainhour was a suicidal act. He reached for the gun and wrestled Spainhour to the floor.

Spainhour picked up a brick and began to hit Ash across the forehead. Ash kicked him, scrambled on top, and rushed to the back of the house. Spainhour picked up the pistol and grabbed a shotgun, running out the front, shouting, "I'll kill them all!"

Ash ran out the back and up the street to a small neighborhood store. He had to find a gun.

Spainhour ran to the bushes beside the Tolbert kitchen window.

Ila heard four thunderous noises from the kitchen.

She unplugged the iron and ran towards the explosive sounds. She heard the children crying in the next room. She thought her heart stopped.

She was not prepared for the acrid smell of gunpowder that choked her, or the blue mist that teared her eyes. She felt faint. For one moment her mind seemed blank and all she could think of was a line from the play she had read many times over: *One daughter, even now, was killed in secrecy and pain beside Achilles' tomb.* Maureen lay on the floor, her feet toward the stove, a smoking furrow of flesh across her back.

David leaned on the table as if he were asleep. Blood was spurting from his neck onto the tablecloth.

Ash's children, three-year-old Robert and two-year-old Cathy, came into the room crying.

Got to get help, Ila thought, as she raced to the front door. There was no phone. She would flag down a car and get help.

She opened the front door and there he was.

Spainhour.

"You bastard," she screamed, slamming the door and pushing in the lock bolt.

Two blasts from the shotgun caught her in the wrist and pelvis.

She fell to the floor and Spainhour jumped off the porch, running toward the downtown area.

Ash broke down the back door and saw it all.

Ila could not move. She could only weep, her mind numbed, as she thought of the words of another: *O hear me, it is your mother who calls. I lean my old body against the earth and both hands beat the ground. My husband is dead, graveless, and forlorn. You know not what they have done to me.*

The snow began to cover everything.

In the confusion with the police and ambulance, Robert and Cathy ran into the cold. A neighbor heard Ila say, "My babies, my babies," and with a length of rope, the police tied the children to the house until more help could come.

Sixteen

Nedar, South Carolina, December 26, 1947

THE SNOW TURNED to sleet, frosting the trees in front of the solid cabin, bending the naked yellow-bell branches to the ground, icing the pond. Mayzelle had been trying for at least half an hour to start the kindling in her mother's fireplace. The flames caught quickly around the wood, caressing and fierce, then smoldered in a dark cloud that crept along the ceiling.

The older woman walked over to Mayzelle and handed her a small can. "What's this?" asked Mayzelle.

"Kerosene, Baby. You puts it on and the work'll be easier."

Mayzelle smelled the fluid. "Yep, kerosene. You know, Momma, it's a wonder you didn't blow up yourself years ago."

Mayzelle's mother smiled. "At least I keep myself warm."

Mayzelle chuckled. "You a good woman. Tough lady like you, livin' here by yourself."

"I love it. I got rid of six children, and I deserve a rest till the Lord comes."

"Don't you ever get lonely, Momma?"

The old woman pulled the rocker up to the fire.

"Don't get too close now. I'm only gonna use a little of this stuff." Mayzelle sprinkled the fuel over the coals, and a terrific smell filled the air. She threw in a match and pulled back as the flames rose toward the chimney. "There, that oughta do it."

The old lady smiled. "I sees Elvin and his boys now and again. And I goes to church right regular. Not missed a Sunday in, what? Oh, six, seven years, and then only 'cause Nancy was sick up the road. No, don't worry 'bout your ol' momma. I get along the best I can. It's you I worry about. Not bein' around your own kind."

Mayzelle straightened her dress and stretched out on the couch. "Momma," she said with a sigh, "we been through this forty years back. It's not like I'm a freak amongst them or nothin'. In a way, I *am* with my own kind. They need me. You should hear about the messes those folks been in, you wouldn't believe. Ila runnin' away and gettin' married, Vera gettin' the grand mal, Ila drinkin' on the sly. It's amazin'."

"Sounds like the devil's work to me."

"Maybe. Maybe not. One thing for sure, they got it tough, and still they keep on fightin' and hopin' for somethin' better."

"We been through the same trials, child. Your daddy died when you were six. That weren't easy. People made do with what they had around here. You gotta be tough to survive, don't you know?"

"Oh, I know. You forget I worked in them fields like everybody else from the time I was eleven. I remember the smells even now."

"And you think you got it any easier now?"

Mayzelle rubbed her nose and sat up. "No. Not really. But me and Lora, we almost like kin."

"Child, what you talkin'? Ain't no white woman gonna claim you as a sister!"

Mayzelle narrowed her eyes. "It happened, Momma. I can't explain it, but I got me a family—a family what cares."

"You they maid."

"Sure, I work for my bread, same as everybody, but I'm free to come and go as I please. I almost got engaged during the war. Man's name Supine. Supine Rodney his name was. Big man, kind man. First man I ever liked since Reuben."

"What happen?"

"I don't rightly know. Don't rightly remember."

"He probably wasn't sure what color you was."

"Ain't funny, Momma. I know what color I am, but when I look into their eyes, there ain't no color."

"I raised a strange one."

"You raised me like you. I'm you all over, Momma, and you know it. Even gettin' grayin' like yours. See?"

"Sure enough. I don't like it, though. I worry 'bout you so. You ought to be home, settlin' down. It ain't too late. You got your looks and you got your strength. Ten years from now you won't have nothing, and you know it."

"Maybe next year. Maybe next year I'll come home. Lora ought to be gettin' her strength back next year—bronchitis, you know—and Ila, she's tough as nails. She don't need me no more."

The fire had died down when the knock came at the door.

The old lady opened it. A white boy standing out in the wet was cursing under his breath.

"What you want?" said the old woman, a touch of guarded curiosity in her voice.

"Damn it, come all this way, gettin' wet as milk and for what? Damn it, niggers gettin' telegrams, who ever heard of it? Here . . . ." He threw the envelope to the porch and ran back to the car, slamming the door and skidding off onto the muddy highway.

Mayzelle came to the door. "What's the ruckus?"

"Look." Her mother pointed.

Mayzelle picked up the envelope and read the telegram.

"Oh, dear God."

"What is it, child?"

The sound of tree limbs cracking under the ice smothered her answer.

A mass of lights switched on at once, waking the few birds slumbering in the snow-covered branches outside. The fifth floor of the hospital prepared itself for a stretcher with Ila strapped on it. She was pushed down the hall past a Christmas tree and decorations hanging from the ceiling.

No matter how much a hospital staff is acquainted with emergency, there is always something shocking about Christmas Eve pain. Nurses reminded themselves of how lucky they were, their children safe at home.

"But on Christmas Eve?" one of them said. "Is nothing holy anymore?"

"Nothing is predictable," the doctor muttered as he slipped on the surgical gloves.

Ila was not conscious, but her thoughts were paced like lightning in total darkness: *I mourned their father. None told me the tales of his death. I saw it, with these eyes.*

Across town, at another hospital, Spainhour's face was covered. He had shot himself at a fire station near Ila's home.

At the hospital, the doctors allowed the family to stay in one of the waiting rooms. Rossie took a seat by Lora. "Did you send it?" Lora said.

"Yes. This mornin', soon as things got calmed down." Rossie wondered who needed Mayzelle more, Lora or Ila.

Lora shook Lon awake in his chair. "Get up, Mayzelle's comin'. I sent for her."

Lon rubbed his eyes. He had hoped that the nightmare would be over when he woke. He looked around the waiting room: Arthur with Judith's head on his lap, Cathy and Robert asleep on a cot in the corner, Deidre drinking coffee at the window, Ash's arm around her shoulder. And Lora looking straight ahead, a Bible on her lap, those black eyes as bright and undulled by pain as the day Lon married her.

A doctor came into the room and looked around. Everyone stood. The doctor was about the same age as Ila, maybe a little older. He looked nervous. He was searching for a leader in the group, a person of authority to whom he could talk while the others listened.

Lora stood. "My Ila?"

"She's still critical," he said crisply. "We operated all night. She was badly wounded." He wondered why he had said that. Everyone in the room had seen her and they knew. "We're trying to save her legs now. She could wake any time, but we're not really sure when."

Deidre spoke through the tears. "Papa? How about Papa?"

The doctor frowned. Didn't she know, hadn't anyone said?

Lora looked at Deidre and raised her voice for the first time since she was awakened at her home with the news. "David's dead, Honey. You know that. He's dead, and askin' the same question over and over and pretending he ain't won't do nobody no good. You got to straighten up, girl, cause we ain't lettin' no one here drift off. We need everybody."

Lora looked at the doctor, her face stern but confident. "Do you know what you're a-doin'?"

"Yes ma'am, I think I do . . . no, I know I do. We're doing everything possible to save your daughter's life. We're lucky she's made it this far."

"What do you mean," said Rossie softly, "this far?"

"The shock alone should have killed her. She's living because she has something to live for. She's fighting—even though she's unconscious, she's fighting. I suspect she's holding on for you people. You obviously need her, and she needs you."

Rossie studied the man for a moment. "Doctor, ain't I seen you somewhere before? I feel like I know you."

Ash nodded and bit his fingernail. "Yeah, me too. It's like I know you from . . . from where? I don't know. It's strange."

"It's God's will," said Lora. "We trust you, Doctor, to save my little child. She's my eldest, you know, and she's got four children, and grandchildren too. Course, they think they's grown up, but I know different and I think you do too. Save her for the children, Doctor. We'll be a-prayin' for you."

"Pray for her," Doctor Michael Fletcher said somberly.

Lora pushed the soup away. "Hospital food. No wonder everybody in here is sick. You don't see these doctors eatin' this stuff, do you, Lon? Look at 'em, a-smilin' and a-drinkin' their coffee. Laughin'. This is just a game to them, a hobby. . . ."

Lon was tired. The last thing he needed was to listen to Lora complain. "Now, Lora, don't go gettin' upset. A doctor can't live in blood twenty-four hours a day . . . you can look at me with that squirreled-up face all you want to. I just don't want to hear your mouth. We got too much to do today to complain. We got to think of David and Maureen."

Ash put down his juice. "It ain't right. Momma don't even know they're gone. And Spainhour died before I could even get my hands on the bastard. It ain't right."

"Right got nothin' to do with it," Lon said. He picked up his coffee. "Undertaker was supposed to meet us here fifteen minutes ago. Got to make the arrangements.

"Might as well arrange for three," Ash said.

Lora held her chest. "What's that you say?" she said shrilly. Lon reached for her hand. "Don't you ever talk like that, boy!"

"I'm her son. I can talk any way I want to. Momma's gonna die, just like Daddy. Everybody in this stinkin' hospital knows that except you. Might as well get three coffins instead of—"

Lon stood up, his stature commanding respect. His eyes were cold and his voice shaking. "You can leave the table now, young man. Your faith is mighty shaky."

Ash stood. "I'm leavin'," he said spitefully. "But you'll see. All of you will see. You bunch of blind old hicks ain't got sense enough to smell death when it's all around you, but I do! I see it comin'. My wife . . . my wife . . . ."

Lora reached for his arm and pulled him back to his seat. She was surprised that she had that much strength left in her arm as Ash leaned on her shoulder.

The undertaker arrived at their table. With his head cocked sympathetically to one side, he said, "May I be of assistance to you?"

Lora whispered, "Just get the hell out of here for right now."

Where is Mayzelle, she thought. Where?

Ila's eyes opened briefly. The glare hurt.

"Ila? came the soft voice, a woman's voice. "Ila? It's me, Honey. Open up them eyes for me."

Someone turned off the light and Ila lifted her eyes again, trying not to think or care about the quick jabs of pain in her hips.

Who is this? thought Ila, *and where am I? Where is David?* She opened her mouth but no words formed, just spit and slurs, syllables that had no meaning.

"Now, Ila, don't strain, Honey." Pearl reached for her hand. "We're here, we're all here. Judith and Arthur is outside in the hall and so is Lora and Lon."

Pearl. Pearl here? Couldn't be. Pearl is in South Carolina with her husband. What's she doin' here? David. Where's David?

"You know me, don't you, Ila? Nod your head if you know your own lovin' sister," Pearl pleaded.

Ila's chin went down briefly.

"Oh, thank God," said Pearl, weeping. "Ash!" she shouted. "Ash, you come here and talk to your momma."

Ila tried to speak, but the words wouldn't come.

Oh, dear Ash. Poor sweet Ash. Maureen's dead, isn't she? And so is David. I know that. But the babies, my sweet grandchildren, where are they? Are they dead too? Has our world ended? If it has, then let me die here and now.

"Momma," said Ash as loudly as he dared. "It's me, Momma, Ash. We need you bad, Momma. You got to fight this thing for all of us. *I* need you, Momma. I'm alone now. All alone . . . ."

Oh God. The children—Robert and Cathy—they're dead?

"And Robert and Cathy, they need you now, Momma. Their mother is gone now, and they need you worse'n any of us. . . ."

Thank God they're safe.

Doctor Fletcher tugged on Ash's shoulder and motioned him out. "She needs her rest. You've already taken up too much time. You're worrying her when she doesn't need any more worries."

Ash nodded. "You'll be better, Momma. I just know you will."

Pearl leaned over one last time. "We'll be all right, Honey. Old Pearl will take care of everything until you get better. You been asleep for four days, and we know the good Lord's gonna watch over you. We just know it."

And David? Please, somebody tell me about David. If the children are alive then maybe . . . . "Oh." She grasped her sides. The pain shooting from her legs was quick, the pressure unbearable.

"Let's go," said the doctor. "We'll give her another shot."

That voice. Is it David's voice? It sounds so much like David. It's not Rossie and not Arthur. Those hands on my brow are so cold and clean, and his face through the night is so bright. She held her breath and tried to look away. She could not.

"Mayzelle?" she said clearly before dropping into empty dreams.

Seventeen

Nedar, South Carolina, December 30

MAYZELLE'S MOTHER carefully stirred the steaming coffee. "Here, Mayzelle, I just made it fresh. I put in lots of cream, way you always liked it."

Mayzelle walked from the sink to the table and lifted the cup.

"You should go," said the old woman.

"I can't."

"If it's 'cause of me, you can forget it. I can take care of myself. I get along. You should go."

"It's not that easy. I can't go 'cause it's me what causes all their pain."

The old woman rubbed her knuckles. "What you talkin' about? You ain't done nothing but help those folks. What I said before about you bein' their maid, that was just momma talk. I seen the love in your eyes for 'em, and I see the grief all over your face now. Wouldn't be Christian for you to stay away. I don't understand you. First you can't wait to get back to them 'cause you thinks they's your family, and now you just sit here for days a-mopin', sayin' you can't go back. You faced trials before, and you can face 'em again."

"Momma, I been thinkin, ever since I got that telegram. I've done a lot of bad things in my life."

"Baby, now ain't the time to—"

"No, listen to me. I done a terrible thing many, many years ago, and it seems to me that their problems didn't start till then. Maybe I'm the cause of their pain 'cause of what I did."

"Whatever you did, it didn't bring no grief to that family."

"I killed a man, Momma."

The old woman nodded her head. "Why?"

"You don't look too surprised."

"You got to do what you got to do. I figure if you took someone's life then it must'a been to save your own."

"No, not my life. I guess it was to save my dignity."

"Lots of men been killed for less cause."

"I've felt terrible sick about it all these years, waking up in cold sweats, nightmares breakin' my sleep. Sometimes I'd get real happy 'bout somethin', like when Ila and David finally come home from the country during the Depression, and as soon as I felt good, Jeffries' blood seeped into my thoughts. My guilt wouldn't let me alone. That family ain't cursed, I am. I brought the curse with me and it spread out to them."

"Now, Honey, you gettin' all worked up—"

"Momma, let me get it out. Don't you see? Lon and Lora's child, Ila, has always been my responsibility, and my life. I raised that girl more'n her own momma. And God's punishin' me by hurtin' her."

"God don't work that way."

"How you know, Momma? How you know how God works?"

"How do you?"

"It's clear to me now. If I go back there, even if Ila is hurtin', then God will break her right in front of my eyes; and Momma, I can't take that. I can take anything but that."

"What you sayin' is that your guilt is keepin' you away?"

"Partly."

"Partly, my Jesus."

"I can't go, Momma. I can't kill off my Ila."

"So, she may be dyin', a-sufferin', a-needin' you, and you turn your face away, right? You set their house on fire with your guilt, and then watch it burn?"

Ila submitted to three operations. She was not allowed to move, not even roll over. She was drained like an animal, with tubes and catheters. Her face had no color, but at least she could speak.

"Doctor Fletcher, I'm gonna die, ain't I?"

Fletcher handed her a cup of water, maneuvered the straw into her mouth, watched her sip until she choked, then pulled it out.

"Ain't I?" she repeated.

"Not if I have anything to do with it. I've got a special interest in you, remember?"

"That was a long time ago, longer'n I care to remember."

Fletcher studied his charts. "I'm an old bull now, older than I care to admit, but you were the most beautiful, the most fiery woman in the county."

Ila's face was stern. "You should answer my question."

"You aren't improving as fast as we had hoped. Your white count is still way too high. But we're working on it. Soon you might be allowed to go home."

"What?" Ila rasped. "What do I go home to?"

"Love. Lots of it from what I've been hearing."

Can't pay the bills with love, Ila thought. Can't eat love, and now without David, I can't even find where I lost love. "I'm gonna die. Ever since that second operation I been gettin' weaker and weaker. Been seein' things real clear, been resting too much, listening too much, and I been gettin' a no-caring feelin'. Granny Avery used to say that's how old folks get when it's their turn to die."

"Who?"

"Nothin', you wouldn't remember her, just mumbling to myself."

Fletcher smiled and walked out.

Lora approached him in the hall. "How's she doin'?"

"Don't you ever sleep, Mrs. Mitchell? When's the last time you went home?"

"None of your business. I want to know how my daughter is."

"I'm not sure. I think her spirit might be breaking. After that, who knows? She doesn't want sympathy. I'm not sure what it is she needs right now, but I do know that all the pills and injections and operations in the world can't give it to her. She doesn't talk to me much. I'm thinking about turning this case over to someone else. She's hostile toward me for some reason. Maybe I'm too involved to be objective."

"You stay on your job, young man, and I'll stay on mine."

Lora started to the hospital room door.

"No, you're not, Mrs. Mitchell. She needs her sleep."

"I'm a-goin' in, Doctor."

"No, you're not."

A voice from down the hall boomed across the ward. "Doctor, you get your hands off'n that old lady!"

Lora gasped. "Mayzelle. Mayzelle!"

"Come here, old woman," Mayzelle said.

"Who you callin' old? You and me's the same age. Listen, no time here for small talk, you get right on in there and take care of my Ila. She'll listen to you. You wake her up, shake her, anything you have to do except pray over her. She's had enough of that for one lifetime."

Mayzelle pushed Doctor Fletcher out of the way and walked into the darkened room.

Mayzelle felt along the wall for a light switch and, finding none, walked to the window and pulled the shades up. A cold stream of blue light filled the room. Ila lay still, her eyes looking eerily upward for a moment, then squinting at the frail shadow in front of the window.

"Momma? That you?" whispered Ila.

"No, child, but I might as well be."

Ila tried to sit up, but the wounds in her legs prevented any sudden movement. Still, despite the pain, with arms searching the air, she waited for the familiar childhood touch of Mayzelle's firm hands.

"Mayzelle," she gasped. "You've come. They said you wouldn't come and for a while I didn't believe them, and then I just gave up. I need you here. Promise you won't let me die!"

"Die? said Mayzelle sharply. "Die? Here? What you talkin' about, woman? Here, let me get a chair. I must'a been gone too long. I've seen mules worse'n off than you and they pulled through. What makes you think you won't? Huh? Talk louder girl, I can't hear you."

"I was hurt real bad," Ila explained, feeling unsure of herself, almost ashamed of her condition.

"You was hurt, Honey. There's no doubt about that, but you was the lucky one. Mr. Tolbert and young Maureen, they dead. They no longer here to listen to the joy in their children's voices or the light in their earth and sky."

"Don't talk about that, Mayzelle. I'm not ready—"

"When you think you'll be ready? Now's good a time as any to face up to the fight you got ahead. I know you better'n your own momma. I seen you like this before. Ever' time somethin' bad happens, you go hide and try to ignore it. Trouble swimmin' all 'round and you jes' act like it's your burden and nobody else is a-painin' but you. You can't keep that up, and there's nowhere to hide and nowhere to run 'ceptin' the grave, and as long as God gives me the strength, I'm gonna drag you away from there!"

Mayzelle found the light switch above the bed and turned it on. Ila winced and turned her head. She was done with tears. She had cried enough for a lifetime.

Mayzelle worried. In the sharp light Ila appeared pale and more emaciated than she had expected. Her graying hair was wet from sweat, her lips dry and deep brown in color, her glassy eyes almost sunken in their sockets.

Ila asked for some water. "They buried David," she said softly after she had sipped.

"Yes, Ila, I know they did."

"Buried him near his own daddy up near Mortimer. Judith arranged the funeral, with Arthur, Deidre, Dan, and Ash. They picked out coffins for David and Maureen."

"David was a proud man. They didn't bury him in no cheap casket, did they?"

"No, Mayzelle, they didn't."

"Was it a proper funeral?"

"They gave David a fine burial. Course, most of the family couldn't attend, what with me here and all."

"And Maureen?"

"Her folks buried her in the graveyard at Buchanan Baptist." Ila cleared her throat. "It was my fault, you know."

Mayzelle leaned back in the chair, shifting her weight uncomfortably. There was something peculiar about what Ila had just said.

"What was your fault?"

"Mayzelle, come here. I'm gettin' tired and I can't talk too much longer. I feel the sleep comin' on. Easy. My legs feels every shakin'. Even the weight of these sheets hurts terrible. You listen to me. I know it was my fault. Don't say nothin'. Let me get it outa my gut. I didn't love . . . David . . . like I should'a."

Mayzelle frowned. "But he was workin' hard, Ila, to keep you and your babies."

"That was part of it. He came home sweatin' of the field. I smelled the dirt on him and never got used to it. He reminded me of Bradley."

"Who?"

"Old man Tom Bradley. I . . . Well, Bradley tried to make me have him the night Momma's boy died. Don't look so shocked. I was a pretty thing then. You helped me to see that, remember? Course, I didn't know it then, but that was also the day that his boy Vance was killed. Bradley couldn't do nothin' but root over my skin like some—"

"I don't think I should—"

"Yes, you *should* listen. Bradley, he didn't do nothin' that night; but it didn't matter none, 'cause the smell of that old man stayed with me for years. You see, I always remembered that night and that smell whenever me and David was together. I couldn't love David like he wanted. I wanted to give myself to him, like Momma gave herself to Daddy, but I couldn't. I got all messed up. You know what? I even tried to have an affair. Oh yes, *me*—with a doctor, no less. But that didn't work out neither. Nothin' works out. Nothin'. I remember the look in his eyes, and I saw real pain there, empty eyes . . ."

"That ain't so. David loved you more than—"

"Mayzelle, *I was there.* I saw what women my age see but try not to see.

I saw a man I hardly knew. I lost him. I lost him as sure as if I killed him with my own hand. I shouldn't have let Spainhour stay in that house. I should'a called the police as soon as those letters started comin'. I should'a known, and what scares me is that I did know. When I saw David look at me, it should'a hit me."

"You got no reason to feel like that, Ila. Feelin' sorry ain't—"

"Sorry? I ain't feelin' sorry. I'm drained. I'm too empty to feel anythin' for myself but anger. I've already decided to make it up to him the only way I know how. I'm gonna buy the biggest tombstone I can get. My man ain't gonna lay under the ground alone and forgotten. It's gonna say, 'David Tolbert—Beloved Husband.'"

"Ila, Honey, you ain't got the money."

"Yes, I do. I do have the money."

"The only money David left was for the children—their share of the rented property."

"I know."

"Hold on, child!"

"I'm not a child."

"You can't spend money that ain't yours."

"It is mine. It was my husband's money."

"But he wanted the kids to have it! What do Arthur and Judith say about this?"

"Judith and Deidre think it's a good idea. They said whatever makes me happy. I didn't ask Arthur. He still blames himself for gettin' snowed in at Surry with Judith."

"All that makes no difference. The money was meant for the children."

"I've decided."

"You're makin' your children pay for your guilt. You're makin' them suffer 'cause of your mistakes. They need that money. You got no right to pass on your guilt like that."

"Why not?" Ila snapped.

"Ila, you talkin' crazy."

"That's 'cause life is crazy, and I'm not fightin' it any more."

"Ila, you aren't supposed to be alive. Even the doctors say that. You've lived for a purpose, Ila. You been spared for somethin' more important."

Ila closed her eyes.

The doctor opened the door and asked Mayzelle to leave. Mayzelle waved him out. "Ila, let me take a couple minutes to tell you a story about a field foreman named Jeffries, and how guilt almost kept me away from the ones I love."

Mayzelle massaged Ila's legs twice a day for two years. She traveled from Lon's to Ila's every day, making sure that Ila had the help she needed. Neighbors had been good. Some had come in and repainted the walls or repaired window panes. A battalion of doctors did their best, but Ila's legs would be paralyzed. For months she stayed in bed, defying the orders to use the wheelchair.

Mayzelle rubbed her hands in milky lotion. Her fingers were almost raw from massaging Ila's legs. Ila lay on her back on the bed and could feel the cool air from the half-open window next to her pillow.

"You want to try the chair now?" Mayzelle asked.

"No, not today."

"Ila, you got to get up sometime. You gonna get bedsores and then you can massage your own legs."

Ila rolled her eyes.

Mayzelle walked into the kitchen. Getting too old for this, she thought. Haven't got time to be sick myself, much less do all this work.

She leaned in the kitchen doorway and surveyed the scene: dishes and glasses, cups and pans, crowded together like a junkyard in the sink; food stuck to the oven top; windows steamed and dirty. Mayzelle rolled up her sleeves, wiped her hands on the apron, and walked over to the sink.

Must be two dozen dishes in there, she thought, and each one should have a name on it: Judith, Ash, Deidre, Dan, Arthur, and anyone else who wanders in from the street. Those folks are hungry all the time. She tapped her foot. Something's got to give, she thought.

"Ila!" she yelled.

Ila was reading a book. "What?" she said, alarmed.

"Ila," Mayzelle said, trying to sound sweet, "get in here, right now."

Ila stared at the ceiling. Now what's wrong? she thought. "Mayzelle, Dear, how am I supposed to get there, fly?"

"Use the chair," Mayzelle suggested quietly.

"Why? Why can't you come in here? I'm the one who's crippled," Ila moaned.

"Because the dishes are in here, Ila. This is the biggest junk pile I ever seen. How can you live in this mess? I know—you never get to see it. Your company comes in day in and day out, and Lord knows what they must think of you. Uh-huh, must think old Ila Mitchell Tolbert has done turned into a dirty, nasty old pig. Shame, too, 'cause they used to admire you so for your pride in cleanliness. But those days is gone."

Ila pulled herself up by the bar over the bed. "I ain't no pig, Mayzelle. What you talking about?"

"Well, even if I was crippled I wouldn't let no church visitation committee see the curdled milk in the bottom of this glass." She walked into the bedroom and held the glass under Ila's nose.

"What church committee?" Ila said as she pushed the glass away.

"The one comin' by tonight. Shame they going to see this mess. Too bad, I would of cleaned it up for you, too, but I got to be gettin' back to Lora. She needs my help, you know."

"But you can't leave like this!"

Mayzelle pushed the wheelchair to the side of the bed, threw the apron on it, and slammed the front door on the way out.

Ila was shocked. "How you like that," she said. She looked at the glass on the dresser and imagined that she could smell it from the bed. She looked at the chair: wicker, wire wheels, wooden armrests, even hand brakes.

After pulling herself into the chair she rolled into the kitchen by pulling on the tops of the wheels. She went straight to the sink and gasped.

She filled the basin with warm water and soap.

When Mayzelle, rocking on the front porch, heard Ila singing "Footsteps of Jesus," she knew her Ila would be all right.

Eighteen

THE BLACK EARTH was like a sponge; caverns filled with fetus. Life, unchained and angry, constant with energy, rushed to the surface, devouring death along the way, consuming weaker forms left stillborn in bloody tombs. Regeneration, reproduction, all else is unimportant, all else is sterile vanity. To survive is all. The cruelty of the process is a guarantee of existence.

The pines behind the house had stood watch through winter, they and the resilient cedars battered by ice and snow, limbs gnashed by dark storms, green withstanding all.

The wild grass came first, spreading across every field like shiny silk, absorbing the warm breeze from the noisy forests nearby. Then crab apple blossoms, pink and fragrant; lilac, plum, and white dogwood; sweet, heavy-misted scents, pollen swirling across the sky, even into the city itself.

Birch and willow and elm, sensing resurrection, covered winter's carcass. The world became bright and pleasing to the senses. Renewal came with subtle shades of wisteria suspended in air, pictures everywhere painted fresh against the sky like butterflies frozen in time.

April, 1949, and Judith had still not told Arthur. He had, she felt, too much on his mind as it was. He worked second shift at the mill as a cardgrinder, not an easy job. He kept the short bristle-like teeth on the grinder sharpened. Raw cotton passed through the grinder points and was straightened into fiber. He worked the tiny points to a certain specification, not too sharp and not too dull. If he did not do this correctly, then the cotton wadded up and slowed down the rest of the mill processes. The cotton then flowed to a draw frame, and when one string was as thick as a man's thumb, it combined with five or six others into what was called saliva. The saliva was fed into the back of the frame, where it was blended and stretched by rollers. Then the cotton, not quite as thick as a small finger, was twisted even more in the spinning room and finally sent to the looms. Arthur did not enjoy the work, but he did not care to return to farming.

Judith was grateful to Lon, who had fixed the job up for Arthur. Lon was getting older and his sight was failing, but among the mill management he was still respected because he did his job with the fresh incentive of a seventeen-year-old and made a good example for the other, younger workers. A loyal, hard worker, Lon. Loyal and productive. A good company man, they said.

Arthur and Judith lived across the Greenboro city line in a community of tobacco farms and one-room churches called McLeansville. Clusters of mill families bought wooded lots between the farms to build frame houses of pine and oak.

Arthur had built a house with a covered front porch of wood, three bedrooms, a living room, and a large kitchen, all balanced perfectly on cinder blocks painted white. The outside walls were also painted white, and the trim was blue. Arthur hoped to add a picket fence later.

Arthur opened the door and found the kitchen lit by candles in the windows, on the table, and on the cabinet. He pulled off his coat as Judith entered from the other room. Her hair was combed back, and she wore a blue dress that he had not seen before. She smiled and handed him a small box. He opened it. The glint of gold made him wince. He had never owned a ring. He put it down on the table and sat down.

"Arthur, I've fixed you a real nice dinner because I've got some good news for you." She walked to his side and moved his arms so that she could sit on his lap. His arms fell limp to his side. She kissed him, long and wet. She opened her eyes. He was looking down at the table. She had seen that look before, but she could not remember where.

"Arthur, what's wrong?"

"I was thinking about your daddy."

"What were you thinking, Honey?"

"About how really stupid he was."

"What? You know how much my daddy liked you, and I thought you liked him."

"I did, but he was so stupid. Man invested in land all over the county. Penny-pinched so you couldn't have a decent dress or a telephone or nothin'. Saving for his old age, he said. Well, look what it got him. Nothing. He's dead and they sold the land."

She moved away from him and turned on the lights. "Arthur, my daddy worked hard, and it's true that he didn't let his right hand know what his left hand was doin', but that don't give you no call to talk that way about him. It wasn't you and it was no concern of yours. I never heard you talk like this before. Why on earth do you bring it up, anyway?"

"He was always planning for the future. Even when he was living in the future, he kept right on planning. He told me once that he wanted to buy a chicken farm in his old age. Hell, he was in his old age when he told me that!"

"I don't get it, Arthur. You worried about us or somethin'? Honey, we don't have much of nothin', but with time we'll get along fine."

"Your cousins. They live like kings. Always going to the beach or to the mountains, always having a good time. And he wasted you. You didn't do nothing, 'cause he was too cheap to let you do anything."

"I don't resent my daddy for the way he was, Arthur. He required little in life and he felt that we should have little, too. I know I ain't never been nowhere, but now all that's going to change. You've been around the world, traveling and seeing things and doing things. I want part of that life with you. I want to go with you, do things with you, maybe go across the world camping or just visiting. I want us to do those things that I never got to do. And I know you want to do those things, too. Don't you?"

Arthur stood and brought the ham to the table.

"Don't you, Arthur?" She had not meant to sound like she was begging. "Arthur, don't you?" she whispered.

He pushed his fork into the ham and sliced off a piece. "I don't know. I'm not sure."

She pulled her chair next to his. "I love you, Arthur."

"If I hadn't wanted to evict Spainhour, he wouldn't of killed your daddy. I know you blame me for that."

"Arthur, that's not true at all. Spainhour had somethin' wrong with him. Nobody could'a known that was going to happen, especially not you."

He stopped eating and looked to the window. "I saw a one-armed man today at the store before I got in. He was telling some fellows that he used to date you." He said it matter-of-factly, as though reading it from the newspaper.

Judith was stunned and confused. "What? Why, I don't . . . you don't . . . what are you talking about, for God's sake?"

"The man, he said—"

"I don't give a damn what anybody said, I never dated any one-armed man or many other men besides you, and you know it!"

"He was talking. Just talking." He reached for the gravy and she grabbed his arm. He looked at her coldly.

"Arthur, we got to get something straight. I don't need no other man, I ain't even looked at no other man. Don't you believe me?"

"Sure," he said.

She ran crying from the room to the bed and, with her clothes on, drifted into a fitful sleep.

When she woke, he was in her. Frightened and half-asleep, she fought against him, but only for seconds. She watched his face: tight, his mouth open and his eyes shut. She smelled the beads of sweat on his neck. And when he was finished, he wiped the tears from her eyes and kissed her lids, smiling at her as if she were a child needing his protection, pulling her on top of him and holding her close. Her voice cracked with sobs. She kissed him roughly, forcing herself to forget the argument. Then she told him. He was pleased.

"A son?" he asked.

"I hope," she said.

"When did you know?"

"A couple of months ago. You remember when I went to try and get that job at Burlington Industries? I didn't wear any makeup or lipstick. It rained and my hair was so frizzy. The guy that did the employing was a Holiness, and he must have been impressed by my drab look. He hired me right off, remember?"

"Uh-huh."

"Well, I wasn't quite tall enough in the first place for the job, but he overlooked it. All this time it like to have killed me, with that steam in my face, pulling all those hose on the racks. That's why I quit the first week. I knew something was wrong. I just didn't feel right. I was sick. I still get sick now and then. I tried to hide it from you."

"You did a good job of it. Why didn't you tell me?"

"I wanted to be sure. And now I am."

"And now you are."

Mayzelle was sixty-one, tall and proud. Her face was not as firm as it once had been, but her body was as strong as ever. She never stopped working, and her strength was admired by the entire family. She could hurt someone if she chose; she had once, and was ashamed to think about it. She squeezed the soapy cloth and washed around her eyes. The cloth was cool on her forehead. The veins on her hands were taut and fragile. She thought she could feel the blood pump through her neck to her head.

She dipped cold water from a bowl and splashed her face. She breathed deep, and sighed for Judith.

It didn't take long for the news to get around the families that Judith was pregnant. Mayzelle put aside her dislike for Arthur and spent more time caring for Judith.

"I'll never understand why you gettin' so sick, youngun. I been carin' for your grandma's children and your momma's children, and I seen my share of mornin' sickness. But this is somethin' else."

"Oh, I'm all right. The doctor says that I've got a little high blood and they'll have to watch out for me, but that's all."

"That's all? That's all! Just watch out for yourself, Honey. I know. I remember when your Grandma Lora lost her boy. That was worse than anything I ever seen. Now, don't get upset. I don't mean to scare you, but I do mean to enlighten you a little. You do everythin' that doctor tells you to do, and everythin' I tell you to do, and you'll be fine. Don't listen to nobody else."

"I'm afraid of the pain."

"Ain't everybody? Nothin' to it really, like a toothache sometimes—I've heard—sometimes worse. But at least you got a hospital to go to. You'll be the first in this family to go to one to have a baby in forty-five years, I guess, or ever since I been around."

"You been with the family that long?"

"Honey, I been *part* of the family that long!"

"It's strange," Judith said cautiously. "I've known you all my life, and yet I really don't know you at all. There's so many things that make you a puzzlement. I've seen you washin' and cleanin', and no matter what goes on, you're always there, like in the shadows. If a baby's born, you're there; if an aunt dies, you're nearby, in the kitchen, most likely. If Momma or Grandma Lora is ailin', you always seem to show up like a guardian angel or something. You do your work and then disappear. All these years I never knew you to be far away. You're almost like a ghost, wanderin' in and out of our lives, touching us quickly for healing and then movin' on." Judith stared into Mayzelle's eyes for a moment. She took a deep breath. "Why?"

Mayzelle's face showed no emotion. "Here," she said crisply. "Help me fold these clothes."

"Well?" asked Judith gently, afraid that if she spoke too loudly Mayzelle would drift away, like the puff on a dandelion.

Mayzelle heaved some sheets at her. "I s'pose it's 'cause I'm needed. You need Arthur, you depend on him. That's part of love, dependence on others. I learned that a long time ago."

"You depend on us?"

Mayzelle sighed. "For a pregnant woman you sure ask the most innocent questions. What do you think? You think I been hangin' around here all these years 'cause of the great food? Think about it, Honey. I'm an old lady what missed the boat somewhere along the way and instead of endin' up with her own kind got mixed up in a bucket of white paint."

Judith laughed. "I don't know why we never talked like this before."

Mayzelle smiled briefly. "Well, we didn't, that's all."

Judith grabbed her arm. "But we should have, don't you see? All these years livin' together, or nearly together, and everybody knows everybody else like the back of their hand, and *nobody* knows you. That's disturbing, don't you think?"

"I think . . . well, I think that you headin' in directions it's best we not talk about."

Judith pulled a chair up. "Got to sit down. Got to take this weight off. He's kickin' again. He must want to talk with you too."

Mayzelle put her smooth palm against Judith's forehead. "Fever again. I'll open a window. Here, hand me those clothes."

"I shouldn't ask you these questions," Judith said.

"How else you expect to learn anything?"

"I'm just curious. I never was curious before. I don't know why that bothers me now."

"'Cause I'm different from you. Like a bird or a fish."

"No, that ain't right."

Mayzelle frowned. "It's one thing to fool yourself, but don't go tryin' to fool me just to save my feeling. I'm tough as an old bird. I'm not white. I figure you've noticed before, and if it didn't bother you then, it shouldn't bother you now."

"That's not what I'm sayin'. What I'm thinkin' is that I don't see you *black* anymore. I guess I never did, 'cept when you'd have to get on the back of a bus when we were traveling, or you'd go the colored bathrooms at the park, or when they made you do things that we didn't have to do. I guess that's what bothers me. I'm so used to you bein' treated like you were different or not as good as me that I stopped wondering why it had to be so. I been so into my own troubles and my own family messes that I never really cared about yours."

"Honey, you grew up witness to prejudice. It was natural. Acceptin' that as a part of life was the most natural thing in the world for you to do."

"Well," Judith said loudly, "I ain't gonna accept it no more."

Mayzelle wiped her hands on her apron. "You ain't got no choice. You born into your world and I'm born into mine. We can't help bein' the way we are."

"I don't believe that."

"I don't want to talk about it no more—it's depressin' me."

"You sound just like Momma. Even rollin' around in that wheelchair she still refuses to listen to anybody with an idea other than her own."

"Leave your sweet momma Ila out'n this."

"Mayzelle, I feel like a little girl again. Talkin' to you like this."

"You ain't no little girl."

Judith ran her hand over her belly. "No, but I feel like one. I feel good being with you."

"Safe?" whispered Mayzelle.

"Maybe. Let's go get some tea. Any ice left?"

"A little."

"Why didn't you ever get married?"

Mayzelle looked up, startled by the question.

Judith giggled.

Mayzelle grinned. "You makin' up for lost time?"

"Exactly. Gonna ask you questions till the well runs dry. We should get to know each other, like you and Momma and Grandma Lora know each other. Can I ask you a personal one? Did you ever fall in love?"

"I guess I fell in love enough times while I been with your folks. First time was before you were born. Last time was in, oh, maybe 1945. There was this man, a good man."

"Why didn't we meet him?"

"Lord, no. Back then, Lord, even now, you don't embarrass your family."

"*Your* family?"

"Yes, *my* family," Mayzelle said boldly. "My Lora. My Lon. My family. If I had started to bringing young bucks around your house, it would'a caused shame for your family. That's why I just sorta stayed in the background so much."

"For forty-five years?"

"Yep."

Judith leaned back in the chair, her face drained of color.

"Child, you all right?" said Mayzelle. She took a wet cloth and held it to Judith's head. Recognition swelled within Mayzelle. She had seen eyes bright and fiery before—the dry mouth, the numbness. It's too early, she thought.

Lora met Mayzelle in the hospital lobby. "They won't let me stay with her up there," Mayzelle said quickly, with a trace of anger.

Lora nodded. "It's to be expected. Hospital's no different from anywhere else."

Mayzelle nodded.

"But," said Lora, "it's a damn shame."

Mayzelle looked toward the elevator. "Lon comin'?"

"Yes, and Arthur's bringin' Ila. Ila's got a cold, but the youngun insists on comin' anyway."

"Let me know what the doctors say?"

Lora patted Mayzelle's arm. "Of course I will. Here comes Lon. I'll come down as soon as I can."

Lon walked quickly towards the elevator. Lora limped behind him, putting all her strength on one leg. He walked into the elevator and faced Mayzelle. Her eyes repeated the fear in his. He wiped the sweat from his cheek.

Lora passed the newspaper to Lon. "All we do is spend our lives in hospitals. Why is that?"

Lon sat up for a moment. His back hurt from sleeping on lounge chairs. "It just seems like we spend our life at hospitals. When that baby's born, things will return to normal."

"You sure?" Lora asked.

Lon held her hand. "I don't know anymore."

Arthur came in and slumped briefly over the water fountain.

Lora stood. "Any news?" she asked.

Arthur wiped his mouth. His work clothes were too big for him. Looked like he had lost some weight. Two days of working first shift and sleeping in Judith's hospital room had made him haggard and restless. "Not much. They might have to open her up. Something about her blood not being right for the baby. I don't understand it, really. Doctor says he'll do the best he can."

"They all say that," Lora snapped.

Arthur looked to the window and squinted. "Yeah, they do, don't they?"

Lon put his hand on Arthur's shoulder. "They'll be all right, boy. Don't you worry."

Arthur walked to the elevator. "They all say that, too. Don't they?"

The elevator opened and Ila wheeled herself into the lobby. Ash pushed her. "Not too fast!" she snapped. "You gonna break my legs or some-thing!"

Arthur didn't speak. Ila looked past him to the old couple standing in the light. "How's my baby?"

"Weak," said Lon. "Real weak."

"Well," said Ila, "we'll pray. That's all that's left, isn't it?"

Pray? Lon wondered. Almost forgot how. Strange that he should try now. Long time ago he stopped praying, when he saw his dead boy all dressed up on the bed, like he was asleep, the color still in his cheeks. Alone now, my boy, alone with no stone, listening to the creekwater run-ning by the cemetery. Never saw him breathe, never felt my life in his veins. And now this. Arthur's goin' to feel the same. Can tell it on his face. Preparin' himself for losin' his child and maybe his wife. That's why he's bein' so cold. Gettin' himself ready for the hurt. War must'a taught him how to do that.

"Lon? You listenin' to me?" said Lora fretfully.

"Yes, what?"

"Let's get home and get some sleep."

"Can't, got to go to work."

"Work, that's all you men think about."

Lon shook his head. He was too tired to argue. Planned to get a drink as soon as he got to the mill. He'd sneak one to Arthur while he was at it.

The sheriff found Arthur asleep in the back seat of his Buick in the mill parking lot. "Mr. McDowell?" said the sheriff. His voice was filled with patient duty.

Arthur jumped. His sight blurred for a moment. He wondered where he was and why, not quite understanding that the lawman was speaking to him. At first he thought maybe he had drunk too much, maybe beat up on the Callahan boys at the Bloody Bucket . . . but no, that was years ago, when he was young. This was now; he was young no more.

"Mr. McDowell," the sheriff said, "Your wife is deliverin' now, and they couldn't find you, so they asked me to drive around the mill. Now that I found you, I'll take you to the hospital if you want."

Arthur shook his head. "No," he said politely. "I'll drive."

"Congratulations," said the sheriff.

"Thanks."

The Buick sped out of the gravel lot. Damn fool, thought Arthur. Goin' to sleep now of all times. Wouldn't you know it. The one time I catch some sleep, and she goes and has the baby. After two days of labor. Jesus, I don't know how she does it.

The sheriff watched the gravel spew into the air and smiled, shaking his head. "Proud daddy," he said. "I'll let you speed this one time."

Judith breathed deeply, painfully, listening to the doctor as if he were God, exhorting her to breathe deeply and push-push until she couldn't push any longer. She begged for the injections, not realizing that he had given her two already, not knowing that the boy's wet, dark hair had forced its way into the light, the arms into the doctor's arms, the cord cut and body slick upon the sheets.

Later, when Judith woke, Arthur was smiling at her.

"My baby?" she whispered, half afraid to ask.

"Fine," said Arthur.

"A boy?"

"Naturally," Arthur said, wiping his mouth and grinning. "A fine, healthy, skinny, bony little boy."

"How is he?"

Arthur squeezed her hand. "How are you?"

Judith forced a laugh. "Not the same as I was."

Deidre pushed Arthur out of the way. Her hair almost standing on end, she stuttered in excitement, "He's got feet just like mine, doesn't he, Arthur? Just like mine!"

Judith rolled her eyes. A nurse came into the room and thrust the child to Arthur.

"No, I can't," he said.

"It's all right," said the nurse. "He's your baby, isn't he?"

Judith said, "He is." The child was quiet, almost asleep.

"He looks bored," said Deidre, smiling.

"What's his name?" said the nurse.

Judith looked at Arthur. He shrugged. She thought a moment. "Todd."

"What a strange name," Deidre said.

"His name is Todd," said Arthur. "Arthur Todd McDowell."

"Junior," Judith said.

"Sounds better already," Deidre said.

The October moon spread a yellow chill into Judith's room as the child suckled warmly. The bare branches beat against the hospital window, shedding the last leaves to the early winter wind from the north. Dawn brought sleep, erasing memory, bringing life as nature paused. The elms, the willows, and the birch drank the potion slowly while the child grew.

Nineteen

WILL MCDOWELL FOUGHT in Korea for three months, amassing a small fortune from stud poker and achieving a reputation as one of the best sharpshooters in his unit. He did not develop his marksmanship out of the love of guns or of accuracy, but out of a deep conviction that any edge in battle, no matter how slight, would contribute to his survival.

His image of the army was molded of respect for Arthur's service in World War II. Arthur had survived and had brought back Nazi flags, currency, knives, rifles, and other souvenirs of war. He had also brought back memories of terrible things of which he rarely spoke. Yet Will was convinced that war held advantages that outweighed any bad memories. He enlisted because he was certain that there were experiences in Korea that one could never have in Guilford County. On this point, at least, he was correct.

Will gloried in the war. But one day, in one battle, he lost faith in his own judgment, questioning his own immortality. At that instant he hesitated, and he fell critically wounded.

Much of the shrapnel was removed from his legs and chest. But on the left side of his face he would always bear the scars gained in his brief love affair with death.

He was shipped to a veteran's hospital in Oteen, North Carolina, and from there returned home, where he married Ginger Sizemore, a tall, blond milk bottle inspector at Guilford Dairy. Ginger was the perfect mate for Will because she was the only person on earth who could get away with telling him to sit down and be quiet on those rare occasions that he grew restless. The wedding was held in Arthur's front yard. After the honeymoon, Will bought the wooded lot next to Arthur's and began to build his own home. Arthur provided the plans and the beer, and in the evenings, friends from the textile mill took turns in the dissonant orchestration of hammers and nails, saws and two-by-fours, trowels and fresh, crusty cement.

Until their house was completed, Will and Ginger lived in a small, temporary, one-room shed behind Arthur's house. Ginger and Judith became close friends, feeding the work crews and working together in the small garden near the pine woods out back. Ginger took special interest in baby Todd, starting with the day the child turned blue, banged his head on the floor of the shed, and passed out.

Ginger ran to Judith's, holding the child in her arms. Judith dropped a tub of clothes, took the child, and shook him.

Ginger collapsed on the floor. "Oh God, Judith! Oh God! Is he dead? I'll go get Arthur!"

Judith sat down and cradled the child. "No need. He's coming out of it. Just tell me what happened."

"He tottered over for a sip of my Coca-Cola, and I knew it would upset his stomach so I kept it out of his reach, and then—"

"And then he had a fit, right?"

"Yes."

Judith handed her a cool washcloth. "Wipe your face, Ginger. This boy is pure rotten. He scared me to death the first time he did that to me. Holds his breath, turns blue. Faints."

"He does it on purpose?"

"Pure rotten."

Ginger brushed the boy's soft hair. "Bless his little heart. Poor thing."

"Ginger! I'm the poor thing! This baby boy gets everything he wants. Why, his daddy dotes on him all the time, and his grandmother is worse. And Mayzelle? You'd think he was . . ."

"Something special?"

Judith softened. "Well, I reckon he might be, if it weren't for all the squalling every time he wants something . . . course, when he smiles at you like that . . . ." She sighed. "Lord, what am I going to do with another one?"

Ginger inspected Judith's swollen belly. "Boy or girl?"

"I don't know. Arthur wants a little daughter. If it's a boy, I guess we'll keep trying."

"I thought the doctor said you shouldn't have any more."

"He said it was risky."

"Huh," said Ginger, unimpressed. "Isn't everything these days?"

Judith had not one, but two more boys, then at last a daughter, all in quick succession. Arthur was pleased with his children, though he and Judith found that as the children grew into their different personalities, noise and squabbling reigned in the house, and times of rest were rare.

James looked more like the McDowells than Todd. Blond, tall, with a broad Dutch/Scotch-Irish face, he spent the summers in the shade covered with baby oil because he burned so easily. The second son, he competed fiercely for attention. He cried easily when he felt ignored. With time, the tears turned to temper.

Adam was gangly, uncoordinated, and always hungry. He shared Arthur's instinctive love for the outdoors and could often be found collecting frog eggs in a jar in the pine wood streams. He stared at these flimsy collections for hours, watching the contents hatch into tadpoles. These jars forced him to ask questions about life and death that became more persistent as time passed.

Virginia's life among the boys confused and toughened her. She was alternately harassed and protected, depending on the moods of her brothers at the time. Like Arthur, she was a dreamer, and like Judith, a realist; the combination produced some anxiety.

Todd simply went on assuming that he owned the world and all that was in it, and he fought with his siblings when they challenged that view.

Ila rolled her wheelchair to the front door and unlocked the bolts and the double-security doorknob. She peeked through the screen door and saw Todd grinning at her. She smiled back and felt a drop of snuff on her lower lip. She quickly wiped her mouth. Ila didn't like for the children to see her dip snuff. Unladylike, she said.

Judith came to the porch and handed a small suitcase to Todd. "You sure you want him to spend the night, Momma?"

"Course I do. You want to stay, Todd?"

"Yeah," he said. He kissed Judith and ran to the kitchen.

"I'll come get him tomorrow afternoon, all right?"

"Fine."

"And if he gets to be any trouble, just give me a call or wear him out. He's at that rebellious age."

"I know how to handle him. I'll sic Mayzelle on him."

They both laughed.

Ila closed the door. "Hey, hotshot!" she yelled. "You want to help me make lunch?"

"Sure," Todd said.

"Good." Ila rolled to the table, which Arthur had built high enough to accommodate her wheelchair. "Before we feed ourselves, though, I got to feed the baby squirrels. They're in a box under my bed. Go fetch it real careful like."

Todd crawled under the steel hospital bed in Ila's room and retrieved the cigar box where, deep within a bed of old socks, there were two smelly baby squirrels that cousin Robert had saved from the nest when the mother had been run over by a car.

Ila cradled the squirrels in her hand and fed them milk from an eyedropper, talking to them softly, pursing her lips and singing "Footsteps of Jesus," encouraging Todd to sing along.

"These little squirrels remind me of you when you were a baby," Ila said. "Always hungry, always eatin' like a pig. I used to carry you around this house by your diaper between my teeth, like a wolf cub or something. There, they all fat and sleepy now. Put the box back under the bed. In a few more weeks we can let them go back to the woods."

"Then we'll never see them again?"

"Course we will. Like them baby birds that I raised last spring. They still come back, don't they?"

It was true. On summer days Ila would roll out on the front porch to read, and more than once Todd had seen wild birds perch on the back of the wheelchair or eat out of her hands.

"Now hand me that pickle jar," Ila said, "and you go on out and get me some peaches off the tree."

Todd reached deep into the cabinet under the sink and handed her a quart jar of sweet pickles.

"Look at that," Ila said, "the top's rusted." She placed one end of the jar under her arm and with some exertion screwed the jar lid off. "There," she said. "Not even your daddy can open stuck jars like that. Now, you run on and get me those peaches."

Todd walked outside, through the yard, past the old rented house. Ila had had it boarded up years ago and wouldn't allow anyone to stay there. When Todd had asked Mayzelle why, she had said that some things were not meant to be understood. Maybe when you're older, she had said.

He climbed the peach tree, trying to avoid the heavy sap coming from the knobby joints. This was the easiest tree in Ila's yard to climb. The apple tree was larger and had a smooth skin. You had to be barefooted to climb it to the top.

Todd gathered four ripe peaches in his shirt and started to climb down when he saw a beautiful peach, almost out of reach, brown and red and firm-looking. That one he would have for himself. He reached for it, snapped it off the limb—it came easily—and took one great bite.

The pain was searing. Wasps, which had made a nest of the peach, stung his mouth and face. He fell from the tree, scrambled to his feet, and ran crying toward the house, his face swelling. He jumped into Ila's lap, and she could see the trouble. She washed his face with cold water, talking him down from his hysteria and dabbing little wads of snuff from her mouth onto the stings. Todd ate his lunch with dried snuff on his face. He had never smelled anything so nasty. His food tasted awful. He silently vowed never to climb the peach tree again.

After lunch, they sat in the living room. "What do you want to do now?" Ila asked.

"Read to me."

"Don't feel like reading. Tell you what. Go to my top dresser drawer and get that yellow can from the back."

Todd rummaged through the drawer and returned with the can. "Yes, that's it," Ila said, reaching for it. "This is Play-Doh. Keep it in the can and it'll stay soft. You ever play with this stuff?"

"No."

"Well, it's magic."

"Go on."

"No, really it is. I can push it, pull it, punch it, mash it, and make it into anything I want to. What do you want me to make with it?"

"A bird."

"All right. One bird coming up."

Todd watched as his grandmother's hands formed a beak, a head, two wings. His mouth hung open and his eyes were wide.

"See? A dove. A blue dove," Ila said proudly. "Changing nothing into something. It's a gift. You can do it too, boy. All it takes is faith."

Todd reached into the can and pulled out a glob of the Play-Doh, sat on the floor next to the wheelchair, and kneaded the soft dough, wondering if he would ever know all the things his grandmother knew.

That night, after the late show, Ila gave Todd an old army blanket and a pillow, and he lay down next to her bed. In the early morning, when the big trucks came out of Summerfield into the city and woke him, Todd tiptoed to Ila's bed and touched her chest to make sure she was still breathing. He was always afraid she would die while he slept. He didn't want her to die.

Todd did not like first grade. He did not do well in school. His name was so long that Ila had to write it on a card for him to copy onto his school papers. Numbers made no sense to him, although Judith and Ila tried to help.

He did not like riding the school bus, and in the mornings he would miss the bus on purpose so that Arthur would have to drive him to school. Arthur always stopped on the way and bought him some gum.

One afternoon the bus did not arrive at school on time. Todd's teacher, Mrs. Botenrider, told him to wait in the classroom until the late bus arrivals were announced by the principal. He waited by himself. No one else in his class rode his bus.

Todd sat at his desk, coloring a drawing he had made of his home: white lumber siding, blue wooden porch, red chimney with purple and black smoke from the kerosene furnace, tall hickory trees outside, and the dark pine woods carpeted in soft brown mulch.

Absorbed in his drawing, he did not know how long he had been there when a voice crackled over the loudspeaker announcing the arrival of his bus. He hurried to the door and pulled. He turned the knob and twisted the latch. He could not open the door. It was locked.

He panicked. He knew that bus drivers were always impatient to get home. The bus outside would not wait long. He would be alone. He would have to spend the night by himself in this dark room.

He yelled a few times, but the echo of his voice seemed trapped with him, bouncing off the cool green cinderblock walls. He kicked the door furiously. He battered it with his fists until his hands bled. He screamed and cried.

It took a long time for Mrs. Botenrider to calm him when she returned to the room to retrieve her forgotten purse. She promised she would never leave him alone again. She drove him home in her Chrysler, depositing him in the arms of Mayzelle, who was at the house babysitting the others.

Mayzelle held Todd's hand and waved at the teacher's car as it sped down the graveled road. She watched the dust from the road seep into the cedars lining the pasture across the street.

"That's a nice teacher you got, Todd. She must be real special, bringing you home like she did. Now, let me see them knuckles." Mayzelle sat down on the porch and motioned to Todd to sit beside her. "Now, watch where you put them big feet. Your momma's tryin' to get them Sweet Williams to grow. There. Why, you must'a really hit that door hard."

Todd watched Mayzelle cup his hand in hers, letting the strong brown fingertips move gently across his flesh.

Mayzelle took a deep breath. "Well," she said loudly, "I think you'll live. Leastwise I don't think you need any stitches. Course, your momma oughta look at it when she gets back from the Sears store. Meanwhile, you want to help me get dinner ready?"

"I thought I'd be alone," said Todd.

Mayzelle hugged the boy. "Now, youngun, you ain't never alone. Your family done spun a web of love around you. No matter where you at, no matter what you do, their strength follows you around. That's why you so strong!" Mayzelle poked her finger into Todd's side. He put his hands up and laughed. "There," she said. "You must'a given that door some beating, didn't you?"

Todd held his head up. "I sure did."

"Listen, Honey, your momma wouldn't have left you in that school-house all night. Why, I can see it now. Your grandma Ila would'a had me push her all over Greensboro in that wheelchair lookin' for you till the rubber come off the wheels. And your momma would'a dragged half the teachers in Guilford County out of their houses a-lookin' for you. Yes sir, I can see your Uncle Will riding around in his truck, lookin' for you in the cornfields and tobacco rows. And Lord, son, do you imagine what kind of ruckus your daddy would put up to find you?"

Todd laughed.

"Lord," Mayzelle said, her eyes wide. "Your daddy, Arthur Todd Mc-Dowell, Senior, would'a torn that school down with his bare hands, brick by brick, until he found you. And you know what? I'd'a been standing right there alongside of him, stacking up those bricks real nice so he could put it all back together again."

"Aw, Daddy couldn't do all that."

"You seen your daddy hang sheetrock?"

"Yes," Todd said.

"You seen your daddy catch eels and bass and trout and wicked catfish?"

"Yes."

"You seen your daddy wrastle his friends right here in the yard at picnics and such?"

"Yeah, they can't hold him down."

"That's right, baby, can't hold him down. Now come on in and set the table for me."

"It's James's turn."

"Well, I want *you* to help me this afternoon. Now come on in."

Todd followed her inside, glad to be home with Mayzelle there to tell him what to do. And for many Sundays to come, when preachers spoke of the grave, Todd would listen respectfully. He had been there.

Lying in bed that night, Todd could hear Will's beagles wailing in the darkness. He knew that shadows at the edge of the woods or sudden winds brushing against cornstalks in the garden could spook the dogs into manic mourning.

Stupid dogs, he thought, turning his pillow to the cool side and drawing the blanket to his chin. He wanted to yell at the dogs, then close and lock the window. Instead, he pulled the blanket over his head and vowed never to go to school again. They couldn't make him go. No power on earth could make him do what he did not want to do.

He opened his eyes, startled by the sudden suction sound of the refrigerator door opening and closing. He strained to hear his father's footsteps from the kitchen to the living room. After a moment, the soft, heated buzz of the television seeped through the walls. The noise was more comforting than any night light. Todd peeked above the blanket and saw his father standing in the bedroom doorway.

Arthur put his finger to his lips as he walked silently by the double bed where Adam and James dreamed, reaching down to replace the blanket that James had kicked to the floor. Arthur leaned down, and Todd lifted his arms around his neck, wrapped his legs around his waist, and held his breath until safely in the living room.

Arthur retrieved his Budweiser from the top of the television and collapsed with Todd on the old, frayed chair. The television was tuned to "Twentieth Century Presents."

"Actual films about World War II on tonight," Arthur told his son. "You might learn something."

He drained most of the beer during a commercial for Winston cigarettes. Just before the program resumed, he handed the nearly empty can to Todd. "Don't tell your mother," he said.

Todd finished the last bitter ounce, then slipped off Arthur's lap, tiptoed to the refrigerator, opened another beer for his father, and returned to the safety of his lap.

Suddenly, Arthur leaned forward. He sipped his beer quietly, his eyes never leaving the television screen. He tapped the boy on the shoulder. "There," he said excitedly, pointing with the beer can. "I was there. I— yes, around those burning buildings. Good Lord, boy, I didn't know anyone filmed that. I—"

Abruptly, he stopped talking. Todd felt Arthur's arms close around his chest. He snuggled closer.

"Daddy, did you shoot anybody in the war?"

Arthur rubbed his chin across the boy's thick hair. "We put it behind us, boy."

"Mayzelle says we shouldn't put nothing behind us. She says we got to confront, forgive, and love."

"Mayzelle's a smart woman."

"But what does she mean?"

"I'm still trying to find out, son. Mayzelle and your grandmother Ila got strength from hard times. Lot of people like that. Hard times make 'em hard so they can make it through anything. Some people came out of the war like that. I don't know if I got it or not."

"Got what?"

"Nothing. You're too young to be talking stuff like this. Now hush so I can hear the rest of my program."

When the program was over, Arthur jostled Todd, who was nearly asleep. "I'm going up to Nuckles' for a barbecue. You want to come?"

"I don't like barbecue."

"You'll eat it anyway," Arthur said. "Makes you strong." He set Todd on the floor, stood, and reached for his baseball cap. "Come on, boy. On the way home you can pretend to be asleep so I'll have to carry you to bed."

Todd blushed and grinned foolishly. His father knew everything.

The room was bright with morning sun, except the corner where Todd lay wrapped in sheets. He was tall for his age. Arthur almost decided not to wake him. But there was movement there. The boy was rocking silently, deep into the mattress and up again.

Arthur frowned. He's too young for that—isn't he? His pelvis sliding forward, the sheet clinging to his body—an infant's search for manhood? Arthur thought for a moment. No, wouldn't be fair shouting at him. Hell, let him enjoy himself for the moment. It's Saturday. Plenty of time left to get him up.

Judith wandered into the kitchen. "What you waitin' for?" she said kindly.

"The boy."

"You want me to get him up?"

"No," Arthur said quickly. "I'll do it." He put his cigarette out. "Hey, boy!" he shouted down the hallway. "You comin' with me or not?"

"Shhh," Judith said angrily. "Don't wake the rest of 'em. Sometimes . . . . I swear, you just don't think right."

Todd jumped out of the bed, his eyes wide with fear of being caught. He had wasted a lot of time. Daddy might leave him. He pulled his jeans on and grabbed a shirt, buttoning it haphazardly as he slipped down the hall.

Arthur kissed Judith on the cheek.

"Take care of the boy," she said and turned away.

Arthur frowned.

Todd could smell the construction site before he could see it. When they got to the site, Arthur went right to work. Todd carried a box of nails to the house and began to construct a ladder. The sawdust and chalkdust on the new floors spread quickly over his clothes. He liked the smell.

Arthur worked furiously, cutting the sheetrock to fit the walls and crevices. Lifting the pieces on his head, he nailed them into place on the ceilings. If he could get one house done in a day, he would make more money than in three days at the mill. In fact, he hoped to quit the textile mill soon and go into sheetrocking full time.

Judith brought his lunch, barbecue and a bologna sandwich. She parked the car behind his truck. She sat on the porch step and watched him eat.

"When you coming home?" she asked.

"Right now, I guess," he said casually.

Judith looked at him narrowly. "What you mean, right now? Noon? It ain't like you to stop a house when you haven't finished it. You sick or something?"

Arthur put a Pepsi to his lips and sipped heartily. "Go look."

Judith jumped up and walked into the new house. In a moment she returned, her voice shaky. "You finished this house—four rooms and a bathroom—since this morning?"

Arthur looked at the truck.

"Arthur, you could get sick working this hard. There ain't no sense to it."

He stared at her. "You want to come in here yourself and hang this sheetrock on the walls and ceilings?"

"No, that's not what I'm saying."

"You're saying that I'm stupid for hurryin' and wantin' to spend the rest of the day at home on the sofa, sleeping."

"No, that's not what I mean. Look at your hands, all puffy and bloody."

"I hurried because I didn't want you running all over the county this afternoon while I worked myself to death here, not knowing what you were up to." He spit. "You satisfied?"

Judith glanced at Todd. The boy didn't understand. Good. She pulled him to the car. "Your daddy works too hard," she said.

Twenty

December 1958

ILA WAS STUNNED. She grasped the arms of the chair until her knuckles turned white. Anger flashed across her face.

Judith poured a cake mix into a plastic bowl, calmly stirring in milk as if nothing unusual were occurring. She cracked an egg. Her voice was strained but controlled. "Momma, we can't go on living the nightmare."

"I forbid it!" said Ila, pounding the table with her palm.

Judith breathed heavily. "You can't stop it. Me and Deidre already sent out the invitations. We ain't had a decent Christmas since . . ."

Ila raised her head and looked out the window.

". . . since the accident."

"It weren't no accident. It was murder. Your daddy *died* on Christmas Eve. I hate the thought of laughter on that day. I hate the whole Christmas season."

"But Momma, the family's been split enough. The mourning's over. We can't go on grieving."

"You have no right," Ila snapped, "to do anything else. He was your father, and I don't think it's too much to ask that on one day a year we remember what happened."

Judith threw a spoon into the sink, the loud ring of steel cutting across the room. "Momma, I know this is gonna make you mad, but I'm tired of not seeing my children laugh on Christmas Eve. I'm tired of bein' ashamed to smile or laugh again. I'm tired of feelin' guilty for somethin' I had nothin' to do with."

"Don't raise your voice."

"I'll raise my goddamn voice anytime I please!" Judith wanted to stop, but the gate was open at last, and her words came out in a rush. "I'm gettin' to be *old*, and I don't take kindly to bein' told what to do by my mother. We're going to have a Christmas party for the whole family at my house. We're going to have laughter again, Momma. And if you think you're going to ruin it, you've got another think coming. If I have to drag you there screaming, I'll do it."

The color had drained from Ila's face. She started to wheel back to her room, but she turned back, biting her lip. "You mentioned your guilt, your being guilty," she said. "You can't know the meaning of the word." She began to cry.

"Oh God, Momma, don't cry. I've been on edge lately. Arthur thinks I blame him for Daddy's death, and now you're goin' on. My patience is about worn out. Seems like everything's gone wrong since Daddy died." Judith paused and put the cake in the oven. "It's got so I don't even pray anymore, can you imagine that? It's like God is punishing me . . . or us . . . and He won't stop till we guess what it is that made Him mad in the first place. A real swell game. Momma, I'm tired of guessing. I'm tired of playin' the game. God can find another partner."

"It ain't nothin' to joke about."

"Who's joking? I swear, sometimes life gets real heavy, and I would just rather laugh about it than cry. I'm not goin' to let this get me down. Me and the kids deserve more than what we're getting. I guess I'm just tired. Day in, day out, living with everybody's unhappiness. It ain't good for a person. We gotta break out. It's like we're trapped in a cage and our children are being born in the same trap. Don't you feel that way sometimes?"

Ila had poured herself some tea. She played with a slice of lemon. "Yes. I just figured it was part of growin' up. Just part of livin'. You don't fight it. That's what I learned. You just sort of bend with the wind or get broke, and believe me, there's been times in my life when I near got broke bad, especially when I tried to fight the hard times. The Depression, my best friend drowning, David dying . . . Now and again I wish *I* was dead, put six feet under up there on that mountain with David. Sometimes I feel like the only happy people is dead people."

Judith took the lemon from Ila's hand. "Don't you see?" she pleaded. "I don't want to spend my life feeling like that; and from the looks of things, that's why I've got to break out, break away, while me and the children have a chance."

"Your life ain't all that miserable," Ila said in a hurt tone.

"I know! That's just it! I feel like I'm drifting toward a fire, and I just feel the heat now. I'm not gonna take a chance on feelin' the flames."

"So," Ila said cynically, "what you plannin' on doin'?"

Judith paused. "I don't know for sure. But I figure that the best thing to do is laugh a little more; for the children's sake, try to pull this family away from black thoughts. We need to have the best damn Christmas party ever. Let's wash the clothes clean. We need to have hope again."

In the dawn shadows the forest appeared blue, the mist gently brushing against the snow-covered branches. Todd surprised a thin rabbit in the path. The animal froze, quivering. Todd looked into its eyes and saw a frantic moment of madness, fragile and delicate. He moved and the rabbit bounded away.

Arthur laughed and pushed Todd deeper into the woods, past the acre of pines, beside the dark swimming hole with its thin black ice.

After a lot of searching, Todd saw a tree he liked: a cedar tree, tall and fat, warped, with a top as misshapen as the bottom.

"Son, that looks more like a cotton bush than a tree."

"Momma will like it," Todd said.

"I'm not so sure. Let's look some more."

Todd went up to the tree and leaned close to smell the fragrance. He broke off a short branch and carried it to his father.

"Smell it, Daddy, it smells just like Christmas."

Arthur sniffed at the branch. "Yep, it does. All right, we'll chop it. But if your momma don't like it, then you come back here by yourself and chop that one over yonder. You understand?"

"Yes, Daddy."

"Good."

Arthur tried to trim the stray branches from the tree on the front porch. After half an hour he gave up. "Damn tree's bound and determined to stay round. Looks like a bush."

"I think it's beautiful," Judith said, peering out through the screen door.

"Got any coffee on?"

"I can put some on."

"I think it's going to be a long night," Arthur said.

Judith laughed. "I think you're right about that. Here comes Momma and Deidre now."

The car pulled into the driveway and into the slush in the middle of the yard.

"I wish you'd tell Dan not to drive all the way into the yard. No wonder we ain't got no grass out there," Judith said.

Arthur smiled. "Wouldn't do no good. They'd drive up there anyway."

"Still, I wish you'd tell him."

Arthur pulled the tree into the house and Judith went to the car and opened the door.

"Deidre! You watch out for the ice. It's awful slippery out here."

Deidre supported herself by leaning on the car until she reached Judith; then the two women walked slowly to the house.

Judith stopped and turned. "Dan, you need any help? I'll send Arthur out to help you bring Momma in."

"No need," said Dan, his voice slurred.

"No need," mocked Deidre. "That man drinks a couple of ounces and swears he can do anything."

Dan leaned over Ila and put one arm around her back and one under her legs. "Now, when I say go, you hold real tight, old woman."

"You better be the one who holds tight, Dan, 'cause if you fall, then I'm a-fallin' with you."

"Wouldn't that be a sight?" Dan said as he lifted her. "Me and you a-rollin' around in the snow."

Judith held the door for them.

"Watch the door!" shouted Ila. "Watch my legs! Don't hit my legs!"

"Lord, I'll be glad to dump you, woman," Dan huffed.

Arthur opened the small portable wheelchair.

"Come on, Arthur," said Dan. "Help me bring in the gifts and the food."

"To hell with the gifts," said Arthur. "Let's get the food!"

"Careful of them cakes!" shouted Ila. "They're not wrapped too good."

Lon and Lora arrived next in a taxi. Lon shook the snow from his hat and placed it near the radiator to dry. His face was red from the cold, and his skin seemed to have drawn tightly across his high cheekbones.

Lon was seventy-one, but he looked ten years younger. In fact, the managers of the mill were convinced that he was sixty-four. He did not walk stooped and bent. Traces of auburn lingered in his gray hair. His stride was quick and his reflexes sound.

Lon smiled and waved at the chattering children as they ran from kitchen to bedroom, squealing with childish secrets.

His smile dropped for a moment when he saw Todd standing in the corner of the living room, his arms crossed, the back of his head propped against the wall. The boy had learned not to get in his great-grandfather's way. He didn't understand Lon's coldness, but he had learned to live with it.

Lon caught his eyes for a moment. Todd's eyes were like his own: cold and bright, yet distant, unmoved, and serious.

Arthur pulled Lon through the crowd toward the back porch, whispering. Judith shook her head. Somewhere on that porch, or out in the tool shed, was a gallon—no, two gallons—of liquor. Grandpa Lon ought to have better sense at his age, Judith thought.

Lora picked her way through the children, patting their heads and demanding kisses. She saw Todd and smiled impishly. She crooked her finger and motioned him over. He looked from side to side, embarrassed. He didn't want to be mothered in front of all the other kids. He wanted to be on the back porch, with the men, with Arthur, Dan, and even, at a safe distance, with Lon.

"What, boy?" shouted Lora, her purple eyes flashing. "You too big to give me lovin'?"

She grabbed his bony shoulders and pulled him to the kitchen.

"What you been feedin' this boy, Judith? He's a-starvin' to death. If'n you want, I might be able to get y'all some welfare food."

Judith laughed. "That boy grows an inch every month. He eats us out of house and home."

"But," added Deidre, her dark eyes squinting, "he'll be worth it some day."

"What you say, Deidre?" Lora shouted. "This house is so noisy you can hardly hear yourself think."

"I know," shouted Judith. "Ain't it great?"

After Ila had checked to make sure that the food was cooked to her specifications and satisfaction—which meant tasting every dish from the cranberry sauce to the potato pie—she rolled into the living room. The children had made the sofa into a playground. Will and Ginger had arrived, along with Esther McDowell. The voices in the house grew louder and more shrill.

Todd walked into the kitchen. "Momma?"

Judith sighed. "What you want?"

"It's Grandma Ila. She's cryin'."

Judith threw down her dishtowel. "Damn." She brushed past the boy and hurried into the living room. The children were quiet. Lora shrugged as Judith caught her eye.

Judith pushed her way through the crowd of women, all helplessly staring at each other as Ila sobbed with spasms that shook the wheelchair. Judith knelt down and wiped the tears. "Momma," she said, barely concealing her exasperation. "It's Christmas, Momma. It's my party—our first party in years. Now, what's the matter? We can't spoil everybody's time like this. It just ain't right."

"I can't help it," Ila said, her voice, though soft, carrying through the silent house. "I just got to thinkin', and I just now realized that Ash ain't here. He's late. He should'a been here hours ago!"

Judith threw up her hands. "Sweet Jesus!" she said angrily. "Is that all? Why, Momma, people are late all the time and we don't go around cater-waulin' because of it. My sweet Lord, is that why you're a-cryin' and a-carryin' on? Well, I swear I've had enough. You just clean off your face and stop it right this minute."

"But," Ila said quickly glancing around from face to face, "don't you understand, Judith? Ash was late that other time, too."

It was true. Judith remembered. She swallowed hard. "Momma," she said carefully, "your memories have rust on them, like the children's swing-set out back. Ash promised he'd be here, and he will." Judith tried to smile but could not. This had been her effort. Every nerve in her body seemed swollen from planning this party, this final break from lives ravished by unfair changes. "Momma," she said, pleading, "I promise that Ash will be here." She clenched her fist. "You hear me, Momma? I swear to God he'll be here!"

Ila sniffed. "Of course," she said, smiling a little and drying her eyes with Lon's handkerchief. "The food's gettin' cold. We can't hold it much longer. We just got to trust in God, now, don't we?"

Judith hesitated. "Sure, Momma. That's what we got to do."

Todd walked to his grandmother and offered her a Coke. "Can we open the gifts now, Grandma?"

Ila smiled. "In a few minutes. We oughta wait on Ash and your cousins." She looked around. "Well," she said, her voice rising, "show's over. Every-body relax and have some fun. I'm just an old woman. I don't want to ruin Judith's nice party for everyone."

The contented buzz of relatives' voices gradually resumed. The children began to scream with delight at the prospect of opening the gifts at last.

Judith was relieved. Maybe the night could be saved after all. Her eyes roamed the living room. She saw Arthur laughing with Rossie. Ginger and Esther were talking in a corner. Dan was sitting in a chair, asleep. Lon and Lora held hands on the sofa.

A noise on the porch surprised Judith. She instinctively reached for her heart. The front door opened, and a wild cheer rose in the room. A dozen voices shouted, "Ash!" "Robert!" and "Merry Christmas, Cathy!"

Ash hugged Ila and handed her a package. Todd went to the tree and began reading the names on the other gifts. Soon the room was a flurry of ribbons and torn paper flying through the air as the children and their parents tore open the packages. Ila opened her presents cautiously, refolding the paper so that it could be used again next year.

Arthur again lit the lantern in the tool shed. "Listen to 'em," he said, "they're singing carols."

Dan laughed. "I can hear old Deidre's voice over everybody's."

"Yeah," said Arthur, "but she's havin' fun."

"Pretty soon she'll be talking about the movies she's been to see during the last month. Deidre likes movies and shows. You and Judith ought to get out more. We saw Bill Monroe last week at the National."

Arthur took another drink and passed the bottle to Lon. "Saw that tobacco prices are goin' down again."

Dan nodded. "Yep. Bet you're glad to be out of farming, huh?"

Arthur didn't answer.

"Arthur, pass that stuff over here," said Rossie. "I got a feelin' ol' Lon's hoggin' the booze."

Lon gave the bottle to Arthur, who passed it to Rossie.

"Ain't seen you and Pansy in a couple years. How y'all been gettin' along?"

"Fair," said Rossie, closing his eyes. "We just don't travel much anymore. Pansy's gettin' old."

Dan laughed. "Hell, we're all gettin' old. Arthur's thirty-three, Judith is at least thirty-one, Ila's fifty-three, and Lora is seventy or seventy-one."

"She's twenty-two," Lon sputtered.

Everyone laughed.

Arthur's eyes reflected the flame as he lighted another cigarette. "How you know all them ages, Dan?"

Dan pulled a lawn chair from the hanger on the wall. "Deidre. She keeps me posted on birthdays, anniversaries, and things like that. I swear, that woman has her nose in more people's business than a root hog."

Again the men laughed. Arthur tapped the bottle with his finger and put it to his mouth. He took several quick gulps. "You better not let Deidre hear you talkin' like that," he said. "She'll bust your ass." More laughter.

"How's Ila doin'?" Rossie asked.

"Looks good," said Dan. "Me and Deidre visit 'bout every other day. Considering that this is her first attendance at a Christmas party since . . . that time, I'd say she's doin' real well. Says she has to be strong for Deidre and Judith." He chuckled. "Can you imagine, *she* has to be strong for *them*? Deidre and Judith is tough as nails, ain't that right, Arthur?"

Arthur hadn't even noticed that Todd had slipped into the shed. Todd waited for him to answer Uncle Dan, but he didn't. He just stared. Todd was suddenly chilled. He remembered the look in the eyes of the rabbit that he had frightened that morning. In his father's stare, Todd knew, was something that sons should not see.

Twenty-one

June 1959

ARTHUR WAS PROUD of his wife, his children, and the house he had built with his own hands, each board stained in his own sweat. This was his duty, to reap the benefits of his sacrifices made during the war. Like all returned soldiers, he wanted to enjoy the good life promised to all after they won the war; the spoils of war were to be evenly divided. Of course, Arthur expected to work for his share. He didn't expect anything to be given to him. That was not his way. But he firmly believed a person could obtain anything—anything—if he was willing to work and sacrifice, and Arthur knew the meaning of both words.

He read the newspapers and magazines. He knew that the good life consisted of beach trips and coastal fishing in baggy shorts and plaid shirts, ice chests filled with beer and bait; drive-in movies with a warm wife and dozing kids on the back seat; ball games at the Memorial Stadium, cold Pabst in a cup, Todd devouring hot dogs and Cokes; wicker armchairs for the back porch, Davy Crockett coonskin caps for the boys and hula hoops for Virginia; supporting MacArthur, cursing Truman, worshipping Ike and Gary Cooper. He wanted a barbecue pit, a garage in the back for his car, a flower bed for Judith, a fireplace addition to the living room, a cabin in the mountains, and an understanding of what the women saw in James Dean.

As the years went by, he realized that the distance between his dreams and his paycheck could be considerable. He was willing to sacrifice, and, in his spare time, to enjoy the RCA television bought on credit.

He wanted strong sons. He took them into the pine woods to help fell trees, to drag the timber home behind a borrowed mule to be wedge-cut in a front yard denuded of grass by four children. He took them rabbit hunting, on sheetrocking jobs, to turkey shoots, and once, on impulse, to Nags Head to watch them play in the surf.

Arthur could not strike his children. No matter the provocation, all matters of punishment were turned over to Judith. She was stern with the children, sparing no rod when James hit Virginia across the back of her head with a brick or when Todd locked the children in a closet. After punishment the children sought their father, waiting impatiently for him on the front porch. When his car came heaving into sight, they scrambled to the mailbox, screaming in the middle of the road as he carefully guided the car into the driveway. There he gently pushed through the small mob of frantic sons and daughter, listening to tears and sobs and complaints of unfair and severe punishment. I have been unjustly accused, was the essence of their cries, and found guilty without trial, even if I did accidently pull the refrigerator door off its hinges . . . why wasn't the cat punished for licking Adam's you-know-what right there on the front porch when Aunt Ginger visited?

Arthur sighed and picked up Virginia, his princess, who was always pushed aside by the competitive boys. With Virginia under one arm and a bag of groceries under the other, he soothed their fears and confronted their mother, who, having gone through this a hundred times, would be found shaking her head and crying in the bathroom, wondering if she were indeed the witch her own flesh described.

The bathroom was clouded with steam.

"Another rough day, huh?" Arthur said.

"Could of been rougher," Judith answered as she washed her face. She looked at him through the beads of hot water. "And if you go in there and pamper them, I'll be rough on you!"

He laughed. "What's for supper?"

She frowned and threw the washcloth to his chest. He dropped it in the clothes basket by the sink, trying to decide what approach this greeting deserved. If he held her and kissed her and let her cry, then she would be spoiled and expect it all the time. If he told her she was too rough on the kids, she would claim he was siding with them and that they need a stern hand. If he walked away without another thought, she would claim he didn't care. Even worse, she would think he was angry, and that, in turn, would make her angrier. Around and around it went.

He turned on the cold water tap and cupped his hands under it. Then he turned to her and wiped her brow with his huge palm. Her face relaxed. Her tired eyes turned to the window and toward the trees behind Will's home, into the pasture around the pond where little James and Adam were standing, eyes wide and wanting.

She grabbed his shoulders. "Look at them out there, wonderin' what's goin' on in here. Arthur, we've got some fine young brood, don't we? They cry when I hurt them, and they cry when they think you might be hurting me. Lord, Lord, what's goin' to become of them?" She looked at Arthur's face as he followed the movements of his children outside.

He's wearing his summer face, she thought, bright and pale with blotches of red on his cheeks, his eyes bright and clear, and his hair full and clean, almost shining. This man still looks like the boy I met, still slim and powerful, still strange and frightening.

After supper, the family gathered in the living room. Arthur dozed on the couch while Judith read the Bible to the children. She read about hell and damnation and explained that the wages of sin is death. Then the peace of the room was broken by a mighty wail.

James stood crying. This was not like James. He reached for his mother's neck, shouting, "I don't want to go to hell!" Judith dropped the book and waited patiently for the other children to join in the chorus. They didn't. They looked at each other amused. If anyone had to go to hell, who was more qualified than James?

Arthur turned his head and looked at Judith. She shrugged. She decided that the children might be too young to worry about the more frightening aspects of religion. Best let them think about tooth fairies and Santa Claus a little while longer. Judith felt it was best for now to leave two subjects alone: hell and money. They might be able to handle hell, but money was another matter.

Judith pulled the sheet back as Arthur's invisible frame slid into bed. She found his shoulders and pulled him to her. He turned to her at first touch.

"Arthur?"

"Mmmm?"

"Arthur, I've been thinking. With you going on third shift at the mill soon, it's going to get pretty lonely around here."

She listened to his breathing. She had learned that you could tell a lot about what a man was thinking by the way he breathed.

She reached to her side, groped until she found the lamp switch, and yanked it. Arthur covered his eyes and breathed deeply.

"Honey," she said, "I want to go back to work."

"What?" he said, surprised.

"Hear me out first and then decide. You'll be on third, and Momma said she could take care of the kids during the afternoon while I worked. It would be good for all of us, all the way around. Me bringing in more money and God knows we can use it. We've got bills all over the place, what with that new car that we can't afford."

"We needed a car," he said defensively.

"I know, I know," she said quickly and soothingly. "But we can't afford it. Sooner or later we've got to cut back or else they're gonna start taking things back, and you don't want that, and I don't want that . . ."

"I don't want you workin'."

"Oh, Honey, it wouldn't be but for a year or so. Besides, you'll be sleeping during the day while I'm at work. And you don't want those children waking you up every five minutes for something or other, and that's exactly what would happen and you know it. Now, think about it, really, that's exactly what would happen."

"Well, maybe you're—"

"Right! Course I'm right. I've been talking to Ginger. She saw in the paper that there's a cashier job open at the hospital cafeteria. From ten to six. I can handle that. It wouldn't be too tiring, and besides, it would be good for me, getting away from the kids for a while, on my own, helping—"

"Okay, okay!" Arthur was laughing. "You've convinced me." Then he said, his voice deep and soft, "I don't like it, but if you're bound to do it, then give it a try. But if it don't work out, if I don't like it, then you've got to quit, right?"

"Sure. That's fine. Just a chance to do it, that's all I want."

"I'm still not sure, Judith. But you go ahead and try it. I guarantee you won't like it for long. One, maybe two weeks, is all you're gonna take, then you'll be back where you belong, raising those kids."

She wanted to say something from inside that needed saying, but she could not find the words to make it sound right. So she said nothing. She turned out the light and felt his arms force her shoulders back.

Arthur was right. The work was not easy.

Arthur was wrong. She enjoyed the work.

She had never met so many people. Hundreds of hospital employees, hundreds of different faces, and none of them family. She rang up their bills and helped in the kitchen after the cafeteria closed. Sometimes the supervisor marked chipped dishes and cups to be thrown away. Judith laughed at the waste, and she managed to take some of the dishware from the incinerator boxes—thick brown mugs with blue lines around the top, the chips barely noticeable, more like indentations or scars than dangerous, jagged edges.

The work was long and tiring, but the cooks and serving ladies were nice people—hard-working, laughing, sensitive. For the first time, Judith found that she was attractive to others. She had not thought much about it before, with her long hair and freckles. The men in the kitchen were nice to her, helping her carry the register into the office in the morning and at closing. They always noticed her, smiled at her, complimented her.

"Good morning, Sweetheart!"

"Hello, Gorgeous, what's on the menu today?"

"Will you look at that dress! Beautiful woman, get us a cup of coffee, will ya?"

She watched the customers flow down the line, pointing to potatoes or beans or chicken or steak, doctors and nurses talking about children and pets and furniture, families waiting for operations upstairs to be completed. She listened and learned of a world all too familiar: heart attacks and pneumonia, the old man in 311, and the child with two broken legs in 110. Ministers plying a mother with coffee, talking about God's will. Fearful teenagers in a corner with their hands over their mouths, shaking their heads. Laughing attendants discussing the bowel habits of the rich.

The heavy voice from the kitchen was persistent.

"Another cup of coffee, Sweetheart!"

She heard the plaint and turned to the kitchen shouting, "Just a minute, you guys, I'll get it when I'm free up here."

There was no one in the line, but she liked to make the kitchen help wait. She poured the coffee and pushed the kitchen door open with her foot. It swung easily. Sam Diapolas, the chief cook, saw her coming and made a gracious bow.

Sam's dominant physical feature was hair. Reddish-brown fuzz protruded from the sleeves and collar of his undershirt. His knuckles were layered in great mounds of hair, which he washed often. He would be bald within a year. "There she is," he said. "Our saving angel."

She handed him the coffee.

"Hold it just a minute, Dear." He reached over the grill and wiped his hands on a cloth that must have been there since the hospital opened twenty years before.

"Now I'll take it, Judith."

"It's hot. Don't burn your lips."

"The only place I could burn my lips would be on yours."

Judith blushed. "I think Arthur would want to burn more than your lips," she replied quietly.

Sam laughed loudly. "Judith, you're something, really something. I think you're the only girl in this kitchen that's got any good sense."

"Thank you," she said.

"No, I mean it," he said. "You got class, kid. I like that. Listen, does your husband hunt?"

"A little."

"Tell him I've got a good Winchester shotgun that I got to get rid of."

"I won't tell him."

"Huh?"

"We can't afford it."

"Oh, well, never thought about that. You keep a tight rein around your man, don't you?"

"I take care of him, if that's what you mean, Sam."

"Yes, that's exactly what I mean, my dear."

"Sam, there is something we need."

"What is it? All you gotta do is ask."

"You do some plumbing part-time, don't you?"

"Yeah, how'd you know?"

"Myrtle Bond in Dietary told me. I don't know how to ask you, we can't pay much, but we need some pipes put in for the washer, and Arthur doesn't have time to do it . . ."

"And you were wondering whether I could do it?"

"Well, I know how much trouble . . ."

"Not another word. Just give me the specifications."

"The what?"

"The specifications! The number of feet of pipe you'll need and the size. Never mind, I can measure that myself."

"That's sweet of you, Sam."

"Yeah, I know," he said agreeably. "Now, you better get back outside on the line before Brains finds you."

"Brains?"

"Yeah, you know, our leader. Mrs. Duckworth."

"Oh, her. She's out today."

"She is? That's a wonder. Bring us some pie. This calls for a celebration."

"No, I better not. Lunch shift's comin' any minute. Thanks again, Sam."

He nodded and unwrapped some chicken livers. She went back to the register.

Judith woke at dawn and reached for Arthur. He was not there. She kept forgetting that he was at work and would not be home until later.

She rose to wake the children. It was September and they were back in school. She went to their rooms and told them to rise and shine. Todd hated those words and Judith knew it. If he did not get up, she repeated them until he did. She went to the bathroom and washed her face, looking outside through the trees as she dried off, to see what new expression the rising sun would take on today. She fixed breakfast—gravy, fried bologna, eggs, and biscuits—and pushed the children out the door to the mailbox where the school bus would soon arrive. As the sounds of Captain Kangaroo spread throughout the house, she went to the porch to wave goodbye to Todd, James, Adam, and Virginia as they boarded Guilford County Public Schools bus number 229.

Judith had noticed a little sack of flesh under her chin of which she tried in vain to rid herself by restricting her intake of fluids. Soon she faced a choice between an ounce or two of unwanted flesh or anxiety caused by caffeine deprivation. Every time she thought about curtailing liquids, she would brew another pot of coffee.

Besides, she thought, these kids'll keep the weight off; and my eyes, though a little sad, still tell all I am.

She dressed for work and waited for Arthur. He was home at seven-thirty. She fixed another breakfast and helped him to bed. Then she sped to the hospital.

Sam rushed out of the kitchen. He was not wearing his apron.

"Where you goin', Sam?" she shouted cheerfully.

"You mean where are *we* goin', don't you?"

"Huh?"

"The pipes! We got to get the pipes!"

"I can't do that, can't lose the money."

"Hell, Sweetheart, neither can I. I sweet-talked Duckworth. She's gonna take your place for a couple of hours if I fix her damn toilet at her house this weekend. So, why not?"

"Well, I don't know. I haven't even mentioned this to Arthur."

"Come on, Doll, it's all set. Let's hurry."

"Do I have to go?"

"Unless you want me to wake up Arthur and have him tell me where to put the pipes."

Judith laughed at the thought of Arthur being awakened. He would probably punch Sam across the room. "Okay, you talked me into it. Let's go."

They walked to the employees' parking lot behind the kitchen. The sun was soaking up the last pools of water on the pavement from last night's rain.

"Judith, you're goin' the wrong way!"

"But my car's over there."

"And my truck's over here. We've got to go by my house and pick up the pipe first. Come on, time's catching us."

She climbed into the seat of Sam's old truck. The interior smelled damp and sour. The dash had rusted to the color of her dress. Sam turned the key and pressed the choke, and a tremendous backfire echoed across the wall of the hospital.

"Well, Sam, I guess you woke every patient in this building."

"'Bout time they got up. Lazin' around ain't good for nobody."

She smiled and rested her arm on the cool door frame.

The truck wheeled out of the parking lot onto Church Street and within minutes screeched to a halt in Sam's backyard. He jumped out and ran into his storage shed and returned carrying a great load of pipe, which he threw into the bed of the truck. After several more trips, he climbed back into the seat, and again they were off. They drove down Phillips Avenue, and Judith glanced quickly at Dan's house as they passed. Deidre was in the front yard trimming some bushes. Judith waved, but at first Deidre did not see her. Just before the truck went out of sight around a bend, Deidre caught sight for a moment of the unmistakable freckles and hair and expression of her sister, laughing in the cab of a truck that was definitely not Arthur's.

While Sam crawled around under the house, taking measurements and placing the pipe, Judith sat in the bedroom, not taking her eyes from the man in the bed. He sleeps so soundly, she thought. Means he's at peace.

When Sam had finished, she went back to the truck and to the hospital.

Arthur did not know how long the phone had been ringing. At first he pulled a pillow over his head, but the dull, whining noise did not stop. He stumbled into the kitchen and picked up the receiver.

"Hello," he mumbled angrily.

"Arthur?"

"Who's this?" he said, not really caring.

"It's me. Deidre," came the whispered reply.

"What the—"

"Arthur, let me speak to Judith."

"For God's sake, Deidre, you know she's at work!"

"Arthur? I could'a sworn I saw her heading toward your place down Phillips."

"Who was he?" Arthur said dryly.

"Who was *who*, Arthur? Look, I guess I made a mistake. Go back to sleep and tell Judith to give me a call when she gets in." She replaced the phone receiver.

Arthur walked across the yard and onto Ginger's porch. Among the spouses of the McDowell clan, Ginger was the first and only blond. Her face appeared cold, even in summer, and her hands never rested, always in motion: washing, kneading, knitting, touching. She pulled teeth, restored confidence, saved burned cakes, inflated bicycle tires, and generally served as nurse, legal agent, and spiritual advisor for the community. Hers was a quiet strength, an engine of energy, always charged and ready to heal.

"Why, Arthur! You're supposed to be asleep! What you doin' up?"

"Evidently a lot of people think I'm supposed to be asleep."

"What you mean, Pet?"

"Got any coffee?"

"Sure I do. Come on in. What's the matter with you, huffin' and puffin' around my door? Now, you be quiet, you hear? I don't want you to wake up my girl. I just now got her asleep. Flu, I guess. She didn't sleep all night. Neither did I."

"Ginger, I got somethin' I want you to do."

"Sure, Pet, anything, you just name it."

"Judith's runnin' around."

Ginger stared at Arthur for a while and leaned back in her chair. "Now, Arthur," she said, "your wife don't run around. Why, we're the best of friends, Judith and me, and I know what I'm talkin' about. It's all in your imagination. She's the sweetest thing—"

He slammed his fist on the table. A brown cup rolled off the table and across the floor.

Ginger rubbed her neck and cast a worried glance toward the bedroom. The child still slept.

She lowered her voice to a whisper, hoping Arthur would get the hint. "Now, Honey, you calm down. You look like a beat cat. Now, I'll listen to you, and maybe we can figure this out together. Just start at the beginning."

"I got proof."

"What kind of proof?"

"Someone saw them."

"Who saw them?"

"Someone called me, someone who don't lie."

Ginger went to the sink and tried to find the sugar. She had put it on the sinktop that morning. Now it was gone. "Arthur, let's assume that someone saw your wife with someone else. Who was the someone else?"

"We don't know. A man. A young man. While she was supposed to be at work."

"Well then, why don't you call the hospital and see if she's there? I'm sure that would clear things up."

"I . . . we already done that."

233

"And?"

"She wasn't there."

"Oh."

"Ginger, you got to do something for me."

"What? What do you want me to do?"

"Follow her. Follow her for a week."

"Arthur McDowell!" She stood up. "That's the most disgusting, un-Christian thing I ever heard of, and I never thought I would hear it from you!"

"Well, now you have!" he shouted.

She refused to let him scare her. "All right, Arthur, if it means that much, I'll do it. But I'm a-tellin' you, I don't think it's right. If you got something botherin' you, you ought to tell Judith, that's for sure. I think you're actin' shameful about some gossip. That's what I think."

"Thank you, Ginger. Thank you. . . ." He walked to the door and then came back, knelt, and placed the cup back on the table. He did not look at her face.

After he left, she breathed deeply, sighing.

A week later, Ginger woke Arthur before he went to work.

"Well?" he said.

"Sit down, Arthur, you're in for a shock."

He sat down at the kitchen table.

Ginger remained standing, with a glass of water in her hand and a nasty look on her face.

"Arthur McDowell, I followed your wife. I know where she went for a week."

"And?"

"She went to work, and picked up the children at Ila's, and came back home."

"And?"

"And that's it."

"Are you sure? Are you sure that she didn't know you were following her and just acted like she was doing all those things?"

"I'm sure."

"She may have recognized you."

"Not in my brother's car, she didn't."

"She might have had him over at night, while you slept and while I was at work."

"Arthur! Your children!"

"Still, I don't know!"

"Arthur, my God! I don't know what to do with you."

"Deidre said—"

234

"*Deidre*? Deidre said what?"

"I don't know, Ginger. I don't know what to believe. Judith said some man helped her bring some pipes over. She said that; I didn't ask her. But still, they could'a guessed that Deidre saw them. Could'a guessed that I knew about it. Could'a made the whole thing up to fool me. Yes, that's it. To fool me! And put the pipes under the house to make it all look convincing."

Ginger threw her glass in the sink and the slivers from it scattered across the kitchen. She pointed her finger at Arthur. "You're wrong, bad wrong."

Ginger left.

Soon Judith would be back from work with the car and Arthur would have to go to work. He had not slept more than two hours in two days.

He was on the couch when the children came running into the room. They dropped their books onto a chair and jumped on top of him, kissing his face and running their hands through his hair. He laughed as they told about the fight on the bus and the whipping that James got for yelling in the lunch line.

He promised he would take them fishing Saturday, if they were good to their momma. They promised they would be.

Todd turned on the television. Arthur sent Todd to the refrigerator several times for beer. When he had finished drinking, he allowed Todd and James to share the last ounce in the can. Todd forgot how many beers he had taken to his father.

At seven, Judith arrived from the hospital. She sat on the couch with Arthur and kissed him on the forehead. He pulled her down and kissed her harshly. She pulled away. The children smiled at each other. She spoke to them.

"Okay, kids, all of you into the bathroom! Bath-time, then bed."

Todd walked to the bathroom and the rest followed. "I'm first," he said and closed the door in their faces.

James came back to the couch. "Can we have a mayonnaise sandwich after?"

"If you hurry," Judith said. She had had a long day. Anything they wanted would be fine as long as they went to bed quickly, so that she could sit with Arthur, in peace and quiet.

Later, Judith ran the water in the tub and Arthur slipped out of his clothes. Soon he was ready to get into fresh workclothes for his shift. "Got a surprise for you tonight, Honey," he told Judith in the kitchen as she made sandwiches for the children.

"Yeah, we gonna inherit a million dollars or somethin'?"

"No, better than that. I'm not going in tonight."

"Not going in? Why not?"

"I figure a night off won't hurt anything. I've never missed a day yet." He touched her hair.

"That's sweet, Arthur. Bills or no bills, you deserve a rest once in a while. It's gonna be nice sleeping with you again."

"Yes," he said. "I imagine so."

She went in and had the children say their prayers, kissed and covered each, left a night light on for Virginia, and separated James and Todd when they started wrestling. With the children's doors closed, she came back to the living room. Arthur was drinking another beer, watching "Gunsmoke."

She watched the show with him, her head on his shoulder, as she fell asleep.

She felt the sting on her face and woke up. The television was off. Arthur was pulling her to her feet. She felt the sting again, a painful slap across her eye. He threw her to the floor and straddled her, holding her head down by the hair.

"*Who is he?*" he whispered through clenched teeth, his saliva falling on her forehead. She started to scream, but he held her down with his knees and covered her mouth with his hand. "I said, *who is he?*"

Her eyes were wide, searching, frightened. She tried to scream and couldn't and bit his hand until she was sure that the sweat she tasted was mixed with blood. Still he refused to release her. He kept talking nonsensically about a man, a man, some man. He *knew* who he was; he had the license number from his truck. He *knew* they met; after dark, when he was at work and the children asleep. He was sure of it . . . sure of it . . . sure of it . . . why, why, *why* did she do it, why did she do this thing to him?

She drove her knee as deeply as it could go. He released his grip for a moment, long enough for her to scream, "*Todd! Todd!*"

The boy was not asleep. He had heard the noise and feared it. Now he had no choice. He jumped out of bed and ran into the living room.

"Todd! Aunt Ginger, God—get Aunt—"

Arthur held her face with his hand.

Todd ran out the door into the night, across the dark yard, and through the rose bushes that tore his feet and his legs and his underwear. He banged on Ginger's door, screaming for her to come. The lights came on much too slowly, and it seemed an eternity before Ginger opened the door.

She pulled Todd inside and he sobbed the command his mother had given. She ran to the phone and called the police. Will walked groggily into the kitchen. "What the hell's going on?" he said.

W

Twenty minutes later, the police car, red lights illuminating the woods on both sides of the dirt road, pulled into the yard and up to the porch. Two officers raced to the front porch and knocked.

Arthur answered.

"Yes?" he said calmly.

"You Arthur McDowell?"

"Yes."

"We got a complaint, Mister. We got to come in."

"Sure."

Judith was on the couch, curled up in a corner. Her face was red and burned, her clothes torn. She sobbed and covered her eyes when the policemen came in. Virginia and James were in the kitchen, crying. Adam was still in bed, shivering with fear. Todd was trying to calm him.

Arthur walked over to Judith and sat down. She jerked.

"Now, Baby, come on, I'm sorry. Really, I didn't know what I was doin'. I'll never do it again. God, but I'm sorry. I don't know what come over me. I love you, Baby. I love you. I love you. . . ."

The taller policeman seemed annoyed. "Ah, you look pretty well beat up, ma'am. We've got to investigate. Mind if we ask some questions? You want to press charges?"

She shook her head.

Arthur smiled weakly. "Can't you see that this was all an accident? We can take care of ourselves."

The policeman was struck by Arthur's polite, quiet manner. He wondered how this gentle man could be this cruel. His eyes moved from Judith's face to that of his partner.

"Well, Kendall, what do you think we ought to do?"

Officer Kendall shrugged. He looked far younger than the tall policeman, and he seemed a little nervous. His eyes darted around the room. He spoke softly, as if afraid to disturb the tension in the air. "Third party complaint. If she won't press charges, not much we can do." He looked at Judith and took off his cap. "Ma'am, we're going to call back tomorrow, when things have calmed down. If he hurts you again, all you have to do is let us know." He seemed unsatisfied with his own words. "Are you sure you don't want to press charges?"

"I'll be all right," Judith said. "Just leave us alone."

"I love you," Arthur whispered, his head bent in submission.

Judith brushed her hair back. "I'll be all right, Officers. Things just got out of hand, that's all. We'll work this out ourselves."

"Come on, Kendall. Not much we can do here," said the tall policeman. "You call us, ma'am, whenever you feel you need help, okay?"

"I'll be all right. We're just tired, that's all."

"She'll be all right," said Arthur meekly. "I can promise you that. I'll never lay a hand on her again, I swear."

Officer Kendall nodded, and he started to say something but shook his head as he closed the door. "Crazy world, isn't it?" he said to his partner as they got into the car.

Arthur told the children to get back in bed. He carried Judith to the bedroom.

She turned on her stomach, her face buried in the pillow.

He talked. For hours he talked. About his love for her. About this strange man who had a name and a license plate and a desire for his wife. Judith, exhausted, drifted into unconsciousness. If I don't wake up, she thought, it will be because he has killed me.

He beat her again.

In his room, under his blankets, Todd could hear the muffled sounds of violence, but the sounds were like seeds in his mind, which his consciousness ignored, for sanity's sake.

The next morning, Judith put the children on the school bus, but she did not go to work. She called the police, explained what had happened, drove downtown, and signed a warrant for Arthur's arrest.

Arthur did not know that he was sought. He had left for work to make up for the time he had lost the night before. The policemen entered the mill and walked up to Arthur, read the warrant, and took him to jail. He was not allowed bail. Court was scheduled for the next day.

Arthur called Judith and asked her to bring him some good clothes. The workclothes he wore were greasy and grimy, and he did not want to appear in public in them. Judith said she would send some clothes by Ginger. Ginger picked up the clothes the next morning and took them to the jail. She left the clothes with the guards, who forgot to give them to Arthur.

The judge's name was Patton, Lloyd Patton. He had a huge belly and his chest was narrow. He had a reddish-brown mustache that seemed to get in the way of his mouth. His tongue licked the ends of the hair. He looked like the nineteenth-century portraits that surrounded the courtroom.

Judith could not speak when she came to the stand. She could not tell these strangers of her humiliation. She only looked at Arthur once. His proud head was bent. When his name was called, he stood uneasily, aware of the eyes taking in his wrinkled, oil-stained overalls.

Judge Patton tried to get Judith to speak up.

"I can't," she said.

The judge looked at the woman and then at the man before him. He glanced around the courtroom.

"All right," he said. "Mrs. McDowell will accompany me into my chambers. Mr. McDowell will stay here until I call him. Bailiff?" The deputy gestured to Arthur to sit down.

Judith did not wait to be told to sit down when she walked into the judge's office. It was a small, gray office, with only two chairs and an old wooden desk between them. The windows were the same color as the walls.

"Now, Mrs. McDowell. Please tell me why you issued this warrant?"

She told him of the beating, and of the lie that her husband believed; of Ginger's shadowing, and of the jealousy that until now she had thought was natural.

Patton nodded without expression, and when he felt that she could say no more, or had said enough, he stepped outside and motioned for Arthur to come in.

Arthur stood behind Judith and rested his hands on her shoulders. For a moment those hands felt reassuring, until she remembered his pleas and abuse. She pulled away from him. His hands slid to his sides.

Patton rubbed his temples. "Mr. McDowell, will you kindly tell me what happened the other night, and why you think you're here?"

Arthur's head shook for a moment, then his face became stony. "I don't know what happened."

Patton leaned forward. "You don't *know?*"

"That's right. I thought my wife was . . . well, you know, that she might have been seein' somebody else . . . and I just lost my temper. That's all. I know that I shouldn't have done it. I know that I did a horrible thing to her, and I don't blame her if she hates me for it."

Judith flinched. Arthur and the judge didn't notice.

"Mr. McDowell, I have decided that if you accept my recommendation for psychiatric evaluation and treatment, if you go to a prescribed number of sessions to be determined by a qualified psychiatrist to help you work

239

out your suspicion and your anger, then we can settle this matter. You must do so voluntarily. If you choose not to do so, then I shall most certainly send you back to jail."

Arthur frowned. "Psychiatrist? You mean you think I'm crazy?"

"Now, Mr. McDowell, I didn't say that. I am saying that you've got to learn to control your jealousy and your anger. You must come to realize that your actions are not rational or reasonable. I am of the opinion that you need professional help to come to these conclusions. If you love this woman, then you'll do it. If you don't, then I think it would be best if you were to forget about her, go to jail, and get yourself straightened out. What do you think?"

Arthur stepped from side to side and swallowed. "I'll do whatever Judith wants me to do."

Judge Patton looked at Judith. She was trying not to cry. "Mrs. McDowell, what do you say?"

"I think he ought to do what you said, go get some help. I can't talk to him. He won't listen to me."

Arthur knelt by her side. "I will now, Honey. I will now." He reached for her shoulders. She did not resist.

Once a month for a year, Arthur went to a psychiatrist. Dr. Sommer seemed malnourished. His angular features and brittle skin offended Arthur. The doctor's eyes were small, even behind thick-rimmed glasses. He never smiled. His demeanor was of a man who had absorbed the worries and complaints of too many troubled people. He had long ago given up hope of single-handedly saving the psyche of the western world. He was a man with no illusions, talking to a man with too many.

Dr. Sommer determined that Arthur had been jilted by a girl that he had loved in his youth, before the war, and that as a result, he could only trust one woman, his mother, who was dead. Arthur agreed that this was his problem, and Dr. Sommer was pleased that his diagnosis was confirmed. Now that the cause was pinpointed, the effect would disappear. Arthur agreed.

Judith wanted to quit the cafeteria, but Miss Broughfair, the family counselor she went to, said that this would be an admission of guilt to Arthur. So Judith continued to work during the day. Arthur took on more and more sheetrocking jobs, still working at the mill at night.

He would not touch her. He would not make love to her, unless he was drunk. Sometimes she thought she saw his youthful habits return, his joy in his children, and his love for her. But that did not happen often and did not last long.

Todd noticed the change. He pretended that everything was fine, but he tried not to get in Arthur's way.

The boy was growing up and he wanted Arthur to notice. But Arthur seemed preoccupied, distant. He didn't laugh much or play around with the kids as he had in the past. He was always tired. He slept a lot.

Work and sleep. Sleep and work.

Everything's going to be okay, Todd thought. What daddy needs is rest. Rest and quiet.

Whatever it was that Arthur was keeping to himself, he kept well from his children.

Soon Todd would be a man. Then Arthur could teach him the things that fathers taught sons.

Twenty-two

October 1960

ILA PHONED Mayzelle at Lora's. "Can you go with me to the Physical Rehabilitation Center tomorrow?"

"I suppose, but I thought Judith was goin'."

"I talked her out of it."

"Why?"

"I'll tell you tomorrow. It's Todd. I got one of those feelings about him."

"Feelings? I don't understand."

"I think you do. I'll talk to you tomorrow. Right now I got a lot of thinking to do."

"But, Ila . . ."

Ila put the receiver down.

Arthur stopped the car. He went to the back and opened the trunk. The wheelchair unfolded easily on the clinic sidewalk. Mayzelle pushed it to the passenger door of the Buick, and Ila grasped the metal arms and pulled her body over onto the leather seat. Mayzelle gently placed Ila's legs on the footrests. "Easy," said Ila, trembling in fear of possible pain.

"You hold on," said Mayzelle.

"When you want me back?" said Arthur, lighting a cigarette.

"'Bout an hour or so," said Mayzelle.

"No," rasped Ila. "Make it two hours. I feel like a real workout today."

Mayzelle shrugged. "Whatever the old lady wants."

Ila smiled. "You ought to respect your youngers better than that."

"Yes ma'am," Mayzelle said as she pushed the chair to the doors.

Once inside, Mayzelle checked in and took Ila to the rehabilitation room. There she lifted Ila to the parallel bars and watched as she pulled herself across the length of the room.

"Touch the floor with those feet!" shouted Mayzelle.

Ila grimaced and obeyed.

Later, on her back, Ila lifted weights even though her legs failed to respond. "Good," shouted Mayzelle.

Ila smiled.

Mayzelle sipped a Coke. "At least you ain't six feet under. I remember a time when you wished you was."

"True," said Ila. "You talked me back to health. This is the only way I can get strength enough to get away from your constant jabberin'."

"Well," said Mayzelle, her voice filled with power and pride, "at least you can get around the house in that chair without anybody pushin' you."

"Fat lot of good that does me."

"What? You want to be helpless? You want to be pitied?"

Ila squirmed. "Don't you go talkin' to me like that or—"

"Or what? You gonna run home and tell your momma?"

"If I had the strength—"

"You'd what?" Mayzelle smirked. "You'd get up and come over and belt me one, right?"

"No," said Ila with a laugh. "I'd roll over there and hit you in the stomach."

"Violent," said Mayzelle. "You gettin' to feel violent all of a sudden?"

"No, I'm gettin' to feel tired."

Mayzelle searched her face for the signs: heavy panting, loose muscles. Enough for the day. Time to stop. Can't let the fatigue set in or she'll get a cold on the way home.

Mayzelle threw a robe over Ila's shoulders and helped her into the chair. "Enough for the day, youngun."

"Wish you'd stop calling me that."

Ila panted as Mayzelle pushed her to the lobby. There Ila reached into her pocketbook and pulled out a cigar.

Mayzelle made a face. "You not goin' to smoke one of those nasty things again, are you?"

"And what of it?"

"Nothing. Just hope I never tell Arthur or Lon or Judith."

"You won't," Ila said smugly, lighting up.

"How can you be so sure?"

"'Cause then I'll tell about the birthday party y'all got planned for Todd."

Mayzelle opened her eyes wide in disbelief. "You know about that?"

Ila shrugged. "I know everything," she said, coughing.

"You better not spoil that boy's party."

Ila shook her head and coughed again. "Why would I do that? You don't tell what you know and I won't tell what I know. That seems like a fair deal to me."

"I think you got a little of the devil in you, Ila Mitchell Tolbert."

"Maybe," Ila said, puffing rings of smoke toward Mayzelle.

"You know what?" said Mayzelle sweetly.

"What?"

"You startin' to look like President Roosevelt."

"I don't know," said Ila. "I figure he looks better dead than I do alive." They both laughed.

Ila fidgeted in her chair. "I hate to sit here and watch all the sick people come and go. Gives me the creeps."

Mayzelle smiled, thinking, They probably feel the same way about you, old girl.

"What you say?"

"Oh, nothin'. I was wonderin' if Lon would be there."

"At the party? I don't know. Daddy don't like being around Todd for some reason. I never did figure that one out. Daddy always loved the children, but he can't abide being around Todd. I don't know why. Todd is a likable grandchild."

"Great-grandchild. Lon's got a lot of them, you know."

"I know, I keep count. But something about that boy turns my daddy rotten, and I don't know what it is. Come on home with me for coffee and maybe we'll puzzle it out."

"Can't."

"Can't? Why not?"

"Bakin' your grandson a cake."

"Oh, well . . . don't put all that sugar in this one, okay? I 'bout couldn't eat the last one you fixed, full of sugar and chocolate, must'a rotted two teeth."

"What does Lora say about Lon and Todd?"

"Nothin' much. She keeps out of it. Hell, the boy walks into the room and Daddy walks out, ain't that a sight? Can't figure it out for the life of me."

"Yeah," Mayzelle said, "Lon's a strange one. But so is Todd."

Ila shook her head. "You know the things that's been happening over at Judith's house?"

Mayzelle frowned. "Who doesn't?"

"Well, for one thing, the children don't know what's going on."

"How can they not know? They ain't stupid. You seen to that."

"Judith raised 'em good. She's been a good mother. Raising four kids on their money ain't easy."

"You raised four on less," Mayzelle said.

"Yes, but all I had to worry about was sickness, accidents, and poverty. My mother gave me strength . . ."

"And you give Judith the same strength."

"Sometimes I wonder, Mayzelle, if that's enough."

"I know what you mean."

"Have you ever watched Todd when we give him a gift, sittin' on the sofa, openin' the box real careful, holdin' whatever little thing it is to the light?"

"Like a diamond merchant." Mayzelle chuckled.

"Yes, just. He looks at things from all angles."

"Probably a bit of a cheat in him. Runs in the family."

Ila lifted her head and stared at Mayzelle. Mayzelle stared back. Neither smiled.

Finally Mayzelle said, "I'm just kiddin'."

"I know it."

"He's growin' like a weed—no, more like a tree. Strong child."

"Takes after me. Strong heredity."

"Oh yes, I forgot; your South Carolina sharecrop blood."

"Sometimes you ain't funny, Mayzelle."

"One day Todd's gonna ask why his great-grandpa treats him like a disease."

"I think I'll talk to old Lon myself."

"I wouldn't try it. I tried and Lon just got up mad. Stubborn old cuss. I'm glad I'm not stubborn like that."

"Yeah," Ila said. "I reckon that would spoil your delightful personality."

Mayzelle nodded. "Exactly."

"I got something for you to do. And I want to ask you before Arthur gets here."

"What's that?"

"I want you to take a wreath up to David's grave."

Mayzelle looked up sharply. "What? That's clear up to Mortimer. That's hours from here. How you expect me to get all the way up there, walk?"

"No, no. I got it all figured out. I asked Arthur to take you. He gave me some mean looks, but he agreed."

"Why me? Why don't you go?"

"'Cause. I can't get up that mountain he's buried on. Besides, there's something else I want you to do."

"What's that?"

"I want you to take Todd—"

"No."

"You listen to me for a minute. I'm gettin' weaker each year. Now, I know the doctor says that, besides my legs, I'm fit to do anything like anybody else for a hundred more years, but there's somethin' special I want you to do. I want you . . . ." She nodded toward the door, then drew Mayzelle next to the wheelchair. "I want you to take the boy to that place and tell him the history of this family."

"Why, that's the silliest thing—"

"No. No, it ain't silly. I'm not goin' to be around much longer—"

"Why don't *you* tell him?"

"'Cause I'm too close to it. I *am* the history of this family. You been standin' on the outside, and sometimes on the inside, watchin' us every day for I don't know how many years. You know more about us than we do, and that's a fact of life that I ain't too stupid to observe. Take the boy with you. Tell him everything about us. That's all I want you to do."

"And Judith? What's she got to say about this?"

"I told her that you and the boy needed a picnic and she needed a rest from the youngun."

"You are shrewd."

Ila smiled. "Thank you. I knew one day you'd appreciate my learnin'."

"So, you want me to go with Arthur and sit that young boy down in a cemetery and tell him the history of this family, right?"

"Exactly."

Mayzelle shook her head. "They say that old people get crazy ideas in their head. I guess you no exception."

Ila didn't smile. "You'll do it for me?"

Mayzelle sighed. "For you."

October is a special and lonely time in the mountains. It is that part of the season between fall and winter when the leaves seem toasted amid layers of pine, and gaunt, charred bones are topped with spider webs. It is the time of the year when the branches wash the blood off their fingers in the cruel waters of the Brown Mountains. It is a suspended time, not a beginning or an end, when no one celebrates, when mists arrive before the sun, and dust sleeps until summer, and cemeteries become as faded as forgotten wreaths. Colors and life seem to fade, bleed into one another, until the remaining view is like an old photograph left too long in the sun.

The only sound on the dirt road was that of a Buick avoiding the sharp-edged rocks in the path along the river. Arthur was careful not to steer too close to the riverbank on his left, nor to the mountainside on his right. Waterfalls stood suspended in ice around them. The car pulled into a clearing littered with bits and pieces of fallen limbs and the remains of a campfire long extinguished.

Mayzelle wrapped an extra scarf around her head, pulled herself out of the back seat of the car, and motioned for Todd to follow. She looked toward the hill for a long time, searching for the place where the path should be, but the path was covered with leaves. Mayzelle's back hurt a little, and she dreaded the climb up the mountain to the secluded cemetery. She leaned on the car for a moment and watched Arthur as he lit a cigarette.

She cleared her throat and said loudly, against the wind, "You sure you don't want to go up there with us?"

Arthur shook his head. "Nope." He repeated the word, louder this time. Seen enough death, he thought. Don't need to be reminded of it, not up close anyway. He put the car into gear and slowly pulled away.

Mayzelle began the long walk, with Todd behind her. From time to time she looked back to make sure he was still following. Quiet child. He didn't say anything on the way up; just stopped now and then to examine a rock or look beneath a rotted log. Could be takin' him to a sacrifice, Mayzelle thought, and he wouldn't act much different. She wondered what Arthur would do for the next few hours and hoped he would get back before nightfall.

The ground was slippery with dying leaves, and the wind cut across Mayzelle's face. Gettin' too old, she thought, too old to be walking up a mountain with a ten-year-old white child.

Soon she reached the top and walked to the rusted iron gates. Todd followed. Mayzelle sat on the cracked cement bench in the middle of the cemetery. Todd sat beside her.

They sat for a long time, wordless. Mayzelle's eyes moved from stone to stone and name to name until she felt ready to look upon the name chiseled deeply into the Georgia marble: TOLBERT.

"Lord, I wish we hadn't come," she whispered.

Todd looked at her with a frown and walked over to the stone. He turned his back, unzipped his trousers, and urinated, watching without expression as the steady stream spiraled upward across the cold marker. Mayzelle shook her head and smiled. Wouldn't Ila Tolbert have a cow if she saw her grandson pissin' away on his grandpa's grave?

"Probably fry his little ass," she said softly.

The boy cut a glance at Mayzelle and zipped his pants.

"Youngun, come here next to me and let's sit and talk awhile."

Todd grinned briefly and ran into her frail arms. The air seemed to pinch his face as he sought the warmth of her familiar bosom.

Placing her hands up the back of his shirt to warm them on his soft skin, Mayzelle began to rock the boy.

Maybe this boy will know what only a few of us have known, thought Mayzelle. Maybe he will know the whole truth; and somewhere in the tale he may find strength. Or maybe he'll deny his blood. Or maybe he's too young to know what I'm talkin' about. Doesn't matter. A promise is a promise. It is cold up here, way too cold. Storm clouds to the north, and clear, icy blue sky to the south. My veins ain't as warm as they once was.

Mayzelle would tell the boy. No one else could or would. She would have to tell him at that time and in that place. There would be no other chance. Maybe he's only ten, she thought, and white, but he's just as much a part of me as if I had been the one to carry him in my belly. There is no one else for me to give this to, no one else to listen.

She cleared her throat.

"Boy," she said, "I'm gonna tell you some things about people that you ought to know. Things that you 'specially have got to deal with when your time come. And your time is coming sooner than you know. There are two kinds of people: those what gets knocked down and stays down, and those what gets knocked down and gets back up. One of these days, soon, you gonna have to decide what kind you want to be. People is a lot like the deer herds up here in the mountains; the weak ones die, and the strong ones live. I'm gonna tell you about strong and caring men and women who survived against all kind of hard times, survived with their honest pride so they could pass that strength on to their children. And I'm gonna tell you about joy you ain't known yet; and the way things is goin', it's a joy people gets farther and farther away from.

"I didn't want to come up here and tell this to you. At first I didn't think it was my right. I'm an old woman, nearly seventy-three. My memory plays tricks on me. But I love you, and I'm not gonna let this die with me and old Ila. You a young boy and right now you treat me pretty polite, but the day might come when you just pass me off as some old black woman what told you stories like them fairy tales that your momma told you. I hope you never forget what I'm gonna tell you today. I don't have no school learning. What I learned was from my Ila's books, my momma's love, and a good ear for listenin'. Now it's your turn to listen. Mind me good. Nobody is ever gonna tell you this again."

Mayzelle gazed off into the woods and talked fast, so that her words, piling one on another, would help keep them warm. She remembered, turning back to things that everyone else seemed to have forgotten, looking beyond the woods into a land and a time peopled with shadows.

Perhaps the mountain air helped her see things so crisp and clear. She wasn't sure. But she could see, with sharp detail that surprised and excited her, a cotton field, and a skinny, black-eyed girl.

𝕎

Arthur drove to the fork in the dirt road and stopped for a moment. Which way to go? One sign, with the word "gas" painted sloppily on the pole, pointed to the left. Another said "Coca-Cola and other drinks" and pointed to the right. Arthur thought a moment and then turned right.

About ten miles down the road, he passed a fish hatchery and then a dam. Water was low. Must be plenty of trout on the upper side. Should have brought a pole. Then, around a curve, he saw a shack with one gas pump and a screened-in porch with a few homemade two-by-four tables. He brushed the dust off his pants and walked inside. He bought a beer, and then another, and watched the leaves fall toward the river. He thought about his boy and the old woman up on the hill, sitting amid moss-covered graves, telling childish stories—hell, next you know they'll want me to tell him stories, too. Stories I'd rather not tell, but if I had to, I guess there'd be no safer place to deposit them than in my own boy's mind.

Yes sir, I could tell him about the war, and how I met his momma. And maybe one day, when he has hair around his peter and breaks out in hives every time he gets around a girl, I could tell him about the other women I've known besides his momma. Maybe tell him about Milly. He laughed.

He had another beer. Good beer—a bit warm, though.

Then I'd tell him about friends, how you shouldn't get too close to them, 'cause they'll screw you up, too. Maybe not. Maybe he'll get lucky. Naw, nobody's that lucky, especially if he's got my blood in him.

Wonder what kind of man he'll make. Got big hands and long fingers, probably be a good carpenter. Hope he stays out of the mill. He'll bore to death there. Carpenter don't have to talk much, and that'd probably suit him just fine.

Maybe I shouldn't tell him nothing. Let the women fill his head with what they figure is right. Couldn't hurt much. They'll tell him about pretty life; paint life all roses and cheerful, 'ceptin' for their problems, of course. They'll make heroes or somethin' out of themselves. Screw him up real good.

Course, my momma was an exception. Anna never complained, least not much. Couldn't be a better woman than her, nowhere. Shame she's dead. She would'a opened the boy up. Would'a woke him up at night to watch the possums play on the front porch when the lantern's glow spread out of the window. Like pets they were to her, left a pan of corn out for them every night. Daddy never knew.

Arthur wiped his brow, out of habit. The wind was dying down, the clouds drifting in from the north, the river getting colder. He could almost hear it chilling, complaining across the rocks toward the dam. Looks like rain.

Okay, I hear you. No customers here after six. Place probably stays open just to keep the storekeeper from going nuts out here in the wilderness.

Arthur paid for his last beer and climbed back into the car.

Mayzelle was crying.

Todd was crying, too, though he did not know why. He was confused. He did not understand. His mother always said that if a person acted good and thought only good thoughts, then only good things would come to that person. Mayzelle's story didn't seem to work like that.

What if he didn't want to grow up in a world where the good guys didn't always win? What if he didn't want a stone over him like Grandfather David? Todd was full of questions, but he did not know how to put them into words for Mayzelle, so he turned from her and said, "I don't want to talk about this anymore."

"You've got to listen, boy," said Mayzelle.

"I don't want to listen. I didn't want to come up here anyway."

"You didn't have to come."

"Yes I did. Grandma Ila made me. If I had known you were gonna tell me all this stuff, I wouldn't have come up here at all, especially with a . . ."

Mayzelle smiled. "A what?"

Todd didn't answer. He poked at the small fire they had built when the air had grown cold.

"This fire's about out," he said. "I've got to get some more wood. I wonder where Daddy is. He should have been back by now." Todd looked down the trail toward the empty dirt road. "I don't guess many people get back this way."

"You scared?" Mayzelle asked.

"Of what?"

"Of what I'm tellin' you."

"It ain't got nothin' to do with me," Todd said.

"It's your past," Mayzelle said, "and you can't escape from that. The choices your great-grandparents made will shape your life. The choices your grandparents made will shape your life. Fact is, boy, those changes are happenin' right now in your own house. You got to be ready for the fight that's comin' your way. You'll have to be brave and grow up quick in the next few years. All of these stories have a hook on your life. Your grandmother Ila and I hope that we can prepare you for the battle ahead. I know I sound like a cracked old lady, but you got to trust me on this, boy. You can't go through life leavin' out the things that change you from a boy to a man. If you try, then you're lost. You in danger, Honey. Great danger. Ila and me sees it comin'. This time we gonna give you our strength."

"I don't know what you're talkin' about," Todd said. "Nothin' bad is happenin' to me. Nothin' terrible is happenin' in my family. Momma and Daddy have good jobs and they love us and we get along fine. If you know so much, tell me what's going to happen to me."

"What you learn today will decide that," said Mayzelle, "but you have to go through the dark with me first. This is a story that I tried to forget, but Ila taught me to understand hardships, to learn what good can be harvested from bad times. This is a dangerous world. We can all be squashed like the spiders under our feet. We don't have much to say over things, and that's one reason I brought you up here. Ila and I are gonna try to give you some strength, 'cause Honey, you gonna need all the help you can get. There is hope, boy, but you got to learn to recognize it in the middle of the hurtin'."

Darkness filtered through the birches as the Buick pulled into the clearing. A light rain fell on the nearly naked trees. Arthur turned his headlights toward the hill and got out.

"Mayzelle!" he shouted.

No answer.

"Mayzelle! Todd!" he shouted again. Not even an echo. He slammed the car door and walked to the hill. He pulled himself up by young dogwoods. At the top he walked through the open gate of the cemetery and stood staring. Mayzelle was leaning against the back of the bench, Todd held tight in her arms.

Asleep, Arthur thought, in this weather. That old woman and my boy, a real sight, sleeping in a graveyard. Wait till his momma hears about this.

He walked quietly to the bench and shook Mayzelle by the shoulder.

Judith worried. They should have been back long ago, she thought. Judith had been looking at the picture of Arthur for at least an hour—a thin smile forced toward the camera lens, in Paris or somewhere, during the war, his face painted pink, his hair a dull yellow. He looked like summer then. She could not think about Arthur without also thinking of summer, because it was only during that season that he seemed to wake from some sad and lonely sleep. He was never old in summer. Sometimes she felt she had married a child, until winter, and then the child with boundless energy changed suddenly with the season, his face tight and drawn, his eyes piercing, dulled by the lack of sun. She placed the photo back in the album and went to the window. Deidre and Dan had fallen asleep on the sofa.

Judith looked out the window but saw only her reflection in the blackness. She was not as plain as once she had been. She felt more a woman every day. Why did I let them go? she thought. Todd's just a baby, and Mayzelle's too old for this weather. Mortimer is such a long way to go. I must have been crazy to let Mayzelle and Momma talk me into such a thing.

She closed the curtains and sat down at the table in the kitchen. She looked at the coffee pot, but the thought of any more liquid brought a sick taste to her mouth. She moved back to the chair near the window and picked up the picture album. She had leafed through it a dozen times that night, and still she always stopped at the picture of Arthur in uniform. He'll take care of them, she thought. But who will take care of him? Silly thought. I must be getting tired.

Shouldn't have buried Daddy that far away. But, no, Momma wouldn't have it any other way. Ila gonna put him with his folks, and what Ila says, goes. How will you visit, I said. I won't, she said.

Put up an expensive tombstone that nobody will ever see?

Yes, said Momma, but at least I'll know it's there. I can see it in my brain.

Judith closed her eyes and tried not to think about it. Got to think of nicer things. Think about my boy, playing on that mountainside.

Wish I'd gone with 'em.

The drive to Greensboro would take some hours. Arthur knew that Judith would be awake, waiting.

He looked briefly at the long hair of his firstborn, soft and gentle. The boy's hands were smooth, not yet soiled by oil or clay. His mind was filled with love and frailty, not yet scarred by pain. His breathing whispered softly against the harsh, grinding engine noises. Arthur laid his hand on the boy's neck.

"I wish," said Arthur aloud but softly, "that you could see these mountains." He looked back to the road. "They live just like you and me. They never die. They give life and sometimes take it, but never die. That's right, you sleep. Sleep while you can."

Judith heard the sharp cracking noise as the album hit the floor.

She rubbed her eyes and wondered where she was and what she was doing there. Then she remembered: Arthur, Todd, and Mayzelle. The cemetery. She picked up the scattered pictures on the floor and went to the window. Dan and Deidre came in from the kitchen.

Deidre put her coffee down and came to Judith. "Now, Honey, he's all right. It takes several hours to get back from Mortimer."

"They should have been back hours ago."

"Now, Sis, they'll be fine. Arthur'll take care of them all. And Mayzelle may be old, but she's tougher than any of us, and you know that."

"Yes, well, I'd feel better if they hadn't gone."

"Now, come on over here and sit down with me and Dan. Arthur will be here soon. He's a good driver. Let's give them another hour, okay?"

Judith looked at Deidre. Deidre smiled. Judith tried to smile back.

"I guess I do worry," sighed Judith.

"Yes, and who is to blame you for it?" said Deidre. "Mothers are supposed to worry."

Judith picked up her sewing box. Deidre went into the kitchen to make more coffee. Dan cleaned his pipe.

An hour went by, and then another. Arthur opened the door with Todd in his arms. Deidre put her finger to her lips. Judith was asleep in her chair. Dan carried Todd to a place by the fire.

"What took you so long?" whispered Deidre.

Arthur stared at her and shook his head. He left the door open and went to Judith.

"She's been worried sick," said Deidre. "You and that old woman dragging all over the state. Where's Mayzelle?"

Arthur said something but Deidre could not hear him.

"Where's Mayzelle?" she repeated, an urgency in her voice.

Judith stirred awake. She looked at Arthur.

Arthur spoke. "Todd's fine, just fine. A little cold, but he'll be fine. He fell asleep, that's all."

Judith looked relieved and went to her son. She took him to his bed, undressed him, and pulled the blankets to his chin.

She walked back to Arthur. He was sipping black coffee.

"Where's Mayzelle?"

"I dropped her off at Lora's a little while ago," Arthur answered. "Those two were sleeping like babies up there. She's too old for that kind of stuff. I don't know why I let Ila talk me into taking them."

The dawn of his eleventh birthday was approaching, and Todd couldn't sleep. The moonlight cast a glow on every object in the room. He thought about the story Mayzelle had told him.

He had often seen Lon and Lora as drab and quiet older people, with nothing interesting to tell or give. Great-Grandma Lora laughed at most anything. And Lon seemed serious and distant. Todd wondered whether these were the same two people Mayzelle had described, young people in love, with hopes and dreams, living in a tent on the banks of the Catawba. He could hardly believe their strength, always picking themselves up and moving on.

And Ila. Ila had been in a wheelchair for as long as he could remember. He had taken it for granted, like the sun coming up and going down—nothing special or important. Ila and the wheelchair were one, always had been, always would be. How could she have gone through so much and still laugh with the grandchildren growing up, and cheat at cards, and read racy novels, and look forward to rides in the country?

I'm not like them, Todd thought. Whatever it is they have, I don't.

At breakfast, Arthur asked Todd what he and Mayzelle had talked about.

"Nothing," Todd replied.

Twenty-three

THE NEIGHBORHOOD children came to Todd's birthday party. Sawbucks were set up in the backyard and covered with long boards, which in turn were covered with tablecloths and an endless variety of cakes and meats. Todd accepted the gracious congratulations of his neighbors and held up his present, a .22 rifle, for all to see. Arthur and Judith had argued about that gift. Judith said he was too young. Arthur said he was becoming a man and should own a man's things; besides, the boy read too much. Judith said that she didn't like guns.

"But he wants it so badly," Arthur said. In the end, they gave Todd the gun, along with two boxes of ammunition.

Dan brought the liquor and the men adjourned, as usual, to the tool shed, where the real party took place—poker and booze, lurid jokes at the expense of an absent wife's dignity, and a camaraderie that relieved the tensions of marriage.

Lon wasn't feeling well, so he sat down in a corner of the shed, refusing the potent refreshment.

"What's the matter, old man?" Arthur asked. "Gettin' so you can't keep up?"

Dan smiled. "I bet old Lora's wearin' him out these days."

They all laughed, especially when Lon said, "I wish she would." He reached for a beer. "The damn union mess is gettin' me down."

Arthur shook his head and took a long gulp of bourbon. "Union's a good thing. Mill been needin' a strong union for a long time."

"Maybe so," said Lon sadly, "but I've had enough of unions in my day. Don't cause nothin' but trouble."

Arthur grinned. "Progress. Unions will bring better wages."

"And union dues," Lon said, shaking a finger.

"Yes," said Arthur, "but better workin' conditions and all. It'll be worth it."

"Communists," said Lon. "Communists upsettin' everything in this country. Everybody wants more money. More of this and more of that. Nobody cares that we're all goin' downhill. Those unions are all full of communists."

Dan held the bottle up to the light. "Lon, you been sayin' that for a long time, long as I can remember. Everything's going to hell, you say, all the time. I ain't seen no fires yet."

"You will," Lon said. "You can count on it. Bring those unions in and old man Alexander and his boys will fight, yes sir. I seen mill fights, and they ain't no picnics."

Arthur choked on the bourbon. "Lon, you ain't seen shit. If those asses want to fight us when the union comes in, we'll lick 'em, fair and square."

Lon stretched his back and wiped his brow with a handkerchief. "There'll be blood, Arthur. Lots of blood. We got lots of family working over there, and I don't want to see any of 'em getting hurt."

"Well," Arthur said quietly, "when the trouble comes, why don't you just stay home in bed and let us men take care of it?"

Lon turned his face against the scene. "I never backed away from nothin' in my life, Arthur."

"Come on," said Dan, "don't get your blood pressure up, Grandpa. Arthur was just baitin' you. Right, Arthur?"

Arthur squinted. "Maybe. Maybe not."

Lon walked to the door. "I'm goin' to get myself some tea. This liquor's makin' y'all mean. Especially you, Arthur."

"Mind your own business," said Arthur.

"I will," said Lon. "You can be sure of that."

"Go to hell," Arthur said.

Outside on the lawn, Judith helped the children bob for apples and play tag. Ila stayed near the grill with Deidre, turning the hamburgers. Mayzelle peeled potatoes on the back porch.

Ila looked up to Deidre at the first shouts.

The children were bursting balloons, and Ila had to strain to make out the noise coming from the shed. Arthur came running out and kicked over the tables.

When Lon saw the grin on Arthur's face, his mind raced across more than forty years. He had seen that smile before, but only once, long ago, and he remembered a fear that he thought was forgotten: Vance Bradley, with a bullet in his head, smiling.

Arthur began to scream. "I know he's here! I know it! Where is he? You're hiding him from me, all of you! You're protectin' that slut over there!"

No one moved. Arthur walked up to each parent and child, demanding an answer. *"Where is he?"*

"He's drunk," whispered Ila.

"He's mad," said Deidre.

Deidre and Ginger moved toward Judith so that if and when he charged her, they might be able to stop him.

Dan walked silently behind Arthur's back and grabbed him. Arthur easily shook him off. "No! He's here and I know it! Now we'll all see him and all of you will know who's telling the truth!" He threw a bottle to the ground and walked deliberately towards Judith, his eyes locked on hers. She held her head high, eyes drawing him nearer, away from the children.

As Arthur pulled his arm back to strike, Lon shouted, "No!" Lora closed her eyes. Lon pointed toward the garage.

Arthur turned and saw Todd poised on one knee, eye fixed on the rifle bead, the barrel pointed toward Arthur's head.

"Oh my God," Arthur whispered.

Todd let the rifle fall to the ground. He watched the children, his friends, cautiously make their exits while Ginger took Judith inside the house.

Ila watched Arthur walk like a man in a dream over to Todd. The boy would not look at his father.

Arthur shrugged, looking up to the breeze from the trees, trying to find a word of explanation. He opened his mouth several times but could not speak and cupped his hands over his face.

Todd, numb with a cold confusion sweeping over his body, began to tremble. He tried to pretend that this was just a dream and that he would soon wake. He stood.

"Look at me, boy," Arthur said.

Todd looked at the ground.

Arthur slapped him across the face. A small trickle of blood flowed from Todd's nostrils. When the blood reached his mouth, Todd looked into his father's eyes and knew what Mayzelle had known.

Todd looked to the porch. She was watching him, a witness to his shame.

At dawn Todd was awakened. He was told to put on his clothes, gather the other children, maintain their silence, and get into the car. This done, Judith left Arthur.

She vowed never to return. She was done with him. She and the children would stay with Ila.

Ila rolled to the table in her kitchen and lifted the steaming coffee pot. "You're makin' a big mistake."

Judith was too tired to be surprised. "What you mean, Momma? What mistake?

"Leavin' Arthur ain't gonna solve anything. I know you ain't done a lot of thinkin' about this, or else you wouldn't have run away."

"I didn't run away," snapped Judith. "I left him. He ran away from me in his mind a long time ago."

"Still," said Ila assuredly, "I don't think you've really thought this out."

"What's to think out?" she said dryly. "You think maybe I should stay around there until he hurts me, or worse, one of his own children?"

"Oh, Judith, it ain't that bad."

"Momma, how the hell can you sit there and tell me that it ain't that bad? He almost killed me last year, and I'm not going to take the chance of being put in the ground—not while my babies is alive."

Ila shook her head. "It's a bad thing seein' a family end like this. First time in our family history—"

"If you start talkin' about family history I'll throw up. Our family ain't been much up to now, and it's about time I wrote myself out—if you don't mind."

Ila nodded. "It's your life."

"That's right," Judith said. "Mine, not yours."

"You said it, daughter, not me." Ila poured more cream into her coffee. She ignored the tears falling down Judith's face onto the table. She hesitated before speaking. "Judith, listen to an old woman. You still love him, don't you?"

"I don't know," Judith replied in a whisper. "I just don't know."

"Well, I wondered for a long time about whether I loved David. The love in my marriage got lost somewhere during the Depression, or at least I misplaced it. It wasn't until too late that I figured that I hadn't loved your daddy like I should have. I kept it from him. I didn't love him enough. Figured later on that maybe David's dyin' was God's way of punishing me for being so hard on him. No man can live without love. Love makes you complete. David was empty. You suppose that might be happening to Arthur?"

Judith almost laughed. "You really believe that, don't you, Momma? I am really amazed. You're a-sittin' here tellin' me that I don't love Arthur *enough*?"

"Could be, couldn't it?"

"Momma, I don't know what kind of world you livin' in, but it ain't this one." Judith swallowed. "Arthur has had nothing but my love ever since I've known him. You couldn't know. Nobody could know how much I needed that man. The only people that ever took time out to care—and I mean really care—about me was Arthur and Mayzelle."

"But it ain't too late, Judith. It ain't too late to give him the love he needs."

Judith cringed. "Momma, I just don't want to talk about it anymore. It's done and over with, you hear? You really don't understand, do you? You don't want me to save my marriage. I'm just an experiment to you, that's all. You want me to do what you didn't do, to see if it works or not. Momma, don't you know what you're doing? You're makin' me relive your guilt. You think that by my givin' Arthur love or whatever, it'll make things better. You want me to learn from your mistakes. But I got news for you: Loving Daddy more wouldn't have stopped that shotgun blast from hittin' his head. And loving Arthur won't stop the mess in his head either. So you keep your guilt. You keep it, sleep with it, live with it if you want to. Let it tear you up more than it's done so far, but for God's sake, don't try to pass it on to me, all right?"

"I loved your daddy," Ila said softly.

"I know, Momma, I know. And he knew it too. Anybody who knew both of you knew it. Don't let it eat on you like this. You ain't thinkin' right."

The phone rang. The women stared at each other. Neither moved.

Ila sighed. "I'll get it." She rolled the wheelchair into the bedroom.

She shouted into the kitchen. "It's for you," she said sweetly, but her voice cracked.

Judith put the receiver to her ear, watching Ila's face. Ila looked sad and old. I wonder, thought Judith, when a person first realizes her mother's getting old.

"It's me," Arthur said.

"I know who it is," replied Judith.

"I want you and my babies back. I want you back now."

"I'm sorry, I'm really and truly sorry, Arthur, but I can't stand to live like that anymore. You never believe anything I say. You're suspicious of everyone and to me that's not love, Arthur. I'm not a thing that you own. I'm your wife. You've got to trust me."

"If you don't come back, I'll kill myself."

"I can't, Arthur. I can't go through that anymo—"

The sound was deafening. She dropped the receiver and screamed. She fell to her knees. "Momma! He's shot himself! Arthur's killed himself!"

Todd ran into the room.

Ila reached for the receiver. Todd handed it to her. Evidently the phone was still off the hook over at Arthur's. Ila listened but could hear nothing. She told Todd to run next door and call the police and an ambulance and send them to his father's house. This time she would do the right thing, she thought. She would not hesitate like she did over the letters from Spainhour.

Thirty minutes passed and then Arthur walked into the living room, panting, out of breath, as if he were merely visiting for the first time, a cocky smile on his face, a brilliant glow in his eyes. And when Judith saw Arthur, saw him laugh like a child at his perverse joke, his feigned suicide, she threw up her hands and sobbed on the floor.

Judge Patton did not spend too much time explaining anything to any-one. He ordered Arthur to commit himself voluntarily to Chatham Mental Hospital for thirty days. If not, he would lose his freedom by forced in-carceration in jail or in the mental hospital.

Ginger and Judith rode with him to the campus-like structure. He signed himself in and was told he could have no visitors for two weeks.

Judith rolled up the window of the car as she arrived at the Mitchell house near the mill. Mayzelle walked out to the car with two Pepsis in her hands and slipped in on the passenger side.

Mayzelle sipped her Pepsi through a straw. Ice slush came up near the top of the bottle. "You done what you could," she said. "Maybe the hospital will help."

"What if it don't? He doesn't listen to me. It seems I can't do anything right by him. He complains about the grocery money, the car bills, the doctor bills, and he demands to know where I'm at every second of the day."

Mayzelle sighed. "It seems to me," she said slowly, "that you only got two choices: Leave him for good, or stay and help the doctors make him better. But you know, Judith, that sometimes hope got to be a part of nature's plan. And when nature takes its course, we all follow or we all get crushed."

Judith moved some of the beds to Ila's and rented her house to a young couple. She began working more hours at the hospital. She arrived home at midnight, slept, and rose to see the children off to school. Finally the two long weeks drew to a close and she prepared to visit Arthur. She found herself worrying about him. She wondered if she had done the right thing. What would he be like when she saw him again? Would he be cured and happy and loving again? Or would he be ashamed beyond repair? He was a proud man, the proudest she had ever known. He survived on that pride. Without it he would not be the man she had wrestled with on summer afternoons, had loved with a passion she had not known could exist, had worshiped from the day she had first met him. He had become a part of her; every muscle and every glance and every rise in spirit and every smell of his was part of her. She summoned these memories at will, always real, always painful.

Judith read his letters alone in her room. She stayed there a long time. When she came out, Todd could always see the worried look on her face. She handed the envelopes to him.

Arthur's handwriting was scratchy. His fingers held hammers and screwdrivers with the precision of a surgeon, but a pencil always gave him trouble.

October 28

Dear Judith

I will try to write you a line or to and I hope this letter will find you and the kids all well and Still loving me because I love you very much and the kids.

Darling I saw the doctor today and we talk a long while and Darling I think everything is going to be all right and when I come home you and I are going to the coast for a week how about it?

I am doing okay and I hope to improve more before my 30 days is up. Darling dont ever stop loving me and tell the kids I love them. I took a test today and I hope I make out all right. I am getting along fine and I mean it. The doctor said you can see me on the 15 day and he is a nice doctor and I want him to meet you and see for himself what a good looking wife I have and I mean ever word of it, Honey. I better write Todd a letter now because I love all our family. God bless you allways.

Love Arthur.

I am thinking of you my dearest allways.

October 28

Dear Todd

I am OK. I will answer your letter and I was proud to hear from you and I love you all. Don't forget that, Son. Todd, tell James Adam

and Virginia hello for me and I love them to Todd write me ever time your mother write and be good and watch your brothers crossing the road. Good night Todd and may God watch over you all.
Love Daddy.

October 30

Hello Darling

Here I am again. People are nice here and this is no bad place and I feel that I should be home because they have some sick people here.I was not sick I needed rest and now I know it. Darling I think what a fool I have been and you will never know how much I miss you. I don't know anything to write except I cannot wait until the 15 day when you visit. All I want is your Love and the Kids Love and If I got that I can do anything and you know that, don't you?

When I get home we will build a new home, not just a house.
Love Arthur.
Don't forget Honey we are going on a Honeymoon when I come Home. All my love to you my Darling.

October 30

Dear Todd

Todd my son and all of you James Adam and Virginia I love you all and I miss you all very much. Good night to you all and God bless you all Love Allways Daddy.

November 2

Dear Judith

They have moved me to three wards since I come in but now I have a room to myself. I will try to write you a line but I am Blue today and Darling today is Sunday and the longest day of my life. How I miss you you will never know. I am going to ask the doctor to let you bring the kids on the 15 day. I will stay my 30 days but that is all and if I need to come back I will Darling.

I can't stay away from you all I love you all so much and remember that Darling.

I went to church today and I want you to take the kids to. I am not nervous anymore but I think of you all the time.
Love allways Arthur.
Answer soon.

November 2

Dear Todd

I will try to answer your letter that I got last night. My Son I am proud of all of you and I love you James Adam and Virginia and your mother more than she will ever know. Don't ever forget that.

Todd study your homework and if you don't understand something ask your mother. She will help.

Love allways your Daddy.

November 3

Dear Judith

I hope this letter finds you all well.

I talk to the doctor and I will tell him the truth about anything that he wants to know. He is a fine man. As long as they treat me okay I will tell them anything they want to know and Darling if they ask me if I love you you know what I will tell them, don't you?

I stayed in all day today and what a long day. I don't want to loose my outside card, that is a card that you have to have to go outside and walk around the grounds with and you know I cant stand to be inside all the time. I'll close for now and write me soon. Take all mistakes for love. I'll love you forever.

Arthur.

From the man who loves his wife and is true.

Dont forget to bring the kids on the 15 day.

On the morning of the fifteenth day, Judith kept the children out of school. She loaded them into the old Buick and drove to Chatham Memorial. The road was part concrete, part asphalt, and part holes. She got lost driving through several small towns.

She thought about the children, wondering what all this was doing to them. Maybe the kids shouldn't even be here. No, that wouldn't be right. No one should keep a man from his children.

The children were strangely quiet. No fighting on this trip. Daddy was not well. That was all they knew.

On the morning of the fifteenth day, Arthur walked alone in the garden, went to the library, and sat in the lounge, where he could watch television. He did all these things because they told him he should. He walked, and read, and watched, and listened. Yet he could not bring himself to talk to the others, the weak men in tattered robes, wandering, always wandering, from one hall to another. He watched them until he realized that he was doing the same. They were all searching for the same thing.

He tried to keep busy until Judith arrived. He took two showers that morning. He did not feel clean. His face was gray. He hated to look at it. Where had he gone? Where was Arthur?

Soon the doctors would stop playing games with him and he could go home. And when he got home he would spend as much time on the land and in the woods as possible. The open woods would clear his head.

The hospital was unlike anything Todd had expected. It looked a little like the university campus in Greensboro. The buildings were one-story, motel-like structures, built of a light orange brick with green trim. The place was surrounded by a green hedge, but there were no walls. The complex reminded him of a shopping center near the battleground, except this looked more like a complex of modern funeral homes.

Judith walked to the visitors' desk and signed in. The children were taken to a library to look at magazines.

Within a few minutes, Arthur came into the lobby.

She had never seen him cry. He kissed her until she could take no more. Then his face turned red and his eyes turned upward.

"God!" he shouted. "*Where have you been? I've been waiting for hours! Where have you been? What did you do—walk here? Didn't you even care? Didn't you want to see me? What have you been doing? Who have you been seeing? No, don't answer that! I know. I know what you've been doing. They won't tell me, but I know. You've been seeing other men. I'm sure of that. I've always known that, you know . . . but if you had just told me, I would have understood. . . .*"

Judith walked away as he screamed after her.

The doctor's hair was thick and white. He looked like a kind man; Arthur had said that he was. His eyes looked a little like Arthur's, ice blue with small pupils floating darkly. He had a pencil in his mouth. Judith wanted to warn him that he might stick himself with the pencil and get an infection. Todd had done that once.

But no, she thought, he's a doctor. He'll think I'm being silly.

"Sit down, Mrs. McDowell." The doctor was foreign. She didn't know the nationality, German or something.

He told her some things that she did not understand and then tried to explain the terminology: "paranoia" and "schizophrenia."

She listened impassively to his explanations and then asked, "What can I do for him?"

"Do you love him?"

She was surprised by such a simple question after all the medical jargon. "Yes," she answered.

"Then forget him. Because he will never get any better. He resists our every effort to help him. He can't be cured. We can't cure him, and if you've got any sense, you'll go home and concentrate on raising your family without him, because he is never going home again."

She was stunned. Her body had no feeling whatsoever. What was it this man was saying? Never going to get better? Not coming home? Like he was dead or something?

"Exactly," said the doctor, his eyes never blinking.

She found Arthur with the children in the hospital library. He was telling them stories about the strange-looking people in the halls. The children laughed easily.

The doctor gave Arthur a pass. It was a warm and sunny day for November, and the family went to a nearby lake for a picnic. While the children played on the shoreline, Arthur and Judith walked the wooded paths, talking in whispers about his progress and his hopes. She did not tell him what the doctor had said. Instead, she promised to visit as often as he wished, which was every day.

Back in Greensboro, Judith worked the late shift, slept a few hours, and drove to Chatham Memorial every day.

The children bunked in Ila's living room, amusing themselves wrestling with cousin Robert, climbing apple trees, or pulling spikes out of the railroad bed behind Ila's property.

In their prayers they asked God to bless their daddy and make him well again.

On the twentieth day, Judith met again with the doctor.

"But he seems so well in his letters," she said.

"Just an attempt to confuse us."

"Can't I change, won't that help? What can I do?"

"You could be the queen of England and he would still find fault with you. The constant talking is his way of trying to convince himself. It is my opinion that the committee will never release him. Mrs. McDowell, you must begin to change your life. Make plans for a future without him. That is all I can tell you."

On the drive home, she thought of the jealousy and possessiveness, of the arguments and criticism, of the outright lies that sometimes crept into Arthur's head. And once in a while she thought of old Spainhour, and the look on his face that Ila described when he was told of the eviction notice long ago. She wondered briefly how Spainhour could have become so disturbed and murderous. No one had thought to ask at the time of the massacre. No one could have predicted it.

They were not going to let Arthur out. She would have to get used to it and prepare for the day when they told him. She would continue working and providing for her family. The children would have to be told someday, but right now that was too much to think about.

Judith was asleep when Ila called her to the phone. She stumbled out of bed and leaned on the doorway.

"Who is it, Momma?"

"Long distance," Ila answered.

The two women looked at one another for a moment, expressionless. Judith walked quickly to the phone and just as quickly said, "Yes?"

"Mrs. McDowell?"

"Yes . . . but you'll have to speak up, I can't hear you so well."

"Mrs. McDowell, I called to let you know that we will be releasing your husband next week."

Judith felt her knees buckle and she sat down on Ila's bed. She couldn't think of anything to say.

"Mrs. McDowell? Are you still there? Mrs. McDowell?"

"Yes. Yes, I'm here." She swallowed. "Doctor, I thought, I mean, you told me to . . . change my life and . . . forget him. You said that he would never be well again, and now, and now you say he's being released? I don't understand. Doctor?"

"Yes, I know what I said, Mrs. McDowell, and as far as I'm concerned, what I said is still true. But the law thinks otherwise. The man, your husband, signed voluntarily. We can't keep him beyond thirty days. I don't think we can cure him. I'm afraid my colleagues have overruled me on this. I'm sorry, the law says we can't keep him. The other ones—the other doctors here—think he should be released. I'm sorry. Please come at noon next Wednesday to pick him up."

"Doctor?"

He hung up.

Ila waited. Judith rubbed her face and leaned over. "Momma, they're letting him out. Releasing him next week."

"My God," Ila whispered.

"I've changed my life, Momma. I've got a new way of living. They told me—damn them—they told me he could never leave that place."

Ila rolled toward the kitchen. "It's the Lord's will," she said as she disappeared into the dark foyer.

Twenty-four

TODD, JAMES, ADAM, and Virginia could not leave him alone. They followed him everywhere, from room to room, to the car, upstairs, and to the shed behind Ila's house.

"You kids!" shouted Ila. "Leave your daddy alone. Can't you see he needs to be alone once in a while?"

Arthur turned and looked at her for a moment, confused by what she said. Left alone, he thought—that's the last thing I need. He lifted Virginia and walked to the walnut grove. The children laughed at his laughter and rolled in the piles of cold, brittle leaves, throwing rocks at thick squirrel nests high in the branches.

To Arthur, lying on his back, covered by his children, the tree limbs against the winter sky looked like bundles of white nerves. The dogwoods had lost their virginity. The white pine looked the same as always, except for a few inches of new branch, tender and worm-like.

The clouds swirled gray and blue, somberly announcing bitter winds. Brief, chilling rainstorms caused the children to tremble in their beds. And the last smells of fall lingered briefly before reluctantly seeping into the earth.

On Thanksgiving Day, Arthur took Todd to a turkey shoot, somewhere down a dirt road deep within the gray forests and decaying, spiked tobacco fields of McLeansville. Todd rode in the back of the truck and peered through the cab window. Arthur motioned for him to sit down and hold on. When they neared the Longview Grocery and Service Station, Todd banged on the window, and Arthur stopped to buy a pack of cigarettes for himself and a brownie for the boy.

When they reached the turkey shoot, Todd instinctively stood at a distance when Arthur pulled the shotgun from the back of the pickup truck. Arthur opened the breech as a sign that the gun was unloaded, and Todd resumed his place beside his father.

Old farmers in mud-stained overalls and flannel shirts competed side by side with lanky younsters in baggy gray work pants and baseball caps, shattering the paperboard targets, admiring the echo of clean, tight bull's eye-shots.

Arthur won a turkey. Todd was disappointed when he saw that the prize had not been alive for some time. He had hoped for a pet.

For Christmas Todd asked his mother to ask Santa Claus for a Ben Hur Roman Circus Maximus set, complete with plastic chariots, charioteers, horses, and a Roman legion. He had learned early that Santa Claus lived in the revolving charge account office at Sears.

After Christmas, Todd left the set in the tobacco field, and Will's tractor plowed it over. For years, little plastic Roman helmets would come to the surface with the spring rains.

Though the freezing rains of January often made construction work unprofitable, Arthur measured houses for sheetrock and did what work he could. Todd watched from the porch as Arthur loaded the fragile, chalky sheets onto the bed of the pickup and tried to get the truck up the icy road. One day he lost an entire load of sheetrock when the truck slid into a ditch. He did not take risks like that again.

One morning, cries of joy from the children announced a snowfall that canceled school. Arthur stood silently by the kitchen window and stared at the ice forming on the cold steel of his truck bumpers. He watched as a Jeep from the hospital came over to pick up Judith along with other workers for the day. He sat in front of the television all morning, cleaning his guns, sketching plans for a new garage, and answering the phone to explain to Ila that until the roads were scraped he couldn't get the truck out to bring her some groceries. Then he heated up a pot of beans canned the summer before and made tall sandwiches of bologna, onion, and mustard for the kids.

After lunch he gave in to the demands of the children and bundled them up as best he could, depending on Todd to select the proper shirts, pants, and socks for each child. James wore socks on his hands and Virginia wrapped a towel around her head. Adam tied towels and short ropes around his shoes for traction. Todd held the door open as they walked cautiously onto the porch and then, one by one, stepped through the thin crust of the snow, giggling with delight.

Arthur walked around the yard, inspecting the white pines on the boundary between his property and Will's. He strained to see the ice-covered pond through the crackling woods. The chill hurt his throat. He tried to think of summer and found that dreaming no longer warmed him.

"You will quit your job," Arthur said slowly.

"How will I do that, when I—we—don't have the money to pay bills that grew while you were away?"

"I don't care. I need you. The kids need you. I've got my old job back on third shift, and I'm thinking about sheetrocking full time."

"That would be great, Arthur. Really great," Judith said sarcastically. "I understand your desire to quit a job where you had friends and a boss who kept your job at the mill while you were away. I understand completely your thinking when you quit a paycheck and a forty-hour week to take up sheetrocking where you will not be able to work when it rains and you may not get enough houses to sheetrock. I see your doing all of this at a time when we are in real bad money trouble. I mean, we are doing *so well*, living with my momma while strangers rent our house. Have you seen our house lately? Holes in the roof? Ruts in the front yard? Broken windows? Yes, I can see taking a chance on sheetrocking while everything else around us goes to hell. . . ."

"You finished?"

"No! I'm not finished." Then she looked at his face, calm, rested, glowing. "Yes, hell. Hell, yes, I'm finished. I've been finished for some time now."

Arthur pulled her to him. He had been gentler since he had returned. She had been afraid of him at first, yet he had given her no cause for fear.

"Okay, Arthur, you win . . . as always. I'll quit, and you go full time on construction."

"Thank you," he said.

Arthur picked up his coat. "One more thing, Judith. We're going to move back home."

"I thought you liked it here at Momma's."

"Well, it's all right. She's been nice to us. But we got no privacy. I need privacy. She's got people runnin' in and out all the time. It's not my house—not ours—you can understand that, can't you?"

"Oh, Arthur, I know it's been hard on you—everything has. I don't guess there's any harm in gettin' out of here. To tell you the truth, Momma's been gettin' on my nerves a little anyway."

"Mine, too," Arthur said, smiling.

After Judith and Arthur moved back to their own home, Ila fell out of her wheelchair trying to catch the parakeet Arthur had given her, which had escaped from its cage. She broke her leg. She moved in with Judith and Arthur until the leg could heal. After a month she was allowed back in the wheelchair. Ila decided to show her appreciation to Judith and the children by making breakfast for them: country ham and eggs, fresh biscuits, and redeye gravy. Arthur smelled the aromas and woke. He looked at Judith sleeping peacefully next to him and realized that the old woman was in the kitchen. He pulled on his pants and raised the window shade. Something smelled strange. He ran to the kitchen. Flames from a pan of grease leaped to the cabinets. He rushed over and threw his shirt over the flames, then grabbed a canister of salt and threw its contents on the fire.

The cabinets were ruined and would have to be replaced. Arthur tried to get Ila to stop crying, but she couldn't. The fire had started while she was in the bathroom.

A few weeks later, a check from the insurance company arrived to pay for the damage. It required two signatures, Arthur's and Judith's. Judith refused to sign it until Arthur agreed to its use.

"The money should go to pay those doctor bills we owe," she said. "There's not a doctor in town that will see our younguns 'cause you won't pay what we owe."

"If we cash it," said Arthur, "I'm gonna buy a carburetor for that truck outside."

"Arthur," she said, tearing the check in two, "you're crazy!"

The next few moments were like some half-remembered dream. She saw the pained look on his face, and then she saw someone else, *something* else etch lines across his brow as a dark shadow fell across his eyes.

The tabletop caught her back; her face struck the wall.

She woke up in bed.

That night, while Judith and Arthur slept, Ila phoned Ash. Ash parked his car up the road and crept into the house and carried Ila to his truck.

The almost naked children followed. Todd asked if he could talk to Arthur, but Ila refused.

In the morning Judith drove to Ila's and called the sheriff. A warrant was issued. The sheriff's department agreed to serve it.

Arthur was alone. He spent the morning watching the television and reading the newspaper, but he could not concentrate on the game shows or the sports section. His mind kept playing over yesterday. How could it have been avoided? Why had he lost his temper and let the rage out? Why couldn't he keep it in?

He was depressed, much more depressed than usual. He couldn't go to work and he was too nervous to stay at home. He thought of a compromise. There was a house over in the southern part of Greensboro that was ready to be measured for sheetrock. He phoned Ash's son, Robert, to ask if he would like to go along for a ride.

Robert was seventeen and had been working with Arthur since quitting high school. Robert still had his father's looks, but construction work had put some bulk around his arms and chest. His black curly hair was thick and rarely cut. His mustache was new and gave the impression of a tall boy in search of manhood.

Arthur worked Robert hard, paid him fair, and treated him with respect. Robert responded with a manner more like a friend than an employee.

After measuring the house for the sheetrock, Arthur returned home. He washed his face and combed his hair. He was not pleased with the sheetrock measurements. His mind was still on Judith and the kids. He told Robert, who had come home with him for a beer, that he was afraid Judith might take out a warrant.

Robert said that Judith couldn't do that. Robert always liked to be optimistic.

Arthur did not hear the deputies' car pull in front of his house and beside the garage.

But soon he heard the muffled demand to come out of the house: "We have a warrant."

"Mrs. McDowell? This is Cone Hospital. Your husband has been injured. Could you please come out here to fill out some forms?"

Judith felt her grip on the receiver loosen. "Hospital? What's wrong? How badly? How?"

"Could you please hurry, Mrs. McDowell?"

"Yes, I can . . . I've got to . . . yes."

Judith put on another dress and fixed her hair. The children were told to get ready. The phone rang again.

"Mrs. McDowell? This is the emergency room at Cone Hospital. Your husband's condition has worsened. Will you please hurry?"

The children were left sitting in the hospital corridor, and Judith was taken to a large room where several stretchers stood, separated by drapes hanging from the ceiling. In one of the cubicles she saw him. A doctor came to her. "Mrs. McDowell? Good. We're going to have to operate. It may take several hours."

"What happened?"

"He shot himself, Mrs. McDowell. I'm sorry."

"Will he live?"

"I've never seen a healthier body on anyone. He should pull through just fine. You can wait outside. I'll get back to you as soon as I can."

"Can I talk to him?"

"Yes, but only for a moment. He's terribly weak, and not fully conscious."

She walked to the stretcher. The nurse at his side would not move. Judith leaned over him as close as she could. Tubes ran to his chest and his neck.

"Arthur?" she whispered.

His eyes opened and he looked at her. His throat made soft noises.

"Arthur," she said loudly, "I love you, Arthur."

"I . . . love you," he mumbled.

Two interns pushed Judith back and rolled the stretcher away.

The man who stood in front of her wore a dark blue suit and a gray tie. "Mrs. McDowell?"

"Yes," she said.

"I'm Reverend McElvery, from the Methodist church near River Bethel. The nurses explained your trouble to me. I was wondering if there was anything I could do to help."

Judith glanced at Todd across the room. He had not taken his eyes off her for two hours. She looked at the plastic couch near the door. James held Virginia, while Adam stood in the corner.

"No," she finally said, "I don't think so."

"I'll be around for a few more hours. If you need me, ask the nurse at the desk and she can find me."

"Thank you, Preacher."

He turned to leave but hesitated. "Mrs. McDowell, I will pray with you if you wish."

"Thank you, Preacher, but I've been praying for him to live for a long time now, and I don't think anybody else doing it could do any more good."

"Mrs. McDowell?"

"Yes," she said, irritated.

"Don't pray for him to live. Pray that God's will be done, that God does the best for him."

"Yes, Preacher."

She clenched her fist and prayed for Arthur to live.

Todd allowed his eyes to close, pulled his knees to his chin, and let the weight of his body push against the back of the chair.

It isn't real, he thought. It isn't happening. He'll be all right, and the doctors will have him safe soon.

I won't cry. He wouldn't like that. I want to tell him that I wasn't going to pull the trigger on that rifle on my birthday when I was eleven. I just wanted him to stop—but not like this. I'll be strong for him. And for you, Mayzelle.

He can't die. You can't be a son without a father.

Ash took the children to Ila's.

Five hours later, the same doctor Judith had seen in the examining room stepped into the hallway.

She stood.

He smiled. "He made it. I think he's going to be all right. You can sit with him for a while. I'm going to send you home for some rest. Then you can come back and sit again."

"Thank you. Where is he?"

"The attendant will take you to him."

She walked into the intensive care unit. There were few lights. Different tubes were attached to his neck and chest. A taped piece of steel and rubber covered his throat. She pulled a chair next to the bed and watched him. He was covered by an ice blanket. A nurse came over and felt his pulse and turned some knobs on the machines. She looked startled. She turned one switch on and off several times. She looked at Judith. Then she leaned over Arthur's chest and began to move her palm up and down the center, pushing steadily back and forth. Another nurse came in and told Judith to go home. Doctor's orders: freshen up, get some sleep, and then come on back.

Reluctantly, she left for Ila's. There she washed her face, put on some lipstick, and changed clothes. Ila brought her some tea. The back door opened and Ginger came in, followed by Esther, Dan, Diedre, Will, Lon, Lora, and Mayzelle.

Judith felt relieved that they all cared enough to come and be with her. She went to Arthur's sister. "Thank you, Esther. I'm glad you came. Do you want to go back to the hospital with me? I know that when he wakes, he'll feel better knowin' his sister is there."

Esther turned toward Ila. Lon walked behind Lora and put his hands on her shoulders.

Mayzelle whispered, "He's dead, Judith. He's dead."

Todd listened to the women's wails.

Someone told him he would have to be a man now.

He walked outside, away from all the noise, to the bushes that lined the road.

Ila rolled her wheelchair back into the house. It might rain, she thought. Earlier in the morning the sky had been filled with red and brown-hued clouds, clouds that had pulled behind them a gray sheet until every patch of blue was hidden.

Mayzelle met Ila in the foyer and knelt, gently pinning an ivory cameo of the three Graces on Ila's dark dress. "I found it in the box with your baby pictures," she said. "Lora said you should wear it."

Ila nodded and held a handkerchief to her eyes for a moment.

"You ready, child?" Mayzelle asked.

Ila reached up and pulled Mayzelle's hand to her shoulder. Mayzelle could feel the sharpness of Ila's rings.

"Let's go in," Ila said.

She rolled toward her bedroom, where the children were being dressed. She opened the door and looked in. Deidre and Ginger were putting ties on the boys. Virginia sat in a corner, wearing a pink and white dress, her face swollen and red. Judith knelt in front of Todd to straighten his cuffs.

"I'm not going," Todd said suddenly, sternly.

Judith stood and combed his hair.

"I said I'm not going, Momma!" His voice cut through the heavy air.

Deidre looked quickly at Ginger. Ginger hid her face in her hands.

"Momma, do you hear me? I ain't goin'!"

Judith held his head for a moment and looked into his eyes. He does not look like his father, she thought. The nose and teeth are the same, but the face doesn't seem to belong.

She picked up his jacket from the bed and handed it to him. He threw it on the floor.

James and Adam watched silently. Virginia stopped crying. Judith reached down, brushed off Todd's jacket, and handed it to him again.

He took the coat and folded it carefully.

"I ain't goin', Momma." This time the strength and finality were missing from the young voice. He was begging not to go. "Please . . . I . . . I can't go."

Judith shook her head. She had done with crying. She would not cry now; no matter that her hands were trembling and her mouth twitching. The boy Todd had never begged for anything in his life. Never. Except this.

"Why?" she whispered.

"Because he's not dead."

Ginger left the room. James and Adam came closer to Todd. Virginia started to sob and choke.

"He is," said Judith loudly. "He is . . . dead. There is nothing that we can do about it. You're old enough to know that. You're old enough to know that talk like that scares your brothers and your sister. You're old enough to walk out to that car and pay your respects to your father and be the man in this family. You are, you know. The man. Now that he's gone."

Judith left the room.

Deidre walked over to Todd and let her hand cradle the back of his head. "You do it for your momma. She needs everybody now. If you desert her, then she can't make it. You might not understand that now, but one day you will . . . one day you'll see."

"I'll go," he said, "but not because you're making me. I'll go but I won't watch."

Mayzelle pushed Ila's chair over the threshold to the kitchen. She looked back at Todd.

"Come here, boy," she said. "Push your grandmother's chair to the funeral car. I'm riding with Lon and Lora."

Todd walked over and leaned into the wicker back of the wheelchair, steering past the laundry porch to the row of cars waiting in the backyard.

He stared at the colorless sky as he rode to the funeral home.

Dan and Ash lifted Ila's wheelchair up the gray steps to Ivy's Funeral Chapel. Judith and the four children followed. There were a lot of people standing about, but they took their seats as soon as Judith began walking slowly down the aisle toward the flag-draped coffin. Todd held Virginia's hand. James and Adam walked behind Todd. They stared into the upper portion of the box. Todd reached out and touched one hand.

Judith breathed deeply, the only sound in the room. She took a comb from her purse and gently recombed Arthur's hair. As she did so James cried out, "Goodbye, Daddy."

"Goodbye, Daddy," Adam and Virginia repeated in whispers.

Todd turned and walked to the back of the chapel. Mayzelle, standing in the back, reached for him. He evaded her and ran out the huge white doors to the family car. He jumped in and slammed the heavy door behind him. With the window up, he could not hear the muted voice of a preacher whom no one in the family knew. He could not hear the rough singing of the man the undertakers paid to sing at funerals. He did not hear the leaves falling quickly from the trees, nor the rain knocking on the pavement and on the roof of the car.

Yet he could not ignore Mayzelle's tapping on the window.

He shook his head. "Go away," he said softly, then relented and opened the door.

"You gonna be all right, boy," Mayzelle said calmly. She put her hand on his knee and shook it. "You remember those talks we had up in the mountains? You remember us talkin' about carin' and lovin' and family?"

"Yes," Todd whispered, his eyes dim. "I remember, Mayzelle."

Mayzelle hugged him. "You gonna be all right, boy," she repeated. "You hear? Your hurt can't kill that great heart of yours. You just remember what I told you."

The doors of the funeral chapel opened and Mayzelle stepped to the side. Todd sat immobile and barely noticed the others returning to the car or the driver starting the engine. He was faintly surprised when he was pulled gently out of the car at the cemetery in Mortimer.

The cemetery had not changed much since Todd had been there with Mayzelle in the fall. The cracked cement bench had fallen over and was covered with vines. A new hole had been dug beside the tombstone marked TOLBERT. Todd wondered what his father would have thought of this last resting place. He suspected that his father and his grandfather had not gotten along.

Todd wished that Mayzelle could sit on the steel chairs on the green carpet with him and the family. Was this what she had been preparing him for? Todd did not feel ready.

His father was not dead. It was not his father in the box. The man who had liked warm fires in winter and clean, cool mountain air in spring could not be the man they were lowering into a hole in the ground.

A soldier put the folded flag into Judith's hands, and Judith passed it to Todd. He put the flag to his face and bit into it, his tongue bleeding. He would not cry. He did not cry. There was nothing to cry for, nothing to mourn.

He is not dead, Todd told himself over and over.

A minister said some words about eternal life for those who believed. Todd didn't know if his father had believed or not. Arthur had always stayed home and read the paper when Judith took the children to Sunday school. Todd didn't think Sunday school was such a big deal. John Ledo, class treasurer, always announced the amount everyone had contributed to the Sunday school fund. Todd's dime or quarter sounded small next to the others' dollars. John Ledo always looked at Todd funny when he read Todd's name, as though accusing him of being cheap with God.

Todd had questions that no one would answer. Everyone looked stupid at the word "suicide," like their brains had stopped working or something. People whispered about Arthur shooting policemen, or holding hostages, or being drunk, or whatever else they could think of when they didn't know the answers. Todd's head was so full of questions that he did not feel Lon's arm around his shoulders.

It began to rain. Ila was getting wet, so Rossie and Ash made a basket with their arms to carry her down the trail. She kept her back straight and her head high while she was carried.

Todd did not see her go. He never took his eyes from the graveyard until the car carried him away. The last thing he saw, through the window of the car, was Deidre standing over the grave, and Dan trying to pull her away as she fell to her knees. Then the big empty tree branches hid the scene; then the bushes, some with tiny new buds, hid the trees; then the rain hid it all.

There would be no tombstone. There was no money for one.

In McCleansville, all the contents of the house had been taken out onto the lawn to air out the sickly-sweet, dogwood smell of tear gas. Mattresses were covered with heaps of clothes and toys. The smell of the gas licked Todd's face and stung his eyes. Todd had never seen a house turned inside out like this. But he knew how the house must feel.

He watched Mayzelle carry Arthur's old army blankets and fishing poles to the hickory tree, arranging them in neat piles.

I never had a chance to tell him goodbye, he thought.

But I will never forget him.

The death certificate read, "Twelve hours exsanguination, two hours cerebral ischemia." Massive bleeding, deprivation of blood to the brain.

Twenty-five

THE MAPLES *retained clumps of dried brown leaves. A few squirrels' nests could be seen against the moonlit night. A thick mist covered the ground, weaving in and out among the stones, as broken patches of earth glimmered with a bright red dew. Todd walked along the cold, hard ground, looking for his father's grave. He couldn't find it. It was unmarked. But there was a tree there—a tree unlike all the others. Its branches reached down to touch the earth covering his father and his grandfather. Its roots, strong and thick, hardened by wind and rain, cradled the coffins. Todd remembered the special tree and saw it. He ran and tripped across an exposed root as large as his leg. He fell headfirst into the dead grass and rolled on his back.*

The clouds of winter were so close he could touch them. He felt the moss near the tree bristling against his naked skin. His body was red and perspiring, covered by a slick veil of water. He watched the light from the sky travel across his skin, turning his flesh blue and then pale white. Still on his back, he lifted his legs to the tree and allowed his toes to feel the rough old bark. The crisp, dead skin of the tree peeled and covered his legs and mingled with his hair. He jumped and swung on a branch, the longest branch, thick, with smaller branches reaching down. And he followed the pointing branches to the hole below and looked in and saw his father.

He reached for the boy but could not touch; the hole was too deep and black. He would not speak even though the boy begged him. He motioned the boy to follow, but the limbs wrapped around Todd's hands and would not let go. His father's eyes glowed in sorrow and in anger, and Todd broke away and ran into the woods and found that he could not run as fast as the mists, his legs leaden, his chest heavy. He jumped into a stream and fell writhing into the mud below.

He woke.

Todd's face was covered with night sweat. He pushed the heavy quilts off his body. The light from the moon covered the sheets like silver. He sat up, trying to remember where he was and how he had gotten there. He saw his bed, his room, his brothers sleeping in the next bed. He was home, and yet he was alone.

A dream, a bad dream. He would wake again in the morning and not remember.

He lay down and turned his pillow so that the coolness cleared his head and dried his neck. He realized that he was naked, even though he had worn pajamas to bed.

Will had cut pine into tall brush heaps for the rabbits. Now those green and brown sticks of flesh had dried and crumbled into heaps of bark and dust long abandoned by any rabbits that might have lived there.

The paths had grown over with branches from either side of the trail, covered with wild grass and briers as tall as a man, or a boy. Will took his machete and cut a new path, throwing the limbs into the woods as he went, searching out the old trail, clearing out ruts made by years of hunting the same forest. Deeper and deeper he went, stopping now and then to listen to the activity in the woods. He could hear cars roaring down a highway no more than a mile away where five years ago there was a lake and brim streams.

Will would not go that far. He would rather stay back and remember the way things were when the woods were filled with squirrels jumping from limb to limb.

He approached a path that he did not recognize. The trail did not cross rabbit or opossum tracks. It zigzagged toward a hill where running cedar seemed to hold the dirt and grass in place, where inches of pine needles formed clumps of moist, black topsoil. There on top of the hill sat Todd.

Will watched for half an hour. Todd was wearing white pants. They must be wet and black-bottomed by now, Will thought. The boy was sitting on the ground. Didn't he know any better? His hair was thick and uncut. He refused to let his momma cut it, said it didn't look right at school. So he saved up money and wasted it uptown on a fancy haircut. Doesn't look like much to me, Will thought, brown hair stacked up on his head like hay. A face not too much different from a million other kids. Seen that face in the navy and in the bars with Arthur, seen that face in the fields and in jails. Skin tanned and dark and burned in places.

He must like that book he's reading. Skinny kid, should be working, putting a little meat on them bones, not wasting his time with his head buried in a book, probably about knights or kings or some such stuff.

I've seen deer like that boy, stand there or lie there for hours without moving, as long as I don't move. But as soon as I breathe or turn my head or blink my eyes, they're gone. I can never resist blinking my eyes to see if that always holds true.

Will took a step forward.

Breathing the dusk air, Todd looked up.

Will stopped.

The boy's eyes froze. His face tightened. He turned his head. He saw the man. Their eyes locked.

Todd stood and brushed off the seat of his pants with one hand and closed the book with the other. Will climbed up the hill.

"Didn't mean to disturb you, boy."

"Oh, no problem. I was just sitting here, you know. Just reading."

"What you reading?"

"Oh, nothing much."

"Oh."

"You're looking good, Uncle Will."

Will stared at him and reached for the book. Todd hesitated but handed it to him. "Grandma Ila loaned it to me."

The Trojan Women, by Euripides.

Will frowned. "What's this about? Some king or somethin'?"

Todd smiled, then dropped the grin from his face. Will noticed.

"No, Uncle Will, it's about this woman who can tell you what suffering means."

"Oh," said Will, "a prophet."

"Sort of," said Todd seriously, not wishing to offend.

Will grinned. "Colder than a witch's tit, ain't it?"

Todd laughed, and they walked home, by way of the creek that ran to the clam beds where the raccoons had met years ago.

"They're all gone now," said Todd. "Highway, you know? New highway to the shopping center . . . scared them away. Things ain't like they used to be. Even the air's starting to smell bad."

"Modern times," Will said. "The old way's dying. One day all the farmland will be just a bunch of parking lots—or worse, maybe a city dump." He glanced at Todd. "And you're always readin'. Ever think about your future? Ever think about goin' off to college somewhere, instead of farming or working in the mill like the rest of us?"

Todd shrugged.

Will looked him in the eyes. "You gonna be all right, kid?"

"Yeah," he said. "Yeah, I think I'll be all right."

"I'm goin' to visit the old homeplace up in Surry. You want to go along?"

"I don't know if Momma will let me."

"She'll let you. You need to get away for a while. We all do. I got a big tent and a couple of sleeping bags. We can camp and fish for a few days."

"Sure, why not?" Todd said, grinning.

The waters of the Yadkin River are wide and lazy, blindly feeling the shores towards the sea, feeding on farmland and marshes. Will and Todd set up camp on the river bank, and for two days sat quietly beneath the shade of elms, drawing in catfish that didn't want to die.

At night Will cooked the fish after Todd cleaned them. Then they drank. Will sipped the bitter beer, and Todd gulped it. Todd found that the quicker he drank, the less offensive the taste. Will worried about Todd's age and watched for signs of too much alcohol. Todd seemed unaffected.

At night they burned dead pine that crackled and hissed throughout the rapid conversation that developed as the beers were consumed. They slept on rocks and roots, which crept beneath the blankets and sleeping bags before morning.

On the third night, after catching nothing all day, Todd placed several logs on the fire and washed his face in the river. Will pulled a beer out of the ice chest. The boy did the same. They stared quietly into the flames, each immersed in his own thoughts, until Todd, after the fourth beer, spoke.

"Will, why did he do it?"

"Why did who do what?"

"Daddy."

"Oh, that."

"No one ever said why he did it."

"Probably because no one will ever know."

"Huh?"

"Nothin' you would understand."

"You sound like Momma."

"Your momma's got a lot of sense, boy."

Todd stood and walked over to a tree to see if his blankets were dry. A rain the night before had soaked them.

"Will, Grandma Ila says that Daddy was *not right* . . . you know?"

Will shifted and moved away from the fire. The heat seemed to burn a smile around his face.

"None of us is *right*, boy. None of us can say that about anybody else.

Arthur went through a lot. Much more than you'll ever know about—more than many men could take. It's a wonder that he lasted as long as he did. He's dead, and that's all that matters. Let the dead rest in peace. That's what—"

"Don't say that," snapped Todd.

"Say what?"

"Don't say that word."

Will thought a moment. "Word? You mean *dead*? Is that what's botherin' you? He is, you know. Dead. Not really a bad word. Not really all that frightening when you think about it. Do you think that by not saying it, life will be any different? It happened, boy, and there's nothin' you or anybody can do to make it unhappen."

"But why did he do it?"

"Lots of reasons. I ain't got the right to tell you what your momma's gone through. She can tell you that when she's ready, and some day she'll be ready."

Todd looked around uneasily, shaking his head.

"You don't believe that, do you?" asked Will cautiously.

Todd drank the beer quickly, glancing at the darkness beyond the trees, listening to the echo of water crashing over smooth boulders.

"Will, I got to know *why*. I don't want to wait any longer. It gets to me sometimes. Even Grandma Ila—and Ila will tell me most anything—even she clams up when I ask about it."

"Have you ever asked your momma?"

"Once, but she got sick right sudden in the face and I figured that she wasn't gonna tell me. She didn't."

Will looked at him closely. "I reckon you have a lot of memories of him."

"I remember everything about him. His hair and his eyes. Sometimes when I was little, in the night when everybody else was asleep, he would come and get me and bring me to the television and we would watch the late movie together. I remember things like that. I haven't told nobody else what I remember. I don't know why I'm telling you."

Todd waited for Will to respond and when he didn't, he continued. "I was at Grandma's house when all those cars came driving up. Funny thing. They had said Daddy was bad sick, and so I prayed. I prayed real hard for him to be all right. And when I finished that prayer . . . here comes those big cars and all that crying. I promised myself right then and there that I would never forget him, like he was some kind of pet dog or cat that had run away." He saw Will frown.

"What was he *really* like?" asked Todd.

"No one knew," said Will. His voice was deep. He quickly changed his tone to loud and cheerful. "No, no one knew, I guess, except me and Esther. He was handsome, probably too handsome for his own good. I remember the girls always fell in love with him, and he always went from one to another, never did stay with one for long till your momma came along. She was innocent and she was honest and he really loved her. Oh, he said he loved the others, but not for long. A pretty ass always moved him from one to another. I guess he needed to feel that someone needed him, and everybody in town knew that she was head over heels in love. She was honest. That meant a lot to him. I remember once I told him a lie. Told him that Ma was mad at him for skipping school. I lied. Hell, Ma didn't know he had skipped. Well, he went right to that house and told her he was sorry. She said, 'For what?' and he said, 'For skipping school.' She walloped him hard. That was before we moved to this county. Whopped him good and hard. He took it pretty good, came calmly out of the house, asked me to go fishing with him and I laughed and said all right. Easygoing, that was your daddy. We no sooner got out of earshot of that house than he lit into me like a hungry bear. Like near to killed me! While he was bangin' my head on the ground, he kept telling me to promise never to lie to him again. I promised. And, you know, boy, I don't think that I ever lied to him after that. He didn't like liars." Will stopped for a moment and came to the fire. He kicked more wood in and went back for another beer. He sipped on the can for a few more minutes, hoping that Todd would talk about something else.

"What else do you remember?"

Will wanted to tell the boy to be quiet. He wanted to tell the boy that all was past and of no importance, but when he looked into the wide eyes he couldn't refuse.

"He felt pretty bad about Ma dying. It tore him up real bad. We all looked up to her, depended on her for strength and love. I don't think he ever got over that. None of us did.

"Ma worked too hard. Her only aim in life was to keep us happy, and we were a demanding bunch. Sometimes we look back and wonder what we could have done to have made life a little easier on her.

"She had tuberculosis anyway. It killed her slow and vicious. Arthur, he went on believin' that it was the best thing for her, to be dead and peaceful and happy—until he got back from the war. It was almost as if he expected to find her waitin' for him at that big black stove we had, workin' on dough or fryin' fatback." Will frowned. "Judith always reminded me of our momma," he added thoughtfully. He was silent for a moment, then went on.

"You sleep with a man until you're ten or so," he said, smiling again, "then you hunt and fish with him, compare your peter with his and share the same girls, and gets to be that you don't have to have a direct conversation to figure somethin' out. Arthur didn't have to draw me a picture. He never let people see him suffer. He would go off into the woods or wherever and sit for hours or days and then come back in. You knew somethin' was wrong when that happened, you just knew it, and it didn't take no genius to figure it out. We never talked about it. Never.

"Then I guess the really big event was his friend in the army—the one he killed by accident. I forget the boy's name. Arthur only mentioned it once. After he came back, he would have nightmares and one night I woke him up . . . let's see, that would be around the time he was dating your momma. He told me about this friend of his that he had killed in the war. He felt guilty about that. Remember, in my family you never had much money or much of anythin' else, but you always had your friends, and they meant a lot more to you than your car or your dog or your money. That hurt him bad. Can't forget a thing like that."

Will stood, but almost fell back down. He braced himself on a tree. "These beers'll get you once in a while, won't they, boy?"

Todd stood to help him.

"No, boy, you sit down. I can do it." Will went into the dark for a moment. When he came back, he drank another beer and sat next to Todd with his arm around the boy's shoulder.

"And then your momma's daddy was killed. Arthur blamed himself for that, too. He knew that somethin' was wrong with that old buzzard Spainhour." Will threw the empty can into the river and watched it float quickly out of sight.

Todd did the same. He didn't feel drunk, he felt—excited—he had heard this before. "You mean all those things made him feel guilty enough to kill himself?"

"Not, not all separately. I guess when you add 'em all up, they must'a put a lot of pressure on my brother. My *brother*. You know, maybe you're right. He must not be dead, or else we wouldn't be talkin' about him like this."

He reached for another beer. "Of course, there was one more thing," he added. "He wasn't going back to that mental hospital for nobody."

"Will, what exactly happened?"

"I got there after work, too late to do anything except call the ambulance. Arthur was on the grass, bleeding. The air smelled of tear gas. Burned our eyes. It had happened about five minutes before I got there. I guess they tried to take him; I heard there was a gun battle, they used tear gas, and . . . I don't know . . . it's hard to remember. I heard he went into

286

a back room and killed himself. And that's all. Short, quick, finished. Least, that's what they said."

Todd closed his eyes. He opened them to see Will watching him. "Something isn't right," Todd said and spit into the fire.

"What's that, boy?"

"Nothing," Todd said, "just thinking."

Twenty-six

September 1962

WHEN DOWNTOWN, Mayzelle always stopped for a Coke at Woolworth's and felt some sense of satisfaction at each slow, cold draw from the bell-shaped glass as she studied the signs pasted on the walls above the grill: Lemon Meringue—15 cents, Coffee—10 cents, Burger—35 cents.

People still stared at her. It had not been long since those A and T University students had pulled the swivel counter chairs around, eased back in their seats, and scandalized segregated Greensboro.

She stopped here at least once a week to honor those young men and women who, with grim determination, let the world know what she had always held to be true: Human beings are not defined by color, like subspecies. She gave a quarter to the black waiter, leaned over to pick up her bags, and leisurely strolled down the aisles, basking in self-respect at having done her duty.

The next evening she turned on the radio to hear frantic reporters describing rifle shots, tear gas, wounded U. S. Marshals, and hysterical college students at the University of Mississippi. She eased down on her bed as she heard rioters complain about the registration of a new student, a colored man—a black person—or, as one angry sophomore said, "that nigger, James Meredith."

She had seen it all before, and she wondered how much longer she could hold out hope for a better day. Her black friends called her foolish and idealistic. Her thinking, they said, was muddied by working too long with white people. Sometimes she wondered if they would feel the same if they had shared her life, and the life of the only real family she had known since childhood.

Judith sat as close as possible to the front of the city bus. The fumes made her choke and gag for breath. When the bus doors opened at a stop, she breathed deeply and exhaled slowly, catching as much of the outside air as she could.

The gears and brakes squealed as the bus stopped before crossing the railroad tracks that separated the downtown area from the shopping area of Greensboro. Judith stepped slowly off the bus, holding her hair so that the draft from the engine did not tangle it. She walked purposefully, looking straight ahead, until she saw the blue and white sign above the large dirty windows. She pushed the white frame doors open and found herself in a dark storeroom with clothes hanging from the walls and clumped together in masses of dirty blues and reds and soiled whites piled high on unpainted tables.

"Clothes and Fabrics," the sign read. Clothes for the poor. Other women, some with faces carved of stone, with heavy bags of flesh dripping from their chins and arms, fought over this dress or that. Children stood near the dimly lit dressing rooms, waiting to be pushed behind old screens and drapes, their nakedness hidden by dirty underwear.

Judith walked from table to table looking for clothes that would fit a tall, gangly, brown-haired twelve-year-old, a blond eleven-year-old, a curly haired ten-year-old, and a nine-year-old girl. She inspected the used clothes for signs of age, calculated the effort needed to fix them up, marked the material for durability, and wondered, though she tried not to wonder, who had worn such clothes and when. With a little soap here and a thread and needle there, with a cut along this seam and a little more material around the sleeves, with ironing and stretching, they might do. They might do.

She looked around, eyes darting to the door every time the bell rang. The perspiring faces entering were pained faces, painted on with grease-paint, like clowns on strike. She looked for those she knew. She didn't mind at first when a huge, fat-fingered lady noticed a pair of corduroy pants and jumped across the table to get them before Judith could think. Judith understood. Whatever she could gain for her children was worth the cost in compromised dignity.

One thing she could not bear: Lord, she thought, don't ever let me look like these women, don't ever let me lose my soul to the point where my pride is lost forever. My body is the home of my soul. Let me keep it pleasant. She knew that there was a pattern in her life and that one day someone else might look at her with the same thought. Maybe not.

She reached into a stack of clothes and parted them until she found something she liked: a dress, red and white, crinoline, worn and tattered. It could be repaired. Virginia would never have to know. The lady with the mass of fingers looked at the dress and reached for it. Judith narrowed her eyes and silently dared the woman to touch the dress. The woman's face softened, and the huge gray bags swallowed up her eyes as she turned away.

Now what, Judith thought, is the real difference between that woman and me? Both of us seem to be in the same fix, else we wouldn't be here. She thought of Ila. Ila working in the garden in the country during the Depression. Ila fighting to protect us instead of losing her mind when Florence Kellam drowned. Ila fighting death and doctors when everybody gave her up for lost. She showed us how to live, with courage and dignity and hope. Our children are worth that. Their beauty cancels out a thousand tragedies.

Let the other woman have the dress. I've got more than her. More than many. No matter how bad it gets, I ain't gonna be pulled under. After all, what would Mayzelle say?

Who am I to be too proud to take what good people offer for help? My husband fought for this country; my children are good citizens. I'll provide for them. We got a right to live, and if I could help others I would. Ila gave away food to less-fortunates during the Depression, and Lord only knows how many times United Charities has given her a help for the doctors or some government cheese or eggs. A widow's budget is not much payment for all she's done for God knows how many dozens of relatives and friends. But Ila didn't fall on her knees, and by God, I'm not going to either.

The moths rammed noisily against the yellow porch light. Judith ignored them. She reread Arthur's insurance policy. She threw the heavy papers to the ground. The families of suicides get no insurance money. Worthless pieces of paper.

She tore the envelopes open, stoically measuring the contents: tax forms to be filled out in triplicate before social security would pay benefits to widows. She would have to wait several months for those checks. A letter from the bank, stating emphatically that the last two mortgage payments were overdue, but if necessary they would take what she could give. She laughed like a child. Take what she could give? What was there to give? And another letter, nice soft stationery from the attorneys Bevins and Mode, politely informing the "recently widowed Mrs. Arthur McDowell of an impending suit by Lee-Berry Construction Company for invoices past due: three truckloads of sheetrock." The hospital sent a sloppily typed bill for three hundred dollars: "Services for McDowell, A. T." She didn't open the envelope with the red dove in the corner. She knew it was a bill for five hundred dollars from Ivy's Funeral Home.

She couldn't sit and rot on the front porch while the creditors tore her family apart. She didn't have the money. She didn't have a job. That was all there was to it. They would have to understand, for a while at any rate. Maybe the Veteran's Administration could help a little. She would go to them in the morning, after applying for jobs. Where? Anywhere. Greensboro was growing, lots of new businesses from up north coming into town. Going back to the hospital cafeteria was out of the question. There had to be something else.

"What a life," she whispered. "I wonder what it's all about? Probably a big joke, and I'm the punch line. After I'm dead, God will bring us all into an auditorium and tell us the joke and explain why we missed the humor."

She watched the fireflies streak across the woods. Thousands of them, like moving Christmas lights on a tree, blinking on and off with regularity; deep yellow flashes, never in the same place. The crickets sounded angry, their low voices shouting in unison, an orchestra of violins scratching against the bullfrogs' brass.

She stood and walked to the door, glancing toward the woods. Todd was out there somewhere. Boy never slept anymore.

She almost thought about her children's future—but no, not tonight. Tonight was bill night. Tomorrow she would worry about the children. They had to be clothed and fed, but the car had to be repaired first, and the truck sold.

So much, it numbs you all at once.

Yet these were not the burdens that broke her will to work; these were not the causes of her despondency. Somehow, she knew, these money problems could be worked out. It might take years, and she would lose a lot, but she wouldn't lose everything.

She checked on the children. Virginia, James, and Adam slept soundly. Todd would be in when he felt like coming in, when he was sleepy enough.

She walked into her bedroom and undressed. She crawled into the bed and let the night seep into the room.

Night. Night in a dark room washed clean of the old smells. She felt like a stranger in a strange house, in a cold, dark bedroom, huge and clean and empty, like a shell. A dead room—the walls with no pictures, the closet half empty, the corners filled with memories like cobwebs.

She listened to the house and to the wind caressing the eaves of the roofline outside. She heard a voice, muted, spilling out into the hallway and to her open door, stopping there. She sat up. Which one was it this time? Which child was gripped by a nightmare? Which one was alone beneath the sheets, reaching out and not receiving?

She walked swiftly, silently through the house to the source of the moans.

They hide their grief during the day, she thought. They try to spare me the mirror of my own. Alone, all of us alone now. What other hell could God invent that would punish as much as this one?

Someday they'll blame me.

It was Virginia. "Here, Darling, it's all right. Wake up, Honey, you're having a bad dream. That's right, hold onto Momma. Momma's gonna make everything all right. Here, put your head down on the pillow and think of good things."

Virginia rubbed her eyes and whispered hoarsely, "When's Daddy coming home?"

A chilling emptiness gripped Judith. The empty chamber where tears begin filled with stinging warmth. She did not answer. "Go to sleep. I'll sit with you till you're asleep."

I wonder when they'll start blaming me, she thought. They'll be right. I killed him just as sure as if I took the gun myself. If only I had not signed the warrant. Then he would be here, and the breeze from the window would feel good on our flesh instead of harsh. We would be one again, clean again. She pushed the hair out of her face. No, I'm just dreaming— he might have killed us all.

She tucked the blankets around Virginia's chin. The child was asleep now.

Judith looked out the window. The pale moon across the field dimly outlined Will's dog lot. She examined her own reflection: ghostly, shiny eyes. But there was another face there, and Judith turned with a start.

"It's all right," Todd said. "Virginia will be fine."

"How long you been here?" she asked. "You almost scared me to death."

"Sorry, Momma. I always come in when she gets that way. You shouldn't oughta wake her up like that. She's better just to sleep through it, that way she'll forget whatever it is that makes her toss and turn like that."

Judith walked past him to her room and closed the door. I'll stop by Momma's and have lunch with Mayzelle tomorrow, she thought as she crawled beneath the covers. Then she felt a little better.

Mr. Goins at the cigarette factory smiled a lot. He helped Judith fill out the application. He was in his early forties, with chubby red cheeks and dark brown eyes. He was losing a little hair on the front of his head. He was, in an odd sort of way, what Judith used to call cute. His flesh looked like polished rubber, the kind children's dolls are made of.

He laughed. "Oh, will you look at this!" he said, delighted. "*Four* children. My, that is hard to believe, Mrs. McDowell. I'll bet they're fine ones, too."

Judith nodded. "Do you think I'll get the job?"

Goins frowned. "I surely hope so. Even though you don't have much experience I think we could train you fairly quick."

Judith felt uncomfortable. "I've really had lots of experience . . ."

"Oh, I don't mean *that*. I mean, raising kids and washing dishes is all right and all that, but what I'm talking about is *real* job market skills. But let's not worry your pretty head about that."

No, thought Judith, let's not.

Goins ran his pencil across the bottom of the application. "Tomorrow okay with you?"

"What?"

"Tomorrow. Morning. You can start to work then."

Judith thought of the children. They would be in school; no need for a babysitter. "Well, I don't see why not. Tomorrow morning would be fine."

"Good enough. I'll have a word with the personnel manager. He owes me one. We'll get you set up in the morning."

"What will I do?"

"Uh, probably assembly work. I'm not sure right now. I'll let you know in the morning. All right?"

Judith almost smiled. "That would be fine."

Goins nodded and stood. He extended his hand. "Here's to a long and valuable relationship with the company."

Judith sat on a stool in the quality control room. She took random cigarettes, placed them in a machine, and wrote down the numbers that appeared on the machine's windows. She didn't know what the numbers meant and she didn't care. There was no thought involved, no problem solving, no decisions to make. The most boring job imaginable. The work allowed plenty of time for daydreaming, and she took advantage. She faded into the past, until by noon she could no longer see the numbers because of the mist across her eyes.

Arthur. Always Arthur. He wouldn't let her alone. Wouldn't let her forget.

The hand on her shoulder pinched harder.

She turned in fright. "Oh . . . Mr. Goins. I'm sorry. I was just daydreaming."

He showed no expression. "Now, Mrs. McDowell, uh, Judith—this job is very important. I took a big chance with you and lately, quite frankly, I think you've been letting me down." He wagged his finger at her.

"I'm sorry," she said shrilly. "I just have to pull myself together. It's hard to get back into the world again."

"Yes, yes," he said sympathetically. "What with your husband's death and all, you obviously need some time for mourning. But," he said, looking around uncomfortably, "there's plenty of time for that sort of thing after work."

Judith made an attempt at humility. "I understand. I'll try not to let it happen again. Really, I'll do better." You better, she thought, this paycheck puts food on the table.

"Listen," said Goins, popping a stick of chewing gum into his mouth. "What you need is a break. I mean, you need to get out, you know? Get out and enjoy yourself."

"Yes, I know. I don't really get out of the house enough."

"Why don't you . . . uh, I mean, why don't *we* get together for dinner sometime. I promise you a good time—you know, a good dinner, maybe a couple of drinks or something."

Judith was surprised.

Goins offered her a stick of gum.

"No thanks," she said. "I don't know what to say."

"Say you'll go out with me."

"I'm sorry. It's . . . too soon."

"Thought I'd ask."

Judith turned away from him.

She wouldn't think of Arthur; she couldn't. Didn't have time. She had to think of the children, had to keep her mind away from the part of her soul that bled.

With time the emptiness within filled with cobwebs, then dust, then fell into a long sleep for many months.

Thirteen. God, that's a terrible time to be alive, Todd thought as he walked around the blackberry briers in the field. He tried to jump the creek at the bottom of the hill, saw a snake on the other side, and fell backward with a loud squishing noise into the mud. His fingers were embedded in the wet grass and his rear soaked in cold water. He stood and surveyed the damage. Soaked shoes and socks, mud-tipped blue jeans, and a slimy feeling around his underwear—and a sudden realization that he was being watched. Without moving his head, he moved his eyes as far to the right as possible. There, in the cedar stand, was a slender boy with a look of curious delight.

Todd reached down to the mud and scooped up a handful of gritty black sludge, a favorite hiding place for the scorpion-like crayfish, and with a true arm threw the meaty glob toward the intruder.

"Augh!"

"That'll teach you to be laughing at me, boy!" Todd shouted as he jumped back for a clear view of the observer. He saw that the mud had made a direct hit on the side of her face.

Her face?

"Oh, God," he said under his breath as he ran to her. "I'm sorry, I didn't—"

"No!" she shouted. "Stay away from me, you crazy jerk."

"I'm sorry," said Todd.

"Why are you smiling then?" she said.

"I could have asked you the same thing when I fell in the creek."

He moved out of her way as she walked over to the creek to kneel and wash her face. He did feel a little bad. After all, some of the guck got in her hair, dark hair, tied back in a ponytail. Probably real shiny—without mud in it.

His eyes followed the curve of her shirt, a flannel thing with a tear near the bottom. She was about Todd's size, except—except there seemed to be a softness there, barely outlined, as she knelt on the creek bank in the straw grass.

Without moving his feet, he cocked his head to the side for a better view. He was surprised by his own blush. He had seen almost-naked women in the magazines at Franklin's Drugstore. But this girl, with all her clothes on, looked more attractive, was more of an *attraction*, than any of those pictures.

He couldn't help wondering if she could look much better with her clothes off.

"Probably," she said.

"What?" he blurted.

She seemed perplexed. "I said, this junk will probably not come out of my daddy's shirt."

"Sure it will," he said, embarrassed.

She stared at him. "You live up here, Mister Coordination?"

He laughed. "Yeah, beyond those oaks across the field, near the pine woods. But I haven't seen you around."

"I haven't seen you either. What you staring at?"

He looked at her face. "My name is Todd. Todd McDowell. Uh, I wasn't starin' at nothin'."

She lowered her eyes. Her voice was softer than a moment ago. "Want to see a bunch of frog eggs?"

No. "Yes, where?" He knew every frog nest in the water for a mile.

"Over there, past those birch trees, near the pond. Come on, I'll show you."

She's got the cleanest face I ever saw, he thought as he tripped across logs and underbrush to keep up with her.

Within a few minutes they were side by side on their stomachs, peering over an outbank of tall grass and dry moss into a deep hole in the creek. The hole was crowded with thin webs of green branches covered with white sacks of frog eggs.

"Never seen so many in my whole life," he lied.

"Me either. Really makes you think, doesn't it?"

"Yeah." He moved his leg closer to hers, hoping she wouldn't notice.

She noticed. He could *feel* her notice as her calf tightened, then relaxed. He let his hand move to the small of her back.

Oh God, he prayed silently over the noise from his heartbeat, don't let this be a dream.

Todd dreamed about Arthur again. This time the dream was different; there was nothing but water and sky, and someone else in the cemetery shoveling dirt and rocks into the grave. Todd ran toward the intruder but woke to the sound of his own labored breathing.

Twenty-seven

June 1963

JUDITH PULLED on her robe and headed for the front door. She stumbled over a chair and wondered who had left it in the hallway.

"I'm coming! I'm coming!" she shouted.

The rapping on the door ceased.

She opened the heavy lock and shielded her eyes from the morning sun piercing through the wire mesh of the screen door.

"Yes?" she said.

"Mrs. McDowell?"

"Yes. What's wrong?"

"Nothin's wrong, ma'am. It's just that I was wonderin' if you had any odd jobs to do around here."

Judith tried to focus on the man's face. "You kiddin'? What's this, a joke or something? Me with three strong boys and you're askin' me if I have work to do? Wait a minute . . . aren't you Simpson? Your momma, she's . . . let's see . . ."

"Mabel."

"Right." Judith snapped her fingers. "Mabel. I haven't seen her in so long. How's she doin'?"

"Well, she's sick, you know. Cancer."

"Yes, I heard. I'm sorry."

"She talks about you all the time, though."

Judith couldn't help smiling. "She does, does she?"

"Oh no ma'am, not *that* way, she talks about how much her and you did together when you first moved here."

"Yes, I remember." Judith tried to think of exactly what she had done with Mabel when she first moved here. She could think of nothing. "Well, come on into the living room and have a seat. I ain't got no jobs for you, wouldn't be able to pay much if I did."

He walked in.

"You're taller than I remember," she said.

"Yes ma'am."

"Broader shoulders. I guess you got that from your father. How old are you now, Freddie? Twenty-two or three?"

"Twenty-five, ma'am."

"Twenty-five? You're kiddin' me! You're not twenty-five!"

"Yes ma'am," he said, grinning. His dark face seemed very smooth. His hands were huge and surprisingly fleshy; they didn't go with such a bony body.

"Well, I must say that you do make me feel old," she said.

"Old? You ain't old," he said earnestly.

He really doesn't think I'm old, thought Judith. His brown eyes—or are they darker than brown?—seem so deep and large. Must be his father's eyes. Course, no way to tell. Boy's father ran away fifteen or sixteen years ago. "Sit down, Freddie."

He crossed his legs and knocked over a lamp. He caught it just in time to keep it from hitting the floor. He looked at her with a scared expression, as if expecting to be hit.

"Oh, don't worry about that old thing, Freddie. My kids have been slowly destroying this house piece by piece for years. You know my kids, don't you? Todd and James and—"

"I seen 'em about, but I don't get over this way much. Been helping around the house, you know, doing odd jobs."

"I see," Judith said.

"Well," he said, smiling politely, "I guess I better be going."

"Thanks for dropping by, Freddie, you come back again."

"What?"

"I said, come back again."

"You mean it?" he stuttered.

Judith laughed, confused. "Of course I mean it. James and Adam are always looking for somebody to hunt with. You do hunt, don't you?"

"Oh yes ma'am, all the time."

"I figured as much. Those brier cuts on your hands give you away. Spend a lot of time in the woods, don't you?"

"Yes, I like to get my quota of rabbits when I got time."

Judith thought a moment as she opened the door. "You read a lot?"

He frowned. "Read? No ma'am, not too much."

"Ummm. I just wondered."

"I read the newspaper, though," he added quickly. "And sometimes I get a book that I like. I've read *Huckleberry Finn* dozens of times, and—"

Judith laughed and held out her hand with her palm up. "Sometimes," she said, "a man can read too much."

Freddie sighed. "Yes ma'am, that's what I think, exactly!"

"We'll see you, Freddie."

"Yes ma'am." He backed out the door onto the porch.

"Freddie, you all right?"

"Well, I don't know, but I think you ought to know that your roof needs reshingling."

"Probably," said Judith. "Not a thing I can do about it. Shingles cost money."

"Well, maybe so and maybe not. I think I can get you a good deal on them, and what with your boys a-helpin', we could reroof the whole thing in two . . . maybe one week."

Judith walked out into the yard and looked at the house. The shingles were torn and rotting halfway across the roof. That was one of the things Arthur had meant to fix.

She walked back to the porch and opened the door.

"Mrs. McDowell?" Freddie said. "I think that it wouldn't cost much. Just a few dollars. I've got a friend . . . ."

She stared at him for a moment, watching his face and his eyes, so motionless and innocent. He wasn't a boy and he wasn't a man. His hair was neatly combed, although his part was a bit too high, and his arms were covered with thin black hair.

Judith frowned. "We'll see. You come back next Saturday morning and we'll see." She closed the door.

He smiled and walked away, reaching down to pick up a handful of rocks which he tossed down the road as he cut across the woods to his own house near the new shopping center.

Judith forgot about him in ten minutes.

The next Saturday, Todd woke before the rest and walked out on the front porch. There, boxes of shingles were piled neatly in five stacks. On the ground against a tree were a bucket of nails and some hammers.

Todd walked around the house and saw the ladder leading to the roof. The ladder was made of old planks. He shook it. It seemed sturdy enough, so he climbed to the top. There, standing next to the chimney with his back toward Todd, stood a young man in blue jeans, scratching his neck.

"Hey, you!" shouted Todd. "What you doin' up here?"

Freddie turned around, stared for a moment, and then smiled.

"I'm waiting for you and your brothers to help me reshingle this old roof." He reached down and effortlessly pulled a shingle from the roof and dropped it. Todd watched the shingle shatter into pieces and scatter down the roof to the ground.

"When did all this come about?" asked Todd.

"I suspect your momma can tell you that," Freddie said.

"I suspect she can!"

Todd carefully crawled back down the ladder and went into the house. He banged on Judith's door. "Momma! Get up! There's this crazy man on top of the roof and I think you better come and see."

He heard the bedsprings sag within.

Judith opened her eyes and reached over to the clock, pulling it to her face. Seven o'clock? Monday? No, *Saturday* morning.

"Momma? You up?"

"Yes," she mumbled. Her mouth was dry. She had a headache. She pulled a blanket around her slip and walked to the door, opening it slowly, just enough so that she could see Todd.

"Todd? What's wrong?"

"I think you better get dressed and come see. Listen." He pointed toward the ceiling.

She heard the scratching noises above.

"My God!" she said. "What's that?"

"A man. Tearin' up the roof."

Judith frowned. "Yeah, yeah . . . I remember now. I don't understand. What's he doin'?"

"Says that me and the boys are gonna reroof the house."

Judith laughed and leaned her head against the door. "Really? I didn't expect him to come back. Freddie Simpson. I told him to come back today if he wanted to roof the house and we would *talk* about it."

"Momma, he don't want to do much talking. He's got all the shingles out front, and it looks like he means to start soon."

Judith closed the door and pulled a dress over her slip, brushed her hair, then went to the bathroom and washed her face. Todd paced nervously in the hallway.

"Momma?" he shouted at the bathroom door. "If you want, me and Adam and James can go up there and throw him off."

He heard his mother laugh softly. "No," she said. "We do not throw visitors off our roof. It's just not done in polite society."

She opened the door and walked down the hall. "Still," she added, "you might wake James and Adam just in case."

Judith cautiously placed one foot, then the other, on the ladder rungs and started to climb. When she reached the top, Freddie came over and pulled her up.

"I'm not sure I want to come up here."

"Aw, come on, Mrs. McDowell, you can do it. Besides, it's really pretty up here. You can see the sun coming over the trees and the fish ponds across the street. And if you look real hard, you can see the top of my house."

"No, I better not."

He pulled her up.

At first she crawled to the top of the roof and then he supported her as she reached for the chimney and stood.

She brushed back her hair. "Whew! It *is* nice up here, so cool."

"It might look nice up here, but watch . . . ." He kicked at the roof with his boot. Several shingles, rotten with age, broke into pieces.

"Oh dear, I guess they do look bad."

"Yes ma'am, and the next thing you know, your wood under here will rot and cave in, then your floors and walls will rot, and the whole house will go."

Judith looked at him. "Really?" she asked innocently.

"Yes ma'am," he said proudly.

"Then, Freddie, I suppose we're gonna have to do something about this dangerous situation, aren't we?"

"Yes ma'am," he said somberly. "Just glad we caught it in time."

"How much?" asked Judith.

"Fifty dollars."

"What?" she shrieked. "Fifty dollars to reroof a whole house? What you gonna roof it with, loafbread?"

"No ma'am. I got a friend who works at a construction company and he gave me a good price on the shingles. All we got to do is get the shingles up here with the tar paper and start working."

"Got it all figured out, don't you?"

"Yes ma'am," he answered, grinning. Her foot slipped and he reached out and caught her arm.

"Don't call me 'ma'am,'" she said, regaining her footing. "I'm not that much older than you."

He nodded.

"You got a deal, Freddie," she said. "I'll get the boys. They'll gripe for a while, but at least it will get done. How long's it going to take?"

"Well," he said, looking around, "we'll have to strip the old roof and tack on the new tar paper and then nail on the shingles. Probably a week or two, depending on the weather."

"For fifty dollars? That cheap?"

"Yep, fifty dollars."

She shook her head. "That's hard to believe, but I guess you know what you're doing . . . you do know what you're doing, don't you?"

"Oh, yes ma'am! I've worked construction for years. I roofed our own house—see?" He pointed across the tops of the pines. There in the distance was a neat white frame house with gray shingles.

"Looks good enough from here, Freddie. You're some businessman. Help me down and get to work."

Freddie held her shoulders, squatted, and helped her down the side of the roof to the ladder. There she gripped the sides and eased her way down to the ground. James, Adam, and Todd waited on her at the foot.

Todd helped her off the ladder. "You want us to throw him off?" he asked quietly.

"No," said Judith. "I want you to go up there and help him."

James groaned. He and Adam started toward the house.

Judith followed them and grabbed their shoulders. "Wait a minute, you two! I'm gonna keep a dry roof over our heads and you're gonna help me. Neither of you is gonna get out of this. Take your time and follow Freddie's instructions, and I'll cook those fish Adam caught for supper."

Adam grinned. "That's good enough for me."

James spat. "I hate fish."

"And frog legs for you?"

"Well, all right, but I ain't gonna like roofin'."

"No," said Judith, "I don't suppose you will. But you ain't doin' it because you like it. You're doin' it because I asked you to. Because the men in this family are all I've got to keep us dry and warm."

James blushed. Adam left to carry the shingles.

Todd climbed to the top. "What do you want me to do?" he asked Freddie.

"Bring up a hammer and we'll start stripping the old shingles and paper on the corner over there. Get a move on and we can get plenty done before dark."

"Dark?" said Todd. "It's only seven-thirty in the morning!"

At noon, Judith called the boys down from the roof. Todd came down slowly. Blisters had broken on his hands and the water ran down his wrists. James and Adam were sunburned and slick with sweat. Freddie came down last. He seemed cool and relaxed, his eyes wide and bright despite the strength of the afternoon sun.

Judith turned on the outside water faucet and told them to wash up for lunch.

Todd let the cold water run over his hands for several minutes, but the burning, itching pain continued to make his joints throb. The water felt heavy.

After two plates of tomato sandwiches and a pitcher of cold tea, the boys followed Freddie back to the roof. James and Adam stayed near him, watching his moves, how deftly he removed the shingles in one pull, how expertly he tacked down the new tar paper after removing the old.

"Where'd you get them muscles?" asked Adam.

"You're stupid," said James.

Freddie pulled up a bent nail and eyed it for a moment. "I got these muscles at Sears and Roebuck. Yes sir, ordered them out of the wish book a few years ago. Paid for 'em, twelve ninety-five plus tax."

Adam laughed. James saw that Freddie was smiling, so he laughed also. They liked this man.

Todd did as he was told but said nothing. The stranger laughs too easily, he thought, and is too friendly. Who does he think he is, ordering everyone around like slaves?

At six o'clock the perspiration was gone and the work had slowed down. Adam rigged a rope to pull up the shingles instead of carrying them on his shoulders. Red sores were appearing on his neck and back.

Todd walked into the house. James and Freddie covered the unused shingles with plastic and came down. They walked into the house as Todd walked out with a book.

James touched Freddie's arm. "Don't mind him. Bookworm. Reads about Roman Empire and World War One and stuff like that."

Freddie nodded in silent understanding. James seemed pleased.

Judith greeted them in the kitchen. "Freddie, you can stay for supper, can't you?"

"No ma'am, I've got to help Mother tonight. I promised I'd wash her hair. Maybe some other evening?"

Judith smiled. "Sure. How much longer, you think?"

"Oh, I dunno. I'll work on it as fast as I can—without sacrificing quality. I like to do my best work."

Judith felt a flush across her face. She didn't quite understand why. Just the way he talked. There was something suggestive in his voice. Maybe she just imagined it. She said goodnight.

Repairing the roof took two weeks, not one. Freddie was at work shortly after dawn every morning and didn't finish working until four or five in the afternoon. He took a lot of breaks to help Judith after work.

When he was not working on the roof, he repaired little things around the house: the toilet apparatus, the well pump, the carburetor on the car. Little things.

Judith fed him, encouraged him, treated him more and more like one of her own. Every evening she asked him to stay for dinner, and every evening he politely declined.

When Judith wasn't washing clothes or working at the cigarette factory, she helped him carry shingles to the roof or screwdrivers to the garage in back.

"You really do too much, you know," she told him.

"What d'ya mean?" he said, sounding hurt.

She smiled. "I mean you work yourself to death for us and you know I can't pay you nearly what it's worth."

He looked sheepish. "Oh, I don't do it for the money. I get pleasure just helping out when I can."

"Hot in here," Judith said. "This storage room is so cramped. One of these days I'm going to clean it out."

"I'll do it," Freddie said. "Soon as I can."

Judith shook her head. "I'm not used to a man working this hard around the house. Most men would rather be inside watchin' a ball game on television or out chasin' their dogs."

"Not me," Freddie said seriously.

"Let me get over for a moment so I can open a window in here. I'm suffocating."

"Sure," Freddie said, leaning over the lawnmower parts on the floor.

She felt her leg brush against his back, and for a second he stopped working and for the same instant she stopped moving.

Twenty-five, she thought. This is silly. To feel this way. This is wrong. Damn window. Can't get the damn window opened. She sighed.

"Here," he said. "Let me get it."

He moved across the junk on the floor and effortlessly opened the window.

The cool air filled the room quickly, but she did not feel it. Instead she felt the warmth of his body behind hers. She left the room. She needed time to think.

That night Freddie stayed for supper.

Judith fixed chicken pie. Freddie ate quickly. Judith laughed and talked and told Adam to go to bed because he kept falling asleep at the table.

"Ma'am . . . I mean, Judith," said Freddie. "That was a real good supper. I best be goin' on home now."

"Oh, come on, Freddie," begged Adam. "Momma? Make him stay!"

Judith smiled and went around collecting the plates. "Why, of course he'll stay. Freddie, we're goin' to watch Red Skelton on television tonight, and I think the kids would enjoy having you around."

"Well, I don't know." He seemed confused.

"Oh, come on, Freddie," pleaded James.

He laughed. "Well, if I'm wanted."

Judith smiled. "Of course you're wanted. You worked hard, now's the time to relax and enjoy."

"You're right, Judith. I'll stay, but just till the show is over. I don't want to overstay my welcome."

Judith slapped him on the back of the head as she passed. "No need to worry about that, is there, boys?"

Adam and James exchanged gratified looks.

Adam fell asleep before the show started, and James spent most of the half hour talking about fishing the nearby streams and ponds.

"Ain't like it used to be," said James. "I remember when we was little Daddy used to take us clean across those woods—must'a been ten miles or so, into the deep woods too, I mean. We kids didn't fish none. We just followed him so that we could help carry back all those fish he caught. You remember that, Momma?"

"Yes," she lied.

The show ended. Adam woke, and he and James left for the kitchen to scrounge around in the refrigerator. James pulled out a jar of mayonnaise and Adam pulled out the milk carton with his name scrawled on the label.

"Whose turn to wash the dishes tonight?" Judith asked.

"Todd's!" the boys shouted.

"No, that's not true," said Virginia, quietly combing her doll's hair. "It's James's turn and he knows it!"

"It's awful dark out there," said Judith. "Is Todd back yet? I put his supper in the refrigerator."

"He's in his room, sleeping," said Virginia.

Funny, thought Judith, I didn't see him come in.

"Well, kids," said Judith cheerfully. "Time for you all to say goodnight to Freddie until Monday. Time for bed."

James took his milk and sandwich to the bedroom. Adam followed.

Judith sat down on the couch next to Freddie.

"James?" she shouted.

"Yes," came the muted reply.

"You say your prayers, you hear?"

"Yes, Momma, I will." He never did.

"Nice kids you got, Judith," Freddie volunteered.

"I'm proud of them," she said. "Though they have been a mess since their father died."

"I guess it's been hard on you, too."

"Yes," she said. "Hard is not the word, but it'll do. But let's not talk about that. It's too pretty to talk like that—what with the crickets in those woods and the moon out all white and blinding."

Freddie started to get up.

"Where you goin'?" she said quickly.

"Oh, to get a glass of water."

"You stay right here," said Judith. "And I'll get it for you. That's one good thing about this place, we don't have to drink city water. Nothing like cold, fresh well water pumped out of the ground."

"You can say that again, Judith. I like it better than most anything."

She came back and sat down on the chair across from him. He stared at her for a moment and then looked away.

"Yes? What's the matter?" she said.

"Well, the water . . . uh . . . ." He pointed to her hand.

"Oh!" She laughed. "The water! I would'a held it for an hour if you hadn't said somethin'."

He smiled.

They sat and watched the television, but neither knew what was on the screen. Finally Freddie twisted and looked around at the ceiling and said, staring at the lightbulb above them, "You want to go outside and listen to the night sounds?"

She swallowed the question piece by piece until she was sure that she understood it. "All right, I don't see why not. It's so pretty out there, I wouldn't want to waste it."

He stood and went to the door. She walked behind him. They walked across the yard, across the road, and onto the path descending into the woods. The path led to a pond deep in the woods. They walked to it and sat on the log that Will had felled so that the children would have a place to sit when they went swimming. No one had been swimming here for more than a year. Now the water was black and shiny, overtaken by frogs and turtles and numerous animals that made strange noises beneath the tall grasses.

They sat quietly for a few minutes, talking about the air and the calmness around them. Freddie could smell her perfume cutting through the thick pond air. His mother, Mabel, once wore a scent like that before the cancer scent arrived. His mother's skin was once that smooth, without blemish. Judith was so alive, so filled with smiles. She brushed her hair back, and he could tell that the cool air was pleasant to her.

Judith felt good here. Freddie brought back a lost youth. She wasn't that old, come to think of it; lots of good years left. Time had not left too many scars, and the night filled those in with soft dark touches. He looks so innocent. Twenty-five. He looks so familiar. There is an innocence written about his fingers.

She felt the hair on his arm before he touched her.

The boy hidden on the knoll crawled back home in the dark. There he sought the peace of his own small bed.

Todd bit into the wet bark and spit the sour taste out of his mouth. His cheeks rubbed the skin of the tree fiercely. He concentrated on the pain. His body was not as strong as he wished and so he stopped and walked to the depressions in the soft earth. All color was blotted by the rain, except for brief flashes of quiet lightning above him, sending the clouds across the sky, lighting up the blood-red dogwoods across the field, and bouncing light from stone to stone.

He covered his eyes and fingered the long wet hair that fell across his face, listening to the meaningless voice that called him, and he looked down and saw his father reaching from the grave.

He woke. He rolled out of the bed and walked quickly toward the bathroom. He glanced to the other bed. His brothers slept.

Todd slammed the jelly on the table as Judith entered.

"You don't look like you got much sleep," Judith said.

Todd took his place at the end of the table.

Adam wandered in with Virginia. They washed out a couple of glasses and sat down.

Judith put a pan on the stove and cracked eggs into a bowl. "We got company coming for breakfast," she announced mysteriously. Adam looked at James and smiled. Todd poured a glass of milk.

"Who?" asked Virginia.

"Freddie," said Judith.

Todd's face tightened and he put the glass down slowly, deliberately.

No one spoke when they heard the knock at the back door. Virginia let him in.

"Todd?" said Judith.

"Umm."

"You don't mind slipping down a little and letting our guest have your seat, do you?"

He moved to another seat.

Judith smiled at Freddie and pointed to the empty chair at the head of the table. Freddie sat down and rested his elbows on the table. His face was clean and bright.

Judith brought the scrambled eggs to the table and asked Virginia to say grace.

"God is great, God is good, let us thank Him for our food."

"Amen," said Judith.

"We gonna work on the roof today?" Adam asked.

Judith looked at Freddie.

"No," said Freddie firmly. "Today is Sunday and it wouldn't be right."

Todd crammed a piece of toast in his mouth.

"Todd?" Judith said sweetly. "Don't eat like that, you'll choke."

I hope so, thought Todd.

Judith filled Freddie's plate and then passed the eggs on down the table. Todd watched with disgust as Adam filled his plate and then passed the empty bowl on to Todd.

Todd stared at the bowl and then at Adam's plate. Adam was eating quickly. Judith was watching Freddie eat.

Todd rose as quietly as he could and began to walk out the door.

"You not hungry?" Judith asked.

He shook his head and slammed the door.

He walked across the yard to Will's house. Will, sitting on the back porch, was cleaning a piece of equipment with gasoline. A fuel pump or something. Todd didn't know much about cars.

"Have a seat, boy."

Todd sat down on the ground and picked up a rock.

"Lazy Sunday, eh?" said Will.

"Yeah."

"That's the trouble with summer and you being out of school. Lazy days can bore you some, can't they?"

Todd nodded.

"Why the long face?"

"Nothin'."

Will stopped scrubbing the steel and wiped his hands on an oil-stained rag. The smell of gasoline was strong in the brief gusts of wind from the dirt road.

"Nothin'? Nothin's botherin' you? Must be a powerful nothin'."

Todd sneered. "Not funny," he said crisply.

"I know it's not," said Will.

"Momma's new friend thinks I'm his slave. Thinks we're all his slaves."

Will frowned and looked away. He stood, brushing the dirt from his overalls, then looked down at Todd. "Don't let this eat on you, boy. Spit it out."

"It ain't his place."

"Your momma's earned the right to choose her friends."

"No she ain't," Todd said, rising and walking away to the pine woods.

Twenty-eight

August 1963

TODD SEARCHED the yard for the Sunday newspaper. "Where is that thing at?" he said aloud. Then he remembered that James had been out earlier. He was probably hiding somewhere, reading the comics. I'll beat his ass, Todd thought. He hardly noticed the car driving up. A large man, sweating from carrying his own weight, pulled himself into the sunshine.

A visitor, thought Todd, this early in the morning? His eyes moved quickly across the man as he walked to the porch: a shiny blue suit, a tight white shirt, and a gray tie. He looked as though he weren't breathing well. "Can I help you?" Todd asked. "We don't need no insurance," he added. Figured he'd save the man some time.

The man laughed and blew his nose into a rose-colored handkerchief. "No, I ain't a-sellin' no insurance, ain't a-sellin' nothin' but the Lord this beautiful Sunday mornin'."

Oh, God, Todd thought, a preacher. A fat preacher.

"I'm not sure if we want any of that either," Todd said.

The preacher frowned. "Is your momma at home, boy?"

"Yeah, but she ain't up yet."

"When do you expect she will be gettin' up?"

"Anytime now."

"Well, I'll just wait out here, then."

"Suit yourself," said Todd. "But sometimes—sometimes she don't get up until eleven or so on Sundays. Ain't you gonna miss church or somethin'?"

"Got a substitute today," said the preacher. "My own daddy's leadin' my congregation. I'm from New Table Baptist, up the road a few miles."

310

"Baptist, you say?" Todd held his hand up to his eyes and walked out of the sun. "Well, then I know we ain't interested. You see, we're Catholics. Holy Roman Catholics."

"That's sure a funny thing to hear," said the preacher, walking toward Todd. "Your Aunt Esther and your Aunt Ginger said you nice people were Baptists, even though you used to go to another church."

Uh-oh, thought Todd. "How you know them?"

"They go to my church, young man. Now, let's be frank. We're two gentlemen, standin' in the Lord's bright sunshine, and one of us is tryin' to keep the other one away from his momma. Now, why would one of us want to do a thing like that—lie to a preacher?"

Todd said nothing.

"I'll answer that," Judith said from the window.

"Hello, Judith. How you gettin' along?" the preacher said as he walked to the porch.

"I'm doin' all right, and you, Preacher Millfont?"

The preacher laughed easily. "You remember me? Ain't that a miracle. After all these years."

"It'd be hard to forget you, Preacher. Won't you come in?"

"I'd be pleased to."

"And you too, Todd. Come on in."

"But Momma, I got things to do."

"Now," Judith said with a trace of anger in her voice.

The preacher sat on the sofa, and Todd heard the springs within groan.

"You want some coffee?" Judith asked politely as she sat down on the piano stool.

"No, thank you. I just dropped by for a minute to see how you were getting along."

"This is a visitation?" Judith asked seriously.

"Well, no. Not exactly. This is the Lord's business."

"Well," said Judith, "I don't expect the Lord would mind me having a cup of coffee, would He?"

"Go right ahead, Judith. You don't mind if I open a window, do you? Mighty hot this morning, don't you think?"

Judith looked at Todd. "Open the window for the preacher, Todd."

"Judith, I've known your momma Ila and your grandmomma Lora for a long time, and I've always taken an interest in their younguns. It really bothered me when you dropped outa church."

"No time, Preacher. I got these kids to raise, by myself."

"We all got time for the Lord, Judith."

"Yes, and I think the Lord understands that some of us praise him better by keeping our families together."

"Now, Judith, you talkin' bitter."

"I just don't mince many words anymore, Preacher. I don't have the time to be as nice as I should."

Preacher Millfont grinned. "You come by that natural. Your momma's the same way."

Judith didn't know whether to take that as an insult or a compliment. She chose to ignore it. "Well, I know I should go to church. And I guess I should send the kids, but I don't feel right makin' them do somethin' that I don't do. I make them read their Bible stories at night, once in a while. They're God-fearin' children, and I'm a God-fearin' woman. What more can God want from me?"

The preacher narrowed his eyes. "Judith, that's what I'm here for. The children. I'm really concerned about them. People been talkin'—"

"They always do."

He continued. "They been talkin' about you and that Simpson fellow."

"Now, Preacher," Judith said softly. "I am giving you my hospitality. Don't go abusing it by bringing in gossip to my own door. I hear enough of it by and by."

"Yes, Judith, I realize that. But I feel it's my Christian duty to point out that your soul, and the souls of your children, may be in mortal danger."

Judith stood. "And how might that be?" she asked coldly.

"You livin' in sin, Judith," he said. "Yes, you, a widow. You temptin' God. The home of the widow may become stained with—"

Judith rubbed her eyes. "I'm tired. I was up all night ironing clothes and I don't need to hear you talk to me like this in front of my boy. My sins are between me and God."

"Freddie's mother, Mabel, come to see me. She's dyin', you know . . ."

"You can leave now, Preacher. Todd, open the door."

". . . and she's a-sufferin' not just from the cancer but by seeing her sweet boy drawn up in this web of sex . . ."

Judith left the room.

"It ain't good for the children!" the preacher cried behind her.

Todd held the door open and gazed across the yard. The preacher wiped his face and patted Todd on the shoulder.

Todd froze in shame, hating Freddie with all his heart.

◊

Judith placed the coffeepot on the table and handed the plate of eggs to Freddie. He scooped out a large clump and passed it down to the boys. Judith stared at her plate.

"Ain't you hungry?" said Freddie.

312

"No, you go ahead," said Judith meekly.

Todd stuffed a biscuit in his mouth and hurried from the table.

"Where you think you're goin', Mister?" asked Judith.

Todd chewed quickly. "Gonna help Will build that storage shed he wants."

"Well, all right, but don't think you're going to get out of helping Freddie build that front fence—you hear?" Todd walked out the door. "You hear?" Judith shouted.

She turned and sighed. "That boy. Sometimes I don't know what gets into him."

"That boy needs a good ass-whippin'," Freddie said.

A cold chill stirred in Judith's chest. "No," she said. "Not that. He'll be fine."

"He's worryin' you to death. You ought not to think so much of him. You know that."

James threw a biscuit to Adam. "Yeah, Momma, he's just stuck up. Even at school he don't talk to nobody. Nobody wants to be his friend. He can't keep a girlfriend for more than two or three days."

"Yeah," said Virginia.

Freddie pushed his eggs away.

"Can I have 'em?" Adam asked.

Freddie smiled. "Sure, kid, but eat 'em slow. You're gonna choke, the way you eat."

Freddie cranked up the truck.

Judith came out of the house and kissed him. "James can't go with you to pick up the lumber, but I guess we can round Todd up."

"That'll be fine," said Freddie.

"Now, where is that boy?" she said.

"Next door, remember?" Adam said as he crawled onto the truck bed.

Judith walked to Will's house.

"Freddie needs your help to haul lumber for the fence. He's goin' now. James is sick, got a fever."

"But I'm helping Will," Todd said.

Judith breathed deeply. "*Now*," she said slowly, "you can help *me*."

Todd threw his hammer to the ground and walked to the truck. He jumped into the cab and shut the door. Freddie backed the truck out onto the dirt road and drove to the highway. Soon they were in the city, starting and stopping at one traffic light and then another.

They turned at the World War I Memorial Baseball Stadium with its two fortress-like towers, pulled across Summit Avenue at Saint Leo's Hospital, and soon passed the O. Henry Hotel and the Jefferson Standard Building. The Jefferson Building had been completed in 1923. Todd remembered Mayzelle describing the skeleton of steel being clothed by clean, simple stone, rising to windows on twin towers that resembled the high arches on a Gothic cathedral. The city was growing into an urban center of commerce as one by one the neighborhood blocks were torn down.

After half an hour, they were on the road to the lumberyard. Freddie rounded a curve and had to slow the truck when he came up behind a car that was moving very slowly. The double line indicated no passing. Freddie tapped his tanned fingers on the steering column and reached over to turn up the radio. Country music whined out the windows and Freddie mumbled.

"Why don't you pass them?" Todd asked. Freddie said nothing.

Stupid, Todd reminded himself, we can't pass on a yellow line.

The car in front sped up and slowed down again. A family? Had to be, thought Todd. A man and his wife. The old lady in the back seat is probably a grandmother, and the kids are her grandchildren. Must be poor, he thought. Old Chrysler, covered with dust. No wonder it can't go fast enough on these hills.

"Damn niggers," Freddie whispered.

Todd looked out the window.

"What's your books say about damn niggers?" Freddie snarled. "Actin' like they own the damn road. Black sons-of-bitches drivin' that crate." He leaned on the horn. "Get off the road, you black bastards!" he shouted.

Todd leaned forward. "My books," he said thoughtfully, "indicate that those people in front of us probably have better manners than you."

Freddie gripped the steering wheel and turned sharply, passed the car, and then slowed down in front of it.

"What are you doing?" Todd asked.

"What's it matter to you, nigger-lover?"

Todd blushed.

Freddie stopped the truck in the road. The car stopped behind him.

Freddie jumped out of the truck so that the car could not pass. His muscles were thick and tight beneath his torn undershirt.

The driver of the car, an old man, opened the door. Freddie walked to the car and jerked the door toward him. He stuck his head up to the driver's face.

"What you think you doin', you dumb black-assed nigger? You own this damn road or somethin'?"

The elderly man, startled, tried to reach for the door handle. Freddie

314

grabbed his arm and jerked him up. Eyes wide and unblinking, the women in the car sat tense and quiet.

Todd jumped out of the truck. Adam stood on the truck bed.

"Let him go," Todd said quietly. Freddie grinned.

The old woman in the front seat of the car got out and rushed over. "Leave him alone!" she shouted. "Can't you see he's not feelin' well? Shame on you, Mister, pickin' on a man what's three times your age!"

"Yeah," said Todd. "Come on, let's go."

Freddie looked at the old woman's face and felt the old man's arm tighten. Perspiration dripped down the old man's face and he shook his arm free. He got back into the car and drove around the truck.

"What was that supposed to prove?" Todd asked.

Freddie laughed shortly. "Go read a book," he said.

"You should of seen him, Momma," Adam shouted as he piled chicken on his plate. "Freddie grabbed that ol' nigger by the arm—" he shook with laughter, "—and pulled him out of the car. It was the funniest thing I ever seen. Yes sir, funny! You should of been there, James."

"I wish I was," said James sadly as he coughed into his handkerchief.

"I wish *I* was there," Virginia said, smiling at Freddie. "Did you kill that old nigger?"

"No," said Freddie. "Your big brave brother here couldn't stand the sight of blood."

Virginia laughed. "Is that so, Todd?"

Todd left the table. He slammed the door and walked up the road.

I'm not a nigger lover, Todd thought. I'm not. I don't know why I bother to make a fuss. I don't know why.

That woman.

That woman was so strange looking, so tall and skinny. She looked at me . . . I've seen her . . . I could swear I've seen her before. When?

The look on a face, years ago, at Mortimer. She looked like Mayzelle, intelligent and proud. And Freddie knew it. He looked at me with contempt and hate like he knew she was . . . special.

If only I could wish him dead.

But I can't.

He kicked the stones in the road, jumped the ditch, and ran through the woods, along the old rabbit trail.

"I'm a coward," he panted. With every other breath he tripped on the words. "I'm a coward," echoed through the deep woods.

He ran until he could run no longer. Then he fell across a dried-up creek bed and pushed his forehead into the dirt. "And *he's a bastard*. Freddie's a son-of-a-bitching bastard and . . . ," he choked on the words, ". . . and my mother's . . . ."

He sat up and wiped the dirt from his face. His mind raced back and forth between images of Freddie sneering at the old black man beside the Chrysler, and of the tough black woman who stood up for him.

And then the dream returned: wet tombstones.

Suddenly, he felt comforted with the thought that there was someone with him in that lonely place. An old woman. An old black woman holding his hands, whispering stories in his ear and rubbing his back to keep him warm, surrounding him with secrets and love, her love and the love of others half remembered; images of Lon and the death of his baby son, images of a man stone dead in a railroad station, and another man with pieces of colored glass in his face.

"Mayzelle!" he shouted. "Mayzelle!"

What was it? What was she trying to tell him on that mountaintop? What half forgotten lesson was she trying to give him? What strength, buried in his subconscious, could save him now?

What could kill the shame, the curse, and the guilt?

Judith phoned. She had to work overtime.

"Fine," said Freddie. "I'll watch the kids."

Virginia pulled her chair closer to the television. Adam brought the popcorn to the couch and shoveled portions into small plastic cups. He passed one cup to James and Virginia, and another to Todd and Freddie. Then he poured Coke into tall glasses of ice. They had all seen the movie before and were bored by it.

"Tell me about that nasty nigger again," Virginia said.

Adam laughed. "Yeah, it's more interestin' than this movie."

Todd sipped his Coke. "They ain't niggers, y'all. They're people like me and you. Their skins are different, that's all."

"They're niggers," Freddie hissed. "And don't you forget it, Virginia." He retied the bow around her hair.

"They're *people*! Call 'em colored or black or Negro, but don't call 'em nigger. It'd be the same as other folks calling us white trash."

Freddie stood up. He smiled at Todd. "Want to come with me for a minute?"

Todd put his Coke down and walked into the hallway.

Freddie placed his hand on Todd's shoulder. Todd flinched. Freddie pushed him hard to the bathroom door. "Get in there!" he shouted. "I've had enough of you!" He grabbed Todd's arm and pulled it to his back, pushing him to the sink. Todd kicked and scratched, but the stronger man had his head in the sink and turned on the cold water tap.

Todd felt the rush of water. His scalp burned. He would not scream. He would not scream until he died. He would not. He struggled to free himself but couldn't.

Freddie pushed him to the bathtub and walked out.

"Don't do that again," said Judith slowly. "I know you didn't do what Adam said you did . . . least not that way. The boy exaggerates. I know how Todd can provoke. But don't touch him again. I'll do the discipline in this house. It's not right that you should."

He kissed her. She moved back. "You hear?" she said sternly.

He kissed her again. "I hear," he sighed.

Blue jays attacked the smaller sparrows with deadly accuracy. Will's dogs witnessed the clashes and barked until they choked and rolled in the dirt. Adam pushed Virginia off the front porch and she cried while James begged her to pretend it didn't hurt.

Todd stretched on his bed, drawing pictures of soldiers, priests, and fast cars.

Will saw Freddie and walked over. The car was up on jacks, and Freddie was underneath.

"How you doin'?" Will shouted cheerfully.

"Fine," said Freddie. "Hand me that wrench, will you?"

"Sure," said Will. "Listen, Freddie—while we're alone here—I understand that you got upset with Todd yesterday."

"Yeah," said Freddie. "He was smart-assin' around. Spoiled rotten, that kid. Needs to be put straight once in a while."

"Yeah," said Will. "I guess that's true. Kids without a daddy just naturally grow up wild. Gotta keep 'em in line, you know?"

No answer came from beneath the car.

"Oh, Freddie? One more thing." Will fingered the jack handle.

"Huh? What's that?" sputtered Freddie, trying to spit the dust and oil off his face.

"If you touch any of those kids again, I'll kill you."

Todd stared into the mirror, feeling the whisper-thin hairs on his chin. He looked at the door latch to be sure that he would not be interrupted. He held Freddie's can of shaving cream up to the light but could find no printed directions. How would he know if he were doing it correctly? Did one shave from the bottom up, or from the side? Should the razor handle be grasped like a shovel or like a fountain pen?

The pounding on the door broke his trance. He dropped the can trying to return it to the medicine cabinet. He didn't want Freddie to know that he had touched the shaving cream or the razor.

"I'm in here!" Todd shouted. No one left him alone, not even in the bathroom. Sometimes James leaned on the door and asked questions, or Adam slipped notes under the door. No privacy around here, Todd thought. How can a person grow up if he can't get any privacy?

The knob on the door shook.

"Go away!" Todd shouted. "I'm not finished yet."

"Todd?" Virginia said.

Todd opened the door. "What's the matter, Virginia, can't you—" His mouth shut tight. Virginia was crying silently, pointing to Judith's room. Todd stepped into the hall.

Freddie, standing at Judith's bedroom door, made no attempt at discre-tion. He was angry, his voice rising and falling like static from a radio with weak batteries. Freddie caught Todd's glance and turned away.

"And another thing, Judith," Freddie said, shaking his finger in Todd's direction. "I'm tired of his mouth and his attitude and his crap. Todd stands in my way every hour of every day, criticizing and smirking, look-ing at me with those eyes, and . . . no, Judith, you know what I'm talking about. Those eyes . . . you know damn well that look, that stuck-up, snotty look of his, like he's better'n me or something."

Todd couldn't see Judith, and her voice was only a wounded, pleading murmur.

Freddie picked up his suitcase and walked through the kitchen, slam-ming the screen door.

Judith came to her bedroom door and closed it. Todd couldn't see her face.

Todd put his arm around Virginia's shoulder. "He's gone," Todd whis-pered, not realizing that he was speaking aloud. He smiled, though he knew it was inappropriate. He couldn't help himself. Then he laughed.

"He's gone!"

Todd pushed the front door and smiled at Adam, who was on the front porch sorting fishing tackle. "He's gone, Adam!"

Adam looked up, his dark eyes curious but distant, until he saw Freddie kicking rocks beside the cedar trail. Adam stood and stared at Todd with an expression of disbelief and wonder.

That evening Virginia came from Judith's room and asked Todd to cook something. Momma wasn't feeling well.

Todd boiled potatoes, heated lima beans, and cut a tomato. He was a little embarrassed by his earlier rejoicing and was feeling more subdued. He went to ask Judith if he could bring her some supper, but she lay with her face to the wall and didn't answer. So he retreated to the kitchen and pulled the chair from the place where Arthur had always sat at the head of the table—the place he had watched Freddie take so many times.

Life can return to normal, he thought, if that is what life has been so far. Freddie is gone. This was Arthur's chair. And now it is mine.

He ate with energy, until he heard Judith sobbing softly in her room.

James, Adam, and Virginia picked at their food. When Adam didn't eat, there was cause for concern. Todd sighed and put down his fork. He was no longer hungry. His stomach seemed dry and tight.

The rain on the roof was not loud enough to drown out Judith's crying.

Todd got up from the table. He couldn't think any more. He couldn't feel any more. He wished the rain would come down harder.

Damn, he thought, why did Freddie have to go?

He kicked the chair, which to his surprise had not been comfortable. The view from that seat had not been what he had expected.

He walked to the window and looked into the dark. James, Adam, and Virginia watched him in the reflection, their faces expectant. Something had to happen.

Twenty-nine

THIS TIME he was aware he was in a dream, but he couldn't wake. This dream was different. It was a nightmare as fresh and vivid and stinging as life itself. A touch like ice pulled him away from sleep, and in one moment, the form in the dream merged with the reality of the room, moved from the chair beside Todd's bed to the shadows, and was gone.

The life of the house collected above him: wind whistling beneath the eaves, mildew creeping across the south end of the roof shingles, pipes sweating, pine studs bending, soft-colored thoughts moving in one room and out another—yellow kitchen, the boys' blue bedroom, Virginia's green bedroom, a brown family room, the private white of Judith's room. Time drifted across pine floors scrubbed clean of wax by small, scuffling feet, and sofas and chairs made comfortable by wrestling, ice spills, and nervous fingers.

Todd lay there, his mind drifting through the house and back again to his own skinny body—flat stomach, no chest, no muscles on bone, big feet, and long, hairless legs. A collection of dependent cells and tissue, all working for a single purpose: to confuse him, to separate his senses from the dark and strange things that he knew were outside, but which his body, in a conspiracy of protection, would not let him see. His eyes closed gently, then opened again. He pulled the blanket off his chest.

He jerked the car keys from Judith's pocketbook hanging behind the door. He didn't have a license, but at this point he didn't feel that he needed one.

Lon opened the door to the old, dark house.

"Well, what you want?"

"I want to see Mayzelle," Todd said.

"Mayzelle's sleepin'. She's not well. Go away." Lon shut the door.

Todd heard loud voices behind the door. It opened again. Lora leaned up to the screen door. "Todd McDowell, you come on in here. Lon, tell him you're sorry."

Lon walked into another room.

Lora smiled. "Come on in, Todd. I got some cake in the kitchen, and maybe some milk. You like that?"

"Yes, Great-grandma," he said politely. He walked softly into the dark hallway. The only sound he could hear in the old house was the heavy beating of a clock in the living room. Memories weighed heavily in the silence.

"I wondered if I could see Mayzelle."

"Honey, Mayzelle's real sick. But me and Lon takin' good care of her. Even old Ila gets around here once in a while to see her."

Todd smiled at hearing Lora call her daughter "old." "Think she might be able to talk to me for a few minutes?" he asked.

"Maybe so," Lora said. She put her hand on his shoulder. "I wondered when you would be around."

"Huh?"

"Just a hunch. You stay here and I'll go upstairs and see if she's wantin' company."

Todd sat on the sofa. He could hear Lon moving a chair in the other room. He heard a door shut upstairs. Lora shouted down the stairwell, "Come on up, boy. She's expectin' you."

Todd walked softly up the stairway, one slow step at a time. The stairs were hand-waxed to a gleam that Todd found unusual, even in an old home. No dust in the air or on the banisters. The thin rug rested on each step, its faded reds and blues showing no stain after twenty years of use. Everything in here stays the same, he thought. He wondered who the babies were in the portraits along the wall, stretching from one floor to the other. Children, grandchildren, great-grandchildren.

He stopped. Never noticed that baby photo before. What an ugly child, all puffed up with a cotton shirt, drooling and incoherent. It was Todd.

The light grew scarce at the top of the stairs. He noticed that some of the lamps attached to the wall had no bulbs in them.

Place needs a little light, he thought. He had never been in this part of the house. He was afraid to disturb the quiet. Lora met him at the top of the stairs and pointed to the door. "You go in there. I figure what you got to say must be private."

"Yes ma'am."

Lora looked at him for a moment, watching his eyes. At first he looked the other way; then a safe feeling came over him. She knows, he thought. She's known all along. Her violet eyes mesmerized him.

"Go on in," she said softly. "There ain't much time."

He pushed the door open and walked in, carefully closing it behind so he made no noise.

The shades were drawn, and Mayzelle was sitting up in bed. Her head was wrapped in a scarf. Todd could tell that her face had been freshly scrubbed. He could smell the soap.

She smiled at him but made no other movement. "Sit down, boy, in that chair. I been waiting on you."

"You know, don't you?" he said.

"Yes. You want to talk about it."

"Mayzelle, I don't know what to do. I have these dreams . . ."

"What do you dream, child?"

Todd told her about the nightmares. Mayzelle only nodded.

"And I wake up and I think I see a movement in the dark," Todd said. "And he comes to me. He's trying to tell me something. He won't let me alone."

"He's not at rest, is he, Todd?"

"He's still hurting."

"And so are you."

"Mayzelle, I just wonder sometimes if I'm . . ."

She raised her eyebrows.

He held his head up. "If I'm going crazy too."

"He killed himself, Todd. He was different from us. Lora and me survived many a storm together. We survived because we could depend on each other. Families today are just breakin' apart all over. Nobody has anybody to lean on, to share with. All those television shows teachin' our kids about happy endings to every program. Kids grow up expectin' easy endings, happy endings just like on TV. Life ain't that way, boy. Lot of younguns gonna grow up and at the first sign of trouble, they gonna collapse." She shook her head. "But you gonna survive. I gave you the gift. You figured it out yet?"

He was embarrassed. "Yes."

"Tell me."

Hesitating, fumbling for words to express thoughts he could barely grasp, he told her. He knew that the others were in him. He was Lon's boy who died. He was David, plowing in the sun. He was Sossomon, mourning his wife . . . Will, loving the fresh smell of the river. And he was

Arthur's son; the father lived as long as the son had memory. The blood of them all was in his veins. Their lives and deaths were his.

He stopped. Mayzelle smiled. "You leavin' anything out?"

He was tired. He rubbed his eyes. "I suppose," he said slowly, "that I got some of Ila and Momma in me. I don't think I could have survived otherwise." He looked at his shoes and noticed that one was not tied. "And . . . whenever I think about all of them, I think of you, too. You're part of me too, aren't you?"

She winked at him. "Maybe a little."

He laughed. "Maybe a lot."

She spoke softly but sternly. "And maybe a lot more of Judith in you than you know. Your momma's had a raw life. Your daddy's love for her turned sour; she's been cheated out of a love that gives us strength and purpose. You can't give her that kind of love and neither can I. Frankly, I didn't much care for that Freddie fellow, but at least he did seem to care about your momma, and she smiled again and for a time was happy. And I hear you begrudged her that. When your daddy died, she was left with nothin' but memories of a man whose love had turned to sickness, and she couldn't do nothin' but watch and worry about what might happen to you children. You remember all the good times—the picnics and the fishin' trips—but your mother had to live with the nightmares. And have you forgotten that it was you who aimed that rifle at his head on your birthday? Deep down, you knew then that something was wrong."

She paused.

"I'm gonna die soon."

Todd said nothing.

Lora came into the room and sat at the foot of the bed. "Mind if I listen in, old girl?"

Mayzelle stuck her tongue out at Lora. "If you quiet, which I doubt you can ever be." She turned to Todd. "Me and Lora have decided that even when we die, we gonna live forever. Do you know how we gonna do that?"

Lora nodded. "Through you and the other children," she told Todd.

Mayzelle laughed. "See? I told you she couldn't keep quiet." She smiled at Todd. "Arthur knows you ain't gonna forget. He's tryin' to tell you not to look in the grave for him. He's not there. He's in you and with you, and with all the others he ever loved."

Lora smiled. "You lucky, boy. Took us a couple decades to figure all this out. Mayzelle knew there was something wrong with your daddy. I guess she could sort of feel it. She saw it comin', her and Ila. There's no shame in what he did. You know that now. We're all cut down, some more violently than others, some more slowly than others. The seed of his death was planted a long time ago, but he was allowed to live long enough to pass on his special strength to you and your brothers and sister—his gentleness, his kindness, his love for his family."

Mayzelle picked up a glass of water from the side table. "I'm rested now."

Lora took a brush and walked to the head of the bed and began to unwrap the scarf around Mayzelle's head. She gently brushed the white hair, then bent over and kissed Mayzelle's brow.

"Can I stay?" Todd asked.

"Yes," Mayzelle whispered. "You stay as long as you want."

Old Lon Mitchell stood at the foot of Mayzelle's bed. The morning light streamed through the window over his shoulder and shone on the framed picture over the bed. It showed a rotten wood bridge spanning a bottomless pit. A small boy and girl were crossing the bridge, unaware of danger. Behind them stood a protecting angel with just a trace of a smile. Ila had given the print to Mayzelle years before. Each time Lon looked at the picture, he felt as though he were seeing it for the first time. This morning the children looked fragile and old.

He watched his wife as she leaned over Mayzelle, gently washing the arms, the legs, the face, then crossing the hands over the chest. He was suddenly afraid that Mayzelle would open her eyes and ask Lora to come with her, and that Lora would go—would walk from the room and out of the house, all the way to a cypress-hung river near a trestled bridge, where night trains sent warm rushes of wind through the flaps of a tent, close and warm with the smell of love-making, where two weak and happy teenagers had created a world.

Mayzelle was gone. How much longer was Lora's stay, or his?

He heard movement behind him and saw Todd sitting up in the chair in which he had fallen asleep. The boy was staring at the bed, dazed. Lon walked to him and handed him a glass. "Drink this."

Todd sipped and immediately looked back up at Lon.

"Don't look at me like that, boy. Mayzelle's always known about me drinkin' once in a while. Never bothered her when she was alive and—" He broke off and turned away.

"Why do you hate me?" Todd asked.

Lora glanced up. "Lon," she said, "open the bottom drawer of the dresser. Find me a nice clean sheet."

Lon found the sheet and handed it to her before looking again at Todd. "I don't hate you, boy."

"Then why do you treat me like a stranger? If Mayzelle hadn't told me about you, I never would have known you, except as some ugly old man in this ugly dark house."

The edge of a smile came to Lon's face. "Ugly?"

"Sorry."

"If you two gonna fight, do it out in the hall," said Lora, looking at the bed. Lon walked to her side. Lora reached out and stroked Mayzelle's hair.

"She's gone," Lon said.

"No she ain't," Lora said softly. "Not as long as I live."

Lon looked at the bed, at Mayzelle, and then at Todd. "I can't help feeling like she can still hear us," he said. "Let's go outside to the hall for a minute, boy."

On the dark stairwell, Lon hesitated, then put his arm around Todd's shoulders. Todd flinched but let the arm stay. "Lora says I'm just a bitter old man," Lon said. "Thing is, I *should* like you . . . a lot. But I can't help being the way I am. I don't want to get too close because you remind me of what I should have had and didn't—a son."

"Grandpa," said Todd, "you've got a lot of grandsons and great-grandsons. You don't treat them like you do me."

Lon nodded. "I know. But when I see Lora and Ila and . . . Mayzelle . . . giving you the kind of love that by right should belong to my own flesh . . . ."

Todd straightened. "We're all your flesh. Mayzelle taught me that."

Lon pulled away from Todd and eyed him sharply. "Just what all did Mayzelle tell you?"

"She told me everything. She told me that denying yourself love and life because of some stupid guilt is wrong; that sometimes the choices we make ain't right or wrong or good or bad. And I'm trying to tell you that we ain't got much time left to know each other, and wasting it like we do don't make much sense. You ain't got no son—I ain't got no father."

Lon's fingers suddenly tightened on the boy's shoulder, as if he had finally trapped something that had eluded him many times. He cleared his throat. "You're right, I lost a son and you lost a father, and neither of us will let 'em go. When you were a baby, I couldn't even look at you, because you looked so much like my boy. I thought that if I loved you, you might take his place, and I didn't want you to—just like you didn't want Freddie to take your daddy's place. But you know something, Todd? We got to let 'em go. Got to let 'em rest. If we chain ourselves to those graves, we're just cheatin' the living. Listen, I heard you and Mayzelle talking last night—don't look so surprised—when you talked about your daddy. Tell me something. Who told you how it happened?"

Looking puzzled, Todd answered, "Well, Momma don't know much about it. She was in shock and nobody ever explained much to her. What I know, Will told me once."

Lon nodded. "Yes, but Will wasn't there."

"He called the ambulance."

"Yes," Lon said, "but you ain't listenin'. Will wasn't there when your father killed himself."

"Well, the sheriff's deputies were there, they surrounded the house. I remember the tear gas . . ."

"Robert was there."

Todd fumbled for the banister and leaned on it. "Robert? Cousin Robert? My God, that's right. Cousin Robert worked for Daddy on construction back then. But why didn't he tell me?"

"He hasn't told anyone anything about it," said Lon.

Todd ran his hand through his hair. "I've got to talk to him. He knows."

"I wish I'd known this was bothering you," said Lon. "You should have come to me years ago. I think you would have if I'd let you," he added, more to himself than to Todd, because Todd was already running down the stairs toward the front door.

Robert had served two years in the navy and worked at Alexander Mills. He had saved his money and rented a new apartment near the Summit Shopping Center.

Todd drew in a breath and knocked on Robert's door.

The door opened. Robert smiled. "Todd? What you doing here?" Robert and Todd had not seen each other in a couple of years. "You've grown, boy, at least up if not out." He laughed, then turned serious. "What you doin' here?"

"Lon said you were there when Daddy died." Todd did not look into Robert's eyes. Instead he looked around him, at the photograph of Robert in a navy uniform on top of the television.

"Come on in, Todd."

Robert picked up a beer. "I guess you're too young to drink." Todd shrugged noncommittally.

"Why you want to know about that?" Robert asked.

"I heard things."

"What kind of things?"

"I heard that there was this gun battle with the police and Daddy killed himself."

Robert looked grim and leaned forward. "He did kill himself, but there wasn't a gun battle."

Todd tried not to show his surprise. "Would you mind telling me what happened, Robert?"

Robert sighed. "It was a long time ago, but I'll never forget it. I was there and I was young, but something like that will always stay with you.

"I was with your daddy. I knew he and your momma had had words and you kids were with Ila. Your dad had a nervous disorder. He had more problems than a person could deal with—business problems and home problems. I was aware that there was something wrong, but when you're that young, you don't see things very clear when they're happening.

"Well, anyway, your mother did get a warrant. I guess she was scared for herself and you kids. The deputies came out while me and Arthur was talking in the living room. Arthur took a look out the window after somebody shouted for him to come outside. He grabbed me by the back of the shirt, and I'll never forget it as long as I live—he told me to get out because there was gonna be trouble. I'll never forget that he was concerned about *me*.

"There I was on the front porch with Arthur behind me inside the living room shouting at me to get out of the way. I was young, and here I was between the police and your daddy. The police were tense and you could tell they were primed. They had been told there were guns and that your daddy had been in a mental hospital. I guess if I had been in their shoes, without knowing your daddy like I did, I might have done the same."

"Done what?"

"Oh, shouting for him to come out and go downtown with them. There must have been four or five cars; eight men, maybe. I begged them not to do anything until your uncle Will got in from work, which might have been five or ten minutes since he worked nearby. But they kept hollering for me to get out of the way and for Arthur to come out. One even tried to grab me, but I knew that I was the only thing between them and Arthur.

"Anyway, your Aunt Ginger drove down the road about then, and Arthur told me to leave with her. I begged them again to wait for Will.

"Arthur kept shouting, 'Leave me alone, this is my house and my property, just leave me alone.' Then they said, 'We come to take your guns and go downtown.' And he said, 'No, this is my property, you got no right.'

"Aunt Ginger had stopped the car, and she told me to get in, and when your Aunt Ginger says jump, you jump. Everyone was scared. Deputies were scared. Ginger was scared. I sure was, too, with all those police around.

"We drove back up the road and met Will coming the other way. I guess all this might have been two minutes at the most . . . and as we came back down to the house, we heard the shotgun blast."

Todd felt a cold shiver rush across his chest. His eyes were moist and his lips as dry as dead pine needles. For a moment he had been in his father's place—his breathing short, his throat tight, trapped in a house surrounded by armed policemen. He lifted his hand and smoothed the hair that was rising on the back of his neck. He tried to speak to Robert, his voice breaking. "You were only gone . . ."

"Just two minutes at the most," Robert repeated. "He must have run back into the room and got the shotgun and shot vertically, full into the nipple. And then he walked at least sixty feet to the porch, because when we got there he was on the lawn, and Will called the ambulance."

"No gun battle."

"No. One shot—only one."

"He didn't try to kill anyone except himself."

"Right."

"Why didn't they wait for Will?"

"I've asked myself that question a hundred times."

"And he didn't try to kill anyone."

"No, Todd. No one."

"I guess that always bothered me. There's part of him in me, and that part made no sense."

"You hear so many things, so many rumors. At the time everybody just wanted to get it behind them."

"I never could."

"You know, Todd, everyone has degrees of mental health. Your father wasn't a harmful man. But something in him snapped, and it could happen to anyone. He loved your mom excessively. He was strong, gentle, and had a real joy for people. But the pressures were just too much: making a living for four younguns, the memory of the mental hospital, and the pressures of a jealous mind. He was more afraid of losing love than of losing sanity—and in the end he lost both."

Todd sat in the car outside Robert's for a long time, his hands on the steering wheel. He felt relieved, yet he knew his heart was beating fast because he could feel the rush of tension across his face. Words from Ila's beloved, tattered book ran through his mind.

Then was Hector's fate so sad? You think so. Listen to the truth. He is dead and gone surely, but with reputation as a valiant man.

Todd knew the truth, and nothing could ever again approach the fresh feeling of peace and calm as his veins were cleared of a poison that had threatened to keep him a prisoner of the past. The last obstacle to growing up had been removed.

He remembered Arthur with pride, without shame.

Todd opened the screen door and found Judith alone in the living room, drinking a Coke, eating a Three Musketeers candy bar, and reading a *Life* magazine. She didn't see him.

He watched her finish the candy and gaze out the side window toward the pine woods, lost in her own thoughts. She looked so alone, and so lonely.

"Momma?"

She turned her head, picked up the soft drink, and put on her parent mask. "Umm?"

"Think there'd be any way I could go to college?"

"You got the grades, son?"

"Not yet, but I could get them. I read more than anybody I know except for you and Grandma Ila. Person can learn as much from books as from school, don't you think?"

"Cost a lot of money. Take a lot of hard work."

"I can handle the work, but I don't know if we can handle the money."

"No one in this family ever went to college before. You'd be taking a big risk, considering our financial circumstances. But . . ."

"Yes?"

"I'll do everything I can to see you through college if that's what you're sure you want. With me and you both working, we might be able to do it."

"You really think so?"

Judith smiled. "There's always hope, isn't there?"

He laughed with her, and at that moment they both knew where to look for it.